something like spring

Jay Bell Books
www.jaybellbooks.com

Did you buy this book? If so, thank you for putting food on our table! Making money as an independent artist isn't easy, so your support is greatly appreciated. Come give me a hug!

Did you pirate this book? If so, there are a couple of ways you can still help out. If you like the story, please take the time to leave a nice review somewhere, such as an online retail store (my preference), or on any blog or forum. Word of mouth is important for every book, so if you can recommend this book to friends with more cash to spare, that would be awesome too!

ISBN-13: 978-1494430917

Something Like Spring © 2014 Jay Bell / Andreas Bell

ALL RIGHTS RESERVED. This book may not be reproduced in whole or in part without permission. This book is a work of fiction and any resemblance to persons, living or dead, or events is purely coincidental.

SOMETHING LIKE® is a trademark registered with the U.S. Patent and Trademark Office and is the sole property of the author.

Cover art by Andreas Bell: www.andreasbell.com

-=Books by Jay Bell=-

The *Something Like...* series

#1 Something Like Summer
#2 Something Like Autumn
#3 Something Like Winter
#4 Something Like Spring
#5 Something Like Lightning
#6 Something Like Thunder
#7 Something Like Stories - Volume One
#8 Something Like Hail
#9 Something Like Rain
#10 Something Like Stories - Volume Two
#11 Something Like Forever
#12 Something Like Stories - Volume Three

The *Loka Legends* series

#1 The Cat in the Cradle
#2 From Darkness to Darkness

Other Novels

Kamikaze Boys
Hell's Pawn

Other Short Stories

Language Lessons
Like & Subscribe
The Boy at the Bottom of the Fountain

To Jordan - I'm sorry your spring was cut short. You spoke your beautiful words, and those without heart came to silence you. But you sang your song anyway, and I have no doubt you're singing it still. I look forward to the day when I can sit by your side again and listen.

Something Like Spring

by Jay Bell

Part One:
Houston, Texas
2006

Chapter One

My name is Jason Grant, and today is the first day of the rest of my life. Or so I've been told. Many times, in fact. Caseworkers like to put a positive spin on everything, as if a cheery smile is enough to change the world, make it the kind of place that welcomes a guy like me. Not that I mind. I want *it to be true. Part of me, way down deep, likes to believe this time will be different. It won't, and I think you know that too. I'm sorry if the words in this journal sting, Michelle. I like you. I've had a shitload of caseworkers, but in the months we've known each other... I don't know. You're different somehow.*

But I know what you're doing. I know that asking me to write down my thoughts is your way of figuring out what's wrong with me. You want to know why I keep getting kicked out of foster families. Twenty-three times now. The family you're about to take me to is number twenty-four. Once it all falls apart, this one will be the last. I'm almost sixteen, and I'd rather focus on finding a job than finding a family. Besides, there's a very good reason it won't work out. Remember the old building? The group home with the shared rooms? My roommate, Mickey, he told me the reason why. He said—

"Ready to go?"

Jason jerked, the pen scratching out one final line. Not that it mattered. His handwriting was so messy that Michelle Trout probably wouldn't be able to read it anyway. He looked up to find her leaning against the doorway, her gentle smile matching the warm feeling inside his chest. Maybe it was the ash-blonde hair that reminded him of his mother, or the well-maintained figure. She was probably the same age Jason's mother had been, when last he'd seen her.

Michelle nodded at the open book in his lap. "You're writing in your journal? That's great!"

"Yeah," Jason said sheepishly. "Just started."

"Well, today's the big day!"

Jason broke eye contact with her. Why couldn't they let him stay here? He made sure not to cause trouble for that very reason. Orphans belonged in an orphanage—not that people used such terms anymore. Instead they skittered around the word, but sometimes Jason felt like embracing it, wearing it with pride. He was an orphan. Nothing wrong with that. Regardless, some people were remarkably good at making him feel ashamed. The woman at his most recent foster home kept calling him a bereft child. She was so overcome with pity for him that she would say this with tears in her eyes. *Oh, my poor bereft child!* By the end of Jason's stay, she had called him a little bastard instead, those wet eyes full of fury.

"You okay?"

"Yeah," Jason lied. He considered begging Michelle, trying to explain that he felt more at home here, where everyone understood that he didn't have a family, where people didn't pretend. Instead he closed the journal and stood up.

Michelle pushed away from the door, fully entering his room. "Gosh, maybe I should have rented a moving truck." She glanced around, as if seeing stacks of moving boxes, when in reality there was only a small suitcase. And a battered old guitar. Jason slung this onto his back, the frayed strap tight and reassuring against his chest, like a permanent hug. He grabbed the suitcase when Michelle reached for it.

"I've got it," he said. "Oh. Here."

He tried to hand Michelle the journal, knowing she'd want to read what he wrote, but she shook her head.

"That's for you," she said. "It's private."

Glancing at her to make sure she was serious, he tucked it under his arm. Then he studied his shoes—seeing them shuffle nervously as Michelle checked his room for anything he might have forgotten. Afterwards he watched the scuffed leather lead him down the hallway, step by step, as he followed his caseworker outside.

Michelle was quiet, which was unusual. Jason wondered if she also felt sad, or if his own silence was making her uncomfortable. Once standing beside her car, he stared at the interior through the passenger-side window, waiting for her to dig the keys from her purse. He'd ridden in her car once before when she took him out for McDonald's, the light smell of her perfume slowly overwhelmed by greasy burger aroma as they sat in the car and ate. He'd liked that—how the car had become a private restaurant for two. Easy chitchat had spilled from her lips, none of it probing, none of it asking for explanations. That had come later, or so he had thought, when she'd given him the journal.

The door locks popped up. Jason put his suitcase in the back seat and brought the guitar with him to the front. He'd ride with it between his legs, which wouldn't be comfortable, but at least the instrument would be safe.

"Okay!" Michelle said, buckling herself in. "You ready? Scratch that. Are you excited?"

Jason gave a hollow smile. "Very."

Michelle chuckled. "You're a horrible liar, you know that?" Her happy expression faltered for a moment as she reached out to brush the bangs from his eyes.

Jason wanted to grab her hand and press it to his cheek. He didn't know why, but he suspected it would bring him comfort. Instead he remained absolutely still until she pulled her hand away.

"Want to get a haircut?" she asked. "Dazzle them with your good looks?"

Jason reached up and brushed the bangs back over his eyes. He liked hiding behind his hair. Seeing the world through a tangled brown curtain wasn't always easy, but well worth the sacrifice. Like wearing sunglasses, this created a sense of detachment, transforming the world into a distant movie on a screen.

"Is that a 'no'?" Michelle prompted.

"I don't want it cut," Jason said, "but maybe a perm. A really tight one. So tight that if I hit my head on anything, I'll bounce right off again."

"A head full of springs." Michelle's eyes sparkled as she started the car and pulled out. "That would save you from having to wear a bike helmet."

"Too bad I don't own a bike." Jason smiled, feeling a little better. As they drove, he realized he was making a big deal out of nothing. He'd been in this situation plenty of times before, enough to make this routine. He was a pro. If there were such thing as the orphan Olympics, he'd have a gold medal in manipulating foster families. He'd be there for a week, maybe two, and when he got tired of it, he'd finish up with one of his famous stunts.

"I know you're going to behave this time," Michelle said, having similar thoughts.

"Of course."

"No pearls in the clam chowder?"

Jason smiled, for real this time. He'd been proud of that one. *Foster home number twenty-two*. The mother there often wore a double string of pearls. Jason had stolen the necklace just to upset her. He'd had no intention of keeping it or selling it. When the woman made a giant pot of clam chowder for him and the other kids, he found inspiration, cutting the pearls loose and returning them to the original owners—the clams.

"She could have broken a tooth," Michelle said.

"Most people don't chew their soup," Jason replied. He had been careful not to swallow any pearls, but a few had been lost before anyone figured out what he'd done. The only way to recover the precious objects was to wait for them to come out the other end again. Since nobody could be certain who had swallowed what…

"Think she's still making the other kids poop into a pasta strainer?" Jason asked.

Michelle shook her head, trying her best to look stern. Or to hold back laughter. Eventually she gave up, and they shared a good chuckle. Outside the car, the buildings of downtown Houston gave way to an old suburb. The trees here had grown tall and strong next to equally robust houses.

"Found me a rich family, huh?" Jason asked.

"Yup!" Michelle said. "Absolutely loaded. That's not the best thing though."

"Oh yeah?"

Michelle bit her bottom lip, slowing and pulling over to the side of the road to park. "I shouldn't be telling you this. I really *really* shouldn't, but this family adopts. If things work out, well, there's a very good chance."

Jason leaned back in his seat, feeling uncomfortable again. Adoption was the jackpot for people like him. The chance to not only have a foster home, but to be knighted as an official member of the family. An orphan no more! Anyone else at the children's home would have been thrilled with this news. For some reason, all it did was make him uneasy.

"That's why, this time," Michelle said, "I'm hoping you can give your new foster family a chance. You'll be an adult soon, and this could be a really good start for you."

"The first day of the rest of my life?"

Michelle nodded, believing in her own convictions. "They'll be able to put you through college. I'm not asking you to love total strangers like they're your real parents. I know it doesn't work like that. But I *am* asking you to think of yourself. Do what's best for you and don't—"

"Screw things up again," Jason said, finishing for her. She shook her head in protest, but they both knew the truth. Michelle didn't need his journal because she probably had a big fat file with his name on it that explained everything wrong with him.

You never learned to shut your mouth. That's what Mickey, his former roommate, had told him. Mickey was twelve, had a nose like a boxer, and was constantly breaking out in hives. He wasn't an easy sell. He'd seen Jason get placed in three foster homes before someone finally gave him a chance too. Mickey was packing his bags when he shared what would be their parting words. *You never learned to shut your mouth. You've got everything going for you, but you'll never make it, because you never learned to play the game.*

Mickey was right. Jason never could keep his trap shut. He couldn't help himself. But Jason *had* learned to play the game. He just wasn't after the same prize.

"Which one is it?" he asked, nodding through the windshield at the street.

Michelle pointed. The house was twice as wide as the one he'd grown up in, the one belonging to him and his mother. Twice as tall too, since the home was two stories. A huge oak tree shaded the three-car garage, a perfectly manicured lawn wrapping around the house and disappearing beneath a privacy fence. Jason smiled, mostly for Michelle's benefit.

"What do you think?" she asked.

"It's great," he said.

Michelle studied him. "Is it really? Just between you and me, what's it like being sent to a new family? In this line of work, we're taught most kids are nervous the first day, but that they quickly adapt and become well-adjusted members of the family."

Jason snorted and looked away.

"Exactly!" Michelle leaned forward to catch his eye again. "I always felt that sounded too simple. I can't tell you how many times I've wished I could go through the process, convince myself I was going to live with a new family and that I couldn't return to my own. At least then I would have a better understanding of what you and the others are going through."

Jason shook his head in disbelief. "You're awesome. You know that, right?"

Michelle remained somber. "So tell me. Try to explain what it's like for you."

Jason thought about it and exhaled. "What was your first day of school like?"

"Disappointing," Michelle said instantly. "I was dying to go, since my brother is a year older than me and always raved about it. Of course he lied through his teeth about what school was really like. He kept telling me that toy companies would stop by every day to test market their latest products, and that everyone got paid to play with dolls and things. And the playground was supposed to be full of circus animals, like a petting zoo except with tigers and elephants. So when that first day of school finally came, I was practically peeing my pants in excitement. You can imagine how I felt when I actually got there."

Jason laughed. "That's cruel, but not exactly what I was aiming for. Unless you felt really confused and sort of out of your element."

"That would be high school," Michelle said, gazing through the windshield. "Normally when I started at a new school, my brother was there to guide me. The first day of my freshman year, Jace had the flu and stayed home. Even worse, my best friend had moved away that summer."

"Yeah," Jason said encouragingly. "Remember what that first day was like. A new school is always confusing. Everyone seems to know what's going on and how everything works except for you. If you're a stranger, you don't have a friend or family member there to make it fun instead of frightening. After an entire day of mistakes and embarrassing yourself, what do you feel like doing the most?"

Michelle swallowed. "Like going home."

"Except you can't," Jason said. "Going home is impossible. There are no home-baked cookies at the end of that first day. No hug to make you feel secure again."

Michelle glanced over at him, eyes concerned. "Is that how bad it is?"

"Just at first," Jason said quickly, not wanting to upset her further. "Just like at school, after a week or two you get used to everything and it isn't so intimidating. So I guess what the textbooks say isn't so far off. It's rough at first, but people adjust." What he didn't tell her is that the feeling of wanting to go home never went away.

Michelle mulled over his words. "What I still don't understand is why you keep putting yourself through this. If you would settle down with one family, you wouldn't have to feel that way ever again."

Jason nodded. That's all he could really do. He knew she meant well. Her tone wasn't judgmental or scolding. Michelle genuinely cared. And she was right. If he would stop sabotaging his chances of getting adopted, maybe he would find some sort of peace. But what he couldn't communicate was just how badly he wanted to go home. No matter how impossible that might be, he wanted it more than anything. Regardless, he put on a brave face for her benefit. "Maybe this family is the right one."

Michelle looked relieved. "They're going to love you. Ready?"

He nodded again, and the car rolled forward, delivering Jason to a home he knew would never be his own. The rest happened in a blur. A doorbell that sounded like heavy brass bells. The grinning faces of Mr. and Mrs. Hubbard as they ushered him into a living room where other kids waited. Introductions that were totally lost on him. Then Jason was plopped down on an expensive couch—one of three, all facing each other—his butt growing increasingly numb as the adults spoke. Michelle sat next to him, addressing Mr. and Mrs. Hubbard across a wooden coffee table painted white. Jason did his best to ignore the stares of the other kids, who were lined up together on the side couch.

No amount of experience helped with this stage of the process and the pressure it brought. What did these people expect of him? Was he supposed to impress? Should he juggle flaming swords before swallowing the blades? Jason had no idea what they wanted, and so he did what he always did on first days. He shut down.

Michelle did all the talking, occasionally shooting him a panicked glance that said he was bombing. He felt like apologizing to her, but instead all he did was nod when addressed. Most questions in this situation could be answered in the affirmative. Are you okay? Are you happy to be here? Would you like a glass of water? Yes, yes, and yes.

His new foster parents didn't seem perturbed by his behavior. They wore the same satisfied expressions they had when he'd met them at the children's home last month. He knew they were pleased with themselves, rather than with him, and why shouldn't they be? Not many adults were willing to take in a fifteen-year-old, especially one with a troubled past. They weren't exactly young either. Mrs. Hubbard was plain with pulled-back brown hair that had lost its shine. Her clothing and jewelry compensated for her dull appearance. The woman practically had money coming out her ears.

Her husband did too. Mr. Hubbard's dark hair was gray at the temples, his mustache already salt and pepper. He had the successful air of a businessman, despite not wearing a suit. The golf clothes suggested his deals took place at a country club rather than a stuffy office.

Michelle introduced them as Mr. and Mrs. Hubbard, but they immediately corrected her and reintroduced themselves as Mom and Dad. This made Jason's mouth go dry. The three kids seated on the side couch were reintroduced as his brother and two sisters. They had names too, but Jason missed them completely. A young girl of about seven or eight beamed at him, while next to her, a boy on the verge of puberty sized him up. At the end of the couch, an older girl in her late teens seemed bored, like she'd seen one too many of these meetings. This told Jason that not everyone made the cut. Being here didn't mean he would automatically be adopted.

"Ah!" Mrs. Hubbard said, eyes lighting up as she looked toward the front door. "There's your oldest brother!"

Jason followed her gaze. A guy his age, maybe a little older, had a cell phone pressed against his cheek. The device was almost lost in the waves of chestnut hair that spilled over his ears and ended just above his neck. His skin was dark with sun, his eyes almost golden. A loose V-neck shirt made his frame appear lanky at first, but the chest was toned, the exposed skin revealing fine black hair not so different from that on his chin. Jason dared to let his attention dart down to the narrow waist, where the shirt was partially tucked into a white belt—either by accident or design.

"Caesar," Mr. Hubbard said. "Would you like to meet your new brother?"

Disinterested eyes grazed Jason, not even focusing, before the phone moved away. "No." The answer was firm. Final. Caesar returned the phone to his ear, continuing his conversation as he crossed the room and bounded up the stairs to the upper floor.

Jason turned to his new foster parents. They didn't seem

fazed by this behavior. Quite the opposite, in fact. Mrs. Hubbard's eyes continued to shine, Jason noticing how they were the same golden hue. Mr. Hubbard's strong chin—the exact shape and size as Caesar's—didn't clench in frustration. Instead he winced in amused embarrassment as his son disappeared, causing Jason to realize the truth. Caesar was their child. The real deal. Flesh and blood.

Jason glanced back at his would-be siblings. The oldest girl was of Asian descent, the youngest much too blonde and fair. He thought the boy in the middle might belong to them too, until Jason saw him glare bitterly after Caesar.

Jason had experienced mixed families before. Biological children were always treated differently. Not that he cared. Power struggles didn't interest him. He didn't compete for the attention of strangers, so he'd gladly stay out of Caesar's way.

"I believe that's everything," Michelle said as she stood.

Jason shot to his feet, nearly reaching out to stop her. Funny, because Michelle had reached toward him, a hand extended for him to shake. He ignored it and hugged her, feeling embarrassed by his own actions, but desperation had won out. When she hugged him back, he had to steel himself. No tears. No weakness in front of this new family. No more than he'd already shown, at least.

"Try to be good," Michelle whispered. "For your own sake. And if that's not enough, then do it for me."

He nodded once she pulled away. He would try. But only for her. Michelle dug in her pocket and handed him a business card, which struck him as cold. He knew the address of the children's home by heart, as well as the number of the front desk. Then he noticed handwriting on the back and quickly pocketed the card.

"Okay," she said, cheeks slightly flushed. Michelle returned her attention to Mr. and Mrs. Hubbard, a pleasant smile on her face. They walked her to the door, leaving Jason standing there. He decided to make eye contact with each of his "siblings" to show he wasn't afraid. Or intimidated. Each met his gaze. Of course. They came from the same world as he did.

"Can you really play that?" the little girl asked, pointing at his guitar.

"Yeah," Jason answered.

"Do you know any hymns?"

Before he could answer, the Hubbards returned to the room.

"So," Mrs. Hubbard said, clapping her hands together. "I've always found a nice board game is the best way to get acquainted. How about a round of Scrabble?"

Jason thought of all the naughty words he could spell. Then he remembered the promise he'd made to Michelle. He'd be good. Forcing a smile, he nodded eagerly. "Sounds fun!"

Two hours of mind-numbing games. Not just Scrabble, but also Trouble followed by Chutes and Ladders. That last one had been for Amy's benefit—the youngest girl. At least the board game marathon had taught Jason everyone's name, except for his would-be parents. Mercifully, they then showed him to his room. After a brief tour, they suggested he get unpacked and enjoy some privacy, although they left his bedroom door open on the way out. He figured it was meant to stay that way.

Jason hadn't felt this antsy since his first few foster families. Back then he had still wanted to please, working hard to live up to expectations both real and imagined. Now, after all these years, he was supposed to try again. If it wasn't for Michelle...

Remembering the business card, he pulled it out of his jeans pocket, flipped it over, and read the handwritten note. *If you need anything, you can call me. Even at home.* Below this a number was scribbled. Jason smiled at the way the word "anything" had been underlined. Another guy might make this into something it wasn't, show it off at school and brag about the hot older woman who had slipped him her digits. But of course Jason wasn't like other guys, and Michelle wasn't that sort of person. Instinct told him to hide the card somewhere safe, so he examined his new room.

Bedrooms in foster homes came in two flavors. The good ones were neutral, the foster parents trusting their wards to fill the space with their own personalities. The other kind, like the one Jason stood in now, reeked of expectation. A baseball mitt, a bat, and a catcher's mask nestled casually together in one corner. On the wall hung framed posters of sports cars, the makes and models of which Jason couldn't even guess at. The queen-sized bed was generously neutral, but the desk next to it was lined with a crisp collection of Hardy Boys books.

So basically, after having met Jason last month, the Hubbards had decided he was a baseball playing jock who fantasized about zooming around in sports cars while solving petty crimes. He shook his head, gathered up the baseball equipment, and tossed it in the closet. In the liberated corner he placed his guitar. After a moment's thought, he slid Michelle's card between the strings, dropping it in the sound hole where he felt it would be safe.

After swinging his suitcase onto the bed, Jason started moving his clothes into the dresser drawers. That's when Amy padded into the room. Smiling, she sat on the mattress edge and looked around. Nothing had changed except the guitar, which she stared at. Then she cocked her head, blonde bangs swinging to the side as she considered him seriously.

"Do you want to pray?" she asked.

At first Jason wondered if she had a speech impediment. Surely she meant 'play' instead of 'pray,' but he gave her the benefit of the doubt. "You mean to Jesus?"

Amy nodded. "Mm-hm."

"No. Sorry, but God stopped taking my calls a long time ago."

Amy scrunched up her nose. "What's that supposed to mean?"

"That I don't want to pray." Jason grabbed the last two pairs of socks from his suitcase and closed the lid. "How old are you?"

"Seven and a half."

"What does a seven-and-a-half-year-old need to pray for? A Barbie Dreamhouse?"

"I've got one of those," Amy said matter-of-factly. "I pray for things to stay the same. I don't want everything to change again."

Jason understood. She was young, but obviously she still remembered the life she had before. Whatever had put her into foster care, she worried it could happen again. He wouldn't ask her what that was. Instead, he steered her toward more pleasant topics. "You really have a Barbie Dreamhouse?"

Amy nodded eagerly, flashing him a smile that was missing a few teeth.

Jason pretended to be impressed. "The kind with an elevator and everything?"

"Yup! And lights that turn on and off and a hot tub. And a toilet." She giggled. "Do you want to come play?"

"With dolls? Uh, no."

Amy went from gleeful to pouty in the blink of an eye. "Nobody ever plays with me!"

"Nobody ever?" Jason asked.

"Nobody ever," Amy confirmed.

Jason glanced around his room. Unless he planned on losing himself in the innocuous adventures of the Hardy Boys, he didn't have many options. "All right," he said. "But I get to play with the boy dolls. You *do* have boy dolls, don't you?"

Amy's eyes lit up. She hopped off the bed and grabbed his hand, leading him down the hallway. Jason allowed himself to peek into the rooms they passed. In one dark bedroom—the blinds pulled shut—his new 'brother' Peter sat in front of a computer, wearing a headset while he hammered at a keyboard. The door to the next room was only cracked, but he could see Carrie, the oldest Hubbard girl, pacing the room while lost in a phone conversation. The room across from Peter's was obviously their destination, since it was a pink paradise, but Jason's attention was focused down the hall. Unlike the others, the door there was closed. The dull thump of music could be heard from beyond.

"Whose room is that?" he asked, even though Amy was tugging at his arm to get him to follow. "Is that where your parents sleep?"

"No," Amy said, rolling her eyes. "That's Caesar's room. He never comes out. Mom and Dad sleep downstairs."

"Oh," he said as if disinterested, but he strained to hear what song was playing, even as they entered Amy's room and sat on the plush carpet.

"Here it is!" she declared.

The plastic three-story monument was just as princess-powered as their surroundings. Jason tried to imagine living in a real home with so much eye-bleeding pink everywhere and decided it would drive anyone insane. Perhaps that was why all the dolls wore such manic grins. He listened patiently as Amy gave him a tour of the different Dreamhouse rooms and then showed off the accompanying car and horse stable. Afterwards she presented him with the dolls they would be playing with.

"This one is me," she said, holding up the blondest, "and this one is you."

Jason was handed a doll with black hair sculpted in plastic. Nothing like him in real life. He couldn't imagine wearing the Hawaiian shirt and white shorts either. Despite all of this, he pretended to be impressed. "Looks just like me!" he declared.

"This one is Caesar," Amy continued. Caesar's doll had slick-backed hair—synthetic fibers this time— and a tiny pair of sunglasses on his forehead. Jason accepted possession of the doll, feeling oddly intrigued. "And this one is Carrie. They're a couple."

"Caesar and Carrie?" Jason asked.

"Mm-hm." As if to demonstrate, Amy thunked Carrie's doll-head against Caesar's in one of the most brain rattling kisses ever.

Jason glanced back toward the hallway, imagining Carrie sneaking down it at night to Caesar's room. Was that who she was talking to on the phone? Was the music in Caesar's room being played so loud to drown out his responses?

"And you and I are a couple," Amy said, smacking her doll into his with a smooching sound.

"Oh!" Jason breathed a sigh of relief. "Caesar and Carrie aren't *really* a couple."

"No!" Amy giggled. "They're only dolls!"

"I forgot," Jason said, acting silly for her benefit.

"Well, they *do* look real," Amy said, excusing his confusion. "I always make sure my dolls have someone. Mom says I'm a natural matchmaker."

"And have you found that special someone yet?"

Amy raised her eyebrows as she fiddled with her doll's hair. "There's a boy at school, but I don't like him anymore because he won't marry me."

"He won't?"

"Nope. I asked him last week."

"Aren't you a little young to settle down?"

"Settle down?" Amy asked.

"To get married."

"Oh. I'm not too young." Amy said this in all seriousness. "I thought about it carefully. Weren't you lonely before you came to live with us?"

Jason swallowed. Lonely was one way of describing it. Sometimes when out shopping or whatever, he'd see people who seemed to have so much more than him. More friends, more family, and when it came to romance, more love.

"Yeah," he replied. "I was lonely."

Amy glanced over at him. "Me too. I don't want to feel lonely ever again. Do you?"

"No. I don't."

"Getting married means you never have to be. That's why I'm ready. Hey, should we have a wedding for Caesar and Carrie?"

"Maybe tomorrow," Jason said, half-distracted. "The dolls look tired. I think we should put them to bed."

"Oh, you're right!" Amy said, shoving her doll into the elevator.

"I'll be there in a second," Jason said. "I have to brush my teeth."

He stood his doll in the bathroom, moving it around vaguely, when really he was lost in thought. He remembered one lonely night. The worst, in fact. *Foster home number nineteen*. Jason had been in bed, unwilling to sleep. He was waiting until the clock said three in the morning, when he was sure everyone would not only be asleep, but deeply so. When that time came, Jason had crept down the hall, opened the door to Shawn's room, and carefully approached his bed. He only wanted to see Shawn sleeping, wondering if he did so shirtless, or if he lay on his back or maybe curled up into a ball. Jason had spent countless nights trying to imagine something so simple, his curiosity slowly driving him mad. So he had given in, deciding to see for himself. As it turned out, Shawn wore a muscle shirt and slept lying on his side. The curtain-filtered street light outside allowed Jason to see this, along with the buzzed red hair he always wanted to run the palm of his hand along. Shawn seemed like a deep sleeper. Surely one little caress wouldn't wake him.

He was right. Touching Shawn's hair didn't cause a reaction, but when Jason brushed the tips of his fingers along that freckled arm… Whatever deluded hope he had been running on expired the moment Shawn flinched and swung out of bed. Confusion turned to a look of such anger that Jason stumbled backward until he was up against the wall. He mumbled incoherently, desperate to find an excuse. When Shawn raised his hands and clenched his fists, Jason gave up and ran from the room.

At the breakfast table the next morning, Shawn glared but didn't seem intent on telling their foster parents what had happened. Regardless, Jason set fire to the shower curtain that day. Not one of his most creative stunts, but enough to ensure he was sent back to the group home. And away from Shawn.

"You're supposed to make me a midnight snack!" Amy complained.

"Sorry!" Jason said, snapping back to the present. "How about pancakes and ice cream?"

Amy licked her lips and rubbed her belly as Jason made his doll prance around the kitchen, knocking tiny plastic plates and pans around.

"Now you've woken up Carrie!" Amy said. "*And* Caesar. You know how grumpy they get."

"I don't care," Jason said. "I'll make them pancakes and ice cream too. Then they'll forgive me."

"They *love* pancakes!" Amy enthused. "Almost as much as they love each other."

"Oh no! We're out of ice cream!" Jason cried, his doll trembling with fear in front of the refrigerator. "We have ice cubes. That's close enough, right? We can mix them with hand lotion to make our own ice cream. They'll never know the difference!"

He noticed then, that the music in the hallway had grown louder. From the corner of his eye, he spotted a figure in the doorway, one wearing a cyan T-shirt the same color as the one Caesar had—

Jason hopped to his feet, as if he'd been caught doing something wrong. Caesar looked him over, face puzzled. Did the other guy even recognize him? Maybe his arrival here hadn't registered in Caesar's world. Jason felt like introducing himself, but instead he said, "I was just playing."

"With dolls," Caesar responded.

Jason nodded, deciding maybe he could make this into something funny. "Yeah. Can't get enough of them. Don't tell your parents, but I'm a dollaholic."

Caesar raised his right eyebrow.

Okay, so maybe it was a little early for the weirdo banter. Jason grasped for something to say and came up empty. Behind him, Amy continued playing unabashed. "Oh, Caesar," she was saying. "I love you, Caesar. Kiss me. Kiss me!"

Caesar's left eyebrow joined the other, his attention darting between the two of them.

"You're very popular with the ladies," Jason explained. "Or at least, your doll is. He's quite the little player."

Salvation came in the form of a smile. "What's your name?"

"Jason."

"Jason," Caesar repeated, as if trying it on for size. "Well, Jason, next time you want to toy with my life, be sure to let me know first. I like to decide who I kiss." Then he nodded at the dolls that Amy was still smacking together. "Or headbutt."

Then he disappeared down the hall, the music becoming muted again a few seconds later. Jason considered the way those amber eyes had shone when Caesar smiled. He felt lightheaded.

Maybe it was time to set fire to the shower curtain again.

Chapter Two

When Jason woke up the next morning, the first thing he did was check his bedroom door. This was important. He'd shut it before going to sleep, noticing it had no lock in the knob. Now it was open again. He raised his head, surveying the room. His guitar was still in the corner. Nothing seemed to have been touched. If this was some form of initiation... But no, more likely this meant—

"Oh, good! You're awake!"

Mrs. Hubbard stood in the doorway, a pair of slacks draped over one arm. She held up a white dress shirt for him to see. "Always best to make a good impression on your first day of school. You'd better get ready now. There's a schedule for the bathroom, and you only have twenty minutes left."

"It's Friday," Jason said, hoping this would excuse him from starting at a new school. Couldn't it wait until Monday?

"Friday is a school day," Mrs. Hubbard said, gliding into the room and hanging the clothes on the back of the chair. "Hurry along now. Breakfast will be ready soon."

Jason resisted a sigh and rolled out of bed. He was heading to the door when Mrs. Hubbard spoke again.

"The green toiletries belong to you. Everything is color-coded. If you need a towel, washcloth, toothbrush, or anything else, choose green."

With his back turned to her, Jason could safely roll his eyes, which he did.

The bathroom, thankfully, did have a lock. He felt tremendous relief at having some guaranteed privacy. Until his allotted bathroom time came to an end, at least. He leaned against the bathroom counter, hands splayed on the cold marble, and stared at himself in the mirror while willing himself to wake up. His mouth was naturally downturned at the edges, just like his mother's had been, which often led to inquiries of why he was sad when he wasn't. He also had her button nose, although he thought it looked cuter on her, especially the way it crinkled just before she laughed. Tangles of naturally rumpled brown hair made his eyes difficult to see, but he knew they were a bluish-gray like his mother's.

Jason wondered sometimes what he had inherited from the father he'd never known. The chin that jutted out involuntarily when he felt uncomfortable? The broad shoulders? The build that wasn't quite thin, but resisted putting on muscle? He tried to remember what the photos of his father had looked like, but couldn't, so he turned his attention to other matters.

Glancing around the bathroom, he took note of the color-coded towels and such. The pink items no doubt belonged to Amy, the orange to Carrie and the blue to Peter. Maybe. That left green for him, and for Caesar? Jason spun around, searching for the missing fifth color. When he couldn't find it, he shrugged, stripped off the T-shirt and pajama bottoms he'd slept in, and stepped into the shower.

When he was finished and had returned to his room, he put on the clothes that had been left out for him, wishing he could slip into a comfortable old shirt and jeans. Maybe schools in this part of Houston had a dress code. But when he reported downstairs for breakfast, he was no longer sure. He noticed Caesar first, dressed in a loose black T-shirt and artificially aged jeans. Next to him, Carrie was rocking a red blouse, so definitely no code. Only Peter wore an equally dopey dress shirt and slacks.

"Good morning!" Mr. Hubbard said, gesturing for him to sit.

Jason nodded in greeting, then focused on pouring and eating a bowl of cereal. Breakfast passed the same way dinner had last night. Mr. Hubbard tried to force conversation out of them, but only had success with Peter, who liked to talk. Amy did too, but she and Mrs. Hubbard were elsewhere.

"And how did you sleep?" Mr. Hubbard asked. From the way he beamed, he acted like this had been Jason's first night in a real bed and not out on the streets.

Jason's mouth twitched, eager to sting Mr. Hubbard with words, but he'd made a promise. "I slept great," he answered.

"First night in your new home," Mr. Hubbard pressed.

"Yes. It was wonderful. I'm so lucky."

Satisfied, Mr. Hubbard turned his attention to his oldest daughter, freeing Jason to glance across the table. Much like at dinner last night, Caesar's entire attention was on his phone, fingers moving in a flash as he texted. Jason wondered how one person could have so much to say. Was Caesar's head full of countless thoughts he couldn't hammer out quickly enough?

Jason wished, just for one hour, to be on the receiving end of those texts, if only to see what they said. Of course that would require him to have a phone, which he didn't.

By the time Amy and Mrs. Hubbard appeared from upstairs, the other kids had risen from the table and were getting ready to leave.

"You'll give Jason a ride, won't you, Caesar?" Mr. Hubbard said. "And Carrie, you show him around the school. Make sure he gets a nice warm welcome."

Carrie and Caesar exchanged glances, then smiles. "Of course," they said in unison.

"And this is for you," Mrs. Hubbard said, holding out a new backpack. "It has everything you'll need in it."

Jason eyed it with unease. "Thanks, but I already have one upstairs."

Mrs. Hubbard shook her head. "That old thing? I'll throw it out. Here. We want you to have a good start."

Jason wanted something familiar around, even if it was just a ratty old backpack, but he thanked her and took the new one.

"Ready?" Peter asked him. "Come on, we'll wait out front."

Jason followed him out the front door, surprised when Peter kept walking past the cars in the driveway and headed for the sidewalk.

"Wait. Aren't we supposed to get a ride?"

Peter turned, but kept walking backward. "There is no ride. They put on a sweet and innocent act around Mom and Dad, but trust me, they won't give you the time of day. Carrie's a snob, and Caesar…" Peter shook his head and turned forward again.

Jason paused and thought about heading back to the driveway to see for himself, but two things stopped him. Mostly it felt good to be away from the house. Every step he took was liberating. And Peter liked to talk, which made him an easy source of information.

"We can take the bus," Peter was saying. "Or we can walk. It's not far. Sometimes walking makes me late, but who cares?"

"Do we even go to the same school?" Jason asked, catching up and walking alongside him.

"No, but middle school is right next to the high school." Peter glanced over at him, freckles covering his pug nose. "You're putting on an act, right? This whole quiet and polite thing, it's not the real you. Or do you have some sort of mental disability?"

Jason felt uneasy at this sudden inquisition, so he played innocent. "Huh?"

Peter watched him a moment longer before snorting. "Almost had me for a minute. How old were you?"

Jason let himself relax fully for the first time since Michelle had dropped him off. "Seven," he said. "You?"

"Six years old. Parents were crackheads, although not until after I was born, thank god."

Jason nodded, the pieces falling into place. He didn't ask all the usual questions about relatives who might have taken Peter in, since he knew firsthand that life sometimes dealt nothing but cards with low numbers and mismatched suits. "My mom fell in love with the wrong guy," he offered. "And I don't mean my dad."

The explanation was vague, but sufficient. Jason didn't like to talk about his past. Most of the kids he'd met while in care didn't. At a certain point, you decided that your life was split into two distinct halves. There was Before—no matter how good or bad it had been—and there was After. Only so much crying could be done over Before, especially since the game of After was so complex and demanding.

"I didn't get adopted until recently." Peter said. "I'm twelve now, so I spent plenty of years in the wilderness. I don't want you to think I'm like them."

"Fill me in," Jason said, glad he could dispense with any pleasantries. "What are we dealing with?"

"It's safe here, if that's what you mean," Peter said. "Nothing creepy."

Foster home number five. That had been a hard lesson for Jason. The father there, camera in hand, had come into his room one day and asked him to take off his clothes. He had said Jason's caseworker needed proof he was being fed and in good condition. Jason had been trusting enough to take off his shirt, but when the man demanded his shorts go too, Jason had known something was wrong. The man blocked the door when Jason lunged for it, but he didn't let that stop him. Jason fought, hopelessly overpowered, but he managed to gouge one of the man's eyes and earn his freedom. When he made it to a neighbor's house, his chest was covered in red scratches. He didn't need to convince anyone of his story. Jason had escaped before the worst could happen, but it had been a turning point for him. He hadn't trusted another adult since. Not completely.

"There will be plenty more of this," Peter said, tugging at the collar of his dress shirt. "The Hubbards want perfect little children, but play along and they'll ease up eventually. I'm no saint and they still adopted me. You seem smart enough to make it. Unlike the last two."

"What did they do wrong?"

"Big mouths and lots of attitude. Nothing like you and me, I'm sure." Peter grinned. "Just keep yourself in check until you become their problem permanently."

Jason took a strange comfort in knowing he could get kicked out of this placement. There had been other Hubbard kids who hadn't made the cut. That was good. A few of the foster homes he'd been in had parents who lived for lost causes and were determined not to give up on any child, no matter how bad their situation. Such homes took a lot of creative destruction to escape from.

"So tell me about Amy and the others," Jason said, hoping Peter would start with Caesar.

"Amy gets treated like a princess. Do yourself a favor and never ask her about her past. You don't want to know. Believe me. But at least this was her first and final placement. She got adopted almost right away. Carrie is a total snob. She's the first kid the Hubbards adopted, way back when she was Amy's age. She likes to pretend she's biological. Practically treated that way too."

"Practically?" Jason asked, knowing where the conversation was headed.

"Yeah, because only Caesar gets the star treatment. He's blood, if you haven't figured it out yet. Mrs. Hubbard couldn't have any kids after she gave birth to him. His ego was probably too big. Tore everything up on the way out."

"Gross!"

Peter laughed shamelessly. "For real. Wait until you get to know him. If he'll ever talk to you, that is. You can tell what the Hubbards think of their son from what they chose to name him. His bedroom is the biggest in the house, he has his own bathroom, and have you seen his car? Anything he wants is handed to him on a silver platter. I hate him."

"Only because you envy him."

Peter considered this sullenly and then nodded. "Yeah, fair enough. I'd switch places with him in a heartbeat. When he goes off to college to drink himself to death, maybe I *will* replace him."

"You want his room?" Jason asked.

Peter glanced over at him, eyes surprisingly cold for someone so young. Then he blinked. "Hey, you ever play World of Warcraft?"

"Nope."

"It's never too late to learn. You'll need a computer. Better yet, you can have mine. It's a good starter machine. I want to upgrade to—"

Jason half-listened to him rattle on about computers while he considered what he had learned. His new foster home was safe, and he shouldn't have any trouble with the other kids. Amy was troubled, Peter was bitter, Carrie was a snob, and Caesar was distant—which was probably for the best. Jason thought he could deal with all of that. He just needed to keep his head down, get adopted, and do whatever else Michelle thought would give him a good life. College probably.

As Jason laid eyes on his new school for the first time, he realized how empty all of this sounded. A fake family and an education he didn't want or need. What would he do with a degree? For that matter, what would he do with the rest of his life? Jason had been offered so many fresh starts previously—so many blank canvasses—that sometimes they were all he could see in his future; one giant white void. This begged the question of what he wanted to fill that empty space with. The answer that came from inside sounded an awful lot like Amy.

I don't want to feel lonely ever again. Do you?

"You have something against my car?"

Jason was shoving his new textbooks around in his locker, pretending to get organized before heading to his next class. That way he could avoid awkward conversations with other students about who he was or what he was doing there. With his head almost totally inside the locker, his ears needed a moment to register the familiarity of that voice.

Peeking around the locker door, he found himself face-to-face with Caesar.

"Uh?" Jason managed to say.

Caesar grabbed the locker door and opened it wider. "Was that a yes or a no?"

"I like your car," Jason said, not knowing if he'd ever seen it.

"Then why didn't you ride in it this morning?"

"Oh. Uh... I didn't want to be a burden," he said, recovering slightly. "Anyway, I'm used to walking. Helps maintain my girlish figure."

Caesar's eyes traveled down said figure and back up again. "If you want a ride home, I always park right up front."

"Okay," Jason said.

Caesar's brow furrowed. "Okay, you understand, or okay, you'll be there this afternoon?"

"Both," Jason said.

Caesar nodded as if satisfied and turned to walk away.

Only one class remained, and Jason's stomach clenched all through it as he wondered what the ride home would be like. Would the car be loaded with Caesar's friends, Jason pressed between two of them? Or would they be alone, Jason grasping for words to fill the silence? No matter which way it went, he was okay with it. He'd be nervous during the drive, but he'd also have ample opportunity to check Caesar out and add new details to the steadily building fantasy in his mind.

When the final bell of the day rang, Jason took his time reaching the parking lot, not wanting to appear desperate. Caesar was easy to spot, since he was in the center of an entourage. That was the best way of describing them since they all wore the same casual and yet carefully planned clothing, like a gang spawned from a middle-class suburb. If this little clique had a leader, Caesar was it, since all heads were turned in his direction.

Walking toward this group went against every instinct Jason had. Not because they were cooler than him. Even if Caesar had been surrounded by the school's chess club, Jason still wouldn't have wanted to approach because having so many friends was alien to him. Occasionally Jason made a friend at the group home, another hard-sell like him, but eventually everyone went away, either finding a family or aging out of the system. Jason made his peace with not having friends long ago. And yet, standing here now—watching as people listened to what Caesar had to say, laughing at his jokes or shaking their heads—Jason felt a sort of yearning.

Caesar turned to find him, amber eyes lighting up in recognition. "Hey," he said, raising a hand, "there he is!" He gestured for Jason to come closer, putting the same hand on his shoulder when he was within reach and pulling him near.

Jason turned around at the last moment, realizing this wouldn't be a hug. That left him side by side with Caesar, who adjusted his arm, draping it over Jason's shoulders as he faced a bunch of strangers. A girl with black hair spiraling down her shoulders voiced the question posed by their expressions.

"Who's he?"

"Jason," Caesar said, as if this made everything obvious.

Most of them only feigned understanding, but a few heads nodded, telling Jason this had happened to other foster kids before him. He wondered if he was about to become victim to some horrible prank. Instead, Caesar started blabbering about a public argument two teachers had gotten into that day.

As Caesar talked, Jason kept sneaking sidelong glances at him. Two black discs covered his lobes. Just earrings, but maybe Caesar planned on gauging them next. An equally dark line of stubble outlined his chin. Jason wondered if that was intentional or if his facial hair just happened to grow that way. He found himself wishing the day was warmer, that spring had transformed into summer, forcing Caesar to wear a tank top. He imagined how the exposed arm would feel pressing against his neck, sweat sealing their skin together like they were—

"So what do you think?"

Jason came back to reality. A guy with a buzzed head, arms crossed over his chest, was staring at him expectantly.

"Me?" Jason cleared his throat. "I'm thinking I have no idea who any of you are or what you're talking about."

"Very honest!" Caesar laughed, squeezing him closer. "Unfortunately, that means you'll never fit in with this crowd."

The girl with the spirals of hair stepped forward. "I'm no liar! Although I might have stretched the truth a few times, if only to spare your feelings."

"You're cruel, Steph. So terribly cruel." Caesar hooked her with his free arm, drawing her in much as he'd done Jason.

Except Steph didn't turn around. She pressed herself against his chest, raising her head for a kiss. Jason found this extremely awkward, since Caesar still had an arm around him. He'd never been this close to a kissing couple before. If Jason strained his neck a little, he'd be right in the middle of the action, not that he had such an urge.

The arm around him tightened, probably reacting to Caesar's other arm that was now wrapped around Steph. As exciting as it was seeing Caesar's tongue slide into a girl's mouth, Jason mostly felt like disappearing.

Thankfully, Caesar broke the kiss and gently released them both. "I gotta get home."

"Aw!" she complained.

"You know how my mom is with the new ones. She'll be worried if I don't have him back on time."

"I can walk," Jason offered, causing Steph to perk up.

"Nah. It's no problem. Hop in."

Their chariot was a long silver car, the make oddly familiar. Jason realized he had a poster of it on his bedroom wall. Maybe Mrs. Hubbard had intentionally put it there. From the joints in the roof, he guessed it was a hardtop convertible. The car looked like the sort an older business executive would buy—respectable enough to please the wife, but sporty enough to recapture some youth.

As soon as Caesar was seated and the engine turned over, music blared to life. Hip-hop lyrics accompanied their ride home, preaching the hardships of the ghetto and the pain of losing best friends to drive-bys. Jason found this ironic since all they drove by were expensive shopping boutiques and fancy restaurants. He didn't relate to rap music much. Jason preferred listening to Brian May destroy the stage with Queen, or better yet, Eric Clapton coaxing moody sounds out of his guitar. Still, the way Caesar's head bobbed to the rhythm, the way he spat along to the lyrics, made it somehow tolerable. Of course Caesar could probably roll around in dog poop and look good doing so. Only when they cruised into their neighborhood was the music turned down. The car slowed as Caesar glanced over at him.

"So what's the real reason you didn't want a ride this morning?"

Jason hesitated. "I noticed Peter walking and figured if you didn't give him a ride, you probably wouldn't give me one either."

"Peter." Caesar said the name as if it exhausted him. "That

kid is disturbed. No one his age should be so bitter." He shook his head, adding, "Not that I don't get it. I mean *I don't*, not entirely, but I know it can't be easy."

"What?" Jason asked.

Caesar locked eyes with him. "Trying to find the right family. One good enough for you. That's gotta be rough. But Peter hasn't gotten any better since he first arrived." He returned his attention to the road. "In fact, I'd say he's gotten worse."

"He'll grow out of it," Jason said. "Eventually you get used to everyone having a family when you don't. Or getting kicked out of a home for things other kids only get grounded for."

"Yeah, but he's got a family now." Caesar frowned. "You know what? It doesn't matter. I'll admit I'm a dick and I never give Peter a ride, but the kid depresses me."

"It's not like he chose to lose his parents," Jason said, feeling defensive.

"That's not what I mean. You can always talk to me about being on your own or whatever. It's Peter's attitude that gets me down. You seem cool though, like you've got it all figured out."

"Oh, totally," Jason said, repressing a smile. "The world is my oyster. The merest gesture gets me what I want. I wink and the ladies fall at my feet!"

Caesar grinned. "You'll have to teach me how that works."

Jason considered winking, to see if it worked on guys as well—or if it worked at all—but he restrained himself as they pulled into the driveway.

Caesar put the car in park before the engine went silent. "Listen. I mean what I said about being able to sympathize. A lot of kids come through here, and I've seen some of the toughest guys break down and cry. If you need anything, my room is just down the hall."

"Thanks," Jason said, knowing he'd never take him up on the offer.

Caesar seemed to sense this. "I mean it. No need for false pride. Not with me. If you ever— Shit." Caesar lifted his rump so he could shove a hand in his front pocket and pull out a vibrating phone. He glanced at the display and rolled his eyes. "Women," he said.

The telephone took him to another world. Caesar started texting. A moment later the phone rang and he answered, stepping outside the car for privacy. He must have forgotten Jason was sitting there at all because he headed inside, even electronically locking the car doors behind him.

Jason smiled, glanced around the car interior, and resisted snooping in the glove box. He allowed himself a moment to consider the conversation. Caesar had said Jason was searching for a family he approved of, not the other way around. A family had to earn the right for him to join. Jason realized it had always been that way. He kept going from home to home, but none of them had fit. His current situation wasn't too bad. The only problem was an inconvenient stirring inside himself. Jason would have to leave eventually. No doubt about it.

But not just yet.

Chapter Three

"Chore rewards!"

Mrs. Hubbard announced this with such gusto that all present at the breakfast table winced.

Despite it being a Saturday morning, a knock on Jason's door informed him of his turn to use the bathroom. Mrs. Hubbard ran a tight ship. Jason was no stranger to this. *Foster home number eight.* That home had been even worse; a schedule of the day's events—broken down into each hour—was posted in every room. He'd put up with it at first because it was a nice house with a pool in the backyard, but eventually the constant micro-managing had been too much. Jason had gotten up at six in the morning, grabbed a shovel from the garage, and spent the next half hour scooping parts of the perfectly manicured lawn into the pool. By the time the foster parents had risen, the water resembled hot cocoa, Jason happily swimming around in it like the sole marshmallow.

"Who would like to explain what chore rewards are?" Mrs. Hubbard looked around the table, from Caesar's empty seat, to Carrie, who refused to make eye contact, and then to Amy, whose mouth was full of pancakes.

"We each have a list of chores to do," Peter said in monotone. "When we've finished them all, we go out for a reward."

Didn't sound so bad. Jason had done chores his whole life without expecting to get anything in return. When he was finished with breakfast, he was given his list. He had to mow the lawn—which was still pretty tame at this time of year—trim the bushes in front of the house, and do some light raking. His tasks were finished within an hour, Jason not having broken a sweat. He was grinning when he reentered the house.

Mrs. Hubbard looked pleased. "Good job! Of course the goal is to get all the chores done. We do that as a family. A team. Carrie is scrubbing the bathrooms, and Peter is vacuuming. Which one of them do you want to help?"

Jason wanted to ask how Caesar was helping. Instead he followed the sound of droning to the living room where Peter was and helped by moving any obstacles out of the way.

"It's best to work slow," Peter confided as they carried the vacuum cleaner to another room. "Otherwise you end up doing everyone else's work. I'd bet you anything that Carrie is sitting on the toilet right now and texting."

"I noticed Caesar is exempt," Jason said.

Peter nodded. "All he has to do is clean his own room and bathroom. Personally, I think that should be the rule for us all, but whatever."

They took their time with the rest of the house. When they were finished, they helped Amy carry trash bags to the garage. The reward portion of the day was much nicer. Mrs. Hubbard took them out to a Mexican buffet, where Jason stuffed himself. Afterwards they drove to The Galleria, a massive upscale mall where they were each allowed to pick out something. This meant waiting as Amy built her own teddy bear at one store, followed by a number of clothing retailers for Carrie. Peter already knew what video game he wanted, which just left—

"What would you like, Jason?" Mrs. Hubbard looked him over as he drew a blank. "You could use some new shoes."

That was true. At the first store they visited, he found a lime green pair of Converse he was crazy about. "Size ten," he said holding them up. "And they're on sale!"

Mrs. Hubbard swatted his arm and smiled like he was being silly. "Those won't go with many outfits. Or any at all. Let's find something more neutral."

Jason held on to the shoes as she shuffled through the store. When she picked up a pair of boring white sneakers and asked the clerk to bring them in his size, he gave up and left the lime green shoes behind.

"Go ahead and lace them up," Mrs. Hubbard encouraged. "You can wear them out of the store and we'll throw away the old ones."

Jason felt like throwing something all right, but then he thought of Michelle. He wasn't attached to his old shoes anyway. He soon began to miss them though. Walking down the mall corridors, he was mortified as his new shoes squeaked with each step, sounding a bit like a farting duck. His cheeks were burning with embarrassment and anger when Peter started laughing. Somehow this made it funny, and Jason and Amy started laughing too. Mrs. Hubbard just shook her head, as if they were being unreasonable.

Dinner time was nearing when they got home, so Jason

helped out in the kitchen. Caesar showed up briefly at the dinner table, flashing him a smile, but then his phone jangled and he was out the door. Of course someone like him wouldn't stay home on a Saturday night. For Jason, weekend nights were just like any other evening, aside from not having to worry about school in the morning. He watched television with the family, then let Peter show off his favorite video game. Jason could see the appeal of living a virtual life, but he didn't have the desire to be an elf who spent too much time getting drunk in imaginary taverns. Peter seemed very amused by this though.

Eventually, Jason excused himself and went to his room, took his guitar out of the closet, and practiced holding chords without strumming the strings. He yearned to play but didn't want to attract attention, enjoying this rare moment of privacy. Maybe tomorrow would be better. Even the most organized foster families cut their kids slack on Sundays. The day of rest and all that. Maybe Jason could take his guitar and find a nice big park to play in. People usually thought he was trying to earn money, which was enough to scare them away. Yeah, a nice day in the park, a light sunburn on his nose, and sore fingers. Grinning at the idea, Jason flopped on his back and closed his eyes.

"Everyone in this family goes to church," Mr. Hubbard said, his gaze hard.

Beside him, Mrs. Hubbard was still frowning, just as she had been ever since she stalked off to fetch reinforcements. Now that her husband was here, Jason supposed he had to explain himself all over again. Sitting on the edge of the bed, still not having gone to take his turn in the bathroom, Jason crossed his arms over his chest.

"I don't believe in God," he said. The truth was, he hadn't really made up his mind, but Jason had enough experience to know he didn't believe in church.

"You don't have to believe in anything," Mr. Hubbard said. "This is a family activity, and we expect you to participate."

Jason was tired of smiling, tired of holding back, and most of all, tired of being good. He wanted to be alone, and the idea of rushing through his morning rituals and putting on the horrible dress clothes Mrs. Hubbard had brought to his room was simply too much.

Sorry, Michelle.

"I don't have to go," Jason said. "It's one of my rights, and it's in the agreement you signed. I'm allowed religious freedom, and that includes the right not to practice. Maybe I should call my caseworker."

"No." Mr. Hubbard held up his hand. "No, that won't be necessary." He took a deep breath and exhaled. "What exactly do you plan on doing with your day?"

"Catch up with my reading," Jason said, grabbing one of the Hardy Boys books.

"So you'll be here while we're gone? You aren't going out?"

"I'll be here," Jason said, fighting down a grin.

Mrs. Hubbard's frown deepened, but she left the room with her husband. Jason skipped breakfast and stayed in his room until the car left the driveway. Then he went downstairs, grabbed an apple from the kitchen, and walked around the house while eating it. He hadn't seen the downstairs bedroom when helping Peter vacuum, so he made that his first destination, curious what his caregivers made of their most private space. He noticed first the dozens of photos of the Hubbard kids. Most were on the wall, some on the two nightstands. These weren't just for show or they wouldn't be hidden away in here. The Hubbards really did care about the kids they took in. This made him feel a little bad about not going to church, but not much. His eyes lingered on the photos of Caesar. Some were of him as a kid. These, while interesting, didn't do much for Jason. The newer photos of Caesar as he was now—those he stared at long and hard.

Then he went to the walk-in closet, surprised to find a number of hunting rifles in one corner. Unzipping one of the bags, he touched the cold metal barrel, his skin crawling at being close to something that could bring death so swiftly. Finding nothing else of interest, he returned to the kitchen, grabbed a can of Coke, and went back upstairs. At the end of the hall, he stopped in front of Caesar's door, closed even now. He wanted to go inside, wanted to open every drawer, peer beneath the bed, try to discover who Caesar was through the things he owned. Jason knew this would only fuel his interest and create an obsession. Then he'd probably do something stupid like when he'd snuck into Shawn's room that night.

Instead, Jason left the door closed and went to take his first leisurely shower since arriving here. Afterwards he strutted naked down the hall back to his room, where he put on underwear and an old pair of jeans. Then he grabbed his guitar from the corner of the room, sat on the bed, and pressed it to his bare chest.

He closed his eyes as his fingers loosened up and the music found its rhythm. Nothing beat the vibrations rumbling against him. When the music was right, the vibrations were too, carrying with them a sense of tranquility. Everything was good in the world. This feeling soaked through Jason's skin, permeated his bones, got swept up into his blood stream. The music made him high. More than that, it put him at ease. He rested his head against the guitar, pressing his ear against its body, and lost himself in euphoria.

"Nice!"

Jason's fingers fumbled, a discordant sound ending the song as his eyes shot open. Caesar was leaning against the doorframe. Today he wore a white tank top and a matching bandana that obscured most of his hair.

"And then not so nice," Caesar said.

Jason opened his mouth and made a croaking noise. This made his cheeks flush, so he set aside the guitar.

"Don't stop!" Caesar said, taking a step forward. "For real. You're really good!"

Jason eyed him, assessing how serious he was. Caesar was smiling. At him. That was enough for him to swing the guitar back around. He strummed for a moment, then chose *Something's Always Wrong* by Toad the Wet Sprocket, a song he knew by heart and felt comfortable performing in front of someone else.

He closed his eyes again as he played, but not because he was shy. He simply didn't need sight any more than he needed taste or smell. Not while making music. At the end of the song, he almost bridged into another, strong clapping bringing him back to reality.

"Man, I wish I could play like that."

"Do you have a guitar?" Jason asked. "I could teach you."

"No. A friend of mine has one, and I've screwed around with it—" Caesar sat on the bed next to him, eyes on the instrument. "The thing is, my friend doesn't know how to play it either."

"Here." Jason handed him the guitar, feeling like he was giving up something fragile and precious, like a newborn baby.

"I'll teach you a few chords. It's easy." He got on his knees in front of Caesar—who was grinning goofily—to show him what to do. "Put one finger right there. No, your index finger. Okay, now put your middle finger on the next one down."

"Next string down?" Caesar asked, brow furrowing.

"Next string and one fret lower. Right. Now with your ring finger—"

"Another one?" Caesar asked in disbelief.

"Yeah. Just put that one up and to the left..." Jason tried to point, but this obscured Caesar's view and one of his fingers slipped from where it was supposed to be.

"I'm not getting it. Just position my hand for me."

Jason reached out and hesitated, which was a big mistake, because Caesar noticed.

"You okay?"

"Yeah!" Jason said. "Just thinking. Uh. Here."

He took hold of Caesar's index finger, trying to remember the last time he'd touched another guy. Normally he was careful not to because he worried it would make him feel... well, this! His chest was tight, his stomach filled with excitement and unease. Caesar's tan skin made his fingernails appear extra white. Jason clenched his jaw as he placed each finger where it needed to be, ignoring thoughts of how nicely they would intertwine with his own. When he was done, he pulled away.

Caesar's attention was on him, not the guitar neck. "We don't have to do this," he said.

Jason stood and wiped the frustration from his expression. "It's cool. You're ready. Try strumming."

Caesar did, and while his grip on the neck wasn't tight enough and his strumming was too strong, he managed something resembling a chord. "All right!" he said. "This is great. Now teach me everything else." He laughed at Jason's reaction and handed the guitar back. "Honestly, man, I think I'd rather listen to the master himself."

Jason smiled at the compliment. "I'm not sure the rest of your family will feel that way."

"They'll love it," Caesar said. "Where'd you learn to play?"

"My mom. She knew the basics, and we had a neighbor a few houses down who gave me lessons in exchange for help around the house." He glanced down at the guitar adoringly, barely seeing the spots where dry wood peeled or dirty strings needed replacing. "This was hers. When she first gave the guitar to me, it felt huge. It fits better now. Or I guess I fit better to it."

Feeling awkward, Jason ducked into the closet to hide the guitar there. The instrument was one of the only things he still had from his original life, the one which felt more real despite having ended nearly nine years ago, and he was starting to worry Mrs. Hubbard would take the guitar away to make him fit her ideal. When he left the closet, he found Caesar glancing around the room.

"Where's all your stuff?" he asked. "It looks like you haven't moved in at all."

"I travel light," Jason explained, going to the dresser to fetch a shirt.

"You've got to do something to personalize this place," Caesar said. "It's like living in a hotel. Or is that how it feels to you anyway?"

"Foster care?" Jason turned to him and shrugged. "I don't know. I've never stayed in a hotel."

Caesar laughed, but not in a condescending way. "Well, being in a hotel feels like this. There's a room, and it has everything you need, but none of it is personal. Come see my room. It's stuffed full of crap. You can go shopping there. Pick stuff out to bring back here."

"Thanks," Jason said, "but I don't have any money."

"I meant that figuratively. You can have whatever you want, no charge."

"No thanks." The idea made him nervous. Being in Caesar's presence was challenging enough. To be surrounded by him would be overwhelming.

"Then let's go shopping for real. Let me buy you something small. Anything to breathe life into this place." Caesar didn't wait for an answer. He took off down the hall. Jason hurried to put on his sneakers and a T-shirt before following.

He found Caesar sitting in his car, wearing a maroon hoodie over the tank top. Jason settled into the passenger seat, but the engine didn't start. Caesar was texting again. Jason worried this meant others would be joining them for their shopping trip. Caesar's frown of concentration deepened. Finally he glanced up. "Some people just don't understand the need for guy time."

"Your girlfriend?" Jason asked.

"Something like that," Caesar said. He pressed the top of the phone until the screen flashed and went blank. "Oh, look! My battery just died. What a pity." He tossed the phone in the back seat and started the engine. "You ready for this?" he shouted over an explosion of hip-hop music.

"Yeah," Jason shouted back.

The truth was, he had no idea what "this" referred to or if he'd be ready for it. But he did know that being in Caesar's passenger seat sure beat an uncomfortable church pew.

"What's it going to be?" Caesar asked, flipping through framed posters. "Boobs?" Flip. "Trippy black-light mushrooms?" Flip. "Eminem?"

"Sex, drugs, and rock and roll," Jason said.

"You make it sound good, but these posters suck." Flip. "Gwen Stefani impersonating Madonna." Flip. "More boobs." Flip. "Here you go, a bunch of greased-up, shirtless firemen."

Caesar turned to face him, but Jason gave him a practiced blank expression. Inside he was wondering if his slipup during the guitar lesson had given him away. If so, he wasn't about to confirm it now.

"Suit yourself." Caesar shrugged. "If you don't like boobs, firemen, or Madonna impersonators, what do you like?"

Jason took over, flipping past posters of bikini models and cannabis leaves. He stopped on a vintage movie poster and grinned. "This."

"Friday the 13th?" Caesar asked. "You like horror movies?"

"Yeah. Ever since I was a little kid. This series was my favorite because of the main character's name."

"Jason?" Caesar said after a moment's thought. "The guy in the hockey mask?"

"Yup. That's me!"

Caesar's eyes widened. "Don't say that!"

"Not a fan?"

"No. Not of any horror movie." Caesar looked back at the poster apprehensively. "I scare easily."

Jason smiled. "Those movies aren't scary. They're funny. You just have to see them with the right person."

"You really want this hanging on your wall?" Caesar asked.

"I have to look at it every time I walk by your room?"

"It's either that, or you go to a horror movie with me so I can show you how fun they really are. There's a new zombie flick I've been dying to see." Jason nudged him. "See what I did there? Dying?"

Caesar raised an eyebrow. "That's your idea of funny?"

"Too stiff?" Jason asked. "Don't like deadpan humor?"

"All right. Stop with the horrible puns and I'll take you to your movie."

"Today?"

Caesar shrugged. "Why not?"

The mall cinema was showing the right movie, but not for another hour, so they strolled past shops and then hit the food court. Jason wanted pizza, but when Caesar suggested Chinese food, he pretended that's what he wanted too. Otherwise they would have to stand in separate lines.

"So what do you think of life with the Hubbards?" Caesar asked between bites of broccoli beef.

Jason just nodded.

"What sort of answer is that? Come on, be honest with me. I can take it."

"Well, you guys probably won't get a reality show any time soon."

"You're saying we're boring?" Caesar's eyes twinkled. "Just you wait until Amy throws one of her fits. Or Carrie goes through another breakup. The censors will have to bleep every other word."

Jason smiled in response. "I like boring. I've had enough drama to last a lifetime."

"So you're here to stay?"

This made him more solemn. "It's a nice house," he said, "and your family is all right. But that doesn't have much bearing on if I stay or not."

"Sounds like you've been doing this a long time."

Jason nodded again.

Caesar poked his food around with his chopsticks. "We get guys like you sometimes who never settle down. One of them told me he resents us. Like, he understood what we're doing is generous or whatever, but he kind of hates us regardless."

"Hate is a strong word," Jason said. "I can't speak for anyone else, but there's this part of me that still wants to go home. My real home. I want to be with my mom again, and even though I know it's not possible, I can't help what I want. So yeah, when people come to me and basically say 'don't worry, I'll be your mom,' I get angry. Not at them, necessarily, but at the situation. Dealing with it would mean accepting the life I knew is gone. It's much easier to just keep moving, keep avoiding the truth."

"Which is why you pack light."

"Yeah."

Caesar let go of his chopsticks and leaned back. "What happened? Can I ask that? I usually don't, but—"

"But what?"

Caesar shrugged. "I wouldn't mind getting to know you better."

Jason swallowed, telling himself not to read anything into this, not to indulge in yet another hopeless fantasy. But Caesar's open expression was enough to get him to talk about a subject he normally avoided. "Okay, but promise you won't say you're sorry. I hate it when people feel sorry for me."

"I promise."

Jason took a deep breath, then exhaled. "My mom was sixteen when she got pregnant. Before then she was practically a saint. Bible camp and church every Sunday. Or walking door-to-door with pamphlets, which is how she met my father. He was a couple of years older. They went to the same school but never talked. That day at the door they did. Later, after she got pregnant, he enlisted in the Army. Mom said it was to escape becoming a parent, not that it matters, since he died in a motorcycle accident a few years later. My mom kept me, obviously, and my grandma helped raise me until my mom was out of high school."

Jason hesitated, unsure if he wanted to continue, but seeing Caesar's look of pure sympathy prompted him to do so. "When I was six, everything started falling apart. My grandma died of a heart attack, and I think my mother started drinking. I remember she didn't smell right to me anymore. Eventually she started seeing this guy, and in retrospect, I think it was the first relationship she'd had since my father. I guess she was lonely or desperate or maybe just drunk, but something was wrong, because when the guy started hitting me, she didn't tell him to leave."

"I'm sorry," Caesar said.

"You promised not to say that."

Caesar's jaw clenched. "I know, but that's really fucked up. I wish I could have been there. Like as old as I am now, I mean, because I would have beat the living shit out of that guy."

Jason couldn't help smiling. "He was pretty big."

"I'm tougher than I look," Caesar responded. "Don't let these good looks fool you. Beneath this pretty exterior is a tiger!"

Jason shook his head, no longer wanting to dwell in the past when the present had him buzzing. He chose to summarize the rest. "Eventually too many people noticed the bruises and stuff, and Child Protective Services stepped in. That's when I was seven years old."

"What about your mom?" Caesar asked.

"There's no chance of me going back."

"Maybe she's not with that guy anymore. Or—"

"That's enough about my life." Jason said this firmly, but he tried to inject humor back into the conversation. "Tell me about the almighty Caesar. What's life as an emperor like?"

Caesar shook his head ruefully. "You have no idea how often I get teased about my name, although I suppose it is appropriate."

"How so?"

Caesar moved his plastic tray to the neighboring table and leaned forward. "I really am going to inherit an empire. My parents have groomed me since day one to take over my father's business."

"I don't even know what he does."

"Flight computers," Caesar said, sounding unimpressed. "Black boxes and some other specialized equipment that gets shoved into airplanes. Not just civilian but military as well. That's where the real money is. Anyway, ever since I started high school, the pressure has really been on for me to follow in his footsteps."

"Is that hard?"

Caesar waved a hand dismissively. "Nah. I've got it made. I don't take anything for granted, trust me. I'm not spoiled. Stories like yours show how random life can be, how lucky anyone is to have a family, not to mention a successful one. I study my ass off and my grades are near perfect. That's what my parents want. I'm supposed to get into Yale and make the right contacts there before I return to learn the ropes from my father. In return, I get to do whatever I want."

"That's not spoiled?" Jason asked.

"Maybe it sounds that way to you," Caesar said. "I told them church is too much, that I'll get straight A's, but I need some time to myself. I honestly think my father is happy to let me run off with my friends, because being social is a big part of those military contracts. You don't get them without being charming. He'd probably say us being in this food court right now is practical training. Am I charming you?"

Jason shrugged. "Maybe a little."

"Then I'm halfway there." Caesar stole a bite of sweet and sour chicken from Jason's plate with his bare hand. After chewing thoughtfully and sucking the tips of his fingers clean, he continued. "You have to understand how my parents function. They like to decide what their kids do, so I let them. I'm giving up my freedom of choice, and sure, the life that awaits me will be comfortable. But it won't be my own. I won't pretend I've got it hard, but I pay a price for the things I have."

Jason made sure he didn't look convinced.

"How old are you?" Caesar asked.

"Almost sixteen."

"Almost?"

"My birthday is next week."

"Oh, wow. Okay, what do you want to do with your life?"

"No idea."

"Well, I don't mean to play the age card on you, but when you do figure it out, ask yourself how easy it would be to give up that dream."

Jason noticed the tension on Caesar's face. "So you're saying you don't want to run your father's business?"

"No, I don't."

"Why? What was your dream?"

"Doesn't matter. Listen, I know Peter hates me, and maybe the rest of you guys do too, but there's nothing I have that you can't. Amy knows this. She's smart. My parents want her to be the perfect little princess, and she plays that role to perfection. When they're not around, she's kind of weird."

Jason thought of how one of their dollhouse dramas had ended in a quadruple homicide. "Weird is good."

"Yeah, but she doesn't show that side when Mom and Dad are around. Carrie still fights against it, but she's made it this far. Peter stepped into line too. He got adopted, but he still lets my mom dictate how he dresses. Have you considered that?"

"No."

"Peter knows how to play the game. I don't get why he still resents me, but whatever. So I guess what I'm trying to say is you can have my life too. If you want it, I mean." Caesar flashed him a smile. "I'm willing to share."

Jason shook his head. "I still say you're spoiled."

"Says the guy who's getting a free meal and movie out of me."

Jason laughed. "Well you did say you were willing to share. Hey, what time is it? Doesn't the movie start soon?"

"No phone, no clock. Let's head over there anyway." Caesar stood, picking up their trays. "Aren't you going to eat your fortune cookie?"

"Nah," Jason said. "I can't stand the things."

"There was nothing funny about it!" Caesar complained as they pulled into the driveway.

"They made papier-mâché brains and hid explosives inside them," Jason said with a grin. "It didn't even make sense. Zombies must be able to smell when brains are fake."

"Well, that's why they hid them inside the shop mannequins." Caesar shuddered and put the car in park. "Definitely not a funny film."

But Caesar had laughed a lot. They both had, mostly at the bad acting or the snarky lines Jason kept adding to the end of dialogue. A Sunday afternoon horror movie wasn't on most people's agenda, so the theater had been mostly empty. They'd had a good time, even if Caesar had tensed up whenever a zombie appeared on screen.

"Speaking of monsters," Caesar said. He fetched his phone from the back seat and turned it on. "Twenty-six text messages, two voicemails."

"Must be nice to be so popular."

"They're all from the same person."

"Oh." Jason thought of dark corkscrew hair. "Steph?"

Caesar glanced away from the phone momentarily, eyeing him before answering. "Yeah. Things have been pretty crazy with her lately."

Jason swallowed. "Crazy hot, or crazy crazy?"

"Crazy crazy. She and I dated on and off for years. It never works out, so we decided to do the whole best-friends-with-benefits deal. You know what I mean?"

Jason nodded numbly.

"Now she's even more into me. The casual thing was her idea, but I think she still takes our relationship seriously."

"But technically she's not your girlfriend?"

Caesar shook his head, distracted by the phone again. Jason watched the amber eyes dart around the screen, brow furrowing at what was displayed there. Jason felt like grabbing the phone and throwing it out the window so it couldn't ruin the day they'd had together. Finally Caesar sighed, shoved the phone in his pocket, and opened the car door. "Come on. It's almost dinner time."

"I'm still full from lunch."

"Yeah, me too, but we still have to make an appearance." Caesar led the way to the front door. "I won't be able to sleep tonight," he moaned. "I'm coming to your room if I have a nightmare."

Jason smiled at the idea. "You've got nothing to worry about. I'll protect you from a zombie invasion."

"They'd hear you coming a mile away. I didn't want to say anything, but what's with the shoes?"

Jason blushed. He'd been squeaking around the mall the whole day. Every single step was a noisy reminder of the stupid sneakers. "Hey, I worked hard for these. They're my chore reward. I wanted a pair of lime-green Converse, but— Uh…"

"My mom," Caesar said, shaking his head. "Maybe you can try oiling them or something."

"Like cooking oil? I'll take them to Burger King and have them dipped in the deep fat fryer."

Caesar guffawed on their way into the house, which might have been what attracted Mrs. Hubbard's attention. She met them in the living room, eyes wide in shock. Mr. Hubbard was right behind her.

"Where have you been?" she asked, addressing Jason directly.

"We just went—"

"You said you would be here," Mrs. Hubbard interrupted. "We returned home from church to find an empty house. Just imagine how that made us feel."

"Relax," Caesar said, clapping a hand on Jason's shoulder. "He was out with me. I was bonding with my new little brother."

"I'm not your brother," Jason snapped before he could help himself. He hated the idea. Caesar wasn't family. He wasn't blood.

"Oh-kay," Caesar said with a grin. "Obviously we still have a lot more bonding to do."

Mr. Hubbard ignored him. "Jason, you did say you would be here."

"I'm sorry," he managed. "I didn't think it would be a problem."

"Well..." Mr. Hubbard looked to his wife, who pressed her lips together and shook her head.

What did they want him to do, fall to his knees and beg? Jason wanted to tell them where they could shove it, maybe knock a lamp off the stupid end table just to see them flinch in fear. But in the corner of his eye, he could see the concern on Caesar's face, feel the hand tighten on his shoulder.

"I was bored and made him tag along," Caesar said. "You guys always want me to spend more time with the family."

Mrs. Hubbard turned her attention to her son, lips tightening. "Next time leave a note," she said. "Come on. You can help set the table."

Jason was sure that last request referred only to him, but Caesar stayed with him all the way until dinner was served. Shortly after all were seated, Caesar's phone rumbled and the texting began anew. This time Caesar occasionally looked up, eyes darting in Jason's direction as if to make sure he was okay. Only when the meal was over did he disappear upstairs.

Jason, as much as he was beginning to despise his new caregivers, made sure to help clear the table and do the dishes. He sat in the family room and watched television with them too, just to show he could be part of the herd. For the first time in many years, he didn't want to lose his foster placement. Jason laughed along to a lame sitcom, realizing that if he wanted more days like today, he'd have to try harder to become a Hubbard.

Jason's dreams were filled with blinding sunshine. The sound of a child's laughter echoed in the distance, a woman's voice calling out. When he was dragged back to the waking world, he found the opposite. The room was dark, the carefree laughter replaced by a terse whisper.

"Hey!"

Jason's face contorted as he took a sharp breath that felt like his first. As he rolled over, that breath caught in his throat. Caesar sat on the edge of the bed, white bandana gone now and his hair a mess. That wasn't all. The hoodie and tank top were gone too. The street light outside illuminated chest hair, dark nipples, and the gentle curve of pectoral muscles. Desire rose in Jason like a hungry beast, but he pushed it back down and looked up into tropical eyes.

"I had a nightmare," Caesar whispered. "I told you that movie was a bad idea!"

"Okay," Jason said, trying to figure out what to do. He pushed himself up on his elbows. "Shouldn't you be waking up your mom for this?"

"I just need company until the adrenaline goes away. You know what it's like."

Jason yawned. "I had a dream about an elephant on a beach once," he said. "Scared the hell out of me. No idea why."

"Adrenaline," Caesar repeated. "Come hang out in my room?"

Jason felt a familiar mix of excitement and dread. "Okay."

Caesar stood, waiting for him to get out of bed. Jason did some quick equations in his head to help the swelling between his legs die down before he stood. He strategically kept his back to Caesar as he pulled on his jeans, so he wouldn't just be in a shirt and pajama bottoms.

"Hey, bring your guitar!"

"Huh? It'll wake up the house."

Caesar waited at the door. "So play quietly!"

Jason grabbed the instrument from the closet and followed Caesar down the hall, which was even darker, but he could still see the strong lines of his neck, the jutting shoulder blades, the narrow waist. Caesar had a nice build. Not football player, by any means. He wasn't a beefy guy, but he wasn't skinny either. Somewhere in the middle, like Jason himself, except with real muscle.

When the door to Caesar's room opened, light flooded the hallway. Jason noticed Caesar's charcoal-colored boxers as he squinted against the brightness, but soon his attention turned to the room itself. He could see why Caesar considered his room to be bare, since this one was bursting with personality. A king-size bed sat in the middle, dark brown sheets and comforter in a rumpled tangle, but even its bulk didn't monopolize the room's space, which felt larger thanks to the vaulted ceilings. In one corner hung a yellow flag with a black two-headed eagle. Posters decorated the walls, a few of girls, some hip-hop themed, and one of Jimi Hendrix that likely had more to do with what he was smoking than his music. On the far side of the room was a loveseat stained by too much snacking, probably while playing the game console that sat on the floor in front of a widescreen television. Next to this, a door revealed bathroom mirrors beyond.

"Jesus!" Jason said, forgetting to whisper. "You're really slumming it here, aren't you? No wonder you keep coming to my room."

"Yeah, it's a complete dump," Caesar said, standing by the door he had just closed. He wasn't bothering to whisper either. "Like I said, you're always welcome in here."

Jason spun around once more, noticing the car magazines on the side table, the sideways pillow in bed that Caesar might have been cuddling with, and the clothes he'd worn that day piled together on the carpet. Jason's instinct was to sit on the bed, since most people didn't have a couch in their bedroom, but instead he just stood there holding his guitar.

"What's with the flag?" Jason asked, nodding to the corner.

"Ah, that's the flag of the Holy Roman Empire. You know... Caesar? Roman Empire? A gift from my father, or a reminder of what I'm supposed to inherit. Thing is, in Julius Caesar's day, they didn't carry flags. They used standards, like a golden eagle on top of a pole that would be carried into battle. Not to mention that the emperors of the Holy Roman Empire weren't known as Caesars."

Jason stared at him dumbfounded. "You're really into history, huh?"

"Told you I study my ass off. And no, I'm not into history." Caesar flopped onto the bed. Propped up on his elbows, his bare legs hung off the edge. Jason averted his eyes.

"I guess when you're named something like that," he said, "you pay more attention."

"Which is probably why you like those horrible Friday the 13th movies."

Jason grinned. "Are you saying my mother named me after a murderer?"

"No. Hey…"

Jason was forced to look back. Caesar scooted further onto the bed, back against the headboard, and patted the space next to him. Jason, throat feeling tight, leaned his guitar against the wall. When he climbed onto the bed, he made sure there was distance between them.

"I was thinking about your mom," Caesar said. "You were how old when it all happened?"

"Seven," Jason answered.

"That's almost nine years ago. A lot can change. Maybe she's not with that guy anymore, you know? When's the last time you had contact with her?"

Jason looked sidelong at him, sexual thoughts dissipating from his mind. Caesar's eyes were wide with concern, maybe even hope. Jason struggled to understand why he would care, why it mattered if there was any chance of being reunited with his mother. He also found himself wanting to reward that hope with a positive answer, to give Caesar the happy ending he desired. But he couldn't.

"She died. When I was twelve."

"What?" Caesar looked shocked, as if he had known her. Or maybe the idea that everything could go so wrong was alien to him. Regardless, he scooted closer to Jason, their shoulders touching. "Do you want to talk about it?"

Jason shrugged. "There's nothing to talk about. I saw her occasionally. There were visits, and she looked… tired, I guess. Then the visits stopped and after awhile they told me the news."

"What happened?"

"You mean how? She drank herself to death. They hid the truth from me for years, but my current caseworker, Michelle, she's different. When I asked her about it, she told me straight-up. I know people were trying to protect me, but I spent years wondering how she died."

"Oh man," Caesar whispered.

"Yeah," Jason said lamely. Talking about this was always too hard. He felt he should be wailing over her death, even all these years later, or at least crying at little. He really did love and miss her, but it was like he'd developed a tolerance. The pain was still there, but it didn't overwhelm him anymore. Sometimes he felt it should. If he really loved her, that pain should tear him up just as much today as it had back then. Jason changed the subject, hoping to escape these uncomfortable thoughts. "What was your nightmare about?"

"Huh? Oh. Zombies were eating my papier-mâché brain, except in my dream it was stuffed full of Chinese food instead of explosives. Listen, I know you hate hearing it, but I'm sorry about your mom."

"Shit happens." Jason shook his head, exhaling in a huff. "Sometimes I wish it had happened sooner."

"What do you mean?"

"I would have been put into care; I would have been seven and upset, but I wouldn't have been angry. I fought for five years, refusing to settle down because I wanted to go home. By the time she died and I realized I never would go home, I guess fighting had become a habit. Besides, nobody wants a twelve-year-old. Not really. They want little kids."

"Not true. Peter had just turned eleven when he came here." Caesar nudged him. "Or you. Why do you think you're here?"

"To make your parents feel good about themselves."

Caesar's jaw dropped. Then he laughed. "You're cold, man! Maybe you *were* named after an axe murderer!"

"Then you shouldn't have invited me to your bedroom in the middle of the night. Look, I even brought my axe."

Jason grabbed his guitar and began lightly plucking at the strings, the notes gentle, the music minimal. Caesar scooted down, grabbing a pillow and lying flat, but his head was upturned, eyes shining as Jason played. This made him feel special, like he was some sort of treasure, the most prized among everything in this trove of a room. Jason closed his eyes, focusing on making the music the best it could be. When he opened them again, Caesar's were shut, his breathing deep. Jason stopped playing and watched his face for any reaction. When it didn't come, he let his eyes travel over Caesar's body, the black hairs on his arms, the shape of his fingers that gripped the pillow next to his head, the small of his back, the curve of his butt.

Jason sat there and stared until his eyes burned. Then he

set aside the guitar and scooted down so they were on an equal level. If the space between them wasn't there, their lips would be touching in a kiss. He studied Caesar's face, memorizing every detail of this unwilling emperor until his eyes betrayed him and refused to stay open any longer.

Chapter Four

Jason yawned and stretched himself awake. Caesar did the same a few moments later. He sat up, considering the three small windows set into the vaulted ceiling that were the only natural source of light. The muted blue sky suggested morning was still breaking. Caesar rolled over to reach the nightstand and turned the alarm clock to face him.

"Shit!" he said, sitting upright. "Mom will be up soon. You better get out of here."

Instead of replying, Jason just laughed.

Caesar blinked at him. "What?"

"Your hair. It's standing straight up!"

Caesar tried to smooth it down before he nodded. "You should see yours. Hey, you've actually got eyes!"

Jason brushed at his bangs self-consciously.

"You shouldn't do that," Caesar said, swinging out of bed and walking to the pile of clothes on the carpet. "Here."

Caesar held up the white bandana he'd worn the other day. Jason just shrugged at it, not having a clue how to turn a square of fabric into headgear.

"Watch." Caesar folded and flipped the bandana until it became a long ribbon. With one knee on the bed, he bent over and used this to brush back Jason's bangs, tying the bandana behind his head. "Now your hair is sticking up too."

Jason patted the top of his head experimentally. "This is stupid."

"Yeah, but it's nice to see those blue eyes. And the rest of your face." Caesar looked him over. "It's a nice face."

Jason pulled off the bandana and held it out. "I look dumb."

Caesar shook his head. "Keep it. There are tons of ways to wear it." A noise in the hall attracted his attention. "You really should get back to your room."

Jason shrugged, not understanding why it would matter, and feeling weird when Caesar cracked open the door to peek down the hall. Had they done something wrong? All his fantasies were still a secret, so Caesar couldn't know the things Jason wished had happened. To anyone else, the night was as innocent as a sleepover.

"Coast is clear." Caesar opened the door all the way. "Go go go!"

Jason hurried down the hall, glancing backward once. Caesar was still at the door.

"Thanks for keeping me safe from the zombies," he whispered.

Jason nodded, ducking into his room. He shut the door—even though he knew Mrs. Hubbard didn't like that—and sat on the edge of the bed. He considered the bandana in his hands, wondering if Caesar was embarrassed about needing someone to comfort him after his nightmare. Maybe that's why he didn't want Jason getting caught in his room. Or maybe, in Caesar's mind, the night hadn't been all that innocent. As they lay facing each other, perhaps they had been having similar dreams.

Jason held the white bandana up to his nose and breathed in. Then he hid it between the mattress and box-spring before he rose to take his turn in the bathroom.

"Ready to go?" Peter tugged on the straps of his backpack to make sure they were tight and considered him with raised eyebrows.

Jason had been loitering by the front door for the last five minutes, hoping Caesar would hurry up and finish whatever he was doing. After showing up at the breakfast table and sneaking a wink in his direction while wolfing a bowl of cereal, Caesar had disappeared upstairs again. Jason was hoping to ride to school with him and had mostly forgotten Peter even existed. Until now.

"Well?"

"Yeah, I think I have everything," Jason said reluctantly. Perhaps Caesar was waiting for him to leave, not wanting to attract suspicion by them being too chummy. If so, then maybe Jason had been right. Last night had been special to them both.

"Not the best move, skipping church," Peter said as they began their journey down the sidewalk. "But then, you knew that already."

Jason glanced over at him, wondering if Peter could possibly be twelve years old. Aside from his videogame marathons, he seemed much older. Like thirty. Sure, life in foster care could be hard, but Jason didn't feel like it had aged him prematurely. Unless he was too similar to see the truth. Was he just as jaded and calculating?

"I don't like church," Jason said. "That's enough reason not to go."

"Has nothing to do with whether you want to go or not," Peter said. "Mrs. Hubbard—Mom—was upset during the whole drive there. Couldn't stop talking about it."

"Yeah, I know," Jason said. "She gave me an earful before you guys left."

"Then why didn't you go? Unless you're playing the redeemed sinner."

"Redeemed sinner?"

"Yeah. If you're good your whole life, nobody cares. You never get credit for it because that's who you've always been. But if you're bad and then later realize the error of your ways—" Peter made bunny rabbits with his fingers to surround this with quotation marks. "—then everyone makes a big deal out of how hard you've worked to change. I refused to wear these stupid clothes for the first few weeks here, and then showed up at the breakfast table one morning in a starchy white dress shirt. Mrs. Hubbard almost cried."

Holy shit! What a calculating little bastard! "I'm not playing any games," Jason said. "I didn't go because I didn't want to."

They walked in silence for a block. Peter kept glancing over at him, as if trying to read his mind. Jason tried to clear his thoughts, just in case he could.

"You're not staying, are you?"

"Probably not," Jason said, mostly in the hopes that the subject would be dropped.

"Too bad," Peter said, but his expression held a hint of satisfaction. "I'm surprised. I mean, I switched foster families too. There were a few I wouldn't have wanted to be adopted by, and I made sure they didn't want me. But the Hubbards… If a rich family doesn't do it for you, then what are you looking for?"

"The impossible," Jason said.

Peter rolled his eyes. "You should at least milk it while you're here. You have a birthday coming up, right? Ask for something cool like a PlayStation. When you get booted out, there's no way they can ask for it back."

"I've always wanted a dog," Jason admitted.

"A dog? They won't let you take that back to the group home. No, you're better off asking for electronics. Maybe a laptop. Some are good for gaming, you know?"

Jason felt more at ease with Peter talking video games and

kept him on that subject until they parted ways. His day went pretty much as it had on Friday, right up to the moment between fifth and sixth period when a familiar face showed up at his locker.

"Again," Caesar said. "What do you have against my car?"

"Peter wanted to walk with me," Jason said. "Besides, it was wait around or be late."

"I'm never late. That's why I have a fast car. I just need extra time for all of this." Caesar gestured at himself. "Such perfection doesn't come naturally."

But Jason had seen him with bedhead and knew that it did. "I *might* let you give me a ride home again."

"Actually, a couple of us were thinking about knocking some colorful balls around after school."

"Pool?" Jason guessed.

"Nah, we're not that cool. Minigolf. Wanna tag along?"

"Yeah, okay."

Just like the previous school day, Jason had a whole class period to be nervous, mostly because he didn't know Caesar's friends, but even if they were heading out solo, he still probably would have had the jitters. This time when he walked to the parking lot, not as many people had gathered yet. Steph was there, side-by-side with Caesar as they leaned against his car. The guy with the shaved head was also present. Jason got a proper introduction. His name was Kurt, and the handshake he offered was painfully firm. Jason noticed his solid build, which along with the skinhead vibe, made him intimidating. They were soon joined by two other girls who couldn't stop giggling. They all piled into two separate cars, the giggling girls and Kurt in one, Jason and Steph riding along with Caesar.

Steph sat up front, of course, allowing Jason to observe them as they talked. Occasionally she turned to include him in the conversation, but Jason mostly just wore a blank expression like he couldn't hear over the music. What he noticed most from his backseat hideaway was how often Steph smiled in Caesar's direction, how her eyes traveled up and down his features as he spoke, only rarely dropping to his arms or his chest. She loved him. Jason was sure of that. She was attractive too, with pink lips that framed straight white teeth, a pert little nose, and warm brown eyes that shone with confidence. For a brief moment, he wished he could be her, wished more than anything that he was pretty and perfect and capable of leaning over to peck Caesar on the cheek in return for whatever compliment he'd just paid her.

When they reached the miniature golf course, Caesar paid for six clubs and declared that everyone should pair up. The giggling girls stuck together, and Steph took hold of Caesar's arm, leaving Jason with Kurt. He wasn't exactly thrilled by this, but he kept his expression neutral. On the course, Caesar and Steph went first, walking ahead to the next hole when finished. Jason kept his eyes on them as he played. He wasn't alone. Kurt seemed just as interested.

"You know about them, right?" he asked, jerking his head in their direction. "I bet Caesar's bragged to you already."

"You mean how they're together?" Jason putted his ball, groaning when it skirted the rim of the hole and rolled farther away.

"*Together,*" Kurt said as if it were ridiculous. "He broke up with her ages ago, and somehow he gets to keep her. The bastard has everything."

Jason glanced over at Caesar, who was smiling broadly while pretending to club a ceramic dwarf over the head. "Yeah, he certainly does."

Kurt swung hard, the ball ricocheting back and forth. "Leave some for the rest of us."

"What about them?" Jason asked, referencing the two girls bringing up the rear.

"Been there, done that," Kurt said. "The twins come as a two-pack, and I don't mean that in a hot way. They're always together at school and on the weekends. They even tag along on each other's dates. If you can't get one of them alone, what's the point, right?"

"Right."

They played three more holes, Kurt aggressively slamming around his ball before giving up and writing a low number on the score card. Jason stuck with it until he'd mastered each new twist, ignoring Kurt's huffs of impatience.

"Time to switch partners!" Caesar declared.

Jason perked up at this, but Steph seemed disappointed.

"But we're a team!"

"What's the matter?" Caesar asked. "I thought you liked

switching holes." The joke didn't really make sense, but it got laughs anyway. "Kurt, you go with Angela. Steph, you go with Angie. Jason, you're with me."

Everyone but Jason groaned as they swapped places. The hole they were on now included a small stone castle. When the ball went through the drawbridge, it continued to travel through a tube to a lower level. Jason didn't talk much until they hopped down there together, giving them more privacy.

"You guys do this a lot?" he asked.

"Minigolf?" Caesar shook his head. "Nope. I figured it was a good way for you to meet everyone."

Jason felt flattered that this was all for his benefit, but couldn't help asking, "Then why am I with you right now?"

Caesar concentrated on his shot. "To make sure you're doing okay."

"I'm fine. You're the one who scares easily." Referring to last night felt good. He wanted it to be a topic, even though he wasn't sure what more he'd say.

"Hey now!" Caesar glanced toward the others. "Don't sully my reputation."

"I'm good at keeping secrets," Jason said, feeling brave. He wondered if he was being obvious. If so, it went over Caesar's head or else he'd probably be freaking out.

"I'll keep that in mind. Yes! Three strokes!"

While Caesar was distracted with writing down his score, Jason kicked his ball into the hole so they could walk to the next course.

"Windmill," he said. "Total classic."

"Yeah." Caesar gestured that he should go first. "So, you want me to hook you up with one of the girls? Not Steph, obviously, but one of the others?"

Jason's stomach felt tight. He was glad to have the ball to focus on. "They aren't really my type."

"How about Kurt?"

Jason swung, missing the ball completely. He focused on repositioning himself and chose his answer carefully. "I don't think I'm his type."

Caesar laughed. "No, definitely not. You ever been in love before?"

"No," Jason said without hesitation. He was pretty sure love was a two-way street, and that unless the circuit was completed, it didn't really count. "Have you?"

"Move over," Caesar said, setting his ball down on the starting point.

Jason was surprised to see his own ball farther down the green. He didn't remember hitting it. He stood aside, waiting for the answer to his question, but it never came.

"If someone catches your eye," Caesar said, his ball disappearing between the windmill's blades, "you just let me know. I'm sure you can handle yourself, but I'd want to know." Caesar looked up at him. "No matter who they are, I'd want you to tell me."

Jason tried to swallow but couldn't. He opened his dry mouth, searching for the right words. He almost had them when Kurt's voice called out.

"Switch partners! Steph, you're with me. The rest of you, figure it out!"

Caesar shrugged easily. "My own ploy used against me. You take Angela. She's slightly less annoying than Angie."

Jason wanted to demand they continue their conversation—wanted to tell Kurt to go fuck himself—but instead he said, "They aren't really twins, are they?"

"No, but don't tell them that."

Jason was stuck with his new partner the rest of the game. The two girls continued to look at and communicate with each other, even over a distance, so he was mostly left alone. Afterwards they returned to the parking lot. Kurt left with the twins. Jason was in the back seat again and remained there even after they'd dropped off Steph. The moment had passed. Sure, he could still open his big mouth and tell Caesar the truth, but given time to think about it, he knew it was a bad idea. Some moments with Shawn had been like this, odd snippets of conversation or accidental touches that Jason had interpreted as evidence of their mutual attraction. Reality had proven much less romantic.

Then again, those moments had been fewer in number. Even now, Caesar's eyes kept returning to the rearview mirror to meet his. Why? Why did he look at Jason just as often as Jason looked at him? Surely that had to mean something.

"You going to let me give you a ride tomorrow morning?" Caesar asked.

"I feel bad abandoning Peter."

"I'd give him a ride too, if he'd accept."

"What do you mean?"

"I told you," Caesar said. "The kid hates me. Don't ask me why. I don't have a clue."

"Oh." Jason thought about it. "Maybe we'll just keep things how they are. I'll walk with him in the morning and ride back with you in the afternoon."

"Suit yourself, although I have a meet after school tomorrow."

"A meet? What kind? Track?"

The eyes in the rearview mirror smiled. "Wait and see. I'll be by my car at the usual time. You can come with and watch. Cheer me on."

"Okay," Jason said, and feeling some bravery return to him, he added, "It's a date!"

Torture. Absolute torture.

For the second time, Jason sat in the bleachers and stared as Caesar thrust, squirmed, and writhed against another guy. High school wrestling was nothing like what he'd seen on television. Gone were the campy costumes and over-the-top characters giving ridiculous speeches. So far no one had been hit over the head with a folding chair. There wasn't even a wrestling ring! Just guy after guy, wearing skin-tight spandex, rolling around together on a mat.

During the wrestling meet on Tuesday, Jason's impression had been of guys driven to insanity by hormones but absolutely clueless as to how sex functioned. Heads would often be stuffed into crotches, and a certain starting position mimicked doggy-style, and yet none of it was quite right. The two guys on the mat would switch positions countless times, not finding satisfaction in any of them.

Since then, Caesar had taught Jason the basic rules, how pinning was the goal, but that competitors had a number of other ways to earn or lose points. Understanding how the sport worked made it appear a lot less perverted. Regardless, Jason's mind did wander at times. Especially when Caesar was out there on the mat wearing nothing but a sky-blue singlet. The amount of curves that the uniforms revealed was astounding and yet still left so much to the imagination. Jason often found his mouth hanging open. He'd have to practice keeping it shut, and would have plenty of opportunities. Every Tuesday and Thursday, he planned on sitting right where he was. At least until wrestling season was over.

"Thinking of joining the team?"

Jason looked up just as Steph sat down next to him. She had the smiliest eyes ever. He supposed he would too, if he were her.

"No. Sports aren't really my thing."

Steph considered the match in progress. "Then you're the first sensible guy I've ever met. Personally, I don't see the appeal. Unless you can explain it."

Jason could think of countless reasons why rolling around with another guy was appealing, but opted for something he'd heard recently. "It's a time-honored sport. The oldest of its kind."

Her head swiveled back in his direction. "Did Caesar tell you that?"

"No," Jason said. Then his shoulders slumped. "Well, yeah. You probably know more about wrestling than I do."

Steph swatted his shoulder playfully and laughed. "I don't know much either. I tend to zone out when Caesar talks about it. So boring!" A referee whistled loudly before beginning to yell, attracting their attention. "Then again, it is sort of hot."

"Yeah," Jason said without thinking. When Steph looked at him in surprise, he quickly added, "I can see why you would think that."

Jason wasn't in the closet. He didn't feel like he'd ever been. Around age twelve he realized he found guys more attractive than girls. Perhaps one of the few perks of not having parents was not feeling pressure to be someone he wasn't. He didn't fear what his mother or father would think because they were already gone. He supposed he could have told his caseworkers and caregivers over the years, but why would it matter to them? The only people he ever felt like confiding in were the guys he became infatuated with. As for Steph, he'd only obscured the truth because he didn't want anyone to know he was drooling over Caesar.

Especially now. What greater proof could there be that Caesar was straight? Jason wouldn't be able to wrestle like that, be intimately close to another guy without getting hard. Even watching Caesar closely for such a reaction caused a stirring in his pants.

"It's really nice to support your brother this way," Steph was saying. "By being here, I mean."

"He's not my brother," Jason said, still half-distracted.

"Oh. I guess it takes a long time before it feels like family, huh?"

He pulled his attention away from the action. "To be honest, it never feels like family."

Steph's eyes searched his. He was sure she was going to say she was sorry, which would have set his teeth on edge. Instead she nodded, as if understanding. "It can feel that way with blood relatives too, believe it or not. I'm sure it's not exactly the same, but I refuse to believe I'm related to my father."

"Home life not so good?" he asked.

"Home life is great. Dad took off when I was a baby but likes to show up every few years—usually drunk—to remind us all what a loser he is. So I've had a glimpse of what it's like to not have parents. I'm halfway there."

Jason nodded. She couldn't understand completely. No one could unless they had been through it themselves, but he appreciated that she was making an effort instead of pitying him. And perhaps that incomplete home life provided a Freudian explanation as to why she incessantly texted Caesar.

"So what do you think of your new foster parents?" Steph asked casually.

Jason hesitated. If he planned on staying, which he kept seesawing on, and any badmouthing got back to the Hubbards...

"What I mean," Steph continued, "is do you also find them to be overbearing, controlling, and just a little bit creepy?"

Jason smiled. "That's one way of putting it."

Steph nodded. "I got a full dose when Caesar and I used to date. Mrs. Hubbard gave me a huge lecture once on how much makeup a 'young lady' like me should wear. I swear Caesar is adopted. I don't see how else he could be so normal."

As if on cue, Caesar strolled out to meet his opponent. When he noticed them in the bleachers, he pretended to stumble, pinwheeling his arms comically.

"Maybe not normal exactly," Steph amended, "but by way of comparison, he turned out fine."

"So you two used to date?" Jason pried.

Steph nodded. "Off and on. Each time we'd get all starry-eyed for each other, then we'd bask in the honeymoon stage, and later we'd eventually remember why we broke up in the first place. Not exactly a vicious cycle, since we both enjoyed ourselves, but it couldn't go on like that forever. Now we're just good friends. Some people in life—most of them, really—aren't meant to be anything else."

"How can you tell who is who?"

"Friends accept you for who you are," Steph said. "Lovers always want more from you—like your time and affection—or more for you, like they want you to be happier, healthier… just *more*."

"And Caesar didn't want more?"

Steph mulled the question over. "We'd reach a certain point, and he'd be content with who we were. He didn't need it to be more. That's why he can do this whole friends-with-benefits thing and not need to take it to the next level."

"And you?"

Steph shrugged. "Beats being lonely."

"I hear Kurt is single," Jason said helpfully.

"I hear you are too," Steph said, but her attention remained on Caesar, eyes shining as he finished pinning his opponent. Then he leapt to his feet, pumping his fists victoriously.

No, she definitely wasn't ready to move on yet. In that regard, neither was Jason.

Chapter Five

The morning felt faded, the sun higher in the sky than it should have been. Jason lay in bed and contemplated this. Was it Sunday? Had the Hubbards gone to church, leaving him to sleep in for once? But no, Friday was still too fresh in his mind. Saturday was here, and yet he still lazed away in bed. No being summoned to the bathroom for his allotted time, no dreadful chore awards. Could this be a birthday gift to him? If so, it wasn't a bad present.

He lay there another half hour, just because he could, his morning wood rising and falling depending on the thoughts drifting through his mind. Caesar sent it racing up, up, up! Thoughts of another birthday—one without his mother or any true semblance of a family—made it flop over with despair. Originally, he was supposed to spend this birthday with Michelle. They'd talked months ago about what he wanted to do. That was before the Hubbards had shown up at the group home. Still, maybe it wouldn't be so bad. The day was already off to a good start.

Sitting up with a wide-mouthed yawn, Jason got out of bed and trudged to the bathroom. Once showered and dressed, he went downstairs to the kitchen and dining area where the table was empty except for his place. There, an empty plate and clean cutlery awaited him.

He was wondering if this was meant to teach him a lesson for sleeping in when Mrs. Hubbard came into the room.

"He's awake!" she cried, loud enough for the whole house to hear. Then she went to him and pressed her hands to his cheeks. "Happy birthday, Jason! Sixteen is such a special milestone! Did you sleep well?"

"Yeah," he said, more than a little taken aback.

"What would you like to eat? You can have anything you want."

"Pancakes?" he tried.

Mrs. Hubbard nodded but hesitated. "Pancakes are awfully sweet, and you'll be having cake soon enough. Maybe eggs would be better?"

He almost felt relieved that she was still so controlling. "Scrambled?" he bargained. "With cheese?"

Mrs. Hubbard nodded and went to the refrigerator.

"You should have asked for a lobster omelet with truffle fries," said a welcome voice as Caesar strolled into the room. "Or maybe an Irish coffee. Use those birthday wishes wisely."

Jason smiled as Caesar plopped down a present in front of him and took a seat. "For me?" he asked, eyeing the elongated box with interest. He couldn't think of anything he really wanted, but he was curious to see what Caesar had chosen to give him.

"Yup, for you. I can't believe you're sixteen already. It seems like only yesterday that you were fifteen."

"Ha-ha," Jason said, still eyeing the present.

"Go ahead, open it."

"Not until after he blows out his candles," Mrs. Hubbard called from the stove.

Caesar rolled his eyes. "Open it. You'll need them for this afternoon."

Jason glanced over at Mrs. Hubbard, whose lips were pressed together, but she nodded. He didn't need any more prompting. He tore off the paper, breath catching when he saw the Converse logo. Had Caesar really remembered Jason mentioning them? Did he pay that much attention to his words? Surely not! They wouldn't be the right color, but any pair would be better than the horrible shoes he had now. Jason flipped open the box.

Lime green. Just like he wanted.

"I tried telling him you already have a perfectly good pair of shoes," Mrs. Hubbard said.

"These are different," Caesar said. "They're racing shoes."

"Racing shoes?" Jason asked.

"Must you give away everything?" Mrs. Hubbard scolded.

Jason looked up. "We're going go-kart racing?"

Caesar nodded. "Mom called your caseworker for ideas, and she tipped us off. So what do you think of the shoes?"

"They're perfect!" Jason breathed. "I love them!"

Caesar smiled. "Good. I bought myself a pair too." He leaned back and put a foot on the table, Mrs. Hubbard tsking as she brought over a plate of eggs. Caesar's shoes were at least a size larger, and neon blue rather than lime green, but they were the same style. "Now we match. Lace them up!"

"Let him eat," Mrs. Hubbard said. "This is exactly why I didn't want him opening anything yet."

Jason kept the shoes next to his plate as he wolfed down the eggs. Then he carefully weaved the laces through each hole before sliding them on. As he was doing so, the rest of the family slowly gathered in the room to congratulate him, each bringing along another present.

Money can't buy love, but it certainly could rent it. For the first time—and in a completely superficial way—Jason loved the Hubbards. He was used to getting a present on his birthday, and would often be taken out somewhere like McDonalds when he was younger, but he'd never had a birthday like this before. A huge cake almost as wide as the table was set before him, his full name spelled out below *Happy Birthday*. After he blew out the candles, he opened his next present. Peter had bought him a computer game.

"It's an expansion pack for World of Warcraft," he explained. "Not the ideal place to start, but I thought we could run a few quests together and see what you think."

"Great!" Jason didn't have a clue what Peter was talking about, but he was having too much fun to mind. From Amy he got guitar picks and an electric tuner, and from Carrie, an MP3 player loaded with some of her favorite music. Mrs. Hubbard gave him his first suit, which was gray and appeared extremely uncomfortable. Her husband gave him a jacket too, but this one was camouflage.

"For a weekend out," he explained. "Just us men."

If that included Caesar, then it sounded like a good present to Jason!

After cake and ice cream, he was taken to an indoor race track that not only had go-karts, but special ones for adults that required the driver to be at least sixteen. These beefed-up karts included mandatory helmets, which made the experience feel more genuine, like they were part of a miniature Indy 500.

On one of his previous birthdays, Jason had asked to be taken to Chuck E. Cheese's. This was tricky, since the care home couldn't afford to bring the other kids along, so just Jason and his caseworker had gone. He'd been given twenty dollars worth of tokens, which seemed like a lot at the time, but they disappeared into video games in under an hour. Today Jason expected to race on the go-kart track once, maybe twice—which they did. He loved every minute of it too, getting lost in the rush of speed.

When the second round came to an end and he stepped out of the kart, Mr. Hubbard walked up to him.

"Another couple of laps?" he asked.

"Seriously?" Jason asked.

"Sure! We've got all day." Mr. Hubbard peered over Jason's shoulder and squinted. "Actually, it looks like Peter wants us to do laser tag next. I think he's just jealous because he's too young to race with us. What do you think? Quick game of tag and then back on the track?"

Jason couldn't believe his luck. Maybe he'd been a little hard on the Hubbards. Sure they expected a lot, but they gave just as much in return. Mr. Hubbard walked away to make arrangements. Jason was struggling with getting his helmet off when Caesar strolled up.

"The chin strap is twisted," he said. "Here, let me help."

Instead of reaching for the strap, Caesar flipped up Jason's visor and grinned.

"What?" Jason asked subconsciously.

"I'm telling you, you've got a great face. Cut your hair and you could have anyone you want."

Jason doubted that was true. He managed to get the chin strap figured out and pulled the helmet off, his hair flopping into his face once again. Caesar pretended to look crushed by this.

Jason stuck out his tongue in response. "Come on," he said, "I'm about to whoop your ass at laser tag."

"You a pro or something?" Caesar asked.

"Certified," Jason lied. He'd never played in his life, but figured he'd have beginner's luck. As it turned out, he didn't fare so badly. Of course most of his competitors were either little kids or Mr. and Mrs. Hubbard, but Jason managed to stand his ground against Carrie and Caesar. In the end, Peter was the sole survivor, his endless hours of gaming giving him an edge.

The rest of the day passed in this fashion; go-kart races, black light miniature golf, video games, and more laser tag. As the sun was setting, they went out to an Italian restaurant and ate their fill. The Hubbards must have told the server it was Jason's birthday, since a piece of cake sizzling with sparklers was brought to him by singing waiters. The experience was embarrassing, but also made him feel special, in a humiliating sort of way.

Afterwards they went to the movies, and while the animated

feature was one he never would have chosen to see, his head felt on the verge of exploding from happiness. Amy's presence saved him from this fate, since they couldn't see something gorier with her around. Regardless, he couldn't take much more of this. They had done more fun stuff in a day than he usually did in a year. By the time they returned home, he collapsed straight into bed, a permanent smile plastered on his face. Still fully dressed, feet feeling heavy in his new shoes, he lost himself in dreams of racing birthday cakes and singing lasagnas.

"I can understand you not wanting to go to church last week," Mrs. Hubbard said. "I know how overwhelming it all must have seemed. But this time you really have no excuse."

Things were back to normal. Jason almost felt relieved, since this was familiar territory compared to yesterday's endless perfection. As much as he appreciated being treated so well, he didn't intend to let it change who he was. "I told you, I don't believe in God. Not having a religion *is* my religion."

Mrs. Hubbard turned her head to the door, as if to call her husband, but then changed tactics. "This is about family time. That can take place at church, a restaurant, or a go-kart track. Sometimes you'll like where such things take place, sometimes you won't."

Jason could read between the lines. If he liked the good things, he had to put up with the bad, and part of him did feel guilty for denying such a simple request. He could easily daydream through a church sermon and had previously… And yet that would mean not being alone with Caesar again.

"Sorry," he said. "I feel strongly about this."

Eyebrows raised and lips pressed together, Mrs. Hubbard left the room. That wasn't so bad. Jason flopped back into bed, waiting until the house went quiet. Once sure that everyone had gone, he got up, took a shower, and went downstairs for a bowl of cereal. He walked the house as he ate, finding no sign of Caesar. Afterwards he went upstairs to the end of the hall, standing motionless as he listened for any sound on the other side of the door.

Nothing. Dead silence. He must have stood there ten minutes working up the courage to knock.

"Hello?" he tried first. "Caesar? I'm bored. Want to go

shopping or something?" No response. Maybe he was sleeping in? Jason knocked once. Then twice. Frustrated, he went downstairs and looked out the front window. Caesar's car was gone. He felt discouraged by this, but soon another opportunity sprang to mind. Jason went back upstairs, placed a sweaty palm on a doorknob to a bedroom that wasn't his, and turned it.

The first sensation was a lingering scent. He found it hard to define. A little cologne maybe, mixed with whatever shampoo Caesar used. Below this was the somewhat musky smell of a room that had recently been slept in. Jason shut the door behind him, wanting to keep this essence trapped. He felt a pulling in his stomach, a strange cocktail of excitement and anxiety. Holy shit, this was desperate! But he didn't truly care how it reflected on him.

Jason walked around the room, running his fingers along the spines of a movie collection, searching the titles and his memory for anything even remotely homoerotic and coming up empty. He opened dresser drawers, shifting clothes to find hidden porn magazines that revealed Caesar as anything other than straight. Nothing. Then he entered the bathroom for the first time, not sure what he was looking for. Hope, he supposed. Hope against all evidence pointing to the contrary, that Caesar kissing Steph was a ruse to fool any onlookers, that Caesar might want to kiss him instead.

Jason explored the room, his despair increasing as he continued to come up empty-handed. As he flopped backward onto the bed, grabbing and hugging a pillow to his chest, he had to accept the truth: Caesar was just a normal guy. Handsome and sort of charming—sure. But normal nonetheless. Jason closed his eyes and sighed. How nice that must be. None of the desperate struggles, misguided fantasies, or lonely nights. Just a sea of potential girlfriends and an eventual wife and kids, followed by the standard happily-ever-after.

"Hey!"

Jason jerked back to reality, surprised to find Caesar standing over him.

"What are you doing in here?"

"Sorry. It's just..." Jason blinked, glancing around for an excuse. "You know how much my room sucks. It's way more comfortable in here."

"Obviously," Caesar said, glancing at the pillow Jason was

still hugging and shaking his head when he shoved it away. "I've had the morning from hell, man."

Jason sat up, making room for Caesar to sit on the end of the bed. "Where were you?"

"With Steph. She woke me up this morning, crying on the phone, so I went over there to see what I could do."

"Her father?" Jason asked.

Caesar looked surprised. "Yeah. You guys have really gotten to know each other, huh?"

"A little."

"Anyway, the asshole resurfaces occasionally, making her life hell. Yesterday was one such occasion."

"Oh." Jason swallowed, trying to imagine Steph crying in her bedroom, her tears giving way to relief as Caesar took her into his arms. "Did you guys do it?"

"It wasn't a booty call. You're such a perv!"

Jason laughed in relief more than anything. "I'm just trying to figure you guys out. I mean, do you love her?"

Caesar exhaled. "Only in the way you do after you've realized you can't be with a person, you know what I mean?"

Jason shook his head. "Nope."

"Oh. Well, I still have feelings for her, but they aren't the exact same emotions I had when we were together. Or maybe they are, but they're sort of hibernating. Not active, but not gone. Maybe someday they'll fade away entirely."

"That's sad," Jason said.

"Is it?"

He nodded, because he could picture what it must be like to be Steph—to have once been loved by Caesar and to now only have a shadow of that devotion.

A sound like an angry bee came from Caesar's pocket. He pulled out his cell phone, pushed a few buttons, and groaned. Jason watched him text something, shaking his head as he did so. Then he tossed the phone aside and considered him. "You know what? Don't fall in love. It's not worth it."

Jason furrowed his brow. "Really?"

Caesar flopped on the bed, rolling onto his back and stretching his arms over his head. "No. Not really. Hey, why don't you grab your guitar? Play me something to ease my troubled mind."

Jason hopped up to do just that and was in his bedroom

closet when he heard the garage door rumbling downstairs. He hesitated, wondering if he should pretend to be doing something productive. What he probably should have done was run down the hall and hide in Caesar's room. Maybe then Mrs. Hubbard wouldn't have appeared in his doorway.

"Could you help me with a few things?" she asked.

His stomach sank, but he nodded anyway. "Sure."

"A few things" turned out to be a number of tedious chores. First he had to help her in the kitchen, prepping for lunch and then doing dishes. He didn't see why they couldn't leave the mess until after they ate, when they would have generated more dirty dishes. Might as well do them all at once. This was nothing compared to what came next. Mrs. Hubbard wanted to clean out the refrigerator, which not only involved checking expiration dates, but wiping down the bottles and jars of food that were still good. Jason suspected this was intended to punish him, and when she mentioned waxing the kitchen floor he decided he'd had enough.

"Why isn't anyone else doing chores?" he spat.

Mrs. Hubbard's response was just as heated. "Because they already contributed to the family this morning by going to church."

He nearly pointed out that Caesar hadn't, but he was loyal enough to keep his mouth shut. The Emperor himself showed up shortly afterwards, car keys in hand. He spared Jason a sympathetic wince before heading out the door. This made the tedious tasks a little easier, since Jason stopped constantly wishing he could go back upstairs and rejoin him. Of course now he wondered where Caesar had gone. Maybe Steph had called him back, and maybe this time Caesar would act on Jason's idea and get laid.

This thought put him in a foul mood that lasted the rest of the day, through lunch, dinner, and the evening television. When Jason was free to return to his room again, he left the door open and plucked at the guitar in a way that he hoped sounded Spanish. To his ear, the music was romantic, and he liked the idea of Caesar stopping on his way down the hall to listen. Jason played until his fingers were numb, ignoring Amy when she sleepily asked how much longer until he was finished.

Eventually it worked. When he looked up from his guitar for

what felt like the hundredth time, Caesar was there, head leaning against the doorway, eyes tired.

"Hey!" Jason said. "You're home!"

This enthusiasm caused a smile, but even it was weary. "That I am. Nice song. What's it from?"

"Nothing. Just a little freestyle." Jason set aside the guitar and stood. "Should we hang out in your room? I can play more for you."

Caesar shook his head. "After a day like today, I just want to go to sleep. See you tomorrow, okay?"

Jason's head nodded, which he considered a betrayal since the rest of him didn't like this plan at all. A whole day until he would have another chance, and every possibility that Steph, Kurt, or someone else would be around. After Caesar disappeared down the hall, Jason paced the room feeling…

Too much. He craved and yearned and needed. He was horny and emotional, angry and vulnerable. He considered excuses, reasons to knock on Caesar's door, but all of them were flimsy. In each scenario, he was sent back to his room. Jason thought of how he'd snuck into Shawn's room just to see him sleeping. Similar emotions had driven him to do stupid things before, but they were a pale imitation of what he felt now. Shawn had been a physical infatuation. Jason had barely known him. Caesar actually talked to Jason, welcomed him into his life, made him feel good about himself.

It's a nice face.

Caesar had said this and something similar on two different occasions. He liked how Jason looked. No guy had ever complimented him like that before. Not many girls either. This was a hint, an invitation. One of them had to make the first move, that's all. And it would seem Jason would be the one to do it, since he had already taken the first few steps. He found himself in the hallway, walking through blissful darkness and glorious silence, which meant the midnight hour belonged to him alone. He stopped when he reached Caesar's door. Hand on the knob, breath held tightly in his lungs, he willed the door to open silently. A familiar smell preceded a room cast in shadow—a form in the bed breathing softly.

Jason shut the door behind him and remained still until he was sure he hadn't disturbed this peaceful scene. Then he walked to the bed. Caesar was on his back, arms splayed out. As Jason's vision adjusted to the dark, he could see the way Caesar's brow was knotted, a frown on his face as if the stress of the day refused to leave him, even in sleep. Jason loved the strong nose, the proud mouth, the narrow chin. How could Caesar ever look at him and see something good when Caesar was so incredibly handsome?

Jason put one knee on the bed, then a hand so he could bend over, bringing their faces parallel like they had been the other night, when they had slept side by side. Except now he didn't let that distance remain. He placed his other knee on the mattress. If he could never kiss those lips, Jason wanted to at least pretend, to get as close as humanly possible so he could imagine over and over what it must really be like. Their noses were on the verge of brushing, Caesar's breath practically his own when it all went wrong.

Caesar's eyelids fluttered open.

For a moment, they locked gazes. Past the initial surprise, Jason saw understanding. They were both holding their breath. If Jason's fantasies held any truth, any invisible hope, they would kiss now. This would be the beginning of everything. Caesar shifted, bringing a hand near his face... but then that hand kept moving, landing on Jason's shoulder and pushing him away. Gently, but still away.

Everything leading to this moment—every dream, wish, and fantasy—cracked and shattered. Reality returned, leaving him all too aware of what he'd done. This wasn't a love story. He had crept into some guy's room, and while he honestly wasn't going to kiss Caesar, no one would ever believe that. Invasion of privacy, of personal space. The breaking of trust, the appearance of sexual assault. Jason had committed so many social transgressions that it made his head spin.

Sitting up on both knees, he tried to find an expression that showed he understood what he had done. "I'm sorry," he said, voice cracking.

Caesar studied him, propped up on one elbow. Was he deciding what to do? Trying to find some suitable punishment?

"Jason," he said.

The lips shaping his name caused emotions to stir. So messed up! So lost! But Jason couldn't help himself. From the nightstand, the phone shook with a half-second buzz. Caesar's jaw clenched.

He closed his eyes, and when he opened them again, they were angry.

"Go back to your room," he said.

"I'm sorry," Jason said, pushing himself off the bed.

"Just go!" Caesar rolled over, turned his back to him and covered his head with his arms like a man protecting himself from a beating. Jason stared for a moment longer before he abandoned stealth and hurried back to his room. Once there, he shut the door, wishing it had a lock. Since it didn't, he sat with his back to it, working hard to fight off the tears that wanted to make the night even more humiliating. He'd been stupid. Just like before.

No. That wasn't true. This was worse, because unlike before, Jason didn't want to give up. He still wanted to run down that hall, find the words to make everything right. But he knew nothing he could say or do would help. Only one option remained, a familiar path that he had walked before. As Jason sat in the dark of his room, he promised himself this would be the last time.

Chapter Six

Jason needed an idea. One that would get him sent back to the group home today. Sure he could call Michelle, tell her he wanted to leave. Or he could say as much to the Hubbards, scream and shout that he hated them and wanted to go. But such methods often didn't work, as Jason had discovered early on. People would mistake his acting out as a cry for help, assaulting him with tedious questions and well-meaning speeches. No, if he wanted to ensure the speediest exit, he would have to make himself a threat to the rest of the family. Like the stunt where he'd set the shower curtain on fire. How could anyone sleep while wondering if he'd burn down the house?

During breakfast, he kept his eyes open for any opportunity. Food fight? Too tame. A butter knife at Amy's throat? Ugh. That might work, but Jason still had to live with himself. He needed an idea that scared people, not traumatized them. By the end of the meal, he still didn't have anything, but at least Caesar hadn't shown up at the table.

Jason was at the front door and wearing his backpack when he remembered the guns in Mr. Hubbard's closet. If he grabbed one, sat on the stairs and refused to go anywhere… that would probably do it. Maybe he could point the gun at himself, get thrown into a mental hospital. Hell, maybe they could fix him while he was there.

"Ready to go?" Peter asked, joining him in the entryway.

Jason was going to say no, march into the closet to begin his ploy, but then Caesar appeared at the top of the stairs and it was too much. Jason needed to get away from him, escape the shame and pain. He was out the door and down the sidewalk so fast that Peter had to run to catch up with him.

"Hey! Slow down! What's going on?"

Jason ignored Peter's questions. Why bother playing nice with any of the Hubbards now? Especially when he was so close to leaving.

"I told you that guy is a jerk," Peter continued. "What did he do?"

Jason shook his head, stomping along the pavement. In the back of his mind, he worried about damaging the shoes Caesar had given him. Such insane thoughts wouldn't end until he got away from here permanently.

From behind he heard an engine roaring, a silver spaceship pulling up alongside him. Jason refused to look. When he heard the hum of a window rolling down and a voice telling him to get in the car, he picked up the pace.

The engine of Caesar's car growled as it launched down the street and stopped. The red brake lights were joined by white before it started to reverse at a frightening speed. Jason thought Caesar intended to run him over. The rear of the car swerved toward him, but ended up pulling into a driveway just ahead. When the car stopped, the passenger door was lined up perfectly with the sidewalk. Jason stopped in his tracks.

The door opened, Caesar ducking slightly to be seen. He fixed Jason with an angry glare. "Get in the fucking car!"

Why? So Caesar could tell him off? Demand an apology? Take him somewhere to kick his ass? Such things would hurt on many different levels, but maybe that's what it would take to get Jason to stop screwing up like this.

He took a step forward, but Peter grabbed his arm. "Let's go," he said. "We can take the bus."

Caesar redirected his anger. "You want a ride, Peter? Hop in. Come on! What are you so scared of?"

"I'm not scared of anything!" Peter shouted. "You better leave or I'll tell Mom you almost ran us over!"

"It's fine," Jason said, pulling his arm free. "Walk to school or take the bus without me. I don't care."

He got into Caesar's car, glancing out the window as he shut the door and noticing the accusation on Peter's face. Not that it would matter. The car lurched, pulling back onto the street.

"What were you doing in my room last night?" Caesar asked, still sounding angry.

"Nothing," Jason said. "I wasn't going to do anything. I was just pretending."

"Pretending?"

"You wouldn't understand."

"It looked like you were going to—"

"I wouldn't have," Jason said. "Believe whatever you want, but I wouldn't have."

The car was silent as they pulled out of the neighborhood and into a busy street. Jason kept his attention on the traffic instead of the driver, waiting for the insults to start. The silence was driving him crazy, so he reached for the stereo. Even Caesar's hip-hop was better than this. His finger only brushed the power button before Caesar knocked it away.

"We need to talk," he said.

"No, we don't!" Jason said. "I can imagine everything you could possibly say. You don't think I know how fucked up I am? I don't need you to tell me that! Save your breath. It won't happen again because I'm leaving."

"What?"

"I'll be gone tonight. You won't see me again."

The car swerved, one tire going up and over a curb as the vehicle screeched to a halt. Jason's heart was pounding, the blood draining from his face as he looked over for an explanation. Caesar's jaw clenched as he unbuckled the seatbelt, but his eyes... Oh hell, his eyes! Those slices of amber were on him in a way Jason had imagined more than once while biting his lip in bed. Caesar brought his face near, and Jason decided that even if he was mistaken, if some horrible violence was about to happen instead, that it would be worth this one happy delusion.

Caesar grabbed Jason's head with both his hands, stared hard to make sure his intent was known. Doubt ceased to exist. Jason felt like crying for joy, almost did as he closed his eyes and felt those lips touch his own. He wasn't passive. He didn't let this moment pass with any uncertainty or hesitation. His fingers sought Caesar's hair, kept him close as his lips tried to make up for their complete lack of experience. At least Caesar seemed to know what to do, constantly adjusting for Jason's clumsiness, air huffing from his nostrils as his tongue slipped inside Jason's mouth.

From behind them a car honked impatiently, breaking the spell. Caesar released him, Jason unwillingly doing the same. The car zoomed around them with a parting honk. Jason could have killed the driver if anger hadn't fled his body so completely. He grinned and started laughing when Caesar did the same.

"Can we try that again?" Jason asked.

"Yes. But not now."

Caesar put the car into drive and pulled back onto the street. A block later, he turned left into a neighborhood and parked along the curb. Then he looked at Jason and shook his head. "You're not leaving." This was a statement rather than a question.

"I thought I had to."

"Yeah," Caesar said after a moment. "I can figure out why you'd think that. But now you don't need to. I'm cool with this. From that kiss, I'm guessing you are too."

Jason wanted another, but there was so much he needed to know. "I thought you were— I mean, you and Steph..."

"I like guys," Caesar said without hesitation. "That's not a secret. You could have asked."

"You could have told me," Jason retorted. "I'm gay, by the way"

"I kind of figured that out."

"Just now, or—"

"Last night," Caesar said. "I suspected before then, but hope and reality can get tangled up, if you know what I mean."

Jason definitely did, but he didn't care about any of that now. All he wanted was to explore this new possibility. He wanted to spend the entire day with Caesar, ask him a million questions, give him twice as many kisses. "Let's skip school," he said. "Go have some fun."

Caesar appeared amused but shook his head. "The last thing I want now is us getting in trouble. You can make it through a day of school."

"And afterwards?" Jason asked.

"Afterwards it'll just be me and you. I promise. Until then..." Caesar leaned forward, his lips so near that Jason could feel his breath when he spoke next, "here's a little something to tide you over."

This time Jason didn't close his eyes.

At the end of fifth period, Jason went to his locker, but only because he'd met Caesar there before. Sure enough, as he was arranging books for the sake of appearing busy, a hand appeared atop the locker door, a face to the side of it.

"After school, right?" Caesar said. "You haven't forgotten?"

Jason considered him and smirked. "Are you that insecure about your kissing abilities?"

He'd said it louder than he intended, not really thinking of the consequences, but Caesar didn't seem concerned. "Insecure?

No. I was worried my epic make-out skills had rendered you nearly comatose."

"I did nearly pass out," Jason admitted. He considered those lips for a moment. "Where are we going? Straight home, or…?"

"Wait and see," Caesar said, pushing away from the row of lockers and strutting down the hall. "Don't stand me up!" he called over his shoulder.

Heart racing, Jason walked to his next class in a daze. He wished he had a manual about all of this, detailing what the next step would be, how dating worked, and of course sex. Maybe that was something most people learned from their parents, although the idea of Mrs. Hubbard lecturing him on the pros and cons of oral stimulation didn't sound appealing.

Class was just beginning when someone knocked on the door. He watched with disinterest as the teacher went to answer it, paying more attention when the teacher spoke his name.

"Mr. Grant, you're needed in the front office. Take your things with you."

Jason felt awkward as he left the room, every head turning to watch him. Once alone in the hallway, he was free to wonder what was going on. He hadn't done anything wrong. Not unless Caesar was bugged and the kiss had been a sting operation. He laughed at the idea, taking it more seriously when he remembered their conversation before class. He supposed another student could have overheard and… What? Rushed to the principle to report two dudes had talked about kissing? That couldn't be it.

Jason didn't know what he'd find when he reached the office. He certainly didn't expect to see a tall woman with long blondish-brown hair standing there. Jason recognized her even before she turned around.

"Michelle!"

"He remembers me," she said with a smile.

"What are you doing here?"

"And yet he forgot our appointment." Michelle scowled at him a little too intently to be serious, her head casually gesturing to the office staff behind her.

"Oh, yeah," Jason said, catching on. "Sorry. You know I can't keep my days straight."

"That's why you've got me." Michelle adjusted the purse strap on her shoulder. "Ready to go?"

"Yeah!"

They were quiet as they left, not speaking until they were a safe distance down the hall.

"It hasn't been two weeks already, has it?" he asked. Caseworkers always followed up to see how things were going in a new foster placement, but not this quickly. And they certainly never pulled him out of class.

"My mom used to do this," Michelle said. "She'd show up at our school unexpectedly, call my brother and me to the office for a dentist appointment or some other excuse, and then she'd take us out for ice cream. We used to love when that happened."

"So you're taking me out for ice cream?" Jason asked.

"Sure! Why not?"

He stopped. "I'm not a little kid. You're trying to soften the blow. I just don't know what went wrong."

"Nothing's wrong," Michelle said, immediately reconsidering her words. "Nothing important, I'm sure. Your foster mom asked for this meeting."

Jason's stomach sank. Somehow he didn't think Mrs. Hubbard wanted to discuss adopting him just yet.

"She didn't sound upset," Michelle said. "Just concerned. All a normal part of adjusting. Unless you can think of anything in particular."

Jason shook his head as they continued walking before he realized what this was about. "Church. She wants me to go, and I keep refusing."

"Ah." He waited for Michelle to judge him, to tell him what he should do, but she didn't seem concerned. "So, McDonald's for a milkshake? Or Baskin-Robbins for some real ice cream?"

"McDonald's," Jason said. "French fries dipped in a vanilla shake. There's nothing better."

"How could I forget?" Michelle asked, holding open the door for him.

He blinked in the brightness of the day, afternoon sun gleaming off a silver sports car in the parking lot. "I was supposed to meet someone!" Jason said. "After school."

Michelle shook her head. "Sorry. One way or another, your plans would have been canceled. Mrs. Hubbard said she would pick you up after school. I told her I'd fetch you on the way over. My early arrival needs to remain a secret."

"Yeah, but..." Jason stared at Caesar's car, feeling the potential fade away. Those jokes about him standing up Caesar would now become reality. Jason slipped off his backpack and dug around in it. "I need to leave a note."

"Okay."

He walked to Caesar's car, spreading out a notebook-sized piece of paper on the hood. The empty white space intimidated as he tried to decide what to write. Eventually he settled on "See you at home. Sorry." After adding his name, he resisted the urge to draw a little heart.

"So you've made a friend?" Michelle asked, watching as he folded the paper and pinned it beneath a windshield wiper.

"Sort of," Jason said. "He's one of the Hubbards."

"One of your foster brothers?" she asked.

"Yeah, but he's not my brother."

This didn't seem to faze Michelle. She turned her face skyward as they walked to her car. "Feels so good. Of course, when summer rolls around I'll hate the sun, but right now it's heavenly."

"It is," Jason agreed.

Once in her car and on the road, Michelle asked him how he was faring in his new placement. Unwilling to talk about his feelings for Caesar, Jason found he didn't have much to say. He focused mostly on his birthday and how amazing it had been, which seemed to make her happy.

They were sitting outside at one of the McDonald's playground tables, Jason dunking a salty fry into his shake, when Michelle became more direct. "I wanted us to have a chance to talk openly," she said. "Whatever you want, I'm on your side. If you don't want to go to church, you don't have to. I'll argue your case, but what I really want to know is if you want to stay. Is it working out with the Hubbards, or..."

"Or am I about to pull one of my stunts," Jason said. It seemed crazy that just this morning he'd been planning to. Amazing how much could change in so little time. He thought of that kiss in Caesar's car and wanted more. "I'll stay," Jason said. "At least, if it's still an option."

This obviously wasn't the answer Michelle was expecting, but she nodded. "Is there something else going on? Mrs. Hubbard could have talked about the church issue over the phone with me."

Jason swallowed a cream-soaked fry and smiled. "You don't know her very well, do you?"

"You're the first kid I've placed with that family," Michelle admitted.

"Then maybe you'll need me to defend you, instead of vice versa."

"That bad?"

"Total control freak," Jason said.

Michelle considered him, shaking her head as he dipped and devoured a couple more fries. "That really is disgusting."

"Want to try it?"

Michelle raised a critical eyebrow, but then nodded. "Absolutely."

Jason swirled a fry around until it was coated and then held it out to her. "Open wide!"

"Religious freedom is covered in the training program that both you and Mr. Hubbard completed in—" Michelle checked the folder she was holding. Jason watched, amused that she was in full-on lawyer mode. Sure she was sitting on the living room couch next to him and not pacing before a jury, but the expression the Hubbards wore implied they were on trial. "—nineteen-ninety six. I understand that was a long time ago, and taking a refresher course is optional, but I can tell you now that Jason isn't required to attend any church or religious service unless he wants to."

Mrs. Hubbard pressed her lips together so tightly that the blood fled them, leaving them white.

"We're really not asking much," Mr. Hubbard said. "An hour every Sunday, that's all."

"I agree," Michelle said. "An hour isn't much, which is why I don't understand why he can't stay at home for that time."

"The issue goes deeper than church," Mrs. Hubbard said, eyes narrowed. They softened somewhat when she turned her attention to him. "Jason, we get the impression that you don't really want to be a part of this family. You'll watch television with us, but that's such a passive activity. Aside from walking with Peter to school every morning, how do you engage yourself with us?"

Besides sneaking into your son's room and trying to steal a kiss?

Jason couldn't say that, but he did feel safe mentioning their activities outside the house, which he did.

"That's very nice," Mrs. Hubbard said, "but what about the rest of us? Have you played with Amy recently or spent time on the computer with Peter? I'm sure Carrie would love to see a movie with you."

He doubted that was true. Carrie hadn't shown the slightest interest in him. "I hadn't thought of that," he said. "I guess I'm still adjusting to living here."

"We understand that—" Mr. Hubbard said, but his wife cut him off.

"Other children didn't need so long. Peter and Amy became part of the family in the first few days. We gave you a wonderful birthday and everything, but you're still fighting us!"

"Everyone adjusts differently," Michelle said calmly, but she was repeatedly tapping the file folder against her leg.

Mrs. Hubbard repeated her position. "Church is about spending time together. Say we went to a restaurant you weren't fond of, or a movie. We'd still expect you to come along, simply because we want you to be a part of this family. If you don't want that, then maybe you should tell us now."

There it was. An ultimatum. If you want to stay here, you'll go to church. Simple as that. No matter what Michelle said, that was the deal. Maybe they wouldn't openly state the reason for sending him away later, but they would find some other pretense.

Jason heard the front door open, saw Caesar poke his head in the living room and take in the scene before making a face of mock terror. Then he retreated. If Jason was sent back to the group home, dating Caesar would become much more difficult. Jason didn't have a car, and not all foster placements were in Houston. Even if Caesar were willing to pick him up from time to time, they wouldn't see each other every day. Not like they did now.

From next to him, Michelle stopped tapping the file and huffed. "Mrs. Hubbard—"

"I didn't think of it like that," Jason interrupted. "I know you tried explaining it to me before, but I didn't understand. Now that I do, I'd be happy to go to church with you."

Michelle turned to him in transparent disbelief, but he ignored her. Mrs. Hubbard remained skeptical too.

"Do you mean that, Jason?"

He nodded. "I'm not used to being wanted. Sometimes the idea scares me. That's silly, I know, but..."

"It's not silly," Mrs. Hubbard said, the ice leaving her voice. "You're wanted here! This is your home!"

Jason hadn't seen his home since Child Protective Services took him away from his mother, but he smiled as if relieved anyway. Michelle went through some formalities next, her tones much more muted. He felt guilty about that but hid his feelings until he was walking Michelle to her car. Even then he kept his back to the house so his face couldn't be seen.

"Thanks for throwing me to the wolves," Michelle said, looking more puzzled than angry.

"I know," Jason said. "I'm sorry. The thing is, I want to stay here, and me sitting through some boring sermon for an hour every week is a small price to pay."

"You don't have to," Michelle said. "Foster care is never about changing yourself to please anyone."

"I won't change. I promise. I'll wear earplugs while in church or something."

Michelle remained tense. "Well, if you have second thoughts and need someone to fight for you, I wouldn't mind another go at Mrs. Hubbard."

"She's a lot of fun, huh?"

"None of my other kids will be coming here," Michelle said, quickly adding, "which is totally unprofessional of me to say in front of you, so please forget I did."

Jason wanted to tell her that things between them didn't need to be professional, that she could swing by anytime and hang out with him if she wanted to, but he imagined that would probably make her feel uncomfortable or obligated. Instead he stood there with his hands in his pockets as she unlocked the car door.

"Still have my number?" she asked.

He nodded.

"Don't be afraid to use it."

He watched as she pulled out and away, allowing himself a sigh before he put on a fake smile and went back inside to be part of the family. Doing dishes with mom, playing dolls with Amy, and sitting next to Peter while he played on the computer. Everything but what he actually wanted to do. Maybe at night, when the house had fallen silent, he would finally be free to take that journey down the hallway again.

Jason gently knocked on the door, wincing at how loud his soft raps seemed to echo through the silent house. He turned to make sure no bedroom lights had switched on, and ended up banging his guitar against the wall. He was still grimacing when Caesar opened the door.

"Not exactly stealthy."

"Sorry," Jason replied.

Caesar jerked his head, signaling that he should enter. Jason did, noticing the room was tidier than usual, a candle lit on the side table. Casual, but still suggestive. He fought down a feeling of panic as he sat on the bed.

"Here to play me a song?" Caesar asked.

Jason nodded but left the guitar where it was—resting between his legs. He watched Caesar expectantly, taking in the muscle shirt hanging off the bare skin of his shoulders, and hoped for proof that this morning wasn't a fluke or a delusion. Caesar picked up on this, chuckling before rewarding Jason with a kiss. His breath tasted minty fresh, implying that he had done the same as Jason and made sure his teeth were brushed.

"So what was all that downstairs?" Caesar asked, sitting on the bed next to him. "Standard check-up or trouble?"

Jason rolled his eyes. "You're looking at Houston's newest altar boy."

"My parents aren't Catholic," Caesar said after a pause, "but I think I catch your drift. Mom's pressuring you to go to church."

"It's that or pack my bags," Jason said.

If Caesar found this surprising, he didn't say so. "So that's it? Your smoking hot caseworker came here to make sure you go to church?"

"It wasn't like that," Jason said, but he found himself distracted by the implications. "You really think she's hot?"

"Yeah! I don't know if she has kids or not, but MILF!"

Jason cocked an eyebrow, not that it could be seen behind his bangs. "So you and Steph, that's not an act?"

Caesar shook his head. "I'm bisexual. I like girls." He reached over and tugged on Jason's earlobe. "And I like guys."

"How does that work?" Jason asked. "I mean, when you get

married or whatever, what do you do about the part of you that wants something else?"

"It's called restraint," Caesar said. "The part that wants to wander is always there, even for straight people. But commitment is commitment. Once I sign on the dotted line, I'll devote myself to that person only."

"I think I have a pen around here somewhere," Jason said, patting his pajama bottoms like they had pockets.

Caesar grinned. "Save it for Vegas." Then he grew more somber. "Listen, whatever this turns out to be, we're going to have to play it carefully."

Jason swallowed. "Your parents?"

"Exactly. I'm not a closet case or anything. My mom knows. She doesn't really like it, but she knows. If she found out that my brother and I—"

"Don't call me that," Jason said. "Even as a joke. It's creepy."

"Yeah, okay. Anyway, I think she'd find it even more offensive than you not attending church."

Jason nodded. "What about your dad? Does he know?"

"Yeah. I'm sure he does, but we've never talked about it. You might want to play straight while you're at home, just so they don't draw their own conclusions."

Jason shrugged. He didn't care if the Hubbards knew the real him or not. "What about school?"

"What about it? You want to go to the prom with me or something?"

"Yeah," Jason said defiantly. "I do."

"Fine, but you have to convince me to ask you." Caesar flopped onto his back.

Jason's stomach felt tense. Was he supposed to… "Convince you how?" he asked with a dry mouth, which certainly wouldn't make this any easier. In the corner of his eye, he could see the dark hair on Caesar's legs, the boxers that probably didn't cover much, not that he'd let himself look.

"You can start by playing me a song."

Jason nearly exhaled in relief. Instead he picked up the guitar and strummed it gently, creating a lazy sort of sound a cowboy and horse might mosey along to. He smiled when this made Caesar laugh, picking up the pace and adding a bit more oomph as the imaginary horse broke into a gallop. Getting into the music,

Jason paused to pull off his shirt so he could feel the instrument against his chest. Then he played more seriously, plucking out *Every Breath You Take* by the Police. Stripped of its lyrics, the song sounded playful and optimistic, and less like a stalker's anthem. Not that he was one to judge.

At the end of the song, he transitioned to freestyle tunes, letting his hands move almost of their own accord as he slowly lost himself in the sound. When he felt fingers touching his back, he seized up. Caesar's hand slid around to his ribs and tried to pull him backward.

"Wait, my guitar," Jason said, setting it down, but he didn't make an effort to lie down afterwards.

Caesar responded by scooting next to him and kissing his neck, shoulder, chin, and lips. Finding himself in somewhat more familiar territory, Jason threw himself into that kiss, nearly reaching the same blissful state he did when playing music. Caesar stroked the top of his hand, taking hold of it and moving it to his lap. Jason felt flannel boxers, something warm and hard beneath them.

"Uh," he said, pulling his hand away.

"Something wrong?" Caesar asked.

"No." Jason's cheeks were burning. All of this was too soon. Not that he didn't want to! That wasn't the problem. He just wanted it not to be the first time. If he could somehow skip over that initial awkwardness, be skillful and confident so he could impress Caesar…

"Am I moving too fast for you?"

"I don't know," Jason answered.

"You don't— Oh!" Caesar chuckled, but it didn't sound cruel. "First time?"

"Nah, I've been with tons of guys," he lied. It was clear Caesar didn't believe him, so he added, "I just don't put out on the first date. Or before the first date."

"Minigolf doesn't count?"

"Nope."

"Go-karts?"

"Nuh-uh."

"I took you out to dinner and a movie. What about that?"

Jason looked at him incredulously. "Lunch at the mall doesn't count."

Caesar still had bedroom eyes. "Very well. Tomorrow, after my wrestling meet, I'm taking you on a date. And no hot caseworkers or annoying parents will stand in my way. Deal?"

"Deal."

"Good. Now you should probably go back to your room."

"Why?"

Caesar pointed at his crotch. "So I can take care of this."

Jason allowed his eyes to flick downward at the tenting fabric. "Oh wow!" he said without thinking.

Caesar smirked. "Oh wow yourself."

Jason glanced down at his own crotch, then grabbed his guitar in panic. As he stood and headed for the door, he held the instrument in front of him like a shield. Hormones flooding his system, he almost turned around, threw aside the guitar, and gave into what his body wanted. Luckily—or perhaps not—enough nervousness remained to see him to the hallway. As he shut the door behind him, he tried not to imagine what was happening in his absence. At least, not until he was safely shut in his own room. Once there, he spent the next half hour imagining all sorts of things.

Chapter Seven

"Going on a date, huh?"

Jason tore his attention from the padded mat where Caesar had a guy pinned on his back. He was surprised. Not because Steph was here. That happened often enough. But he didn't expect her to know about the date tonight.

"Caesar told you about that?"

Steph nodded, rolling her eyes and clapping at the scene below, meaning Caesar must have won. "There isn't much I don't know about him. I've known he was bi since the first time he flirted with my older brother. But I thought you were straight."

Jason blinked. "Even though I'm sitting right here every Tuesday and Thursday?"

"Well, when you put it like that." Steph laughed. "Unlike Caesar, you aren't the most forthcoming guy. You're kind of mysterious."

"Yeah, I do that on purpose," Jason joked. "So, uh, you don't seem upset."

"About you two hitting it off?" Steph shrugged and exhaled. "I figured Caesar would find some other girl eventually. That you're definitely not a girl makes it easier somehow. Besides, maybe now I'll finally move on."

Jason gave a sympathetic smile. "So any tips? Anything I should know?"

"About Caesar?" Steph smiled slyly. "Trust me, he'll tell you everything you need to know. Just try to keep up with him."

Jason wasn't sure what that meant, but seeing as the wrestling meet was coming to an end, he was on the verge of finding out.

"A picnic?" Jason asked.

"Yup!" Caesar walked around to the passenger door of the car and opened it for him. "We've already covered all the typical dates: movies, minigolf, shopping… A picnic is next on the list."

"But it's nighttime."

Caesar glanced around and nodded. "I can see that. Let's go. I wanna get started."

Their destination wasn't far. Caesar drove them to a public park that included a playground, a generic sports field, and farther back, a duck pond surrounded by trees. Caesar grabbed some loaded plastic bags from the trunk after tossing a blanket over his shoulder.

"I can carry something too," Jason said, closing the trunk for him.

"Nah, that wouldn't be very gentlemanly of me. Or very ladylike of you."

"If you think I'm the girl in this relationship," Jason said, "you're sadly mistaken."

"You speak from experience?"

"No, but..."

Caesar shot him a grin as they headed across mowed grass. "Tell you what. We'll wrestle. Whoever ends up on top gets to *be* the top."

"I might leave you wrestling yourself again tonight."

Caesar groaned. "What's the point of this picnic if you're not going to put out?"

"To feed me. I'm starving."

When they reached the edge of the pond, Jason grabbed the blanket from Caesar, kicking away a few rocks and sticks before he spread it out on the ground. He plopped down cross-legged on one corner, salivating as Caesar did the same and started unpacking the bags.

"We've got potato salad. Fruit salad. Real salad." Each item he pulled out was in a plastic container, straight from the grocery store deli. "Loaf of bread. Disposable forks. And of course, something to drink."

From out of the last bag a six-pack appeared. Even in the limited light, Jason could see silvery print on the cans and a swooping font that spelled out a few words, one of them magical. "Beer?"

"Yup." Caesar yanked one free from the plastic rings and handed it to him. "You drink, right?"

"Yeah, of course." As of this moment, at least. "Where did you get this?"

"I popped over to the grocery store during lunch."

"But how'd you get the beer?"

Caesar cracked open his can and smiled. "I have my ways."

Meaning he probably strolled into the liquor store oozing confidence and walked out with whatever he wanted. No doubt his life always worked that way. Jason opened his can, foam splattering his hand, and held up the beer when Caesar raised his in toast. "What are we drinking to?"

"To tonight," Caesar said, a wicked gleam in his eye. "By which I mean *later* tonight."

Yeah, that confidence probably got him everywhere. Jason was tempted to play hard to get, just to deny him something. Then again, the way Caesar opened the potato salad, dunked in a finger, and licked it clean gave Jason other ideas. Assuming he didn't get freaked out again. He brought the can of beer back to his lips, chugging down as much as he could tolerate. Did people really like drinking this stuff?

"You better eat something too," Caesar said. "I want you loosened up, not blitzed."

"I told you, I'm not the girl."

"That's not what I meant by loose!" Caesar said, tossing a slice of bread at him.

Jason deflected it and smiled, reaching for a fork and the fruit salad.

Caesar considered him as he speared and ate a few chunks of watermelon. "You don't have to do anything tonight," he said. "I'm just teasing. Take your time."

Jason glanced up, feeling a mixture of relief that it didn't have to happen and panic that it might not. He just wanted to get it over with so it wouldn't be such a big deal anymore. Being experienced like Caesar must be nice. "When was your first time?"

"You mean with a girl?"

Jason shrugged in response.

"I was fourteen."

Fourteen. Jeez! That meant Jason was already years behind him in experience. "What was it like?"

Caesar thought about it over a bite of potato salad. "Lame. Some older girl I met at a party. I don't even remember her name. We went up to her room, and I was desperate to get laid at the time, so, uh, it didn't last very long." He chuckled while rubbing the back of his neck. "Anyway, I wasn't very impressed. It felt good, but not much more than jacking off did. The next time… *that* was really something."

Jason felt more intrigued than jealous, so he motioned for Caesar to continue.

"The second time was with Steph. We were together for about a year and she was still a virgin. To her it was a really big deal. She used to talk about saving herself for marriage, but eventually she said she didn't want to wait. Her parents were out of town, and we tried to make it special. We had this silly rule about keeping the lights off the entire night, even during dinner. She cooked for me, which was nice, and I did dishes."

"In the dark?" Jason asked.

"We had candles. We lit every single one we could find until the house glowed. Anyway, the time finally came time and Steph got super scared. When I put my arm around her, she was shaking. I ended up holding her the entire night, telling her—" Caesar swallowed. "I told her how I felt about her. My body was dying for action, but I ignored all that as best I could. The sun was coming up when she finally calmed down. She was ready, and I found that I was too, which I hadn't been the first time. Not emotionally. And it was amazing. That night with her was special."

Once again, Jason wished he could trade places with Steph. He was beginning to worry less about his sexual performance and more about competing with her emotionally. How could he ever take her place? He mulled over the details, finding himself at a loss for words. What could anyone say after hearing a story like that? Luckily, the silence was filled for him.

Quack!

He glanced over to find a duck nipping at the bread slice Caesar had thrown at him. The duck quacked happily between bites, or maybe it was trying to scare them off. Either way, this attracted the attention of more ducks, who waddled over from the pond toward them.

"Aren't picnics normally ruined by ants?" Jason said. "I didn't expect an attack by sea."

"Better give in to their demands," Caesar said, reaching for the loaf of bread.

Between bites of salad and swigs of beer, they slowly doled out portions of bread to the ducks. A particularly greedy one spent most of its time trying to chase away the others, not getting very much bread in the process, while another felt brave enough to walk onto their blanket, earning itself the biggest share of the loaf. Even once the bread was gone, the duck continued to walk around them in circles, casting a hopeful eye in their direction. Jason kept turning his head to follow its orbit, laughing more than once.

"You can't take it home," Caesar said.

"Why not? Your parents like strays."

"Hm. Good point. I'm taking the greedy duck with us too. I'll name it Peter."

Jason grimaced. "I don't think he's happy about us hanging out. This morning was tense!"

Caesar rolled his eyes. "He's never happy. I used to think it was his situation, but you seem fine."

"Meaning?" Jason asked.

"That you're happy."

Jason shook his head. "I've got my demons too, believe me."

"What's it like?" Caesar asked. "Not having parents, I mean. I can't even imagine."

"You never asked any of the other kids?"

"Just one guy," Caesar admitted.

"What did he say?"

"He told me to go fuck myself. I figured I might have more luck with you."

Jason thought about it. "Cast your mind back to all those times you had the flu, or got in a fight with another kid while out playing. Think about the times you got in trouble at school, or nights when thunder woke you up and scared the hell out of you. What did you want in each of those situations?"

Caesar answered instantly. "My mom. Except when I got in trouble at school. My dad was always better for that because he thought it was funny."

Jason nodded. "Now remember all those times you were barfing up your guts or scared in the middle of the night, and imagine not having your mom and dad there."

Caesar considered this and swallowed. "Is that how you always feel?"

"No. Not every day. Like anything in life, you get used to your situation. I've been on my own long enough that it's not as upsetting anymore. But there will always be days when I want that safe feeling again, when I wish my mom was there to pick me up when I fall and scrape my knee. Sometimes I still wish I could go home."

Caesar studied him in the limited light. "I know you hate it when I say I'm sorry, so I won't, but I hope you know what my silence really means."

Jason smiled. "Okay."

"Only two more beers left. Want one?"

"Why not?"

Caesar was holding out a can when a light swept across the park, causing them both to freeze.

"What was that?" Jason whispered.

Caesar's attention was on the parking lot. "That would be the police. Stay here, I'll be right back." He stood, grabbing the remaining beer and empty cans. "Uh, better eat some more fruit salad. Seriously."

Jason stared after him as Caesar ran toward the trees. Turning his attention to the parking lot, he saw two flashlights sweeping back and forth across the grass. One rose to blind him briefly, so he grabbed the fruit salad and took a few bites, hoping it would make him appear natural. At least, as natural as a night picnic could appear. He felt slightly better when Caesar rushed back and took his place on the blanket again. After a moment's thought, Caesar grabbed the fruit salad from Jason and tipped the container to his lips, slurping down the excess juice. Then he wiped his mouth with the back of his hand.

"Let me do the talking," Caesar whispered as the lights drew near. Already they could hear the crackle of a police radio.

"Police," a female voice announced, the flashlight momentarily illuminating a badge set against blue fabric before moving back to their faces. The other beam of light was examining their picnic. "What are you boys doing here?"

"Celebrating," Caesar said, smiling like the officers were welcome to join them. "We had a great meet tonight."

"Meet?" asked a male voice.

"Wrestling meet," Caesar explained. "I'm the captain of the team, and if you don't mind me bragging, I was pinning them like an entomologist tonight."

The flashlight started sweeping toward Jason, before it seemed to hesitate and returned to Caesar. "Pinning them like a what?"

"An insect collector," Caesar explained. "Just a little wrestling humor."

The flashlight moved to Jason's face.

"And you?"

"I'm one of the butterflies he pinned."

"And now you're having a picnic," the female officer said, not sounding convinced.

The flashlight remained on Jason, and he made sure to look as indignant as he felt. Of course they were having a picnic! Did they suspect all this was a cover for something illegal? They hadn't done anything wrong!

"Have you been drinking?" asked the male voice.

Oh. Right. Jason's brain felt like it had gone for a swim and forgotten to bring a towel. "Uh…"

"No, we haven't," Caesar said. "Which sucks because I left the Mountain Dew at home. I was thinking about drinking some of that pond water over there. Think it's safe?"

"Stand up," the female officer commanded.

Caesar did as he was told, Jason following his lead. Now the flashlight turned skyward, illuminating a hard female face as the officer stepped close to Caesar and told him to exhale, which he did.

"Sure you haven't been drinking?"

"Absolutely, although the fruit salad is a little ripe. Maybe it's fermented or something." Caesar's teeth flashed at her, and her hard face softened somewhat. "I'm totally willing to take a breathalyzer test. We both are."

"That's exactly what's going to happen," the officer replied.

Caesar shrugged, eyes innocent.

The walkie-talkie crackled again, a hard-to-understand voice coming over the static. "Plates are clear," the male voice said.

The female officer nodded, the flashlight shifting to better illuminate Caesar's features. Again he smiled, like he was totally cool with the situation. The female officer considered him a moment longer before speaking. "The park is closed after eight pm. You boys pack up and go home."

"Will do," Caesar said. The smile remained plastered on his face, even as the officers turned away, shrouding them in darkness once more. The two beams of light bounced back toward the parking lot, accompanied by radio static and dispatch voices.

"I can't believe it," Jason whispered so quietly he was surprised to be heard.

"I know," Caesar responded.

"You're so awesome!"

"Thanks. Now all we have to do is get back to the car without appearing drunk. Oh, and I have to drive us home. And we have to sneak in without my parents seeing us, because my dad can definitely tell the difference between beer fumes and fruit salad."

"I take it back," Jason said. "You're not so awesome."

"Yeah I am. Now pack this stuff up. I'm going to run back and get our last two beers."

Jason shook his head as he watched him go, realizing that Caesar could probably get away with murder, could have anything he wanted, which meant that the rest of the night would be very interesting indeed.

Jason sat on the edge of his bed, an unopened can of beer in his hands. Caesar had slipped it to him before heading to his room, saying it would help pass the time while they waited for the house to settle down. Jason didn't need the beer. What he needed was a plan. He couldn't be Steph. He couldn't imagine being held by Caesar all night and not giving into what his body craved. And yet he didn't want to be forgettable, like that first girl at the party.

Perhaps he could find somewhere in between. Not timid, but also not easy. He needed to offer Caesar something new, and after thinking it over, Jason wondered if he couldn't be his equal—give Caesar the emotional aspect as Steph had done, but also take him on physically, make sex something both special and hot. The only problem was, he didn't have a clue how.

Jaw clenching, Jason stood. Enough doubt and worry! He'd already decided he would need a combination of body and heart. Time to send his brain packing so the rest of him could get this done. Jason set the beer on the dresser, closing it in the room behind him. He didn't think while on his way down the hall, didn't allow himself to wonder if his performance would be good enough. When he entered Caesar's room and saw him turn around and smile—picked-up dirty clothes still in hand—Jason didn't smile back. Instead he approached him with the utmost seriousness and kissed him.

Caesar tossed aside the laundry and reciprocated, lips struggling to keep up until he finally pulled away and laughed, instantly wounding Jason's brave heart.

"What's so funny?"

"Nothing," Caesar said. "I was just thinking about you not wanting to be the girl. Is that what this is? Shouldn't we wrestle first?"

Hilarious. Jason had wanted to impress Caesar, but apparently his behavior was silly, making him want to slink back to his room and reconsider his strategy. Feeling deflated, he sat on Caesar's bed and considered the carpet. "I don't know what you want," he said.

"I'd say you do."

"Then I don't know how you want it."

A finger touched his chin, gently raising his head. Those honey-golden eyes were on him and still amused, but Jason couldn't decide if they were cruel or not.

Caesar took a step back. "Stand up."

Jason hesitated, but then did what he was told.

"Take off your shirt."

His cheeks felt a little hot. "What is this?"

"It's what I want," Caesar said. "Take it off."

Jason glowered at him before complying. "Now you."

"Okay."

Caesar granted his wish, and even though it was a simple one, the act felt extremely erotic. Jason was left in his pajama bottoms, Caesar in a pair of boxers, and it was obvious they were both into this. Jason took a step forward but Caesar raised his hand, stopping him.

"Come to me," he said.

"I was going to anyway," Jason pointed out.

A smile played across Caesar's lips. "I know."

Jason stepped forward, stopping before their bodies could touch. "Now you come to me," he said.

Caesar grinned. "Very well."

One step forward was all it took to connect them, for their crotches to touch, for their bare chests to brush against each other. One of Jason's hands went up Caesar's back, the other travelling south to grab a butt cheek. His brain had definitely checked out. What remained of Jason only wanted one thing. No hesitation remained, which made what Caesar did next extremely frustrating. He moved Jason's hands to his hips, holding them there, but at least he had a counter offer. Caesar tilted his head, exposing his neck.

"Kiss me," he said. "Right here."

Jason did, tasting the natural sweat of his skin, a lingering hint of soap from his shower after wrestling, and a tang of what must have been cologne. His let his tongue curve along the jaw up to the ear, which he invaded briefly before biting on the lobe. Then he went for the lips, but Caesar pulled away.

"Are you sure you haven't done this before?"

Jason grinned. "I'm a quick learner." He moved in again, but Caesar wasn't done talking.

"Hold up. I was enjoying our game."

"Game?"

"I make a request. Then you. Then me. I think it's your turn. What do you want?"

Bashfulness stirred inside of Jason, only to be beaten to death by a violent gang of hormones. "Take off your boxers."

Caesar didn't hesitate. He released Jason's hands and pulled down his boxers, but quickly stepped forward again to wrap arms around him. Jason wanted nothing more than to take a step back so he could see, but Caesar's grip was tight. Regardless, he could feel something pressing against his hip.

"Now what should I ask of you?" Caesar said musingly.

"Come on," Jason said, his patience nearly exhausted.

"Okay." Caesar's grip on him loosened slightly. "Take off your pajama bottoms."

Jason did so, but took advantage of his hands being down there to slide a palm upward along the inside of Caesar's thigh. He felt the weight of warm testicles on the back of his hand before Caesar grabbed him by the wrists and pinned his arms behind his back.

"You have to ask first," Caesar insisted.

"Oh, there's definitely something I want," Jason said.

"Anything goes."

Jason leaned close, whispering his request into Caesar's ear. What he wanted, more than anything else, was to get on his knees.

"I see," came the response, followed by a thoughtful nod. "Tell you what. Grant my next request, and I'll let you do just that."

Jason shook his head, puzzled as Caesar murmured something into his ear. Then Jason's brow furrowed. "Are you serious?"

"Say it, and I'll let you do what you want."

"You're crazy. You really want me to say that?"

Caesar shrugged. "I think it's hot."

Jason smiled. "You would. Ugh. Okay..." He cleared his throat and forced a straight face. "Hail Caesar."

"I'm not convinced you mean it."

Jason glared. "I'm going back to my room!"

"Okay, okay." Caesar released his wrists, took a step back, and waved his hand in a few lazy loops like royalty granting permission. "You may proceed."

At first Jason just stared. He had seen Caesar's bare chest before so his eyes raced down to the narrow hips, to the carefully trimmed pubic hair, to the parts similar to his own and yet so very different. The cock was narrower and a little longer, the balls hanging lower. Jason's was pale, the head pink, while Caesar's was darker with a proud ruby head. His request forgotten, he continued to stare lustfully.

"Uh, that's going to drip on the carpet."

Jason glanced down, face flushing as he wiped at himself. "Sorry."

"It's fine," Caesar said, finally growing serious. "No more games. Come here."

Caesar placed an arm around Jason's hips and guided him to the bed. He took Jason's hand as he rolled onto the mattress, pulling him in. Caesar lay on his side, head on his pillow, like he was settling down to sleep. Jason did the same, facing him in a way that was instantly familiar, except this situation promised so much more.

"You have a beautiful body," Caesar said, reaching out to touch him. Like yesterday, he ran his palm across Jason's torso, but this time he wouldn't be restricted. Regardless, Caesar kept his touches above the waist, Jason writhing in response. This wasn't what he pictured at all, that sex would be about his entire body and not just one part. He reached out to do the same, stroking Caesar's cheek, brushing his fingers along those lips, scooting his body nearer and almost going mad at being so close and yet not quite there.

Finally, Caesar rolled over on his back. "Okay. Show me what you can do."

Jason licked his lips, but not because he was nervous. First he took hold of Caesar, pumping him mechanically until he considered the way he liked to touch himself. Then Jason changed his grip, squeezing his hand tight with every upward stroke. From the way Caesar reacted, he appreciated the effort. Feeling more confident, Jason moved his head down to do what he'd fantasized about so often, but that suddenly seemed different now. In his imagination, he never worried about how to position himself above the other guy, or how he still needed to use his hand to keep Caesar in his mouth. He struggled in the beginning but tried his best, reveling in the idea of what was happening more than the actual experience. Eventually, a hand on his shoulder pulled him up back again.

"Was that all right?" Jason asked.

"I've got no complaints," Caesar said with a wry grin, "but let me show you a few tricks. Lie back."

Jason did so and held his breath. Soon it was released again, exhaled in one long sigh. He kept glancing down, trying to pay attention to what Caesar was doing. There was a lot of slobber, Caesar's hand and mouth working in unison and sliding up and down his shaft. Or he moved them in opposite directions, hand and mouth bumping together somewhere in the middle before separating again. Teeth intentionally toyed with him, or a tongue lolled around the head of his cock. Jason knew he wouldn't be able to remember it all because he was barely able to think. He only managed to hiss out a warning just before he was driven over the edge.

Then he was biting his lip to stop from moaning, pounding the mattress with his fists when Caesar refused to stop. Just before he was about to scream from sheer pleasure, he was released.

"Deep breaths," Caesar said, working his way back by kissing Jason's stomach, his chest, then his shoulder. "You okay?"

Jason nodded, seeing stars. Holy crap! Would it be like this every time? He took a few deep breaths, laughing when his lips were kissed. The face above his was so beautiful, the eyes reflecting the joy he felt inside. He wanted to make Caesar feel that way too, but couldn't while stuck on his back. "What about you?" he asked.

"What about me," Caesar repeated. He moved his legs up until his knees were in Jason's armpits. This left something long and hard pointed directly at his face. Caesar was stroking himself, his body already tensing as he brushed Jason's hair back with his free hand. What was going to happen became clear just seconds before it did. All Jason had time to do was close his eyes and smile.

Hail Caesar.

"Are you sure?" Caesar asked again, shutting Jason's locker door. "For your first time it wasn't exactly… sweet."

"It was awesome," Jason raved. "I wasn't expecting rose petals and champagne. Last night was…" He glanced around a hallway swarming with students. "Uh, are we really talking about this in the middle of school?"

Caesar grinned shamelessly. "I've got nothing to hide."

"Anyway, it wasn't emotionless." Jason swallowed, feeling vulnerable. "I felt things. Did you?"

"Of course," Caesar said. "Come on. I'll walk you to class."

"You aren't going to carry my books for me?"

"Uh-uh. You seem to be one of those newfangled independent women. Dinner's on you next time, by the way."

Jason beamed at him as they walked down the hall, nearly bumping into a few people because of it. "So when *is* the next time?"

Caesar looked surprised. "Well, if you're leaving it up to me, how does every single night sound?"

"That would get expensive," Jason said.

"You're charging me?"

Jason glanced over at Caesar, then elbowed him. "I meant the next date, asshole! Not… you know."

Caesar chuckled. "I know, I know!"

"Anyway, it's Friday night, so I figured we'd catch a movie or something."

"That might be tricky."

Jason led them to a door and stopped. "This is my class. What do you mean tricky?"

"You need to lay low tonight, be the perfect foster son so we don't arouse suspicion."

A tea party with Amy, making peace with Peter, and putting in an appearance for Mr. and Mrs. Hubbard. He knew Caesar was right, but he still didn't like it. "So basically I hang out with your family until our nightly hookup? That's how it is from now on?"

"No. Tomorrow night I'm going to tell Mom about the big

party everyone is going to, and how you found out about it and want to tag along. I'll pout about how you'll ruin my fun and complain that you need to make friends of your own."

Jason grinned. "I'm such a nuisance!"

Caesar rolled his eyes dramatically. "Tell me about it! Unfortunately, my mom will insist that a good place to make new friends is at a party, or maybe she'll lecture me about the family bond. Regardless, in the end I'll grudgingly agree, and she'll pat me on the head for being a good big br— Well, a good role model to you."

"Are you serious?" Jason asked. "There's really a party tomorrow?"

Caesar nodded. "All you have to do until then is play a few video games, brush some Barbie doll hair, and kill some brain cells with reality television."

"And chore rewards tomorrow morning, no doubt." Jason sighed. "Why must my life be so hard?"

"I'll make it up to you." Caesar ruffled his hair and turned away, saying one more word over his shoulder as he went. "Tonight."

Jason could deal with that—could deal with anything, if it meant spending more time together.

Chapter Eight

Jason had always assumed that wanting was the problem, and that getting would cure him. His infatuation for guys usually manifested as sexual desire. Sure he experienced all sorts of crazy feelings inside, but these would culminate into lust. Before Caesar, he'd never had a chance to satisfy those sexual cravings and soothe his heart. Now he was discovering that sex only strengthened the bond. He snuck back into Caesar's room on Friday night, too hungry to talk. Afterwards he felt a little calmer. They murmured words to each other, drifting in and out of sleep until Jason forced himself to return to his room. Then it began all over again. He didn't want to be separated. The hunger remained, and sex was only a side dish to his appetite, not a meal. Jason wanted to be near Caesar, to hear the sound of his voice, to bask in his presence. Or at the very *very* least, he wanted to be able to watch him from across the room, like he was doing now.

The party was exactly what Jason had expected. Someone's parents were out of town—a girl he didn't recognize—and everything had been fairly civilized until her older brother showed up with the kegs. A couple rounds of "Happy Birthday" were sung, so presumably this was all one big present for her. Jason hoped she was turning eighteen because her parents were going to disown her when they discovered this mess.

Still, he was willing to reap the benefits, albeit in a different manner from everyone else here. He wasn't interested in the beer. Jason held a full plastic cup without sipping from it. Getting to hang around with Caesar, *that* was awesome. At first, anyway. Jason had been introduced to countless people, Caesar's arm around his neck the whole time. As the music got louder and the first keg ran dry, Caesar was pulled away from him. So many people knew him, all of them wanting a piece. Jason could relate, but this left him on the sidelines.

Kurt provided some companionship. The guy still intimidated Jason, despite being civil enough, and they didn't have much in common. When conversation ran dry, Jason found a place on the couch. Occasionally the crowds would part just right, like clouds moving aside to reveal the sun, and he would see Caesar.

"That's the same face you make during his wrestling

meets," said a familiar voice as the weight on the couch shifted. "Surprising, because he's not nearly as naked right now."

Jason glanced over at Steph and smiled. "I have a very good imagination."

She crinkled her nose at this before nodding to the room. "Enjoying the party?"

"Eh."

"Same here. This is supposed to be my big night too."

"Oh?"

Steph nodded. "I'm back on the prowl, interviewing potential candidates."

"Any luck?"

"I met a pretty college boy, and things were going well until he opened his mouth."

"Dumb as a rock?" Jason asked.

Steph shook her head. "Breath. Smelled like he'd eaten roadkill."

"You could always buy him a pack of gum."

"Trust me, this guy needed a sand blaster. I don't think he'd brushed his teeth for weeks." She raised her cup to her lips, thin metal loops tumbling down her forearm as she took a sip. "So how about you two?"

"Good," Jason said. "Great. I just wish I could get him alone."

"I know the feeling." Steph smiled at private memories. Then she glanced across the crowd in Caesar's direction, Jason doing the same. Some sort of drinking game was going on involving cups balancing on foreheads. Steph sighed. "Don't let him drive home like that. No matter what he says. He can handle a few beers. After that it's—" She pantomimed yanking a steering wheel back and forth, causing Jason to laugh.

"I'll make sure he doesn't drive. I promise."

"Good." Steph's features grew serious. "Take care of him, okay? I love him, but I know he isn't meant for me. I'm hoping maybe you can help him find his way."

"What, is he lost or something?"

She fixed him with a stare, making him wish he hadn't responded so flippantly. Then she took another sip of her beer. "Does he ever talk about his grandma?"

"No. What about her?"

Steph seemed about to respond. Then her eyes widened

slightly at something farther away. "Put your hand on my leg."

"What?"

"Please!"

Jason put his hand on her knee, Steph moving it up to her thigh. He was about to pull away when someone spoke.

"Hi, Stephanie. I wondered where you went."

Jason glanced up. The guy was huge, hulking, and handsome in a world's-hottest-caveman sort of way. But man, that breath was rancid! Jason moved his hand away and put an arm around Steph. "Who's this?" he asked, trying to make his voice sound deep. "Steph, you haven't been flirting with other guys again, have you? We talked about this!"

"I can't help myself!" she cried.

"This can't keep happening," Jason said. "Either you're mine completely, or you're not mine at all."

"I'm all yours," Steph said, sounding like a daytime soap. "I promise I'll never stray again!" Then she leaned close, pressing her lips against Jason's neck.

He glared up at the caveman while she kissed him, trying not to laugh when she nipped at his neck. Finally the guy huffed and stomped off. Then Jason very gently pushed Steph away.

"No offense," he said, wiping his neck, "but now I'm one hundred percent certain that I'm gay."

"All the good ones are," Steph said. "I think Caesar enjoyed our little show."

Jason glanced across the room to see Caesar giving him a thumbs up. The guy was so drunk that he swayed in place. Jason rolled his eyes at him and turned his attention back to Steph.

"Shame about his breath," Jason said. "He was hot."

"I know." Steph sighed. "Normally I have nothing against a fixer-upper. You should have seen Caesar's hair when we first met. Can you picture him with a pony tail?"

"Seriously?"

"Mm-hm. Very nineties."

Jason laughed. "So what were you saying about his grandma?"

Steph shook her head. "It's nothing important. Honestly."

She changed the subject, and as they continued chatting, Jason decided not to worry about it. He'd rather hear whatever it was from the source. Besides, how interesting could a story about Caesar's grandmother really be?

As the night wore thin, Steph said goodbye and left. After she had gone, Jason felt puzzled. That she loved Caesar and always would was obvious, but she also behaved as if she'd made peace with them not being together. And yet, those text messages still came in torrents. Did she feel differently when at home and alone? Is that when being apart from Caesar hurt too much?

"There's my man!"

Before he knew what has happening, Jason was pulled to his feet and kissing a bottle of rubbing alcohol. That's what Caesar tasted like anyway. Still, a kiss was a kiss, so Jason made the best of it. When Caesar stumbled back a few steps, Jason noticed how many stares they were attracting.

"Let's get out of here," he suggested.

"Yes." Caesar raised an index finger. "The kegs have been sucked dry. So, yes."

Jason got him outside so the inevitable "No, no, I can drive" conversation could take place. Thankfully, Caesar didn't need much convincing that he was too trashed.

"You can drive," he said, pressing the keys to Jason's chest. "I trust you with my baby. I trust my baby with my baby."

"Uh, I don't have my license."

Caesar swiped a hand through the air like a cat batting at a fly. "No problem. Learner's permit."

"I don't have that either. I've never driven before."

This seemed to sober Caesar up somewhat. "Never?"

"Never."

"Well, shit." Caesar considered the night around them. "Okay. Shit. It's going to be a long walk. You sure we can't drive?"

"I'm up for a hike," Jason said. "We can handle it, right? We're tough!"

"Yeah!" Caesar said, throwing an arm around him. "Tougher than beef jerky. Come on."

They made their way down the driveway to the sidewalk… and occasionally onto lawns or out into the street, thanks to Caesar's weaving and winding. This mostly happened when he was ranting about topics Jason struggled to follow, but over the next hour, Caesar slowly became more coherent.

"Are we almost there?" Jason asked.

Caesar stopped, looking up and down the street. "I don't even know where we are."

"What?"

"I was following you!"

Jason covered his face with his palm, leaving it there until Caesar pulled his arm away.

"I think I can get us home."

Jason didn't hide his disbelief. "Really?"

"Yup. Check it out!"

Caesar ran off across a lawn, a security light blinking on as he reached a driveway. There, leaning against the garage door, was a BMX bike. Caesar got on the bike, laughing as he coasted down the driveway. Then he pulled up to Jason on the sidewalk.

"Hop on!"

"Are you kidding me?" But of course he wasn't. "You can't take some poor kid's bike!"

"I'll bring it back tomorrow," Caesar said, glancing at the street corner. "Wandering Oak and Locust. That's easy to remember, because we're wandering around like a couple of locusts."

Jason shook his head. "That doesn't even make sense."

"This will save us so much time," Caesar said unabashed. "Do you really want to walk two more hours?"

"Is that how far away we are?"

"I don't know, but with this we can find our way home quicker." Caesar flashed him a smile. "Hop on. I'll even give you the seat."

Jason glanced back at the house to make sure no one was coming after them. Then he got on the bike, struggling to find a place to put his feet until he rested them on the rear wheel wingnuts. Caesar stood on the pedals to get them moving, and with Jason hogging the seat, he had to remain standing. This left Jason blind as to where they were going, but they were picking up enough speed that he needed to grab Caesar's hips.

"If you're too drunk to drive," Jason shouted over the wind, "should you really be riding a bike?"

"They never warned us against it in school," Caesar shouted back. "Must be perfectly safe!"

The bike wobbled dangerously as they left the sidewalk, went over a curb, and took a sharp left.

"I totally know where we are now," Caesar shouted. "Hold on!"

The lights grew brighter as the neighborhood gave way to a

large street. Before Jason could complain, they wobbled back to the parallel sidewalk. The night was late enough to keep traffic thin, but cars still zoomed by. One, trying to pull out of a gas station, screeched to a halt and honked as they cut it off. Jason kept craning his neck to see around Caesar, always regretting doing so. For the next fifteen minutes, he simply pressed his cheek against Caesar's back and closed his eyes. Then the bike brakes squeaked, bringing them to a halt.

"Uh," Caesar said.

Jason put his feet down to help provide balance and looked around. They were stopped on a high overpass, one with an entrance ramp that veered down to the right and joined with the highway. "We're not going to "

"We have to," Caesar said. "Just one exit and we're nearly there."

"Isn't there a frontage road or something?"

"Uh-uh. Not here."

Jason saw he was right. This portion of the freeway was raised above the ground. The land running parallel consisted of a cracked, weed-covered parking lot, beyond it a field full of rubble where a building had once stood. The bike might have been built for rocketing over dirt mounds, but it wouldn't be able to handle piles of stone.

"Just one exit," Caesar said. "It'll take us five minutes, tops."

"You're going to get us killed."

"I won't let anything happens to you," Caesar slurred. Then he tried to correct himself. "Happen to yous."

"We're doomed," Jason moaned.

"Nah. Well, maybe. Can I sit on your lap?"

"Is that a last request?"

Caesar sat instead of answering. He was heavier than he looked, but at least Jason would be pinned down. He wrapped his arms around Caesar's sweaty torso, his eyes just able to peek over the shoulder in front of him. Already the bike was moving forward, picking up speed as it coasted down the ramp.

"Ready?"

"No," Jason said. Then he started yelling because they were going really fast now.

A car sped past them to their left, then another. A third one swerved away from them as they reached the end of the ramp and rocketed onto the shoulder. There wasn't much room between the rail on their right and the freeway to their left. The late hour made little difference to the traffic here. Cars zipped by them every other second, wind buffeting them each time. Jason imagined them being blown over the side where they would fall who knew how far, or perhaps worse, Caesar would overcompensate and steer them directly into traffic.

"We're going to die!" Jason screamed, grabbing tighter to Caesar.

"We'll be fine!" Caesar shouted. "I'm as sober as a fucking nun right now. Holy shit!"

That last exclamation was prompted by a semi-truck hauling two trailers that barreled past them, honking its horn. As it passed, the world to their left became a dark wall of steel, whirling tires, and the loud hum of rubber racing across concrete. They saw the dimmed brake lights just before the aftershock of air hit them. Now the bicycle really started wobbling, the tips of the right handlebar going over the rail, a pedal skidding against it once, twice, three times before the bike swung to the left toward the road. Jason reached out and grabbed the handlebar, yanking it in the other direction, but way too much. The bike veered toward the rail and seemed certain to collide with it until, miraculously, the rail moved to the right as if wanting to get out of their way.

They had made it to the next exit ramp. Barely! The road angled upward, Caesar letting them coast to a stop so he could hop off. Jason did the same. They looked at each other wide-eyed, dizzy with adrenaline and fear.

"I'll never drink again," Caesar said.

"Funny, I was just thinking of starting!"

Caesar laughed first, Jason soon joining him. Then they pushed the bike to the top of the ramp. Jason recognized where they were now.

"I'm taking us the rest of the way home," he said.

"Fine with me," Caesar said, hopping on the bike and patting his lap. "This is how we should have done it from the beginning," he said as Jason took a seat on him. "Much more natural this way."

"Ha ha."

Caesar wrapped his arms around him, which felt oddly comforting, especially considering how he'd endangered both their lives a few short moments ago. With this in mind, Jason took it slow, pulling into the neighborhood at an earlier turn than usual to avoid traffic. The darkness and silence were welcome after the hectic nightmare they'd barely escaped. Jason leisurely pedaled down the street, coasting as they neared home.

"Are we sneaking in the back door again?" he asked. "Caesar?"

The only response was a gentle snore, Caesar gripping him tighter like he was a teddy bear. Jason shook his head and laughed, wondering how he was going to carry a six-foot-tall wrestler up to his bed.

Church was just as dreadful as Jason had expected. Of course it didn't help that he and Caesar had gotten home at two in the morning, or that the adrenaline from their race down the freeway had kept him wide awake. He alone seemed to suffer from this. Caesar had practically sleepwalked up the stairs with him, fallen into bed, and returned directly to dreamland. Jason had tried to undress him so he'd be more comfortable, a gesture that always looked romantic in movies but in reality involved lots of tugging and shoving around of dead weight. In the end, Jason got him down to his jeans. Afterwards he sat there another half hour, watching Caesar sleep.

Now he was paying the price. Stifling another yawn, he ignored the pastor's lecture on giving back to the community and instead glanced around at the flock. Most had gray, white, or missing hair—older people trying to make friendly with God before they went to meet him. Jason did a double-take when he saw buzzed blond hair, not because of the strong neck, but because the profile was familiar.

Sensing his stare, the person turned to look in his direction. Kurt—his brief minigolf partner and Caesar's closest friend. He looked hungover from the party last night, but then again, Kurt was always rough around the edges. Even now, decked out in a suit, he looked more like Mafia-hired muscle than a wholesome church-goer. After a quick upward nod, Kurt returned his attention to the sermon. Jason tried to do the same, but felt distracted. When this was all over, was he supposed to go over and say something? They were friends with the same person, but not exactly friends with each other.

As it turned out, the decision was made for him. Once he and the Hubbards had spilled out of the church, he saw Kurt walking toward him. Jason met him halfway, glad he did so when he heard what Kurt had to say.

"So, you and Caesar, huh?"

Jason swallowed, remembering the extremely public kiss last night. "Looks that way. Kind of a shock, huh?"

Kurt scoffed. "I've been friends with Caesar since the third grade. Nothing about him surprises me. Not anymore." He dug in his suit jacket and pulled out a pack of cigarettes. "Smoke?"

"No."

Kurt put a cigarette between his lips, talking even as he tried to light it. "What I want to know, is how serious you guys are."

This took Jason aback. "Huh?"

"Like, are you his boyfriend? Or are you doing the friends with benefits thing too?"

Jason's face burned, mostly because he didn't know the answers to these questions. Still, he felt he should at least pretend he did. "We're pretty serious."

Kurt nodded. "That means poor Steph is all on her own again."

Jason relaxed somewhat, seeing where this was going. "Yeah. She was actively searching at the party last night."

"For real?" The cigarette fell from Kurt's mouth. He bent to pick it up, looking hopeful when upright again. "Man, I should have been paying attention instead of getting wasted. She have any luck?"

Jason shook his head. "Nope."

"Maybe you can put in a good word for me. Tell her I'm interested. No, tell her you *think* I'm interested, but that you aren't sure."

"Okay."

Kurt stared at him as he pulled on his cigarette. "What else should I do?"

"How should I know?"

"You're gay, right? You're like half-girl, half-guy. You should know what women want."

Jason raised an eyebrow and laughed. "I'm not half-anything. And I don't know jack about relationships. Caesar is my first… everything."

Kurt smirked. "So no advice?"

"Be nice to her?" Jason said. That seemed pretty safe. "I'll talk to her, all right?"

"Thanks, man." Kurt spit on the ground, then nodded over his shoulder. "Looks like your ride is getting impatient."

He turned to find the Hubbards waiting by the car and went to join them. On his way, he considered the idea of Steph and Kurt as a couple. That would get her safely out of the way, and give her something to do besides text Caesar when she felt lonely. How hard could it be? All he had to do was convince her that Kurt was sexier than he was creepy.

Jason burst into the room. Caesar, stretched out in bed, looked up from his cell phone and gave him a rude "what the fuck?" expression. Or maybe he was just surprised at Jason showing up in the middle of the morning on Saturday, when everyone else was at home.

"I'm on laundry duty," Jason explained.

"Oh." Caesar pointed toward his bathroom. "In there."

He stayed where he was and glared. "Have you even taken a shower yet?"

"No." Caesar cocked an eyebrow. "Are you all right? You look tired."

"Maybe because for the last month, I've been up every night sucking your—"

"Hey!" Caesar said, laughing nervously as he swung out of bed. Then he hurried to shut the bedroom door. When he turned around, he didn't look pleased. "What the hell is going on?"

"I'm sick of doing all these stupid chores while you lounge around. The whole damn week has been like this!" Jason hadn't been doing chores, but the endless family obligations were grating on his nerves. School had been demanding too, which meant all he had time for were quick visits to this room every night. "I'm not your whore," Jason hissed. "And I don't want to be your maid."

"Okay," Caesar said holding up his hands. "I'll help you with the laundry, all right? We'll get it done together. Then I'll take you out somewhere nice."

"Not possible, because I'll have some stupid chore rewards shopping trip I have to go on."

Caesar's eyes brightened and he snapped his fingers. "We'll go to the shooting range! Dad keeps talking about the upcoming hunting trip. You need to learn how to shoot for that."

Jason's anger was replaced by abhorrence. "I don't want to go hunting!"

"You do if you want to be a Hubbard," Caesar said. "Don't worry. It's all just standing around in the woods. Nothing ever happens. Anyway—you, me, and a shotgun. Sound good?"

"No," Jason said honestly. "Although it's better than shopping with your mom. Last time she made me pick out five different ties."

Caesar grinned. "We won't stay long at the shooting range. I'll show you the absolute basics, and then we'll go do something fun. That's what you need, right?"

Jason felt his lips twitch but held back. "That *and* help with the laundry."

True to his word, Caesar hauled the hampers downstairs, and as each load came out of the drier, he helped Jason fold and put away the clothes. Naturally the great and powerful Caesar lifting a finger around the house attracted attention, but they played it off like they were eager to get to the shooting range. This became harder to pretend when they were actually finished and Caesar was loading a long black bag into his car.

"Is that yours?" Jason asked.

"Yeah. We keep all the guns in my dad's closet, but this one is mine. Peter has one too. No doubt you'll have your own someday."

"Oh boy," Jason deadpanned.

"Don't like guns?"

He shrugged. "They're kind of scary."

Caesar shut the trunk of the car. "They can be fun too. You'll see."

He drove Jason to the western edge of the city limits where a large shooting center occupied a portion of an even larger park. As they got out of the car, the air was filled with gunshot so frequent that it reminded Jason of exploding popcorn. Caesar seemed completely at home here, leading them to the registration desk and taking them through the process with bored familiarity.

"You come here a lot?" Jason asked.

"Quite a bit, yeah. Dad likes to shoot, which means I'm

supposed to like it too. What we're doing today is easy. You're lucky Dad is out of town on business or he'd be tagging along and making this more stressful than it needs to be."

They were handed a cardboard box which Jason carried so he wouldn't have to handle the gun. Then they walked through the complex until they were out on a field. Here the gunshots were much louder. Jason flinched at first, but shots were being fired so often that his instincts gave up on trying to warn him. Their destination was a simple wooden structure resembling a doorframe to nowhere. A table sat next to it. He set the box on the table, scooting it over as Caesar unbagged his gun. Jason didn't hide his apprehension.

"Another first for you?" Caesar asked. "I remember you making that face the first time you saw *my* gun."

Jason rolled his eyes. "So what is that thing? A rifle?"

"Nope. This is a twelve-gauge shotgun."

"I thought those had two barrels?"

"They can. This one is a single." Caesar moved the cardboard box to the ground so he could lay the gun sideways. "Let's go over some basics."

Jason tried to keep up as Caesar pointed out each part and explained its purpose. The only information Jason committed to memory was where the safety was. Aside from that, he figured shooting was a matter of taking aim and pulling the trigger. Then Caesar made him hold the gun, which wasn't as intimidating as Jason had expected. Childhood memories of playing with toy versions came back to him, and while the long barrel was heavy and the stock made of real wood instead of plastic, he tried to get into the mindset of this being fun.

The cardboard box held stacks of clay discs called pigeons, which could be loaded into a simple machine one at a time. Jason liked that part. He put a disc in the machine, pulled a lever, and the disc was flung high into the air. Laughing, he did this three times in a row.

"Stop wasting them," Caesar said, shotgun in hand. "Wait until I say 'pull.' Then I'll blow the poor pigeon out of the sky. Ready?"

After they had both put in earplugs, Caesar stepped into the empty doorframe and pointed his gun at the sky. "Pull!" came his muted command.

Jason pulled the lever and watched the disc as it soared into the heavens, muscles tensing as he waited for a loud explosion.

Nothing happened.

He looked to Caesar, who was laughing.

"I had the safety on!"

Jason shook his head and loaded another pigeon. This time when he was told to pull, the clay pigeon was just beginning to drop from its ascent when it shattered into pieces. Jason looked politely impressed, but felt genuinely so when nine out of ten clay discs met their end this way. Thirty discs later, Jason was asked the question he'd been dreading.

"Want to try?"

"Okay."

Caesar had to show him how to hold the gun right, then fix his stance, and finally, adjust his head to be in the right position. Jason was beginning to feel like an action figure by the time Caesar finally returned to the table.

"Pull."

He shot as soon as he saw the disc, even though the barrel wasn't pointing at it. The gun jerked in his hands, the noise not as jarring as expected but still flinch worthy. Of course he missed his target. Caesar gave him a thumbs up anyway and readied another. Jason managed to get the gun reloaded, which felt like an accomplishment, even though he did nearly get smacked in the face by the ejecting cartridge.

The second attempt didn't go much better, nor did the next dozen, but after some coaching from Caesar about shooting the pigeon at the apex of its ascent—and about twenty more tries—Jason finally hit his first target.

"Yes!" he shouted, surprised by the rush. "I did it!"

Caesar laughed. "Congratulations. Today you are a man. Now move over so I can have my turn."

Jason found himself almost unwilling to hand back the gun, discovering a new appreciation for the sport and the skill needed, especially as he watched Caesar shatter another eight. Then it was Jason's turn again. They ran out of ammunition before they ran out of targets, but at the end of an hour, Jason had managed to hit another pigeon.

"Not bad for your first time," Caesar said as they walked back to the complex. "My dad is going to be thrilled you got a head start. A little more practice and you'll be ready for the big trip."

"Hunting for animals," Jason said, his smile fading.

"Like I said, nothing ever happens. Peter might bag a rabbit or a squirrel and think he's hot shit because of it, but mostly it's just us standing around in the woods looking stupid."

"Then why bother?" Jason asked.

"Because we always rent a cabin," Caesar said, "and that means we'll have our own room. Peter will bunk up with Dad."

"Yeah, okay, but there's nothing we can't do there that we don't do at home already."

"We can lock the door," Caesar said. "Then I can hold you in my arms until morning. No more worrying about sleeping in too late and Mom finding your bed empty."

Jason waited for the perverted twist, but that was it. Caesar wanted to be able to hold him without fear of being caught. Suddenly, a hunting trip sounded positively romantic.

When they returned to the car, Caesar's phone was buzzing on the driver seat. Jason waited patiently as Caesar sat there and responded to text message after text message.

"Steph?" he asked after ten minutes of this.

"I'm almost done," Caesar said. Five minutes later, he glanced up and seemed surprised to see Jason sitting there. "Sorry. Wanna grab a bite to eat?"

"Only if you leave the phone in the car," Jason said.

Once seated at a Mexican restaurant, he was disappointed to see the phone had come inside with them. At least Caesar had the decency to shut it off after a few more buzzes.

"What's her deal?" Jason asked. "She seems so together when I talk to her."

"Steph?" Caesar asked. "She has it together. Believe me. Sometimes people get a little needy, that's all. You understand that, right?"

"Yeah," Jason said grudgingly. "But I hope she finds a new boyfriend soon. I don't like competing with a phone."

Caesar chuckled. "She won't stay single for long, don't worry."

"Speaking of which, what about her and Kurt?"

"Kurt?" Caesar shook his head. "They don't have anything in common."

"Nothing?" Jason pressed.

"Not really."

"They say opposites attract."

Caesar didn't look convinced. "Steph is elegant. She never loses her temper, always chooses her words carefully. Kurt is... rough. They both have messed-up parents, but besides that—"

"Messed up how? I already know about Steph's dad."

"Kurt's mom is a pill junkie. She's either wacked out on something or mean because she's trying to get clean. It's always one or the other. Kurt's really good at coping though, and a lot of the advice I give Steph about her dad comes from him."

Jason leapt on this. "Then that's what they have in common! Kurt can comfort her—"

"I can't imagine Kurt comforting anyone."

"—and Steph will round out his edges a little. All we have to do is get them started."

Caesar shook his head and laughed. "You really want her paired up, don't you?"

Jason didn't share his amusement. "When we got back to the car, how many text messages or whatever were waiting for you?"

"Does it really matter?"

"Just humor me. How many?"

Caesar broke eye contact and frowned. "I don't know. Fifteen. Twenty."

"That would be normal if you were writing back after each one. Instead she just keeps hitting you with a barrage of them until you do respond."

"She gets lonely."

"She needs help."

"She's fine." Caesar looked back to him. "You could get yourself a cell phone, start competing."

"Maybe I should," Jason said. "I could text you even when we're together. Might be the only way to get your attention."

Caesar raised an eyebrow. "I'll talk to her, okay?"

"Okay."

"Happy?"

"Yeah."

He wasn't though. As the waitress brought their food, he once again found himself torn between the likable Steph he talked to in person and the intolerable texting maniac who kept interrupting his time with Caesar. Jason had considered gently mentioning the issue to her, but he hadn't seen much of her the previous week. She hadn't shown up at Caesar's wrestling meets like she used to. At the time, he had taken that as a good sign, but now he wasn't so sure.

"Don't say anything to her," Jason said. "Let's just try to get her and Kurt together. See if that helps."

"Fine."

Caesar worked on assembling a fajita while Jason examined the special he'd allowed the waitress to talk him into. As far as he could tell, his meal consisted of cheese-stuffed peppers. Conversation was stilted for most of the meal, Jason wishing he hadn't brought it up. When the table was cleared, he ordered dessert just to buy time. He didn't want them going home and ending the day like this. Luckily, he found inspiration when a group of older women were seated at the table across from theirs. He felt a little guilty because something Steph had mentioned was about to bail him out, but whatever.

"Makes me miss my grandma," Jason said. "How about you? Are your grandparents still alive?"

Caesar nodded. "Most of them. My dad's parents are both still kicking. My grandpa on my mom's side passed away when I was little. I don't remember much about him."

So far, not at all interesting. "I guess I'll meet everyone eventually," Jason tried. "I hope so. I usually like grandmas."

Caesar smiled, which came as a welcome relief. "Just wait until you meet Grandma Annabelle. She's the sweetest. And a total scatterbrain, always forgetting stuff. I don't care though. To me, she's my perfect little angel."

"Awwww," Jason said sarcastically, but he mirrored Caesar's smile.

"Yeah, it's cheesy, I know. She's my favorite. All my good grandparent memories are with her." Despite his words, the happiness faded from Caesar's features.

"You said she's still alive, right?"

"Yeah. I was just thinking of the one bad memory, although it's sort of a good one too." Caesar laughed at his own contradiction. "I was around eight years old and staying the weekend with her. My grandpa was out visiting a friend, so it was just her and me. We were playing in the backyard on a summer day, running through the sprinkler together or trying to make a water slide out of trash bags lined up on the grass. Grandma Annabelle is like a big kid. Even when the other adults were around, she was always happy to play with me. So anyway, we were having fun, but then my grandma couldn't catch her breath. She went to sit down, and I figured she was just old and tired. I kept playing, but eventually she called me over and said we needed to drive to the hospital. When she tried to get up, she couldn't find the strength."

"Heart attack?" Jason guessed.

"Yeah. She told me to run inside and fetch the phone, which I did. Then she called 9-1-1. That's when I understood how serious it was. My grandma kept telling me everything was fine, but then she closed her eyes and stopped talking. No matter how loud I shouted, she wouldn't respond, even when I tried shaking her. I panicked, running around her and freaking out because I didn't know what to do. Then I heard the sirens and ran to the front door. I could barely speak, so the paramedic picked me up in his arms. All he said was 'Show me.'"

"Why are you grinning like that?" Jason asked.

"Because he was the most beautiful man in the world. Blond hair, bronze skin, unbelievable muscles… I didn't notice all this at first, of course, but while watching him give my grandma CPR and bringing her back, well, he seemed like a god to me. This guy had the power to give life, and even though the situation was terrifying, I was blown away when he did it. He brought her back. He saved Grandma Annabelle's life. I remember him turning to me, eyes crinkling in the afternoon sun as he smiled. Then he gave me a thumbs up. I was in awe. I rode with him in the back of the ambulance, and I swear I couldn't keep my jaw shut. He was that amazing, and definitely my first crush. When I was older and started fantasizing about him, I realized that I'm bi. But because of him, I also didn't have a problem with it. Wanting a guy like that simply made sense, you know? Who wouldn't?"

"He does sound hot," Jason admitted.

"Yeah, but it was more than that. He meant something. The guy was my idol. My inspiration."

"Inspiration?" Jason asked.

Caesar shook his head quickly, as if he'd misspoken, but Jason didn't think he had.

"Wait, are you saying you want to be a paramedic?"

Caesar looked embarrassed. "Yeah, I used to. The idea sounds crazy now, but I wanted to be that guy. I wanted to be this miracle worker who showed up on the scene and made everything okay. The idea of being a doctor didn't appeal because I was convinced she would have died if that paramedic hadn't been there. So yeah, I used to dream about being a hero. Sounds arrogant, doesn't it?"

Jason scoffed. "That you want to help people and feel good about it? That's not arrogant. You should do it!"

The twinkle in Caesar's eye faded. "Not going to happen."

"Why?"

"You know why."

So that was Caesar's dream, the one he had given up for his parents' approval. This is what Steph had hinted at, what she hoped Jason could help change. He felt another pang of guilt. She wanted the best for Caesar, and Jason was focusing instead on her texting, making a big deal out of nothing.

The waitress set down a huge portion of fried ice cream, served in a tortilla shell bowl and slathered in whipped cream and honey. Jason's mouth watered, even though he imagined his already-full stomach recoiling in fear.

"Are you actually going to eat all that?" Caesar asked.

"Yeah," Jason replied. "And afterwards—and I don't mean this in a sexy way—there's a pretty good chance you'll get to practice your CPR."

Caesar grinned. "In that case, I'm looking forward to being your hero."

Chapter Nine

"You might want to keep it down."

"Narrrgh!" Jason shouted in reply, almost losing the towel around his waist. His eyes remained wide when he saw who had decided to get chatty outside the bathroom. Carrie. He struggled to remember if she'd ever spoken directly to him before. The eldest Hubbard girl spent most of her time in her bedroom listening to music. When she did leave her room, songs always blared through the earbuds she constantly wore. Even now she had one ear plugged, voices singing from the tiny speaker dangling loose near her chest.

"Did you hear me?" she asked.

"Sorry, what?"

"At night. You and Caesar should be quieter."

Jason froze. Deny, lie, or walk away? The truth wasn't an option, that was for sure.

Carrie sighed impatiently. "Look, I'm trying to help. I don't have a problem with what's going on, but others would." She glanced meaningfully toward Peter's bedroom. "If I can hear you…" Then she plugged the loose ear bud back in and walked away. Jason watched her disappear down the stairs and felt a shiver run down his spine.

He remained tense during church, and like so many others there, his thoughts returned over and over to the sins he had committed. Occasionally he would look over at Carrie, but she no longer seemed interested in him. Peter was behaving normally too. That meant her warning—if it truly was that innocent—had arrived in time. Jason spent the whole day around the family, trying even harder than usual, if only to make sure that everything was okay. He was just a normal guy, part of the team, a happy would-be Hubbard. He definitely wasn't sneaking down the hall every night to do unspeakable things. No, sir. No, ma'am. Of course, when everyone had gone to bed, that was exactly what he did.

"Carrie's cool," Caesar said dismissively. "You don't need to worry about her."

Jason winced at the volume of his voice, which was still loud despite the hour being so late. Jason had crept into his room to warn him, but Caesar didn't seem concerned. In fact, he was tugging at the leg of Jason's pajama bottoms, trying to get them off.

"Stop!" Jason whispered, pulling away. "This is serious. I know she doesn't care, but she said Peter—"

Caesar glared. "What's he going to do? I'll kick his ass!"

"Which would only make him tell on us sooner."

Caesar considered this and nodded grudgingly. "Fine," he said. Then he tried again in a slightly quieter voice. "*Fine.* But I'm not going mute. You know I'm a talker."

Jason fought back a smile. "I noticed that, but I really don't need you telling me what to do anymore. I've gotten the hang of this."

Caesar pretended not to hear him. "Get over here and lay on your stomach."

"Are you serious?"

When Caesar didn't reply, Jason did what he was told.

"Very good. No, no, keep your hands at your sides."

Head on the pillow, Jason rolled his eyes as his pajama bottoms were pulled off and his legs were spread slightly. Caesar put a hand beneath each thigh and told him to raise his rump. Jason did so, and was about to remind the room that he wasn't a bottom, when he noticed where Caesar's mouth was heading.

A second later, he started moaning… but he tried to do so quietly.

Amy considered her options. Then, wistfully, she said, "I've always wanted to buy a black boy."

Jason, feeling a surge of panic, glanced around the toy store to see if anyone had heard, or worse, reacted. Luckily they were alone in the aisle. Except for Caesar, who appeared bored. Jason turned back to Amy, ready to give her a lecture on being more sensitive, when he noticed the way she longingly sighed at the dark-skinned doll on the shelf.

"Why don't you get it?" he asked.

"Because Mom never lets me."

This gave Jason pause. Amy already owned tons of Barbies, including both girl and boy dolls. All of them were white. He was hard pressed to think of an innocent reason why Amy wouldn't be allowed to have a black doll. He glanced over at Caesar for an explanation, but his boyfriend had zoned out completely.

"If that's what you want," Jason said, "that's what we'll get."

Amy opened her mouth to protest. "But Mom—"

"She's not buying you a present today. I am." Of course he was using the cash Mrs. Hubbard had given him for not getting his chore reward last week. Apparently going to the shooting range didn't count. Jason was happy for the money, but as usual, he couldn't find anything he wanted for himself. Instead he decided to treat Amy to something special. As much as Jason had to force himself to be around the other Hubbards, he genuinely liked her. Besides, he'd rather play dolls than one of Peter's computer games.

Amy tugged on Caesar's sleeve. "What do you think?"

"I don't care," he said. "Just hurry up and pick something out."

"This can't be rushed," Jason said, taking the doll to examine it. The dark-skinned version of Ken only included a pair of swim trunks and sandals. "The poor guy is nearly naked. He'll need an outfit. Maybe two."

"Are you kidding me?" Caesar didn't hide his exasperation, shaking his head when he saw Jason was serious. "You guys are weird."

"Oh, go find yourself something. I bet they make a little toy version of your car."

Caesar perked up. "You think so?"

Once he had wandered away to find out, they were free to consider their options.

"He'll have to wear something nice when he takes me on dates," Amy said.

In Barbie terms, this meant a tuxedo. No casual dining in her world! Black was too boring for a kid's line, meaning Amy's new boyfriend would be wearing a silver suit, but she didn't seem to mind. Jason made sure the daytime clothes were slightly less garish, finding a pack with blue jeans and a T-shirt with the words *Fresh Beat!* printed on it.

"Freshly farmed beets?" Jason asked.

The joke was lost on Amy, but she was pleased with his choice. Spotting another outfit on the shelf, Jason grabbed it too in a burst of inspiration.

They found Caesar waiting just outside once they finished paying at the register. Next they stopped for some frosted cookies and cola. Hyped up on sugar, Amy became eager to return home and play with her new doll, so they headed out to the parking lot.

"I can't believe you've never driven before," Caesar said between slurps of his drink.

"Then let's change that. Toss me your keys." Jason's smile faltered when Caesar did just that. "You're kidding!"

"Nope! You have to learn sometime."

Jason swallowed. "I don't think your mom would like me putting Amy's life at risk. Or yours, for that matter."

"You think I'm letting you drive us home?" Caesar smirked. "You're only cruising around the parking lot. That's how everyone starts out."

"Oh." That sounded a lot less intimidating. Jason began to feel excited as he opened the driver-side door and got behind the wheel. "Okay," he said, looking everything over. "Uh, where's the parking brake?"

"Right there," Caesar said from the back. Amy had taken the passenger seat and was digging through her bag. "And you won't need it because we're not parked on a hill."

"Oh. And uh… There's something called a clutch, right?"

"There would be if this car wasn't automatic." After a pause, Caesar added, "You know, maybe this isn't such a good idea."

"Oh, we're doing this!" Jason turned the key. The car was too sophisticated for the engine to roar to life. Instead it went from silent to a quiet hum. "So I just hit the gas and the car knows if I want to go in reverse or not, right?" He looked in the rearview mirror at Caesar's unusually pale face. "I'm kidding! Geez."

But when he needed to back out of the parking space, Jason began to feel nervous himself. He had never so much as driven in a straight line, so navigating backward while not hitting the cars on either side—and while avoiding traffic—made his palms sweat. "How come that car is just sitting there?"

"Because they want your space," Amy said absentmindedly. "You better hurry or they'll honk."

"Okay." Jason pressed on the gas, the car lurching backward. He turned the wheel and hit the brakes at the same time, causing both the tires and Caesar to shriek. Jason had closed his eyes, which probably wasn't a good idea, and when he opened them he found the car parked diagonally in the middle of the lane. "I didn't hit anything!" he said proudly.

"Get out of the car!" Caesar insisted.

Jason ignored him, putting the car in drive and cruising forward carefully. He felt good about keeping the car straight, but when turning at the end of the lane, he made a much larger bow than necessary. He compensated for this at the end of the second lane, turning in an arc so tight that the car ended up pointed at a parked car.

"Amy could drive better than this," Caesar said.

"Maybe you're right," Jason replied. "Amy, get over here and see what you can do."

"Really?" she said.

"No!" Caesar shouted. "Lesson's over. Next time we'll do this in an *empty* parking lot."

Jason insisted on being allowed to park the car in a space again. This time Caesar coached him instead of complaining, giving him tips that helped, even if he did end up over the line a little. Once he and Caesar switched places, Jason allowed himself to breathe out in relief. He agreed that a less busy environment would be better—and safer—but now that he'd had a taste, he was eager to try again.

When they returned home, they found a car missing from the garage and the house silent. Caesar did a quick check to make sure they were on their own. When he was certain, the look he gave Jason was transparent. Amy even seemed to verbalize what he was thinking.

"Want to play with me?" she asked.

"Actually," Caesar said, "I'm going to show Jason a video about driving. In my room. It'll be very boring."

Amy looked crestfallen.

"Who needs a dumb video when I've got such a great teacher?" Jason said. "I'd love to play dolls with you, Amy."

Blue eyes lit up like only a seven-year-old's could. "Really?"

"For sure," Jason said. "I've got my priorities. So does your brother."

"Meaning?" Caesar asked.

"Meaning Amy has a doll with your name right on it. You said you wanted to control your own fate."

"I did?"

"Yup. Besides, we bought something special for your doll to wear. Show him."

Amy dug into the plastic bag and pulled out tiny clothing trapped between clear plastic and thin cardboard. The outfit was for a male nurse. Not exactly a paramedic, but Caesar caught the significance and smiled.

"Okay," he said. "Let's go play dolls!"

Another party, and this one was much more to Jason's liking. Seated on the banks of Lake Houston on a moonless night, they had agreed to burn no fires and play no boom boxes, all in the name of avoiding detection. Regardless, Caesar had begged Jason to bring along his guitar, which he happily strummed as they got drunk off another keg Caesar somehow managed to procure. Eventually they all paired up and found private places in the shadows of the trees.

That's what Jason appreciated about this party. Steph had wandered off with Kurt, which was a promising sign. The giggle twins had found two boys who dressed and talked alike. He imagined they would remain together in a group of four, but still they had gone their own way. A handful of other couples had also slowly drifted farther from the keg, leaving him and Caesar alone. Jason continued to play, sending a tune out in response to the gentle song the water sang. Next to him, Caesar sat with his legs pulled up and stared across the lake, as if he could see the notes disappearing there.

When Jason's fingers grew sore, he set aside the guitar. His empty hand was immediately filled with a plastic cup, beer slopping over the side.

"Where do you get this stuff?" Jason asked.

"Trade secret."

The night was too dark to see a wink, but he imagined Caesar doing so anyway. "You're not having another?" Come to think of it, Jason had only seen him drink one.

"After last time?" Caesar shook his head. "I'm the designated driver tonight. Of course there are more people here than I can fit in my car, but maybe we can fit a few in the trunk. The rest can sleep out here, or something. I have more pressing concerns, such as the one pressing on my bladder."

Jason laughed and watched him go. Then he turned his attention back to the lake and sighed.

"I recognize that sound." Steph appeared from out of the

dark, carrying two plastic cups. "Any left?"

"Yeah," Jason took the cups from her and worked on refilling them, asking as casually as possible, "So how's it going?"

"With Kurt?" Steph sat down next to him. "Well, at first it was weird because all he would talk about was his mother."

Probably because Jason had recently advised him to do just that.

"Eventually, I started to see some parallels in our lives, and the conversation became a lot less forced. He and I have been to the same dark places."

"Really?" Jason said carefully. "Sounds like you guys have a lot in common."

"Which is exactly why you suggested he talk about his mother."

"Uh…"

"Kurt told me. I don't think he understands the meaning of tact."

"Sorry," Jason said.

"No, it's fine! Tonight has shown me a new side to him. And he's an incredible kisser. The best, in fact."

"Better than Caesar?" Jason asked, not hiding his disbelief.

Steph grinned and nodded.

"Wow! I mean… Huh. So are you and Kurt an item now?"

"Yes," Steph said, drawing the word out and not sounding completely certain. "At least I'm willing to give it a try and see what happens."

"Thank god!" Jason said with beer-infused carelessness that didn't go unnoticed.

"You sound more excited for me than I am."

"No," Jason said, chuckling in embarrassment. "It's stupid, but I was getting upset about your text messages."

Steph's head pulled back slightly. "My text messages?"

"To Caesar. I mean, you write him *a lot,* and when we're out on dates, sometimes it's like you're there with us. You can't blame me for being jealous since you're incredible and Caesar is crazy about you. I just don't want to compete, mostly because I'd probably lose!"

He guffawed, expecting Steph to be flattered by his compliments and humility. Instead she was quiet, his loud laugh echoing on the lake before dying a lonely death. The awkward silence stretched on. When she did speak, he struggled to understand the question. "How long has he been texting like this?"

"What do you mean? He's always on that stupid phone."

"Always?" Steph's voice was tense. "You mean ever since you moved in?"

Jason shrugged. "Yeah. Obviously I don't know what he was like before then."

He stared at Steph's profile, but she was no longer looking at him. She seemed angry, but he had the nagging feeling that this wasn't directed at him. She sat there like a statue until they heard feet tromping around in the woods. Then Steph came to life, handing back one of the beers. "I'm done drinking tonight." She stood, Jason doing the same in his nervousness. She glanced at him, toward the woods, and back at him again. "I might text Caesar once or twice a day, if even that. I prefer hearing the sound of someone's voice. That way it's easier to tell if they're lying or not."

"Hey!" Caesar said, reappearing at last. "I nearly got lost."

Steph brushed by him without saying a word.

Caesar stared after her before turning back to Jason. "What's her problem?"

"No idea," Jason said. Brain feeling numb, he sat again and picked up his guitar, mostly to discourage conversation. He needed to think, needed to figure out what was going on, but the alcohol thinning his blood didn't make this easy. All he seemed capable of was repeating the same question in his mind, over and over again.

If Steph wasn't texting Caesar so much, then who was?

"That paramedic guy you liked so much…" The words sounded slurred even to Jason. The streetlights zooming by every few seconds hurt his eyes and made him nauseous but he had to ask. "What was his name?"

"Thom," Caesar answered immediately.

"So did you and this *Thom* ever meet again?" Jason said the paramedic's name with enough disdain that Caesar glanced over at him, but he still got an answer.

"No. I made him a thank-you card, and my grandma promised to give it to him. No idea if he ever got it. Why?"

Jason shook his head. He needed a suspect. In the last few months, he'd spent a lot of time with Caesar. He knew most of his friends and had a vague idea of who they all were. Jason kept thinking of each, trying to find anyone even remotely suspicious. None of them fit. Aside from Steph. He wondered if she was playing him. If so, why had she asked such a weird question? Why did she want to know how long Caesar's frequent texting had been going on? Or maybe she was only making cryptic comments to upset him.

If so, it had worked. Jason couldn't stop obsessing over it, searching desperately for missing pieces and anything unexplained. After awhile, he thought of another. "Where do you get your beer?"

"Why?" Caesar considered him again. "Are you okay? You look a little green."

Jason spotted a convenience store ahead. "I need something to drink."

"Well, it won't be beer." Caesar hit the turn signal and pulled into the convenience store parking lot. "Wait here. I'll grab you a Coke."

Jason nodded, watched him walk into the store, and grabbed the phone. Suddenly he wished he did own one. The screen was dark, so he kept hitting buttons while hoping to bring it to life. Eventually he found the power button on top. After a short rumble, the screen lit. Jason glanced up to see Caesar at the counter. He didn't have much time, and the stupid phone was asking him for a four-digit password. What would someone like Caesar use?

Sixty-nine sixty-nine? That didn't work. Jason struggled to think of anything else vaguely sexual. Eight zero zero eight? In grade school, kids used to type that on calculators to spell boob. Nope. Wrong password. A shadow moved outside the driver-side window. Jason tossed the phone back in the center console just as the door opened. Unfortunately, the screen was still glowing.

"Here you go!" Caesar slid into the driver's seat and handed him a ridiculously large drink and a bag of chips. "These should help you feel better. What now?" Noticing the phone, he picked it up, his fingers moving over the keys with practiced habit.

Jason turned his head forward a little as if he didn't care and sucked on the drink's straw, but he kept watch in the corner of his eye.

One one one one.

Of course. What else would Mr. I'm Number One use? The next screen was a series of text options, which no doubt would have also tripped him up. Caesar swiftly moved through these before shutting off the phone again. "Feel better?" he asked.

Jason nodded, knowing he wouldn't feel better until he got to the bottom of this. Once they were home again, he acted like he needed sleep and went to his room. When he was sure Caesar was safely in his own, Jason went to the bathroom, brushed his teeth, and crept down the hall. The door to Peter's room was cracked, the space inside lit by a battle raging across the computer screen. He knocked gently and the action on the screen froze.

"Yeah?"

Jason entered.

Peter had turned in his chair to face the door. "Hey! Want to play a few campaigns together?"

"Actually," Jason said, "I was thinking about buying a cell phone. Those have games too, right?"

"Yeah," Peter said. "They're primitive, but I can recommend a few that are tactic-based."

Jason nodded. "Cool. Actually, I've never had a phone before and don't even know the basics. Think you can give me a crash course?"

Peter nodded eagerly, unaware that he was signing up to be Watson to Jason's Sherlock. With a little bit of luck, they'd soon crack the case of the century.

Chapter Ten

Jason pressed down the power button with a nervous finger, the cell phone screen flashing before it died again. He thought he glimpsed an image of a red battery. Cursing under his breath, he looked toward Caesar's private bathroom where the door was half-open, the sound of a shower hissing beyond. Jason felt a yearning in his heart, excitement in his body at being here in the morning when he shouldn't be. He could forget all this mystery nonsense, sneak into the shower and reenact what they had done there a few nights ago.

But he wouldn't. Jason glanced around, spotting a charger and hurriedly plugging in the phone. This time the screen stayed lit.

"One one one one," he whispered as he typed it in.

Accepted! The menu that appeared was different from Peter's phone, but he spotted what he needed right away. He toggled down to *messages*, then *texts*. He saw Steph's name, feeling vindicated until he noticed all the messages below it.

Nathaniel. Nathaniel. Nathaniel. Over and over again.

Jason's brow furrowed as he tried to connect the name to a face, but he couldn't. He chose Steph's message first, hoping it would give him reason to shut the phone off and hop in the shower with Caesar.

Not mad. Just wanted to get back to Kurt. Don't you have someone else to text?

Okay. That wasn't too promising. Steph seemed angry about Caesar texting with someone. That person had to be Nathaniel. Mouth dry and pulse racing, Jason toggled to the previous screen. He skipped down five or six messages to get a better idea of the conversation, desperate to see what Nathaniel had to say.

sick of class. sick of studying. sick of everything.

Okay, not exactly damning. Jason's heart slowed a little as he went for the message that followed.

no im not sick of you.

Uh-oh! Jason hurried to the next one.

of course I still want to. when and where?

Oh god! Jason struggled to remember what Peter had said about viewing sent messages. He needed to know what Caesar was saying. Maybe this one-sided conversation made it sound worse than it was. But first, Jason wanted to finish reading these.

ok ill be there.

So they were meeting somewhere.

i love you too.

Bad enough, but the "too" really made Jason's stomach sink. He struggled to find a way of making this statement sound innocent. A relative, maybe? Could Caesar be texting with his grandpa? But it was doubtful an old man still went to classes or texted. A cousin? The next and final message killed this train of thought.

sweet dreams my lonely prince.

The hissing shower went silent, the metal hooks of the curtain clanging against each other. Jason almost fled from the room, but instead he remained motionless. When an electric toothbrush started buzzing, he rushed through menus again. *Sent messages.* He traveled backwards through the history of texts Caesar had written.

Steph! Why did you rush off tonight?

Sleep well my handsome king.

I love you.

Sunday, noon, campus library.

That was everything he needed. Jason shut off the phone and started to turn away, remembering at the last moment to unplug it from the power cord. Then he hurried to the bedroom door, peering through the crack as he quietly closed it behind him. The last thing he saw was Caesar strolling into the room, towel-drying his hair as he went for clothes. One final fleeting image, beautiful and inviting, that made the pain in Jason's heart so much worse.

Clouds gathered above, promising a late appearance of those famous April showers, accompanied by hint of summer manifesting in the form of thunder. Jason wiped the sweat from his brow, cursing the humidity and wishing the storm would break, even if he ended up soaked. Picking up the pace, he wondered if he was headed in the right direction. So far he'd been walking more than an hour. The maps on Peter's computer yesterday had made the university appear much closer than it actually was. If Jason didn't get there soon, he would miss… Well, whatever awaited him.

His stomach twisted with anxiety, just as it had all day yesterday. For once he was grateful for the chores and the rewards that followed—this time lunch out and a movie—since this gave him an excuse to avoid Caesar. Until Jason knew the truth, he didn't want to be around him. But as night fell, he tried a different approach. Or he grew weak. Either way, he went to Caesar's room and spent more time than usual with him, hoping that if they slept together, the morning appointment with Nathaniel would become unwanted. When they had sex, Jason put all of himself into every motion, every kiss, believing it could be the cure. He hadn't spoken much either, providing silence that Caesar might fill with a confession. But he didn't.

This morning Jason had played sick to avoid church. Mrs. Hubbard obviously didn't believe him, but he made it clear that he didn't give a shit. She wasn't happy with the return of his defiance, but that was the least of his concerns right now.

Trying to get his bearings, Jason went to a bus stop to check the map. Still uncertain, he turned around and saw a bus approaching with *University* illuminated on the destination display. He waved it down, which was silly, considering he was at a bus stop, but he didn't want to miss this opportunity. One minute later he was seated, the speed of his pulse increasing along with the bus.

His heartbeat continued working overtime when he reached the University of Houston. After twenty minutes of wandering the campus, he finally found the library, although upon entering, the architecture resembled more a shopping mall that dealt only in books. The floors above were open to each other, high-set windows illuminating the hall. Wings full of knowledge spread out to the left and right.

Checking the clock, Jason saw he still had half an hour to spare, but that now seemed too little time to search this place. Waiting by the doors until Caesar showed up was an option, but that wouldn't reveal what Jason wanted to know. He needed to catch Caesar in the act, if there was anything to catch at all.

Jason began wandering the library, looking at people instead of books. Maybe Nathaniel was here already, waiting with just as much impatience as he texted with. He half expected to see a young guy hammering away on his phone, urging Caesar to hurry. Every handsome face Jason passed—and he saw plenty of them—made him instantly suspicious, but none seemed to be waiting.

With no viable suspects on the first floor, Jason decided to try the second. After walking up and down a few rows, he spotted a guy seated at a table. Blond hair, a chiseled chin, and beefy shoulders. Jason would have done a double take even if he were looking for a book instead of a person. Was this Nathaniel? Whoever he was, the man's attention wasn't on the book in his hands. Instead he kept looking over the rails to the lower floor. From his position, he had a perfect view of the entrance.

Jason kept him in mind as he walked, returning not once but twice. Sure enough, the man's focus remained on the doors below. Having eyed him from multiple angles now, Jason could see that the man's body was just as chiseled as that chin. He hoped desperately that he had the wrong guy, but when the man pulled out his cell phone to check it, Jason knew. This was Nathaniel.

Jason's heart felt like it wanted to implode. He found an aisle to hide in and observe undetected. Copying the very person he was stalking, he took a book off the shelf that he never looked at. He stared over it, trying to fight off crushing despair. How old was Nathaniel? Older than Caesar, that was for sure. He was definitely a student here, if not a teacher. The more Jason sized him up, the more he felt like a boy, because Nathaniel was manly. Stubble on his chin, an all-over tan that came from being outdoors, and those stupid muscles that Jason wished he didn't find attractive.

With nothing better to do while he waited, Jason tortured himself by trying to picture Caesar sleeping with this man. Would he still be a top for someone so much larger? Or did Caesar make an exception when those meaty arms were wrapped around him?

Nathaniel perked up and quickly pretended to be reading, when really he was grinning behind his book. Caesar must have arrived. Waiting for him to appear was grueling. Half an hour seemed to go by before Caesar finally appeared, sneaking up to the table and snatching the book away. Nathaniel didn't look the least bit surprised, which made Caesar laugh. Then Caesar leaned across the table and nuzzled his nose against Nathaniel's.

This little sign of affection was much worse than the kiss that followed. Caesar had never done that to Jason, had never gently touched their noses together like two kittens in greeting. Something so simple and innocent spoke of love, a word that Jason hadn't realized was missing until he had seen it spelled out in a cold cell phone font. He and Caesar didn't touch noses, nor did they say that special little word. And why? Jason simply hadn't known to—didn't have the experience to recognize when such a word was appropriate. Caesar did and had chosen not to use it. The reason stood before him, much closer than before since Jason's feet had brought him out of the aisle and into the open.

Nathaniel spotted him first, reacting with a flicker of irritation at being stared at. This caused Caesar to turn his head. That's when the sound escaped Jason's throat. Like a pained hiccup or maybe air being forced out by a punch to the stomach. All he knew was that it sounded pathetic and communicated perfectly how he felt. Part of Jason felt like running, but then again, he'd come here to learn the truth. This is what he'd expected to see, and rather than flee from it, he would face it. Let Caesar see how much he hurt! Let that expression of surprise turn to one of regret when he saw the damage he'd done.

Much to Jason's surprise, that was exactly what happened. Caesar's expression became one of pained sympathy.

Increased irritation marred Nathaniel's features. "What are you staring at?"

Caesar opened his mouth to explain. "I know him. He's my foster brother."

Jason hated him for drawing that line, for using a term he knew neither of them believed in, but it only got worse when Nathaniel responded.

"Peter?"

"No," Caesar said. "This is Jason, the new one."

"Ah." Nathaniel reappraised him, then he stood, stepped forward, and offered a hand. He was grinning, but there was something ironic about it. "In that case, it's nice to finally meet my new baby brother."

Jason stared at his hand. "You're a Hubbard?"

"No more than you are." Nathaniel's voice was bitter. "How's my old room?"

Jason looked between them, putting the pieces together. At first he felt relief. Nathaniel was just another foster kid, one older than them, one everyone had somehow failed to mention. Caesar being here, their relationship and the declarations of love—they were all innocent. Except that kiss proved they weren't, and the bitterness that hardened Nathaniel's smile implied his history with the Hubbards wasn't a happy one. Caesar opened his mouth to explain, but Jason shook his head. Instead he addressed Nathaniel. "Your old room is about to become available again. Feel free to move back in."

Then he turned, ignoring the sound of his name being called, glaring when it echoed through the library a second time.

Jason walked. He had no need to run. Caesar would never give chase, always expecting Jason to come to him. Only Nathaniel had the privilege of summoning Caesar, the handsome king awaiting his perfect prince. And what was Jason? The way he felt now, he was nothing more than a foolish peasant.

It took Jason three hours to find his way home. He walked the entire way, getting lost in both thought and direction. Anguish seized him repeatedly, but he refused to cry. He focused instead on anger, trying to transmute his love for Caesar into hate. Sometimes he thought he was successful, but that urge kept returning: Jason wanted to be with Caesar. That was impossible now. He knew this. But he couldn't help wishing Nathaniel didn't exist or that Caesar would choose him instead. He kept looking over his shoulder, hoping to see a silver sports car pulling up, a concerned face behind the windshield. Each time Jason turned around, he was disappointed.

By the time he walked in the front door, he was starving and exhausted.

Almost immediately, Mrs. Hubbard stepped into his path. "You're grounded!"

Jason ignored this, walking around her and heading for the stairs.

"Where were you?" she shouted after him.

Jason went to his room, shut the door, and reached for a lock that wasn't there. When he heard footsteps coming up the stairs, he threw himself on the bed and covered his head with a pillow. He could still hear the words, both Mr. and Mrs. Hubbard yelling at him or trying to pull away his pillow, but Jason held on tightly until they gave up and left.

When he was sure the coast was clear, he went to the bathroom and drank from the sink.

"Are you okay?" Amy stood in the doorway, a plush pony under one arm.

"No," Jason said. "I'm not."

"You can hide in my room if you want."

He was tempted to accept, but he knew it would only spark a house-wide search for him, and he didn't want Amy seeing the Hubbards yelling at him. "I need to stay in mine," Jason said, heading for the hall.

Amy didn't move out of the way. "Are they going to make you leave? I hate it when people go away."

Jason swallowed, unsure what his future held, but he didn't want her to worry. "I'm not going anywhere. I got grounded, that's all."

"Oh." A child's mind rarely remained on one subject. When Amy spoke next, it was clear she had moved on. "Will you play the guitar for me?"

"Yeah. But only if you do me a favor first."

"What?"

"Think you can go downstairs and make me a sandwich? You'd have to sneak it up here."

"No need," Amy said. "I have an Easy Bake in my room."

"You mean one of those light-bulb-powered ovens?"

"Yep."

"Uh, okay. If you can make me something to eat with it—something real—then I'll play you all the songs you want."

Half an hour later he was feasting on ridiculously small cookies and brownies, all of which tasted a little powdery, but they got him full enough to refuse dinner when Mrs. Hubbard told him it was ready. Jason was angry at her son more than her, and this rebellion would cost him, but he took satisfaction in it anyway.

Night had fallen by the time he heard Caesar's voice downstairs, and despite Jason not being able to make out the words, his heartbreak increased. He lay in bed as the house grew silent, resisting the temptation to march down the hall and start yelling because he knew it would only be an excuse to interact with Caesar. As much as Jason wanted that, he still tensed up when the door to his room quietly opened. He was facing away from the door and remained that way as he listened to it close again.

One side of the mattress lowered as Caesar sat down. "Don't yell or anything, okay?"

"Afraid someone might hear?"

"Yes!"

The response was so heartfelt that Jason rolled over. Caesar's face was strained, his eyes red, either from stress or tears. Despite this, Jason couldn't feel sorry for him because he felt like shit himself.

"Put your shoes on," Caesar said. "Go for a ride with me."

Jason rolled back over. "No."

"There's a lot you don't know—"

"I think I've figured out the basics!" Jason snapped, sitting up in anger.

Panic appeared on Caesar's face. "Not so loud! Please, just let me explain. We'll hit a drive-thru."

Jason just stared at him.

"Amy told me how she cooked you dinner. You've got to be starving."

"Fuck you." Jason said it quietly, as per Caesar's request. He felt insulted at being bribed with food. Caesar had been cheating on him all this time, and he thought some McNuggets could make up for it?

"I know you hate me. You'll still hate me once I've told you the truth, but you should at least know it. Aren't you the slightest bit curious?"

Jason was, about a lot of things. Like the whole notion of cheating. Didn't a person have to be in a relationship for that to happen? He was beginning to wonder if he'd been deluded this whole time. They had never discussed being committed to each other. If Jason really had meant something to Caesar and wasn't just another friend with benefits—then he wanted to know. Even if it was over now.

Wordlessly, Jason bent over and pulled on his lime green shoes, throat constricting when he remembered who they were a present from. He left them on anyway, feeling miserable enough without wearing the stupid squeaking pair.

The silence required to sneak out of the house accompanied them in the car as they drove. Jason refused to broach the subject. He wasn't the one who needed to explain. That was Caesar's burden, but when he finally started, Jason didn't remain silent for long.

"Nathaniel moved in with us when I was fifteen," Caesar said. "He—"

"—was your foster brother," Jason interrupted. "He ended up seducing you, which you must have liked, because you decided to play the same game with me." He glanced over to see Caesar clenching his jaw and felt pleased with himself.

"He moved in when I was fifteen," Caesar repeated firmly, "but he wasn't my foster brother and he isn't an orphan. He didn't even live with us at first. My parents hired him as a tutor. When high school started, the pressure to get perfect grades increased. My parents aren't good at some subjects and my dad isn't always around, so Nathaniel was called in to be a lot of things to me. More than anyone expected. I admired him. Idolized him. I guess he reminded me of my paramedic. Like I told you before, when I hit puberty, I started fantasizing about Thom in a whole new way. When Nathaniel came into my life, they sort of became the same person in my mind."

"And then he—"

"No! He didn't!" Caesar shouted. "Would you just listen to me? For a long time, I couldn't talk to him. I kept clamming up. But he was a nice guy and got along great with my dad, so he kept making the effort. Eventually, on a family camping trip, he took me out hiking. That's when I finally got to know him. He's not exactly sweet. Nathaniel is like a force of nature. I'd never met anyone so confident, someone who knew exactly who he was and what he wanted. He goes after it too. You've seen the way he texts and…" Caesar sighed. "I'm getting ahead of myself."

"So backtrack to getting molested in the woods."

"He's only two years older than me," Caesar said. "And nothing happened that day. Nathaniel had a rough home life. He confided in me a little, but my dad knew even more. No matter what you think of my parents, they care about people. That's when Nathaniel moved in with us. Not as a foster kid exactly. Not at first. Him being around all the time only made things harder on me. Eventually I broke down and told him I was in love with him. We were out for a walk, and I couldn't keep it in anymore. He didn't say a word at first. He just put his finger under my chin and made me look him in the eye before he kissed me." There was a spurt of laughter that sounded like trying to hold back tears. Caesar shook his head, as if embarrassed. "He just kissed me, right there on the sidewalk."

Jason tore his eyes away. None of this made him feel better. Maybe he didn't want to know the truth after all. "If you love him so much," he asked. "Why did you cheat on him?"

"I didn't," Caesar said, taking a deep breath. "Listen, can the food wait? I'm not sure I should be driving right now."

Jason glanced over at him. "Been drinking?"

"No." Caesar turned the wheel, bringing them to a strip mall parking lot where they pulled up to a store with dark windows. "Nathaniel and I weren't together long. A handful of months, but as you know, that's all it really takes."

Jason's throat grew tight again. Was Caesar implying he felt something for him or only that he knew what Jason felt? He tried to read Caesar, who remained lost in the past, staring hard at the steering wheel. "My mom caught us. You asked if my parents knew about me. Well, what my mom saw didn't leave much room for doubt. I was almost glad. My parents had been talking about adopting Nathaniel, helping him escape his bad situation permanently. He still wouldn't be my blood, but legally..." Caesar shook his head. "I didn't know they would send him away. They didn't send Carrie away when she got in trouble, so I figured Nathaniel would always be there. I didn't want him to become my brother, although I did fantasize he would become a Hubbard eventually."

"When you were married?" Jason asked, his voice cracking.

"I was so in love with him," Caesar said, like he was apologizing. "I'm not telling you this to hurt you. But I need you to understand. If you're going to hate me, I want it to be for the right reason. I wasn't just fucking around with him. Before Nathaniel left, we made a promise. No matter what it took, we would be together again. Even if that meant waiting until we were on our own."

"So you've been together all these years?"

"No. We were young when we made that promise, and so much changed between then and now. Three years is a long time and things happened. People came into our lives—"

"Like Steph," Jason said. "So basically you've always been cheating on Nathaniel."

Caesar glared, brow knitting together. "Betrayal comes in many forms. We promised to get into Yale, and he knew that's where I had to go, but he enrolled in the University of Houston anyway."

"Not everyone can afford Yale," Jason said.

Caesar shook his head. "There's more to it than that. Nathaniel and I were falling apart. We'd been separated for a year at this point, and yeah, Steph was part of my life. She and I kept dancing around each other, wanting more but unable to act."

"She knew about him?"

"Yeah, she knew. The short version is that Nathaniel and I broke it off. So I didn't cheat on anyone. Steph was there for me when I fell, and I still love her for that."

Jason's jaw clenched. He couldn't take it anymore. "What about me?" he shouted. "You sit here and tell me how much you love all these other people, but you never say it to me! How do you think that makes me feel?"

"I love you," Caesar said without hesitation.

"No!" Jason's throat felt raw, but he couldn't stop. "Don't you fucking dare! I don't want to hear it. Not now." His voice was faltering as the tears came unbidden, but he managed one more sentence. "Why didn't you say it before?"

"I didn't feel like I had the right," Caesar said. "What kind of man cheats and then tells the other person that they're loved? So I've been a shitty boyfriend to you, and I'm sorry, but I really do love you."

Jason couldn't respond. All he could do was fight back the tears. He didn't want Caesar or anyone else seeing him like this, but he was too overwhelmed. All the pain combined with the bittersweet acknowledgement that he was loved, that the relationship he had hoped for was real—all of it was too much.

Perhaps sensing his embarrassment, Caesar continued. "The timing was bad. Nathaniel got in touch with me before you moved in. We met up, but kept it strictly platonic. Just friends, even if I did still have feelings for him. Then you came along, and I liked you. A lot. But I wasn't sure what you wanted. What are the odds? My parents must have unintentional gaydar or something."

"Just tell me you haven't slept with Peter too," Jason spat bitterly.

"Give me some credit," Caesar said, making a face. "Anyway, I kept catching you looking at Steph, and you didn't seem to like

Kurt at all, so I decided I didn't have a chance. About the same time, Nathaniel started talking about keeping our promise. Then I woke up one night and you're trying to kiss me."

Jason took a few deep breaths, wiped the tears from his eyes and raised his head. He wanted to face the next question with dignity and wouldn't allow the answer to upset him. "So when did you finally cheat on me?"

Caesar looked away. "A few weeks ago. I was picking up that keg from Nathaniel. That's where I get my beer from, since he looks old enough to buy it now, and uh… Things got out of hand."

"Out of hand?" Jason asked, jaw clenching. "I hope you had fun. Never forget that day. Commit every fucking detail to memory, because it's the reason we can't be together anymore."

Caesar lowered his head, eyes lost in shadow. "I know. I don't expect you to forgive me. But I want you to know that it wasn't just hormones. I love him. He was my first, and that's not something you get over. Ever."

This wasn't the news Jason wanted to hear right now, but Caesar seemed distracted, not realizing the implications. Instead he kept speaking.

"I love you. I really do, even if you don't want to hear it."

Jason looked out the window. He had a headache, his throat felt sore, and his eyes were burning. Gosh, who knew that love could feel so good? "If you love me," he said, his voice a croak, "then why don't you leave him?"

Caesar was quiet long enough that Jason wished he could take back the words because he knew he wasn't going to like the answer. "I didn't ask you out here tonight because I hoped you would forgive me."

In other words, I don't want you, I want him. Caesar had managed to say this ugliest of truths without saying it at all. Jason almost admired his tact. With a silver tongue like that, he'd take the business world by storm. "You're going to make your dad real proud someday."

"What's that supposed to mean?"

Jason tried to swallow the bitter taste in his mouth and shook his head. "It doesn't matter. You can take me home now."

Caesar didn't budge. "I'm glad you still think of it as home. You don't have to leave. My parents will give you a good life.

I'll be off to college this summer, so you won't have to see me anymore. Just a couple more months. Even if you don't like my parents, they can give you a good start. I know how it is. I mean, Nathaniel and you have some things in common, so—"

"Don't," Jason said. "Don't compare me to him and don't tell me what to do. I'll figure it out on my own."

"Sorry," Caesar said. After a thick silence he started the car. "Still hungry?"

"Sure," Jason said with a casual shrug. "Why wouldn't I be?"

"Oh. Okay."

Jason kept this icy act going as they got some burgers, pretending through every bite that he didn't care anymore. Only when they had returned home and he was alone in his room did he let himself cry out the last few tears—and he promised himself they would be the last. No more for Caesar. No more for anyone else. Ever.

"Rough week?"

Michelle was back, no doubt at the request of the Hubbards, but Jason didn't mind. Seeing her was exactly what he needed. She was taking him for a walk around the block, mostly so they could have privacy, although it did make him feel like a pet dog. He imagined a collar around his neck, Michelle holding the leash as he panted happily beside her. Okay, so maybe he liked her a little too much.

"Rough?" he repeated, hoping the word didn't sound like a bark. "I've definitely had better."

"Things were going so well too," Michelle said. "The Hubbards had nothing but praise for you until Sunday. As I said before, if you feel that strongly about church…"

"It has nothing to do with that."

"Oh. Well, something must have happened, and if you feel like talking about it—"

"I fell in love," Jason said. "And it backfired."

"Wow," Michelle said. "Usually the 'if you feel like talking about it' speech doesn't work. Okay. Um, I think I can understand where you're coming from. Few things are as horrible as a broken heart."

Jason glanced over at her. "Been there yourself?"

"Yeah. A long time ago. Most people have had their hearts

stomped on at least once. Not to belittle what you're going through because I know it hurts like hell. Falling in love should be a valid court defense for all but the most heinous of crimes. So you burned down the local Walmart because someone didn't return your call? No need to explain! You're forgiven."

Jason laughed. "Am I?"

"With me, you are. You'll have to manage a half-hearted apology to the Hubbards if you want to restore peace."

"I think I can handle that."

"Good. So besides horrible, crippling heartbreak, are you still content with living here?"

"Yeah," Jason said, surprised by the answer. "I've lived in worse places." And it was true. Amy was adorable, Peter was welcoming in his own way, and Carrie never bothered him. Mr. and Mrs. Hubbard, despite all their faults, really did have the best of intentions. That just left Caesar. Jason knew they couldn't be together, but some treacherous part of him didn't want him out of his life forever. Not yet.

"I'm happy you want to stay," Michelle said. "Let's think up a very simple excuse for your outburst that even Mrs. Hubbard can understand."

"I can't read?" Jason suggested.

"We can do better than that. It's a shame you don't get PMS. I use that one all the time, even if it's not true. You should see my husband tremble."

"You're married?" Jason asked. "That's more bad news for me."

Michelle eyed him and laughed. "I hope you aren't flirting with me. Not that you aren't cute," she added quickly, "but you remind me too much of my brother."

"Right, right," Jason said. "You're just letting me down easy."

"You really do," Michelle insisted. "It's hard for me to put my finger on why... Did I mention I have a daughter? She's only eleven years old, but she's bright. She's in all the gifted classes at school. Maybe we can do one of those arranged marriage things, plan ahead like royalty used to."

"Do I get half the kingdom?"

"I can't promise you that much, but my husband is one of the most successful realtors in Houston. There's at least a house in the deal for you. Maybe a couple of cows and a goat too."

Jason laughed. "In that case, yes. One day I shall marry your daughter." They stopped, having circled the block and reached the Hubbard's home again. *His* home, he supposed, but first he had some bridges to repair. "I was getting picked on at school," he said. "The bully goes to the same church. That's why I didn't want to go."

Michelle thought about his excuse and nodded. "Very nice. Might even be good enough to get you out of going to church altogether."

Which would leave him home alone with Caesar every Sunday, transforming the week's most holy day into one of temptation.

"Nah," Jason replied. "It's time for this old sinner to redeem himself."

The main reason he had shunned church before was to spend time with Caesar. If need be, Jason would become a man of the cloth just to avoid him. His priority now was protecting his wounded heart, which meant he couldn't be alone with Caesar. Oddly enough, it also meant he couldn't stray too far from him either.

Chapter Eleven

No wheelchair can support damaged self-esteem until it learns to stand upright. No cane can help emotions limp along until they can walk. A cast or brace can't protect a vulnerable spirit, and not even the strongest painkiller can stop the ache caused by a failed relationship. No, the only way a broken heart mends itself is with stitches of time and the sticky tape of hastily rearranged dreams.

Jason's recovery didn't come swiftly, but over the next month, he found little ways of coping. He would hang out with Steph, who both shared his feelings for Caesar and understood the agony of having lost him. Or he would spend time with his new family, finding that he didn't have to force himself anymore. Jason was happy for the companionship, since this also made it easier to move on. He would visit the shooting range with Mr. Hubbard and Peter, honing his skill and enjoying the sport. Or he would help Mrs. Hubbard around the house, maintaining an unspoken truce with her. He was always happy to play the guitar for Amy, or help redecorate her doll house.

Throughout all of this, Caesar kept his distance, which Jason was grateful for. Occasionally they would meet, Jason walking into the living room to find him there, but one of them always made an excuse and left. Once Jason spotted Caesar sitting at the kitchen table, eyes on the phone as he texted. Instead of entering the room, Jason had taken a step back from the doorway, remaining near enough to watch Caesar, those old cuts on his heart tearing open again.

Jason knew he would never move on completely. Caesar was right: There was no getting over a first love. Jason tried as best he could. As the school year came to an end, he found his strength tested on more than one occasion. First was the dinner celebrating Caesar's acceptance into Yale, conversation focusing on his plans and how he would soon be far away. Such talk did little to comfort Jason. Later came a party in honor of Caesar's high school graduation, countless relatives and friends lining up to shake his hand and bask in the perfection of his smile. Jason felt trapped in the audience, while on the stage of life, spotlights and applause were directed at the person everyone loved most.

"Isn't he great?" the world seemed to shout. *"Isn't Caesar the most wonderful thing ever?"*

Sadly, Jason couldn't help but agree.

Then came the increasingly discussed hunting trip. Jason hoped Caesar wouldn't come along. With school out, they found avoiding each other more difficult than before. The decent thing would be one of them finding an excuse, but Jason wasn't having much luck. Besides, Caesar could get away with anything. Surely he could weasel out somehow. Or so Jason thought. He was loading his luggage in the back of Mr. Hubbard's Land Rover when Caesar appeared next to him, carelessly tossing in a duffle bag.

"Just one of those things I have to do," he said. "One of my father's dictated obligations. Sorry."

Jason nodded his understanding, his discomfort increasing when they were on the road. Peter insisted on riding up front, which wasn't a surprise. Whenever Mr. Hubbard was around, Peter tended to monopolize him, asking him questions or saying anything to gain approval. Normally Jason didn't care, but with the back of the vehicle full of luggage and hunting equipment, he and Caesar had to share the bench seat in the middle.

While they had plenty of space to avoid touching each other, Jason felt odd not conversing during the nearly five-hour trip. He kept looking at Caesar's exposed legs out of the corner of his eye, wishing the weather was cold so more than shorts and a tank top were required. When Caesar fell asleep halfway through the trip, Jason stole glances at the rest of him. Then, during a break at a gas station, he returned from the restroom to find Caesar standing behind the SUV and texting. That's when he realized he hadn't heard a peep from Caesar's phone over the last few hours.

"You don't have to keep it off for my benefit," Jason told him.

Caesar looked up, as if gauging how serious he was.

"Seriously. It doesn't bother me."

The rest of the trip was easier. With the phone now on, Caesar was frequently occupied, and Jason had countless reminders of why it wouldn't work. He asked to borrow Peter's phone, playing one of the games, but also pretending to send desperately passionate text messages to an imaginary boyfriend. This made him laugh, Caesar responding with puzzled expressions.

One last dreadful challenge remained when they pulled up

to the private cabin Mr. Hubbard had reserved for them. As Caesar had promised, the cabin had two bedrooms, each with two beds. The last thing Jason wanted was to end up in one of those rooms with Caesar. This apprehension was replaced by a new one when they entered. Everything seemed to be hewn from wood or draped with Southwestern-style rugs. The living room was equipped with a large television, an adjoining kitchen styled more like a bar at one end. All of that was fine. What disturbed Jason were the countless animal heads mounted on the walls.

Deer, elk, buffalo, boar, and any other species with antlers or tusks. For a brief moment, he almost laughed. The scene looked ridiculous, like tons of animals had inexplicably charged through the walls of the cabin, busting through with their heads before getting stuck. But then their stillness and the unblinking glass eyes reminded him they were all dead. Jason dropped his luggage on the floor and stared.

"It's fine," Caesar said quietly, stopping next to him. "We never bag any big game. Even if we get a nice juicy turkey in our crosshairs, we can't shoot it because it's not in season. Not much is aside from really small game and animals that aren't indigenous, like axis deer. Unless one of those saunters by—and they never do—it's all shooting at squirrels and missing."

That made him feel a little bit better. After a brief tour—the other rooms in the house also filled with dead animals, even the bathroom—they debated the sleeping situation. Jason wasn't alone in his concern.

"Want to be roommates, little brother?" Caesar asked.

The look Peter gave him wasn't very friendly. "Dad and I always share a room."

"Actually," Mr. Hubbard said, "seeing as this might be Caesar's last trip out here for quite some time, I thought he and I would bunk up. If you don't mind, Peter."

"I guess that's okay." Peter looked over at Jason, seeming to make peace with the idea. "Come on. I'll show you ours."

Down the hallway was a room smaller than the first with two single beds. Jason could imagine him and Caesar pushing them together, lighting the oil lantern on the side table, and spending the entire night in each other's arms. Instead he would be listening to Peter's snores and farts until dawn. Jason glanced at the head of a wild pig on the wall, then looked over at his roommate.

"So, what's the plan?" he asked.

"The first day is always boring," Peter said. "We'll have to unpack, then go to a grocery store for supplies. Dad likes to grill while out here, so no restaurants. Tonight will probably be poker, which sucks. Or maybe some night fishing if we can convince him. Anyway, the real action starts tomorrow. Ready for your first hunt?"

Jason eyed a stuffed squirrel on the window sill. "Can't wait," he lied.

Boring. Wet, miserable, and absolutely dreadfully boring. Jason smiled contentedly. The third day hunting, and this one appeared even more hopeless than those previous. The skies above were overcast, the rain a ceaseless drizzle. So far, hunting had consisted of tromping around in the woods while wearing camouflage, or pausing for long periods when Peter thought he heard something. Or they would take note of trails frequently used by animals, setting up base some distance away. There they stood, kneeled, or lay, waiting for forest animals to make their daily commute to work. Must have been a holiday, because they weren't seeing much.

Peter had managed to shoot a rabbit yesterday, which Jason found upsetting, but then they ended up making a stew of it for dinner. He ate a bowl, feeling disgusted, but also not wanting the animal to go to waste. Later that night in their room, Peter made a good case about this being more honest than how they usually acquired meat. Animals were still dying to make the burgers Jason loved so much, although they had a much less pleasant life—bred in crowded and filthy captivity and dragged off to die a terrifying death in a slaughter house. Jason almost suspected Peter was trying to sell him on a vegetarian diet. But then he pointed out how the animals they were hunting had lived a good natural life in the wild, and even in death served a purpose.

After thinking it over, Jason was convinced, although he didn't see how this meshed with the heads on the walls or the excited chatter Mr. Hubbard and Peter exchanged when browsing through hunting magazines. They oohed and aahed over antler sizes like they were discussing another sort of rack. Since no one would be eating the antlers, Jason struggled to understand their excitement.

At the moment, he and the Hubbards were on their bellies, due to more of the phantom sounds Peter always heard. The guy with the magic ears was to Jason's left, tense as he held his gun at the ready. To his right was Mr. Hubbard, eyes small and intent on the clearing ahead. Past him, Caesar was very casually poking at his cell phone, which he'd hidden among a few leaves.

"Put that thing away!" Mr. Hubbard hissed. "I told you to leave it at home."

"I did," Caesar said. "It followed me out here like a loyal pet."

"This trip is your last chance," Mr. Hubbard replied. "You need to keep your eye on the prize. Do you really want to have a conversation with a client about hunting, only to explain that in all the years you've been out here, you've never bagged any game?"

Wow. Was that the key to good sales? Locker room bragging?

"Gee, that *would* be horrible," Caesar said sarcastically. "How would I ever live that down? Oh, I know. I could lie."

Jason couldn't help smiling. Mr. Hubbard was less amused, glaring at Caesar until he pocketed the phone and picked up his gun. Jason adjusted his grip on his own. What he wanted to do was tie a pillow around the stock so he could take a quick nap.

Next to him, Peter tensed up even more, which seemed impossible. When he spoke, his words were so quiet they were hard to make out, but from the way he raised his gun, their meaning was obvious. Jason looked at the clearing, the breath catching in his throat. Long elegant legs picked their way across the ground. White spots like pinpricks of sunshine shifted as muscles moved beneath chestnut brown fur. Dark eyes sparkled in a way glass marbles in a mounted head never could. And those antlers were huge, covered in velvet that Jason imagined felt soft to the touch. Now he understood the fascination with them because the buck was beautiful. He'd never expected it to be so large, to move so slowly and deliberately like a god inspecting his kingdom. Jason didn't want to steal those antlers or put that head on his wall. He felt like bowing to the sheer majesty of the creature.

"I've got it," Peter said.

"No!" Mr. Hubbard hissed the very word on Jason's mind, but his relief was short-lived. "Let Caesar take it, son."

"But—"

"This is his last trip! You and I have plenty more together."

Jason glanced back and forth between them. Peter's jaw was flexing hard, his brow low. Then Jason turned the other way, saw the look of surprise on Caesar's face before he gave a curt nod, adjusted his gun, and placed his cheek against the stock, just like he had once laid his head on Jason's leg so his hair could be toyed with.

Jason looked back at the clearing, at the buck whose head had turned to consider them, as if asking what they intended to do.

"He'll never hit it," Peter muttered.

He couldn't miss! The animal was ridiculously close, and Jason had seen Caesar pick countless clay pigeons out of the distant sky. Even without the benefit of buckshot splaying wide, the slugs loaded in their guns would be enough to bring down the deer, no matter where Caesar hit it.

The shot rang out, Jason flinching at the same time as the deer. He waited for the beast to cry out in pain, to topple over and never move again, but instead it started running. Not understanding, Jason glanced over at Caesar just in time to see him lowering the barrel, the angle much too high to hit anything but the tree tops. Caesar glanced at him, a hint of warning in his eyes. Jason understood and looked away. Caesar had fired into the air on purpose. He had saved—

BOOM!

Jason's left ear went numb from the sound, his body recoiling instinctively. Next to him Peter was on his knees, eyes and mouth wide with wild abandon. Jason looked at the clearing to see the deer on its front knees, the back legs still kicking as it tried to escape. It toppled over just as Jason got to his feet. He raced across the leaves to reach it, not caring if Mr. Hubbard was aiming a kill shot that would hit him instead. Up close, the buck was gigantic. Jason could smell the musky scent, feel heat radiating off its body. Most of all he could see the panic in its eye as it huffed. The once flawless white crest on its neck was now stained pink with splatter from the hole in its shoulder. Jason saw the wound and acted instinctively, dropping on his knees to press a palm against it, but there was so much blood that his hand slipped off. He tried again, a guttural sound coming from the animal's throat, causing him to worry he was hurting it further. Jason stared into its eyes, wanting to communicate that he was trying to help, but the animal wasn't watching him anymore, its eyes growing dim. The dark orbs became distant, unfocused, and then still.

The tears came then, accompanied by an angry snarl. Jason stood, marching back toward the others who were standing now. He wanted his shotgun, wanted to put a bullet through Peter to see how he liked it. The little shit was laughing, pleased with himself for having taken down an animal with technology it couldn't comprehend. What a fucking hero! Forget the gun. Jason would wipe that smile off his face with his fists.

He was shouting something unintelligible when arms wrapped around him, lifting him off his feet and spinning him around. Confused, he looked up into Caesar's concerned face and the anger inside him broke. The tears really started flowing then, and the snot. Jason pulled away and wiped at his face, smelling copper and tasting it on his lips.

Caesar's mouth kept moving, shaping words Jason didn't hear. He shook his head, looking away, trying to pull free from the hands gripping his arms. Finally, sound returned to his world.

"Jason!" Caesar shouted. "Hold still! You're covered in blood."

Jason raised his hands, saw the buck's blood already beginning to darken and dry where it had smeared across his palms. Caesar stripped off the light jacket he was wearing, then his shirt, using it to wipe Jason's hands, but getting the blood off completely was hopeless.

"What's his problem?" Peter said from behind.

"Quiet," Mr. Hubbard scolded. "Caesar, take him back to the cabin. We'll finish up here."

Caesar put an arm around Jason and guided him through the woods. Jason couldn't understand what had happened, how they hadn't experienced the same thing he had. Didn't they see the beauty? How could they want to cut that down? What Peter had said made sense. This was a better way of getting and eating meat, but the way he had laughed… Jason couldn't comprehend anyone taking joy in this act or how it could ever be called a sport.

His head was awhirl with confusing thoughts and emotions as they reached the cabin. He let Caesar take him to the bathroom, stared with detachment as Caesar washed his hands for him in the sink and dabbed at his face with a wash rag. Then Jason was led into the bedroom, where Caesar made him lie down. After rubbing his back and whispering soothing words, he turned to leave. Jason sat up on the bed, Caesar hesitating at the door.

"You need to rest," he said. "Try to calm down. Maybe get some sleep."

Jason couldn't find the words, could only stare at him in need. Caesar sighed, shut the door and locked it. Then he walked to the bed.

"Lie down," he said.

Jason did so, tensing up when he felt Caesar crawl into bed behind him and relaxing when he felt an arm wrap around him. He didn't feel better. Jason still saw the dark eyes of the buck in his mind, heard the sound of its final breaths. But as he tried to comprehend the coldness of some actions, he was also reminded of a warmth he had once thought lost.

Chapter Twelve

When Jason awoke, he was alone. The light in the room was brighter, the clouds having left the sky. The afternoon sun shone directly through his window on its journey toward the horizon. Despite the cheery atmosphere, he still felt upset. The memory of the buck remained painful, and now he faced other complications, the most immediate being a call of nature and his unwillingness to leave the room. He could hear the others, Peter's voice the loudest. Jason could imagine his smug expression and how cocky he'd be for doing what Caesar had failed to do. Everyone seemed to be in the kitchen, meaning Jason could probably sneak down the hall and return undetected.

Jason successfully navigated the hall to the bathroom and made it back, thinking he had pulled it off, but a few seconds later he heard a light rap on the door. When it opened, he was relieved to see the knocker was only Caesar—which was funny since lately he'd been the person Jason avoided most.

"Feeling better?"

"No," Jason said honestly. "Can I stay in here?"

"For today, maybe. After that..." Caesar exhaled, as if this were a tall order. "I could drain my college fund. Buy this cabin so you can live forever in this room."

Jason managed a fleeting smile. "I don't want to face the others. Are they..."

Caesar shut the door behind him. "Peter is still bragging. He's not really interested in how you acted because he wants all the praise he can get from Dad. He'll probably say something snide when you do come out, but you shouldn't react to it. Don't give him the satisfaction. Dad worries this trip traumatized you, but luckily, he's more preoccupied with his disappointment in me. So really, the heat is off you."

"Sorry," Jason said. "For what it's worth, I'm proud of you. I saw what you tried to do."

Caesar shrugged and leaned against the closed door. "Didn't do much good. You want me to bring you dinner when it's ready?"

Jason swallowed. "Are we eating the buck?"

"Not tonight. Dad had a guy from the hunting lodge pick it up and it's being... uh, prepared."

"Butchered," Jason said. "I'm okay with that. I don't want it to have died for nothing."

"Oh, okay. Yeah, so we'll get the meat, and Peter wants the head mounted, but I can promise you that my mom will make him keep it in his room. She's not a big fan of hunting."

"Fine with me," Jason said. "I won't be hanging out in his room anymore."

"Listen," Caesar said, "about tonight, maybe I can talk Peter into bunking with me. I'm sure he'd love to hold me captive and flaunt his big achievement. Can't say I'm looking forward to it, but that way you don't have to be around him."

The idea of staying with Mr. Hubbard didn't sound appealing either. He wasn't the kind of guy Jason felt like being vulnerable around. The only person he wanted to be with was standing right in front of him. "Let Peter stay with your dad tonight."

Caesar balked. "But that would mean… Oh. I'll take the couch so you can—"

"Stay with me," Jason said. "Please."

Caesar put his arms over his chest, started knocking one heel against the door as if nervous. Then he nodded and turned around. "I'll see what I can do."

Jason stared at the shadows on the ceiling. Outside the open window, bugs hummed in the early summer heat, interrupted now and again by sounds from the forest. The hoot of an owl, a chase through the brush, the high-pitched growl of some unidentified creature. Jason found himself wishing for the white noise that air conditioning provided, but he knew this wasn't the reason he couldn't sleep.

During the brief moments of silence outside, he could hear enough to tell he wasn't alone in his insomnia. Caesar's breathing wasn't deep or restful. He kept tossing and turning. Jason bit his lip before deciding to roll over and face in his direction. The comforter lay crumpled on the floor, only a sheet remaining to cover Caesar's waist. His former lover was lying on his back, one arm draped over his eyes.

Jason felt feverish with desire. He suspected he could creep out of bed and take what he wanted, but only one thing stopped him. Nathaniel. Jason was sure he and Caesar were in a relationship. If something happened tonight, Jason would be the one Caesar was cheating with, instead of on. Revenge? Probably not, because he was pretty sure from Nathaniel's reaction at the library that he hadn't known. Jason couldn't claim such ignorance. Not this time. If he took what he wanted tonight, he would be helping someone cheat.

And yet, Jason still needed what he needed. The comfort physical closeness could bring, the dream of Caesar holding him until morning finally realized. Jason cared about Nathaniel getting hurt, and yet it didn't matter because his own feelings were so much more present and demanding. He wondered if that was how Caesar had felt, if he had considered how wrong and hurtful sleeping with both of them would have been, but still felt compelled by emotion and lust to do so anyway. Maybe this made Caesar's actions forgivable. If he were to sit up in bed right now, turn to Jason and ask forgiveness, he would grant it. Hell, there wasn't anything Jason wouldn't give to him right now.

He *needed* to. Body, heart, and even his occasionally reasonable mind all wanted this. Jason got out of bed, walked to Caesar, and took hold of his wrist to move away his arm. He wanted to look him in the eye before they kissed. Caesar jerked away, but his expression wasn't entirely surprised. Jason bent over to bring their lips together, Caesar dodging. Then he swung his legs around to sit up.

"What are you doing?" Caesar asked.

"You know what I'm doing," Jason replied.

"Don't."

Jason reached out to brush a hand against his cheek, thought fading as his body filled with desire. Caesar grabbed his wrist to stop him, so Jason used the other hand until that arm too was captured. Jason wasn't discouraged. He stepped forward, bringing his body close, using his weight to push Caesar back onto the bed, laying on top of him. Caesar, still holding Jason's wrists, forced him to roll over and pinned him to the mattress.

"I told you to stop," Caesar said.

"I don't care," Jason replied.

He could feel Caesar's hardness pressing against him, so Jason lifted his head to try for a kiss.

"Nathaniel." Caesar said the name like a warning, or maybe a reminder of all that had gone wrong.

"I don't care," Jason repeated. "I need you. Please."

Caesar searched his face. He was clearly conflicted, which hurt and was endearing and didn't matter anymore, because Jason thought he'd go crazy if he didn't get what he wanted. He felt so damn much right now that there was only one way to verbalize it.

"I love you."

Caesar released his wrists, splayed a palm beside Jason's head to support himself before bringing their faces together, but they didn't kiss. Not yet.

"This is the last time," Caesar said. "Promise me."

"I promise," Jason said, and in his heart he knew it was a lie, so he made up for it by repeating the truth. "I love you so much."

Caesar kissed him, and while their lips were busy, Jason put his hands all the places he had longed for. Mostly he held on to Caesar, clutching him tight as the night wore on. Jason did anything he could think of to bring him close, did things that hurt and felt good at the same time. Even after they were both exhausted and Caesar tried to roll off him, Jason wouldn't allow it. The comfort of his weight pressing down was too important, helped maintain the illusion that they could be like this forever—that willpower alone could stop them from being torn apart.

The creaking of the floorboards awoke Jason. He wondered if Caesar was trying to sneak out, or maybe back in after using the restroom. Except Jason was still wrapped in his arms, body warm where their skin touched and chilly elsewhere because they'd lost the sheet sometime in the night. Caesar was breathing heavily into his ear, drool dripping down Jason's neck, but he was too happy to mind. Instead he tugged on one of Caesar's arms to pull him closer, trying to use him like a blanket.

Then the floorboard creaked again. Jason raised his head in puzzlement and saw Peter standing not far away, pocket knife in hand. He was smiling, looking even happier than he had yesterday when he'd taken down the buck. Jason's eyes darted back down to the blade, wondering if Peter had developed a taste for blood.

"Oh, don't worry," Peter said, gesturing at him with the knife. "This isn't for you. I used it to get the door open. My clothes are still in the drawer and I couldn't figure out why you two were locked away in here. Of course, I had my suspicions."

Next to him, Caesar was stirring. Jason had the urge to cover them both, even though it was pointless now. He could feel Caesar's erection against his hip, both exposed to air. There would be no explaining this away, no twist that could make the scene innocent.

"Just go," Jason whispered. "Please."

Peter stopped smiling. He looked at Jason with something nearing pity, and for a moment, he even seemed to consider leaving. But then Caesar woke up, starting when he saw Peter and the knife. He was on his feet in seconds.

"What the fuck are you doing in here? What's with the knife?"

Before Peter could respond, Caesar was on top of him, grabbing his wrist and forcing him to drop the blade before pinning his arm behind his back. Peter was crying out in pain and humiliation, Jason shouting at Caesar to leave him alone. He watched helplessly as Peter was shoved out the door. Caesar slammed it shut behind him, then turned to face the room.

"Fuck!" he growled. As Caesar's brain kicked into gear, his anger turned to panic. "Fuck!" he repeated. "Oh fuck fuck fuck." He locked eyes with Jason and shook his head. "How much did he see? Do you know?"

"Enough," Jason said. "He used the knife to pick the lock. That's all. He wasn't trying to do anything."

Caesar had his hands over his mouth and nose, his head shaking back and forth.

His expression of terror made Jason feel dread. "Do you think he'll say anything?"

"It's Peter!" Caesar said bitterly, moving his hands away. "Fuck! Listen, you've got to get in the shower. Don't put any clothes on first. Just run. That way when my Dad comes in here, I can say—"

"Caesar?"

A fist pounded on the door before it started to open. In his panic, Caesar spun around and shoved it closed again, keeping his hands pressed against it and his arms straight. He must have realized how damning this was because he hung his head. Then he looked back at Jason with an expression of pure apology.

"Put your clothes on," he said. "I have to let him in."

"I'll go out the window," Jason whispered as Mr. Hubbard continued pounding on the door.

Caesar laughed hollowly and shook his head. "Won't make a difference. They'll believe Peter. After all, this has happened before."

Jason pulled on his boxers. "We'll both go. We'll run away."

Caesar turned and pressed his back against the door as it tried to open again. Then he just stared sorrowfully. Jason wanted to comfort him somehow, even to kiss him despite this being the absolute worst time for such a thing. Instead, he locked eyes with Caesar and saw the stillness of resignation. Caesar took two steps forward. Jason thought he was coming to embrace him, but then he stopped. And waited.

Behind him the door opened. Mr. Hubbard took in the scene, then grabbed Caesar by the arm and pulled him out of the room, slamming the door shut. Through the wooden wall, Jason listened to the one-sided shouting, pictured Caesar standing there naked and listless as his father berated him for something that couldn't be changed.

Their voices moved away, so Jason got dressed and opened the door, glancing down the hallway. He could see Caesar on the couch, a blanket covering him, his head low as the lecture continued. Then Jason turned and found Peter standing with his back to the wall, a smug expression on his face. Like he had made two kills this trip.

Mrs. Hubbard stood before him, mascara running. Jason felt uncomfortable—had felt that way the entire day. The drive back had been five hours of awkward silence. Caesar was told to sit in the front passenger seat, Peter taking his place in the back, but even he was smart enough to keep his mouth shut. Why draw attention away from the transgression that had occurred? Mr. Hubbard had nothing to say either, scowling grimly at the road ahead.

Once home, they were each told to go to their rooms. Eventually, Mr. Hubbard had come for Jason. The house was eerily silent as they walked down the stairs. Mrs. Hubbard was crying when they entered the living room. She left a flustered mess, but whatever she did in the other room didn't help, because she returned just as tearful as before.

"We need you to tell us the truth," she said. "When Peter found you this morning…" She shook her head and fumbled with a tissue to blow her nose.

Mr. Hubbard cleared his throat. "We just need to know how all this got started."

"Started?" Jason asked. He shook his head, feeling overwhelmed by the question. "The same way it does for anyone, I guess."

Mr. Hubbard narrowed his eyes. "Meaning?"

"People..." Jason hesitated. "People just fall in love."

Mrs. Hubbard looked at her husband, who nodded meaningfully. She cried some more, but Jason realized these were tears of relief. They were trying to figure out if Caesar had done this against Jason's will, as if he had been molested or something.

"I care about him!" Jason said in his defense. "It's just like when a guy and girl fall in love. There's nothing wrong with it."

"He's your brother!" Mrs. Hubbard said.

"He's not my brother!" Jason leapt to his feet. "And you aren't my parents! What we did isn't sick or unnatural. It wasn't against my will or his! You can't punish us for having feelings!"

"Sit down," Mr. Hubbard said.

"No!"

"Sit down!"

Suddenly Mr. Hubbard looked a lot bigger than he usually did, his chest puffed up and huffing, so Jason did what he was told. Mr. Hubbard watched him to make sure he would stay put, then took his wife's arm and guided her to the other side of the living room. After a hushed conversation, she nodded and left, but not before she shot Jason an accusatory glare. He wondered if Nathaniel had gotten the same treatment before he'd been sent on his way, if all the blame for Caesar's unwanted behavior had been placed on his strong shoulders.

Mr. Hubbard returned to stand over him, arms crossed. What he had to say didn't surprise Jason in the slightest.

"You've struggled to fit in with this family since day one. We like you, Jason. We really do. But considering everything that's happened, I think we both know what would be best, don't we?"

Jason shook his head. He wasn't going to make this easy by being the one to say it.

"Very well. My wife and I think you'd be happier at another home. I'm going to call Michelle in the morning and have her come by so we can all talk. Okay?"

Jason refused to nod or agree to any of this. "Can I go back to my room now?"

"If you wish," Mr. Hubbard said. "We'd like you to stay there until dinner. There are other conversations that need to take place."

Jason stood and went upstairs. Then he pressed his ear to the door, wondering if they would drag Caesar out of his room. Jason couldn't hear anything. Chances were they had questioned him already. When dinnertime came, Jason forced himself to go downstairs, if only to see if Caesar was doing all right. He wasn't at the table. Not wanting to be around the family, Jason asked if he could eat in his room. Mrs. Hubbard seemed relieved to see him go.

Jason spent the rest of the evening packing his things. He left the suit, the squeaky shoes, and the other clothes the Hubbards had bought him behind. That just left his old clothes, his guitar, and a pair of lime green Converse. Jason was sitting on the edge of the bed, considering these few possessions, when he remembered the bandana hidden between the mattress and box spring. He dug it out and tied it around the neck of his guitar. When the house grew silent, he quietly opened his door and walked down the hallway to Caesar's room.

He didn't try to knock. Just as he always did, Jason placed his hand on the knob, felt a familiar stirring in his chest, and turned it. Or tried to. The knob didn't budge. He tried again with more force, stepping back when this didn't work to consider the door. Locked. From the inside. Caesar didn't want to see him.

Taking a deep breath, Jason turned and walked back to his room.

"I'm sorry."

These were the first words Michelle said when he opened his bedroom door. He gestured for her to enter. Instead she stepped forward and hugged him.

"I'm so sorry," she repeated.

"It's fine," Jason said, lump in his throat. "I'm an old pro at this."

"I don't mean the foster placement," Michelle said. She stepped back and double-checked the hallway. Then she shut the bedroom door and sat on the edge of his mattress. "I mean

I'm sorry for what you're going through. The heartbreak you mentioned last time, you were talking about Caesar, weren't you?"

"Yeah," Jason said, maybe a little defensively because she hurried to explain.

"There's nothing wrong with being gay or having feelings for him. You know that, right?"

"You're cool with it?"

"I mentioned that you remind me of my brother. He's gay too, and yes, I'm cool with it. But when I said last time that everyone goes through heartbreak, I didn't mean like this." Michelle considered him and sighed. "What a nightmare."

"It's fine," he lied.

"On the other hand," Michelle said, trying to appear optimistic, "I get to see a lot more of you again. That's a silver lining, right?"

He smiled for her sake, knowing she meant well. "Is there going to be some horrible meeting downstairs, or can we just go?"

"I've already talked to the Hubbards," Michelle said. "We can go. Looks like you're all packed up?"

"Yeah."

"Anyone you want to say goodbye to first?"

Jason looked to make sure she was serious. "I'm not sure if he's in his room or not... Can you guard the hallway?"

"Officially? No." Michelle stood up and went to the door. "I can, however, go over some final details with the Hubbards downstairs. Five minutes, okay?"

"Okay."

Jason was out the door first. Like last night, he didn't bother to knock. This time the doorknob turned beneath his hand. He was worried this meant Caesar wasn't there, but Jason found him sitting on the carpet, back against the bed.

"They told me you were leaving," he mumbled.

Jason eyed him a minute before shutting the door. "Maybe it's for the best. We'll let things die down a little. Then you could sneak out and pick me up. Not every night, but—"

Caesar raised his head. "I'm going to Yale."

"I know," Jason said, "but not for a few months."

"So we just screw around until then?"

Jason hesitated, surprised by the chill in his voice. "I'll get my driver's license. Now that I'm sixteen I can sign up for a work program through the group home. I'll save money, and maybe we can meet halfway. I'd have to get a car, but hell, I'll take a bus until then! Or maybe—"

"Nathaniel got accepted," Caesar said. "To Yale. Getting transferred there is even harder than being accepted as a freshman. He's been working his ass off all year to achieve that. Even before he got back in touch with me."

"So?" Jason wanted to say this defiantly, but the word came out sounding desperate. "So that's it?"

Caesar's tone was pleading. "I've been in love with him since I was fifteen! And I've been waiting, all this time, to be with him." He scowled down at the carpet again. "So yes. This is it."

Jason stood there, lip trembling as he tried to find the right words, anything at all, that would earn him a second chance. When he couldn't find them, when even his heart couldn't offer him hope, his shoulders relaxed. "Goodbye, Caesar."

After a moment of stillness, Caesar looked up one last time, jaw clenching, but only to hold back tears. "Goodbye, Jason Grant."

All that was left, was to turn and walk away. Jason found this easier to do than he might have expected, since staying longer would hurt too much. On the way down the hall, he heard Carrie's music, heard the clicking of a mouse in Peter's room, but he refused to look inside the cracked doors. He wondered if Mr. and Mrs. Hubbard had told them all to stay in their rooms to keep them safe, just in case Jason had a tantrum. Or maybe to shield them from his perversions. Only one door opened as he was passing by.

Amy looked up at him accusingly. He understood, remembering the feeling of abandonment that had once haunted him. Then she thrust something at him—a little bundled-up napkin. He took it, her door slamming shut a second later. Opening the napkin, he discovered a handful of tiny muffins made from a light-bulb-powered oven. Smiling, he opened her door a crack and said, "I love you too, Amy!"

Closing the door again, he popped a muffin in his mouth and went to his former room. Slinging his pack over one shoulder and his guitar over the other, Jason strolled down the stairs, out the front door, and into a hot summer day.

Chapter Thirteen

Home again.

The phrase kept popping into Jason's head all week. At the moment, it made him laugh, since he was sitting in the dining area of the common room. So basically, a couple of tables he needed to wipe down and a few dishes he needed to bring back to the kitchen made him feel like he was home. Not exactly the castle most people dreamed of, but he felt a strange sort of contentment from being in the group home again.

"There you are!" Michelle marched in carrying a manila folder. Caseworkers were *always* carrying manila folders around. This made him laugh too. Michelle smiled in response. "I'm glad to see you're feeling better, even if it is at my expense."

"Sorry," Jason said.

"Is it my hair?"

"No, I'm just in a goofy mood. Wanna sit down? Shoot the shit?"

Michelle remained standing. "Actually, I wanted to bring you the forms you requested."

Jason sat upright. "For the work release program?"

"Yes." Michelle moved the folder away when he reached for it. "I know sixteen seems old to you, but you don't have to give up on finding a family. A good foster parent will be there in an emergency, even when you're on your own as an adult. Two more years is a very long time. Enough to make strangers feel like a family."

"Two years *is* a long time," Jason said. "And I don't want to waste it bouncing back and forth between homes. I want to start building my own life."

"Okay." Michelle placed the folder on the table in front of him, but kept her hand on top of it.

He glanced up at her, saw that she was biting her lip, and shook his head ruefully. "Now what?"

"Remember that brother of mine I mentioned?"

"The gay one?"

Michelle nodded. "Yeah. He's been through some hard times too, and I thought it might help if you had someone to talk to who understands what it's like—"

"I know about the birds and the bees, okay?"

"Not like that," Michelle said, tittering nervously. Then she glanced toward the door.

Jason sighed. "He's already here, isn't he?"

"Yeah," Michelle said. "He came all the way from Austin just because I asked him to. Isn't that sweet of him? So it would be a shame if he traveled all that way for nothing."

"Ice cream," Jason said. "And a movie. This weekend. Me and you."

"Deal!" Michelle said. "Wait here, I'll send him in."

Jason shook his head, then did a quick check of his hair. Messy as always, so that was good. He felt strangely nervous sitting there. He hadn't met many other gay people. Did Caesar count? He supposed Nathaniel did, for what that was worth. So Jason didn't really know what to expect, but when a tall guy—one with the same hair color and high cheekbones as Michelle—entered the room, he felt slightly more comfortable. The family resemblance was obvious, although Jason found the guy version of Michelle a lot more attractive.

Jason decided he should probably stand, which he did, taking hold of the hand that was offered to him and shaking it.

"We share the same name," the man said.

"We do?"

"Yeah, although nobody calls me Jason. My mom used to when she was really *really* mad, but for the most part, it's just Jace. What about you?"

"People call me Jason whether they're mad or not," he answered.

Jace grinned, then glanced around the room. "Should we sit?"

"Yeah, okay." Jason took his seat again, embarrassed when Jace sat across from him and started wiping the crumbs into a tidy pile. "Sorry. I was supposed to clean that up."

Jace looked up. "Don't worry about it. Just a habit from my job. I'm always cleaning up after people."

"What do you do?"

"Flight attendant, although I'm on an extended leave of absence right now."

"Oh."

Jace scooped the crumbs into his hand, realized he had nowhere to put them, and then scattered them across the table again. "Well, that was fun," he said before laughing at himself. Then he turned his full attention to Jason. "Listen, I think my sister wants me to give you a big speech about how you'll be fine, but I'm guessing you've survived enough rough situations in your life to already know that."

Jason shrugged. "I'm not really worried about anything."

"Nothing at all?"

Jason hesitated. "Does it ever stop hurting?"

"When you lose someone?" Jace considered this for a moment. "No. Not entirely. There will always be times when you think of him, and it'll always hurt that it didn't work out... but it won't remain the constant pain you feel now. You might go weeks, maybe even months without thinking of him. Then, on the long sleepless nights when you do, you'll feel a little pang of regret that still stings. That's all."

"Sounds okay," Jason said. "I think I can live with that."

Jace peered at him. "If you don't mind me asking... My sister didn't tell me any details. Do you want to talk about it?"

Jason found that he did, and once he started, he couldn't stop. Jace was a captive audience, or at least a patient one, nodding occasionally to show he was listening and understood. By the end of his story, Jason found himself getting emotional again. "I just feel like if we could be together now, especially since I'm not living there, everything would work out, you know?"

Jace chose his answer carefully. "The first guy I was in love with, there were a lot of circumstances like that. Different from your own, of course, but little things surrounding us that made it difficult to be together. Years later, I went back and tried being with him again."

"You did?"

Jace nodded. "Even though things had changed, and kept changing, it still didn't work. Eventually I had to accept that the world around us wasn't the problem. We just weren't right for each other. It felt like everything but our relationship had changed, which pointed at the true problem."

Jason swallowed. "Do you think it could be different? Do you think people can change enough that they finally fit together?"

Jace thought about this. "I don't know. I hate to rule out anything completely. It's a big crazy world out there, but my own life experience suggests it isn't likely."

"Oh."

"The good news," Jace said, "is that there's a guy out there right now, one you probably haven't met, and he's absolutely perfect for you."

"Really?" Jason said, not hiding his skepticism.

Jace held up the back of his hand, wiggling his fingers. "I've got the wedding ring to prove it."

Jason leaned forward. "For real? You're married?"

"Yup."

"To a guy?"

"Uh, you know what gay means, right?"

Jason's cheeks flushed. "I just meant… It's not legal, is it? Did you guys go to England or something?"

"No, we had a ceremony right here in Texas. When it *is* legal, probably in the year 3025 or so, then we'll sign a few more papers. What matters now is the promise. Oh, and all that love stuff."

"Nice," Jason said, not hiding his envy.

"I'm not trying to brag," Jace said. "I spent years and years thinking I'd never find a guy like Ben. When I was your age, I was convinced it was impossible."

"I know the feeling."

"Thing is," Jace continued, "it's rare to find that person on your first try, or even the second or third. You have to get out there and keep trying."

"So you're saying I should sleep around a lot?"

Jace looked panicked before he understood the humor and laughed. "Just don't give up, okay? Retreat and lick your wounds when you need to, and then get back out there again."

"That sounds… daunting."

Jace shrugged. "If you had a time machine, would you go back and avoid getting together with Caesar? It would spare you the heartache you feel now, but think of everything else you would have missed out on. Would you take it all back?"

"No," Jason said.

"I wouldn't take back any of mine either. Love is worth the pain." Jace started sweeping the crumbs into a pile again, brow furrowed in thought. "Listen, I don't think my sister called me here just to give you a pep talk."

"No?"

"No. The thing is, I have a lot more time than I used to. Ben and I have a really small house, but we could move some things around to make an extra bedroom, maybe put a divider in the living room. Uh, so if you need a place to stay..."

"Thanks," Jason said, surprised by the lump in his throat. "But I think I'm still in the 'licking my wounds' phase. Besides, I want to start building my own life."

Jace nodded as if he understood. "It can be rough when you first start out on your own."

"I have a plan," Jason said, trying to sound confident.

"Okay. Well, just in case... Do you have a pen and paper?"

Jason fetched a pen and tore a lid off a cereal box when he couldn't find paper. He handed these to Jace, standing and watching over his shoulder as he wrote his phone number. After a moment's hesitation, he added another.

"This is Ben's cell phone, just in case I go back to work and am zooming around in the sky again."

"Will he know who I am?"

"I'll tell him," Jace said. "And even if he doesn't remember, all you have to say is that you need help. He won't turn you away."

"Sounds like a great guy," Jason said.

Jace looked up at him and smiled, making him wonder if Ben wasn't the lucky one. Before the cereal box top was handed back to him, Jace flipped it over to see what it was.

"Lucky Charms? Don't let Michelle near those things. She always used to pour them in a big bowl and pluck out all the marshmallows."

"She still does," Jason said. "But she leaves some behind like we won't notice how few there are."

"I'm sure she's only thinking of your health," Jace said. He nodded at the box top. "It doesn't have to be an emergency, or you moving in with us. If you only want to talk or whatever, that's fine. I'll be there."

"Thanks." Jason folded the box top in half and put it in his pocket. Then he sat back down again.

They eyed each other for a moment that felt surprisingly comfortable. Jace was the first to break the silence. "So, what now?"

Jason didn't have a clue, but inspiration soon struck. "Michelle said we'd all go out for ice cream together."

"Did she?" Jace blinked. "Doesn't she have to work?"

Jason shrugged. "She promised. Said something about a movie too. She's always dragging me off to horror movies, whether I like it or not."

Jace raised an eyebrow suspiciously but then smiled. "Come to think of it, I believe she did mention something about ice cream and werewolves. Didn't she also insist on paying for it all?"

Jason grinned. "You know, I think she did."

"In that case, let's go tell her the good news."

Jace stood, offering him a hand to help him up. Jason took hold of it, noticing how warm and soft it was.

No doubt about it. Whoever Ben was, he was definitely the lucky one.

Part Two:
Houston, Texas
2009

Chapter Fourteen

Dark eyes, the pupil and the cornea melding together like a perfect eclipse. Or like obsidian, which was inconvenient, because Jason had a very bad habit of comparing eyes to precious stones. Even three years later, he still couldn't see a piece of amber without all sorts of uncomfortable emotions bubbling to the surface.

"Nearly done," Wyatt said, wiping the sweat from his brow before picking up more flattened cardboard.

Jason smiled and redoubled his efforts to break down the last of the boxes. Stocking retail overnight wasn't exactly glamorous, and going to sleep just as the sun was rising made him feel like a vampire, but the pay was decent. Lately he found himself eager to get to work, which probably wasn't a good thing due to the reason why. Wyatt was handsome. That's how it always began. Jason supposed it worked that way for everyone, but other people seemed to have a lot more luck at actually getting somewhere. This would be another pointless crush. Eventually Jason would ask a few casual questions to find out if Wyatt was straight, and once confirmed, he'd slowly get over it. That was how it always played out. Every. Single. Time. At least since Caesar.

Once finished breaking down boxes and stacking them, Jason took a step back and watched while Wyatt tossed them into the trash compactor. Jason loved the contrast between the dark eyes and bleached hair, even loved the lame barbwire tattoos on each arm, shirt sleeves rolled up intentionally to expose them. Or the pert little ass that always drew his attention. He practically drooled while—

"What are you, a fag?"

Jason's attention whipped away from tight butt cheeks to a face that was leering in amusement. It wasn't a nice face. Maybe Paul could have been considered handsome if he ever demonstrated an ounce of kindness, but Jason's shift manager seemed to delight in making people miserable.

"I bet you are," Paul insisted. "Or were you thinking about stealing his wallet?"

Jason's jaw clenched. He ignored that Wyatt had turned around, because it made him want to lie, and he wasn't about to do that. "I'm not a fag," he said. "I'm gay. Got a problem with that?"

Paul raised his hands. "Hey, obviously it's Wyatt who should be worried. Maybe you shouldn't keep your back turned to Jason here, know what I mean?"

Jason looked to Wyatt, hoping for some backup or at least disgust at Paul's homophobia. Wyatt's pierced eyebrows shot downward, his lip on the verge of curling… but he wasn't looking at Paul.

Jason supposed he had his answer. No more warm feelings for Wyatt. He rolled his eyes at both of them, picked up the last stack of cardboard, and tossed it in the compactor himself. Then he went to clock out.

Working overtime meant the sun was already up when Jason strolled out to the parking lot. Spring was still young enough that the nights were long. Jason struggled to remember the last time he'd seen both morning and sun together. After plopping into his old Ford Fiesta, he clenched his jaw while trying to get the car to start. Even a mild chill gave the engine trouble. He was still trying to get the motor running when he saw Wyatt walking to his own car. Jason averted his eyes, pretending he hadn't noticed him, relieved that Wyatt had already left by the time the engine turned over.

On the drive back to his apartment, he found himself wishing Steph still lived there. He would wake her up with a cup of coffee, let her blink away the sleep, and then whine about his dead-end love life. Like he always used to. Her sympathy knew no bounds, which could be why she'd fallen in love with a bankrupt businessman. Of course, things were looking up for them both, since her boyfriend—now fiancé—had gotten a loan and moved to Colorado to open a microbrewery.

Steph hadn't followed her boyfriend right away, not wanting to leave Jason alone or burdened with rent for a two-bedroom apartment. He'd taken the night hours for that very reason. Not only did it mean a decent pay increase, but working such a crazy schedule ensured they would barely see each other. After a little coaxing, this had been enough to convince Steph to follow her heart. Jason was happy for her, even though he missed her terribly.

With Steph went the last remaining piece of his old life. Aside from her, he wasn't in touch with anyone from that time. She used to act as a bridge between him and Caesar, passing news but not messages back and forth. After Caesar left for college, Steph lost contact with him. Amy wrote a few letters over the summer, but she still had the attention span of a child and moved on to other things. Even Michelle had disappeared, taking a leave of absence from work a few years back and never returning. That had hurt. Jason still wondered what had happened.

Strange how the present could become the past so quickly. At least this cleared the way for something new. The sun was shining, another name had been crossed off the list of his heart, and the future was full of potential. Well, not really, but he could pretend. Jason parked his car and walked up the stairs to his apartment. He was tired enough that the door was unlocked and half open before he spotted the envelope taped to it. The oblong piece of paper caused a jolt of anxiety. This wasn't the first such envelope, although it was certainly unexpected.

Tearing it off and open, he read the contents disbelievingly. He was being evicted. There had to be some mistake! He'd paid rent just last week. Sure he was behind two months, but this letter claimed he still owed three. Sighing, he shut the door, turned around, and walked to the apartment complex office.

The small building wasn't much more than a space for two desks and a wall filled with floor plans of the different apartments. Only one desk was occupied, an older woman sitting there and shifting through papers. He introduced himself to her.

"That was fast!" The woman set aside the papers and considered him from over her reading glasses. "Here to pay your rent?"

"I paid it last week," he said. "I dropped off the check personally."

"For the full amount owed?"

"No, just for one month, but I thought it would buy me time."

The woman sighed and turned to her computer. After some typing and a few clicks, she considered him again. "We got your check, that's true, but when we tried to deposit it yesterday it bounced."

"It bounced?" Jason said, voice rising. "Hold on, why did you wait so long to deposit it?"

"We always make bulk deposits."

Jason's stomach sank. Two days ago his car had been on empty. Fuel prices were up and a full tank had cost him more than he expected, but he still thought he had enough to cover rent. He must have forgotten something, not that it mattered now. Bouncing a check meant an additional fee, which would leave him even deeper in the hole.

"I can get the money," Jason said.

"If that were true, you wouldn't be standing here." The woman said this like she had heard the same line countless times before. "You have until the court issues your eviction papers. We're going to need all the back rent, not just one month. Sorry, but it's company policy when you get so far behind. Best of luck!"

The woman busied herself again with her papers, so Jason took his leave. He was screwed! His next paycheck was still more than a week away, and it wouldn't be enough to cover all three months.

Returning to his apartment, he took a long shower, trying to think of a plan. Call his parents for money? That's what most people would do. The idea made Jason feel wistful. How nice it would be to drive to his mother's house, lay his head on her lap and moan about all his problems. She would stroke his hair and maybe lecture him on being smarter with his money. Then she would rescue him from this miserable situation. A beautiful dream, but an impossible one.

He needed to focus on what was possible. He supposed he could call Steph and see if she could spot him some cash, but he knew she didn't have much, and two month's rent was asking a lot. Getting out of the shower, Jason wrapped a towel around his waist and went to fetch his guitar. Then he sat on the couch and strummed it, intending to think of a solution but letting his mind go numb as his fingers played themselves to exhaustion.

Eventually he set aside the guitar, hearing the business card inside flutter to the bottom. Michelle's home phone number, the one she had given him when he'd first gone to live with the Hubbards. He'd left it in there ever since, like a good luck charm. He supposed he could call her, hear her voice again before confessing what a pathetic life he lived and how badly he needed money. Yeah, that would make them both feel good.

Sighing, he stretched out on the couch, covered his head with a pillow, and willed the world around him to disappear.

Eventually he became tired enough that it did. The real world, anyway. Jason opened his eyes blearily to find himself sitting on an airplane. From the pressure and monotone hum, he could tell the flight was in progress, which was an odd thing to know since he'd never flown before.

Glancing around the cabin, he was disturbed to discover he was completely alone. Surely that wasn't normal. Jason had a middle seat, an empty aisle to the left and right. Straining against his seat belt, he did his best to look ahead and behind him. Nobody there.

A ding sounded overhead, a backlit icon of a cigarette and seatbelt flashing before a voice spoke over the intercom.

"The captain—well, me—has turned off the seatbelt sign. You are now free to move about the cabin."

Jason stayed perfectly still for a moment. When nothing else happened, he unbuckled the seatbelt and stood. Now he could clearly see that he was alone. Except for the captain, of course. Maybe he would be able to explain how Jason had ended up here.

Making his way down one of the aisles, Jason passed a small galley and entered into another section where the seats were larger and looked a lot more comfortable. Ignoring these, he continued to the very front of the plane. The door to the cockpit was open, a figure seated in front of countless instruments.

"Hello?" Jason tried.

No response. No movement. He walked all the way to the cockpit door and tried again.

"Hello?"

Next to him, something started ringing. After flinching in shock, he looked around and found a phone on the wall, the old-fashioned kind with a cord. What could he do but answer it?

"Hello?"

"You were supposed to call us a long time ago."

The voice on the other end was familiar enough for Jason to recognize, which was odd, since they'd only met once. Ice cream and a movie three years ago. That was all. And yet he knew exactly who he was talking to.

"Jace?"

In the cockpit, the captain's seat spun around, revealing the man. Jace smiled at him, but when the voice on the phone spoke again, his lips didn't move. "Why didn't you call us?"

Jason stared for a moment before answering. "Pride?"

He heard a chuckle on the line. "That's very honest of you. Uh, you can hang up the phone now. Even I don't know how I'm doing this."

He turned to hang up the phone, and when he looked back to the cockpit, Jace was standing just a foot away and rubbing his jaw. "That's better. Whew! This is weird, huh?"

Jason nodded. "Am I dr—"

"Don't say it! Whenever I'm—you know—and then I realize, it always wakes me up." Jace tensed, as if waiting for that to happen. When it didn't, he relaxed again. "Okay. So you're lost, looking for guidance, and I just happen to be here to point the way. Think you'll get the symbolism? I thought the phone was a nice touch. You'll call us, right?"

"I don't like asking anyone for money," Jason said.

"It's worse than that," Jace replied. "You don't like asking anyone for help. But everyone has to now and then. Usually they turn to family first. Why haven't you?"

"Uh, because I don't have a family?"

Jace made a buzzing sound like they were on a game show. "Wrong. I told you a long time ago there was someone out there for you, and that you simply hadn't met him yet. The same is true for your family. You need to call them."

"Them?" Jason swallowed. "You're saying I need to call you."

Jace shrugged. "Couldn't hurt to try. I bet you'd get taken out for ice cream at the very least. No more horror movies though; they give you weird nightmares, don't you think?"

"I'll try to cut back," Jason said before laughing. "So am I really dreaming?"

Jace winced. "I told you not to say it! Now you've got to go."

Next to him, the door to the airplane swung open. Outside was twilight, stars appearing in an increasingly darkened sky. Jason felt himself being slowly pulled toward the open hatch, unable to fight against the force of air being sucked through the doorway.

"Wait," he said. "What am I supposed to do, ask you for money? We're talking three months' rent!"

"Buh-bye." Jace wore a mechanical smile, gesturing repeatedly toward the door. "Thank you for flying with us. Buh-bye now."

"I can't expect you to bail me out of my own mess. It won't solve anything in the long run."

"Have a safe trip home now. Buh-bye."

Jason grabbed the edge of the door so he wouldn't be pulled outside. "Seriously! Why would anyone want to help me?"

For a brief moment, the wind outside ceased and the artificial smile left Jace's face. "Ben has so much love in his heart. He won't need a reason. You'll see." Then the force outside returned, too strong this time to fight against. Jace smiled, but this time it was personal and warm. "Goodbye, Jason. It was nice seeing you again."

His fingers lost their grip on the doorframe, and in an instant, Jason found himself floating in a sky sparkling with pinpricks of light. One of those distant lights became brighter until it was blinding.

Jason gasped and sat upward, foot knocking the guitar over and creating a loud *bonngg*. He was in his living room, of course, the blood still pounding in his veins from the dream. Groaning, he forced himself to get up and go to the kitchen for some water. As he stood there drinking, he considered it all, shaking his head at how silly it was. As if he'd listen to a dream. He'd have to be crazy to act on something like that.

Right?

Oh, what the hell! Setting down the glass of water, Jason went to find an old cereal box top.

"The number you are trying to reach has been disconnected or is no longer in service."

Jason turned off the phone and picked up the box top again, palms sweaty as he turned it over and over. Maybe he had dialed the wrong number. Ten minutes later, he tried again, which was fast considering he'd needed an hour to muster the courage for the first attempt. Jason dialed the number more carefully this time.

"The number you are trying to reach—"

Jason hung up the phone and exhaled. Stupid dream! Jace could have at least given him his new digits. Or maybe an email address. That would have been helpful. So much for listening to a sleep-induced hallucination. Jason was about to toss the number aside when his eyes dropped to the two words below Jace's name.

Ben Bentley. Jace's husband. His phone number was there too, but calling someone he had never met sounded excruciatingly awkward. What would he say?

Jason set aside the box top, started tidying up the apartment, and realized he should probably be packing. Just a few short months ago when Steph had moved out, he felt proud at how much was left behind. He actually had his own things now. Sure the couch was pretty gnarly and the television was still the old square kind and not widescreen, but they belonged to him. In addition to a few other pieces of furniture, he had a boombox, some CDs, even a computer. Jason had come a long way in the last few years, which made the idea of failing even more upsetting. A little pride was one thing, but he'd be foolish to let it ruin him.

He supposed he could call Ben and ask for Jace's new number. That would be easier than trying to explain it all from scratch. Before he could overthink it, Jason rushed back to the couch and started dialing. The phone rang long enough that his palms had time to get sweaty again while his heart felt like it needed a paramedic.

"Hello?"

"Hi. Uh. Ben?"

"Yup! Who's this?"

Jason swallowed. "You don't know me, but I was hoping you could help. I'm trying to reach someone named Jace. He's your husband, right?"

The line was silent for a moment. Maybe they had broken up? "Yes, he's my husband."

"Oh, good. Do you have a number for him? Or if he's there, could I speak to him?"

Again the line was quiet for far too long. "Sorry, but who am I speaking to?"

"My name is Jason. Uh, I met your husband once a long time ago. His sister was my caseworker back when I was in foster care. He said I could call if I ever... So..." Jason's mouth was too dry to continue.

"You met Jace?" Ben asked, but he didn't wait for an answer. "Listen, what's the best number to reach you at? And your last name. Please."

"Oh, okay." Jason rattled off his information and was half-tempted to give the wrong number because this was already too embarrassing.

"All right," Ben said, the faint sound of a pen tapping a pad of paper in the background. "You really met Jace?"

"Yeah," Jason said. Was that so unbelievable? "He looks just like his sister."

Ben laughed. "Yeah. He certainly... Yeah. Listen, I'm going to have to give you a call back, okay? It's not a good time right now, but I'll definitely call you back."

"Okay," Jason said, throat feeling raw. "No problem."

He hung up the phone. Another dead end. Something ventured, nothing gained. Shaking off his embarrassment, he stood and set about organizing his belongings. He would pack what he didn't need and try to get an idea of what remained. Maybe he could rent a storage unit for it all and find a shelter where he could stay. Or he could try pawning some of it. He doubted it would be enough to cover rent, but every little bit helped.

He was an hour into this process when the phone rang. The idea of talking to Ben again made him squirm, but maybe it was Jace this time. Maybe he had explained everything to Ben before calling Jason back. That sounded reasonable. Jason hurried to pick up the phone.

"Hello?"

"Jason?" A woman's voice, this one so familiar that his heart leapt. "It's Michelle. Oh my god! I'm so happy you called!"

McDonald's. An outside table next to the playground. Jason felt like he was sixteen again, celebrating another foster care birthday or a rare day out as a treat from his caseworker. The one seated across from him had been his favorite. Currently she was unloading a tray. A salad and soda for herself, and for him—

"French fries and a vanilla milkshake," Michelle said, smiling broadly. "You still like that?"

"Oh yeah!" Jason said, mouth already watering. His food budget had been tight lately, and he struggled to remember his last full stomach.

"I got you a quarter pounder too, just in case. You aren't a boy anymore." Michelle looked him over in a way his mother used to. "I can't believe you finally cut your hair!"

Jason reached up to touch his bangs. His hair was still hopelessly messy, but the tips only touched his eyebrows now. "Steph, a friend of mine, she made me do it. Said the guys would line up around the block."

"And did they?" Michelle asked.

He gestured to an empty sidewalk. "They must not have gotten the memo."

Michelle laughed. "So besides that, how are you?"

"I told you all the important stuff on the phone," Jason said, removing the plastic lid from the milkshake. "Everything was going good. I thought I'd really made it."

"You haven't exactly blown it," Michelle said. "Late rent isn't such a big deal. Better than a massive credit card debt. Unless..."

"No credit company is foolish enough to give me a card," Jason said. "There's only the rent. I guess I'm behind on a few utilities too."

Michelle nodded in an encouraging way, like the situation looked promising. He couldn't help but laugh, being reminded of the countless pep talks she had given him while he lived in the home. He didn't realize how effective they'd been until she had mysteriously disappeared.

"It's none of my business," he said, "but what happened? One day you were there, the next you weren't."

Michelle frowned, fidgeting with the straw of her drink before scooting it away. "I had a breakdown of sorts and needed time off to find myself again. I'm lucky that way. My family doesn't rely on my income or even need it, so I focused on my kids and fixing myself." Michelle raised her gaze. "I'm sorry. This is still so hard to talk about."

"It's okay," Jason said. "You don't need to explain."

"I do because it affects you too." Michelle considered the playground for a moment. "My brother, Jace, he suffered from aneurysms. He'd already been through one when you met him, and well... He didn't make it."

"Oh." Jason wanted to say more but his throat had constricted. Not because of what this meant for his own future, but because the guy who was both goofy and dashing in his own way, the guy who had been so friendly and giving in the short time they had known each other—that he was gone now seemed so horribly wrong.

"I freaked out when it happened," Michelle said. "We all did, because it looked like he'd made it through the worst." She shook her head and busied herself with her salad. "I got selfish. I'll admit that. I felt too tired and upset to give any more of myself. Instead I became preoccupied with trying to keep from falling apart. Before I knew it, more than a year had gone by. My husband made me go back to work because staying at home had helped all it could and I was making everyone miserable. He was right too. It helped, but when I returned to the group home, you were gone."

"Dropped out of high school and got my GED," Jason said. "You know I was itching to start my own life. Once you left, I didn't see any reason to stick around. Not that it's your fault! I don't mean it like that." Jason sighed. "You know what? None of that matters now. I'm really sorry to hear about your brother. And for stirring up painful memories again. I shouldn't have called."

"You were damn right to call!" Michelle said, sounding angry. "You could have left a forwarding number with the home. On the paperwork you just wrote—"

"See ya!" Jason laughed before his face flushed. "I thought it was funny at the time."

Michelle shook her head but managed a smile. "Did you lose my home number?"

"No," Jason admitted. "I didn't want to bug you."

"I wouldn't have minded," Michelle said. "Anyway, all that's in the past now. Eat up and we'll discuss your future."

Jason dunked a few fries in the milkshake and practically inhaled his burger, having to resist a goofy smile between bites. His feelings didn't seem appropriate, considering the news he'd just heard, and Jace's death did make him sad, but emotions were complex things and it felt so good to be around Michelle again. Despite all his problems and the bombshell she'd just dropped, he still found comfort in her presence.

"Ben's worried about you," Michelle said.

"He doesn't even know me."

"True, but after we talked I called him back and explained your situation."

"Did Jace ever tell him about me?"

"We're not sure," Michelle said. "When you met Jace, he was recovering from his first aneurysm and his memory wasn't very reliable. So it's possible he never told Ben or that Ben was too preoccupied to remember. We were all concerned, but Ben was the one taking care of Jace every day. He worried even more than the rest of us. It's a moot point because Ben wants to help you."

"I don't feel right asking for his help." Jason stirred his milkshake to keep the consistency smooth. "All I'm looking for is advice."

Michelle smiled. "Oh I've got plenty of that for you. You said on the phone you don't like your job. You're on the verge of losing your home, and I'm assuming you don't have a boyfriend or you would have turned to him."

"I'm just a poor little orphan," Jason said, making light of it. "Even my best friend skipped town."

"It sounds to me," Michelle continued, "like you couldn't be in a better position to make a fresh start. Ben is willing to take you in. He lives in Austin, which he assures me is the best place on earth, and I'm sure he can help you get a new job."

"Shouldn't I be focusing on getting a second job here? Or maybe a loan? I could pay off the rent and…" He trailed off, unsure what would come next because paying rent had proven too difficult. He was already in the hole and could only work so many hours. Still, it might be worth a try.

"Money isn't an issue," Michelle said. "If it comes down to it, I'll pay your rent and help you get back on your feet. But I think we should address the real problem. You need a support network. When Jace died, my family kept me from going crazy or doing something drastic. Everybody needs that in their life."

"So adopt me," Jason said with a silly grin, even though part of him was dead serious.

"I'm tempted, believe me. But you know what? You're not the only one who needs support. Ben was left on his own when Jace died. Not completely, but if something like that happened to Tim, he would need someone there."

"Tim?"

"Yup. The irresistible Mr. Wyman." Michelle bit her lip. "Geez, it's a long story. Tim and Ben are together now."

"They're in a relationship? Isn't that kind of…"

"Soon? Not really. They've been madly in love since they were teenagers, so in a way, it's taken ages." Michelle shook her head as if exasperated. "I'll let them explain it all. The point I'm trying to make is that you would be helping Ben too. Not that he's considered that. He doesn't need a reason to help you."

Jason's head was swimming as he mulled it over. "Austin?"

"You're an adult now," Michelle said. "This isn't a foster placement. No rules and no obligations. You can come and go as you please. I already explained this to Ben, and he agreed. He's offering you a place to call home until you get on your feet again. Nothing more, nothing less. But while you're there, if you take the time to get to know him, I suspect you'll make a friend for life. One who will always be there for you."

Glancing across the table at Michelle, Jason felt as if he already had such a person. Just like in the old days, he found himself wanting to please her.

"I'll think about it," he said. "Let me try to fix this on my own. One last shot."

Michelle smiled and shook her head. "You haven't changed a bit."

"I have," Jason insisted. "I'm even more stubborn than before."

Jason was running low on sleep as evening fell. Having the weird dream and meeting Michelle for lunch had thrown off his sleep schedule. He managed a quick nap when he was home again, the alarm waking him even earlier than it usually did. Jason hit the shower and put on one of his nicer outfits. Then he reported to work a full two hours early, feeling energized despite the lack of sleep, because now he had a plan. What he needed was overtime. He could take one of the morning shifts. Instead of going home at dawn, he'd put in another six hours or so at the registers, even if they weren't willing to pay him time and a half.

First stop was Human Resources, which turned out to be a room full of filing cabinets and an older man with more wrinkles on his head than hair. Jason knocked politely on the open door to get the man's attention, but first he read the nameplate.

"What can I do for you?"

"Mr. Geoffrey, sir? I was hoping I could talk to you about taking on more hours."

The man smiled, pleased by this notion. That was a good sign! "Come right in. What's your name?"

"Jason Grant, sir."

The smile slid off Mr. Geoffrey's face so fast that Jason stopped in his tracks.

"I told you in the message not to come in," Mr. Geoffrey stammered, standing up. "Your check won't be ready until next week."

Jason shook his head, not understanding. "I'm not here for my check. What I'd like is to work more hours."

Mr. Geoffrey snorted as if he was being preposterous, then peered at him curiously. "I called you this afternoon. Didn't you get my message?"

Jason shook his head. "Sorry, no. Why would you call me?"

"I'm afraid you're no longer employed here."

Jason's mouth dropped open. "What? Why?"

Mr. Geoffrey continued to scrutinize him. Then, like someone avoiding an aggressive dog, he carefully inched around Jason to the door, never turning his back to him. Jason took this as his invitation to leave. Clenching his jaw, he brushed by him, walking into the hallway and making sure he was standing a safe distance away, because suddenly, he did feel like biting.

Jason spun around. "An explanation would be nice," he said. "Please."

Mr. Geoffrey took note that they weren't alone in the hall before he decided to answer. "Your shift supervisor felt you were disrespectful."

"Paul says *I'm* disrespectful?" Jason said, voice raising enough that Mr. Geoffrey flinched. He realized then that it didn't matter. Whatever he said would sound like a lie or only seem to back up Paul's opinion of him. "You know what? It's fine. You want to know why?"

Mr. Geoffrey shook his head, backing toward his office again.

Jason told him anyway. "I'm moving to Austin. Immediately. So you cut me that check right now. I want all the money you and this stupid store owe me. Then you'll never have to see my disrespectful ass again. Agreed?"

Mr. Geoffrey looked on the verge of running or pulling the fire alarm that his hand had drifted toward, but when Jason failed to lunge at him, he nodded quickly.

"Well, since you're moving… I'll see what I can do."

For one glorious moment, Jason thought all of his problems

were solved. Getting his check early meant being able to pay off one month's rent. He had also remembered putting the first and last month's rent down on the apartment when he first moved in, which would take care of the rest. When he suggested as much to the woman in the apartment office, she was happy with his solution, but was unable to let him continue living there without a deposit. Once again, he needed two months rent if he wanted to stay. After he admitted he didn't have the money, management conducted an inspection of his apartment, and Jason was told he wouldn't have to do anything except clean before he moved out.

So much for fixing this on his own.

Once he was alone again, Jason called Michelle and told her he was willing to move and asked what he would need to bring. After she checked for him, she assured him he wouldn't need anything but the clothes on his back. Then Jason really started packing. Anything that didn't fit in a box, such as his bed and couch, was advertised for sale on the apartment community board. When there was no interest, he advertised them as free. That did the trick. Soon Jason was left with his computer, clothes, a couple boxes of random knickknacks, and his faithful guitar. He was driving back from the Salvation Army after dropping off the television and buying a few more shirts, when his car broke down.

Jason rolled the car to the side of the road and walked the rest of the way to his soon-to-be former apartment. He refused to get upset, repeating one word in his mind to maintain tranquility. *Austin. Austin. Austin.* Once at the apartment, he called and canceled his auto insurance. One less bill to pay. The stupid car had cost him more in repairs than its original price, anyway. Afterwards he called a salvage company, arranging for the car to be picked up and earning himself a little extra cash.

After a week of getting his affairs in order, Jason was ready. His life was stripped to the minimum, just as it had been so often before. And he felt fine. He hadn't lost his touch. Jason was still a pro at this.

While waiting for Michelle to pick him up, he allowed himself to feel slightly nervous. If only he knew who he was going to live with. If Jace were still alive, all of this would be so much easier. Instead, Jason was mere hours away from meeting Ben and… What was the other guy's name? Tim? Maybe they were a little too eager to help him out. By the end of the week, they would probably be selling nude videos of him on the Internet.

Jason was laughing at this idea when Michelle pulled up. His discomfort increased when he saw she wasn't alone. The driver-side door of a brand-new SUV opened, revealing a muscular body stuffed into a polo shirt and beige shorts. When Jason finally noticed the head attached to this body, the face was smiling at him like they were old friends.

"Jason, hi!" The man extended a hand. "I'm Greg. How are you today?"

Michelle walked up next to the man and swatted his hand down. "He's not one of your clients. Jason, this is my husband."

"Okay," Jason said, trying to pull his eyes away from the man and failing.

"This all you got?" Greg asked, grabbing a box and heading toward the back of the SUV.

"Yeah," Jason managed after a short delay. Then he turned to Michelle. "I think I'm in love!"

"You and everyone else," she said before smiling. "Is this really everything?"

"Hey, it's way more than I ever had before," Jason said, picking up a box.

"That's right," Michelle said, doing the same. "I'd almost forgotten. Well, it's a good thing we didn't rent a truck, although I could have brought the boys along instead of getting a babysitter."

In a few short minutes, the SUV was loaded. When Jason slid into the back seat, he found it partially occupied. A heavyset girl just entering her teens sat there. She had a handsome face, not unlike her father's, and while that looked a little odd on a girl, he suspected no one had told her because she seemed supremely confident. Smiling at him, she patted the seat next to her. "Slide on in, honey. After all, you did promise my mother that you'd marry me."

Chapter Fifteen

Emma was holding his hand. She'd been holding it the entire trip, and despite the air conditioning keeping the SUV interior cool, the sweat from their palms had long ago mixed together into a bond Jason feared would be permanent. He knew everything about her already, because Emma liked to talk. Nearly fifteen years old, she loved playing football, had aspirations to start her own fashion label one day, and enjoyed croaking out show tunes in a voice devoid of melody. Despite being exceptionally odd, she was immensely likeable. Maybe it was the way she so easily filled what might have been an awkward silence, or perhaps it was the completely uninhibited way she conducted herself.

"Austin city limits!" she declared as they breezed by the sign. "You are going to *love* Uncle Ben. Isn't that funny? Just like the rice guy! I wish Ben was black. How come we don't have any black people in our family?"

"Maybe you can change that someday," Greg answered from the driver seat, directly in front of Jason. "That's why we no longer live in a small town where people marry their neighbors."

"Literally," Michelle chimed in from next to him.

"Not that I don't love my hometown," Greg said, "but there's definitely a lot more culture in Houston. We moved there so you kids would get more exposure."

"Nuh-uh!" Emma said. "We came to Texas because you were gay for Uncle Jace."

Greg looked offended. "What?"

"It's true," Michelle said, laughing when her husband glared at her.

"Anyway," Emma continued. "Uncle Ben is the best. He loves to sing. I'd even say he's nearly as good as I am. He bought me a karaoke machine for my last birthday, and we sing the most incredible duets together."

Greg snorted. "You know he wears ear plugs when you're around, right?"

"He doesn't," Emma said, unabashed. "He's the absolute nicest person in the world. Well, except for that time a kid at the playground called me fat and Ben started chasing him around and throwing rocks at his head."

"It was a teenager, not a kid!" Michelle said quickly, turning around to explain. "And Ben was only throwing sand. I'm sure he was aiming low and didn't mean to get any in the young man's eyes."

Emma smiled. "The guy had to go to the hospital."

"Ben *did* apologize and pay for his medical expenses," Michelle said.

Emma shook her head and mouthed the words, "He didn't apologize."

Jason laughed. "So what about this guy Ben lives with?"

"Uncle Tim?" Emma asked, squeezing his hand tighter.

"Wyman's not your uncle," Greg said from the front seat. "He's the other woman."

"Greg!" Michelle said warningly.

"What? The guy circled Ben like a vulture, just waiting for his chance to swoop in."

Michelle shook her head. "I'll never understand why you two don't get along. If you ever bothered talking to him, you'd find out you have a lot in common."

"The guy's a jerk," Greg said dismissively.

Emma rolled her eyes. "He's just jealous because Uncle Tim is a stone-cold hottie." When a pair of glaring eyes appeared in the rearview mirror, she quickly added, "You're hotter, Daddy! Ain't nobody better looking than you!" Then she turned back to Jason. "I'm sure you'll get used to Uncle Tim."

"Used to?" he asked, but Emma had noticed a billboard advertising a musical and started ranting about it. He half-paid attention while turning his attention to the scenery. From the highway, Austin didn't look so different than Houston. As he watched, they seemed to cut straight through the city and leave it behind before the car finally drifted toward an exit ramp. This brought them to a smaller highway, and after a short jaunt they took one more exit and were…

Nowhere. That's how it appeared to Jason, anyway. The road curved left and right through the trees, but he didn't see what the bulldozers had been dodging when it was built because nothing noteworthy was around. Not that he didn't appreciate nature, but this wasn't what he expected when imagining his future home.

"Sure is nice out here," Greg said with a wistful sigh. "There's a great park not far—St. Edwards—that you should check out. You like to hike?"

Jason considered the scenery. "Usually when I walk, I have a destination in mind."

"Give it a try anyway," Greg said. "You don't know what you're missing."

They approached an entrance to a housing development, hope rising in Jason's chest, but no, this wasn't it either. He began to wish his car hadn't broken down as they continued to drive and drive. Would anything be within walking distance? Anything at all? Finally, the SUV slowed and turned down a tiny paved road barely big enough for the vehicle's bulk. Jason strained to see their destination. After more weaving and winding, they arrived. The trees broke away, revealing cleared land not used for anything practical like crops or livestock. Just tall grass and the occasional tree waving in the light breeze.

"There's Uncle Tim!" Emma said, pointing with her free hand.

Jason whipped his head around but was mostly too late. He saw a riding lawn mower, had an impression of deeply tanned skin and a flash of eyes like ice, but as he craned his neck, the cardboard boxes blocking the rear window made seeing more impossible.

"He'll stay out there until we leave," Greg complained. "He always pulls something like this."

"Only when you're here," Emma said. "Gosh, I wonder why? Could it have something to do with the time—"

"That's enough!" Michelle scolded. Then she looked over at Jason and gave him an encouraging nod. "Just like old times. I even brought your file."

"Seriously?"

She nodded, opened the glove box, and pulled it out. "I thought it would be a nice symbolic gesture. I'm giving it to you. I won't need it anymore because you belong here."

Jason smiled at her, but when she turned around again, he let himself look a lot less certain. He could see the house now, and it appeared nice enough. White and wide, with a slanted roof. He couldn't tell anything about the interior or what sort of people lived there because the structure was fairly anonymous. Only the separate four-car garage off to one side suggested money, unless it was used to store something other than cars. The driveway formed a loop, running parallel to the front of the house and allowing them to stop near the front door.

Michelle unbuckled her seatbelt. "Ready?"

Jason nodded. Michelle and Greg got out of the car first, Jason wanting to do the same, but Emma still held on to his hand. He glanced over at her, noticing an expression of patient amusement.

"I can't believe you let me hold your hand the entire drive," she said.

Jason shrugged, feeling relieved when it was finally released and wondering if it would be rude to wipe it on his jeans.

Emma had no reservations about doing so. "Seriously. I was grossed out in the first ten minutes. I don't even like guys."

"Then why were you holding it?"

Emma laughed. "To see if you'd let me. You're ridiculously nice. Uncle Ben is going to love you. There he is."

Emma nodded out the window on his side, then turned to open her door. Jason glanced out the window, saw someone short and slight. His hair was brown and medium-length, as if he were growing it out, his concerned eyes the same hue. Ben was biting his lip after saying hello to Michelle. Then he noticed Jason through the car window. Their eyes locked and Ben's teeth released his lip so he could smile. Not just a polite upturn of the mouth either. The smile Ben gave him was bright and full of warmth.

Jason reached for the door handle and stepped outside the SUV. He stood there awkwardly as Emma threw her arms around Ben's neck. She was already as tall as he was. Or Ben was as short as her. Either way, Emma turned and gestured to Jason with one arm, as if presenting him. Ben took a step forward, held out his hand, and then dropped it again.

"Um. Welcome home," he said, before looking uncertain. "You are staying, aren't you? Or do you want to look around first, inspect the premises?" Ben's eyes darted to Michelle for help. "Is there a checklist or something?"

Jason laughed. He couldn't help himself. When Ben heard this he smiled and offered his hand again. "I have no idea what I'm doing," he admitted. "Let's start with the basics. I'm Ben."

The hand was cool when Jason took it, making him feel self-conscious about his own that was still roasting hot from Emma's weird test. "Jason," he said.

"Jason," Ben repeated, a strange look coming over him. "Do you go by anything else? I mean, I'm really a Benjamin, but pretty much everyone just calls me Ben."

"I've never had a nickname in my life," he admitted.

"Oh," Ben said, relaxing a little. "Okay. Jason it is."

"He did have a nickname," Michelle chimed in. "At the group home, the staff used to call him Jason the Gypsy because he couldn't settle down."

"Really?" Jason said, turning to her. "I never knew that!"

Michelle looked serene. "You never knew, because I would have twisted their heads off if they called you that directly."

Jason grinned. "Oh, I don't know. I sort of like how it sounds."

"In that case..." Ben gestured to the front door. "Jason the Gypsy, come and see your new wagon!"

Past a simple narrow entryway—a closet for storage on one side and bathroom on the other—was a large open living room. Where tile ended, hardwood steps led down to a sunken space. At first glance, the large room appeared to be all there was. On the far wall, a series of tall windows revealed a backyard with a carpet of lush green grass, the view to the outside interrupted only by a fireplace. On the right, a couch faced a big-screen TV mounted on the wall. On the left were a couple of cozy reading chairs and bookshelves. Jason spun around slowly, confused at first that the entire house seemed to be a single room. Then he noticed the bookshelves built into opposite corners, which framed and partially hid two doorways.

Ben led them through the doorway on the left to the gleaming kitchen beyond. The floor was blue stone, the ceiling exposed wooden beams that matched the rustic table. The space was bathed in light from windows on the front and rear side of the house. Michelle sat at a long breakfast bar situated in front of the stove, while Emma opened a tall cabinet which hid a refrigerator inside. They had lost Greg already, but the sound of a television switching on from the living room gave away his position.

"—so help yourself to anything," Ben was saying. "You don't have to ask. Just treat the place like you own it."

"And don't worry," Michelle said. "It's not usually this clean."

"True," Ben admitted before chuckling. "We actually hired a maid, which was completely awkward. I kept following her around, trying to clean up embarrassing messes."

"Kind of defeats the purpose," Emma said, opening a can of soda.

"That's what Tim kept saying," Ben said. "Ah-ah-ah! Use a coaster!"

Emma's eyes widened before she laughed. "Almost had me there."

Ben grinned at her, then glanced around. "That's it for this floor. I guess we skipped the bathroom by the entryway. Uh... Do you want to see your room?"

Jason glanced at Michelle for permission.

"You're on your own," she said. "I'm your friend, not your caseworker."

"Oh, right." Jason's cheeks grew warm. "Old habits die hard."

Ben led him across the living room to the other doorway, the sounds of explosions accompanying them as Greg lost himself in a movie. Beyond this door was a carpeted stairway, the noise of the television fading as they climbed. The upper floor was carpeted too, making Jason wonder if he should have taken off his shoes, especially since Ben was barefoot.

"Bathroom," Ben said, reaching in to turn on the light and standing aside. "I figure this one will be yours. I didn't know if you used bar soap or body wash or even one of those loofah sponge things, so I kind of bought everything. Same deal with electric toothbrushes versus normal ones. The entire bathroom is stuffed full of my little impulse shopping spree, so you'll have to pick what you want and get rid of the rest to make room."

"Actually," Jason said, "I brought my own stuff."

Ben winced. "Of course you did! Sorry. This is all super new to me. Rather than call Michelle every five seconds and ask a question, I tried to prepare for everything. Everything ever."

"It's fine!" Jason assured him. "I'll use all of it. Nothing will go to waste. I just feel bad you spent so much money on me. When I have a job, I'll pay you back."

"It's a gift," Ben said dismissively, shutting the light off again. "Don't worry about it. What's next? The door here leads to Tim's studio. You can go in if you like. Just make sure to close the door after you so nothing gets disturbed. We want to build him a separate studio on the property and make this a guest room. I don't suppose you're a carpenter?"

"Never swung a hammer in my life," Jason admitted.

"Me neither," Ben said. "Tim and I sleep at the very end of the hall there, the room on the left is our office if you need to use the computers, and your room is right over here."

Jason braced himself. If the bathroom had been overflowing with things he didn't need, he could only imagine what Ben had done with the bedroom. He was surprised, then, to discover how sparse everything was. The room held a queen-sized bed and two side tables … and that was it. Even the down comforter cover was a neutral white.

"I figured you'd want to decorate it your own way," Ben said. "Here."

From one of the side tables, he fetched a small stack of plastic cards and handed them to Jason. Flipping through a couple, he recognized the names of major retailers, all of which sold furniture, accessories, or even electronics.

"Gift certificates?" Jason asked. Then he held them back out. "I can't. Really. I appreciate it, but I'm not here for a handout."

"In that case, rent is six hundred a month and it's due tomorrow," Ben said with a straight face. Then he smiled. "Listen, when it comes to finances, we're doing really well. At least Tim is. I'm still mostly broke and always have been, so I understand where you're coming from. Being on your own can be rough. Jace and I had our own house, and after he died, I was always late on payments and the bank kept threatening foreclosure. Had things played out a little differently, I'd be in your situation. Since I'm not, I'm more than happy to give you a new start. I don't want to be your sugar daddy, and I don't want to make you feel like a charity case. I just want to help, and if that means I get to go shopping with you and have some fun, well, it's a win-win situation."

Jason still wasn't completely comfortable accepting all of this, but Ben's eyes were shining, and he didn't have the heart to turn down his generosity again. "Okay. Thanks. I'm going to write down however much I spend, and I'm paying you back some day, but for now, I appreciate it. Thank you."

"You're welcome," Ben said. "So I guess that concludes the tour. Unless you want to see my room. You're not nosey are you?"

Jason laughed. "Just a little, yeah."

"Me too."

Ben led them to the end of the hall, Jason ignoring the sense of déjà vu this conjured up. The master bedroom was comfortably dark, burgundy curtains keeping out much of the light. A tasteful touch of earthy hues added to the coziness, an archway on one side leading to a private bathroom and walk-in closet. Jason took all this in briefly, his attention mostly focusing on the little creature who was stretching and standing in the middle of the bed.

"You've got a cat!" he said excitedly.

"That's Samson," Ben said. "I hope you're not allergic."

"Nope," Jason said, rushing forward to offer his hand. "I'm definitely not allergic to Samsons."

The gray cat seemed a little stiff and took his time walking to the edge of the mattress. Then he sniffed Jason's hand while keeping cautious eyes trained on him. Whatever the criteria, Jason must have passed, because Samson marked his hand by rubbing his head against it. Then he yawned and hopped off the bed, heading toward a bowl of water in the bathroom.

"He's getting old," Ben said, voice a little terse, "but I'm hoping he'll outlive us all anyway. He still manages to smack down Chinchilla when necessary, so he's got some years left in him yet."

"Oh, so you have two cats?" Jason asked.

Ben shook his head. "Chinchilla is Tim's dog."

"**You have a dog?**" Jason didn't mean to shout, and he felt bad that Samson took off running with ears flattened, but… "I've lived in twenty-four different foster homes. *Twenty-four*! And you know what none of them had?"

Ben humored him. "A dog?"

"That's right!" Jason glanced around eagerly, like the animal would appear out of thin air. "Where is it?"

"In the backyard," Ben said. "She gets a little overexcited when guests show up, but you might be the first one more excited to see her."

"Can we let her in now?"

Ben laughed. "Sure, although you should probably step out back with her instead. Chinchilla is a little accident-prone at times."

He was downstairs so fast that Ben had to rush to keep up. Jason peered out the glass door with his hand on the knob and spotted a medium-sized dog dozing in a patch of sunlight.

"Think you'll be okay?" Ben asked. "I haven't seen Michelle for a while and was hoping to catch up with her."

"Sure," Jason said distractedly as he opened the door.

This woke the dog, who raised her head. Jason closed the door behind him as they considered each other. Then he smiled, which was enough to send Chinchilla rocketing toward him. Well, more like wobbling very quickly. She was a bulldog, meaning she had a big fat head and a body to match. Jason was reminded of cartoons when Bugs Bunny or whoever would plug a smoking cigar with a finger, making it swell up and explode. Chinchilla looked like that cigar at its most swollen, and as he got on his knees to pet her, he decided she was the most beautiful creature in the world.

After getting his face thoroughly licked and laughing until he was out of breath, Jason was slightly relieved when Chinchilla finally backed down. She started walking the yard, glancing back at him like she was continuing his tour of the property. He did his best to follow, looking around and not seeing anything unusual. A patio of cobblestones stretched out from the house and was home to assorted lawn furniture and a grill. The yard was long and wide, and had probably once been bigger before the newly-built privacy fence was installed. Jason assumed that was for Chinchilla's benefit more than anything, since he saw no sign of neighbors.

"If this was my yard," a voice said, "I'd be sunbathing nude every day."

Jason turned around to find Emma approaching. "Well, with two gay guys living here, I doubt they would care."

"Three," she corrected, stooping beside him to pet Chinchilla. "This place is on the verge of becoming a gay commune." She stood again and sighed. "Wouldn't that be nice? They could build extra houses, start a little rainbow community out here where nobody calls you names."

Jason eyed her for a moment. "When you said earlier that you don't like guys..."

Emma donned a mischievous expression. "I didn't mean boys are icky and have cooties, no. Don't tell my parents though."

"Why not?" Jason glanced back toward the house. "Your uncle Jace was gay and Michelle didn't seem to mind. Is your dad the problem?"

"No, he's cool. I'm just waiting for the absolute worst time to come out. Like during a funeral or something."

Jason laughed. "Why?"

"Because people always ask how you came out. It's a story you have to tell countless times during your life. I want mine to be good. So what's yours?"

Jason blinked. "I didn't have to come out because I don't have a family."

"See?" Emma said. "That's no good at all. No rising suspense, no funny ending. You can do better than that. When did my mom find out about you?"

He thought about it a moment. "After I got caught having sex with my foster brother."

"*Now* we're talking!" Emma nodded approvingly. "You start telling that story at a party and the whole room will stop to listen."

Jason grinned. "I'm not sure that's a good thing."

"Maybe not. So what do you think?"

He nodded slowly. "So far, so good. I feel like I'm mooching, which sucks, but past that, the house is great and Ben seems nice."

"He really is."

They took a cue from Chinchilla—stretched out on her belly and panting happily—and sat down on the grass.

"So, did you leave anyone behind in Houston?" Emma asked.

"You mean like a boyfriend? No. What about you?"

"It just so happens," Emma said proudly, "that I landed my first girlfriend last week. She says she's bi-curious, when in truth I'm pretty sure she's straight, but I'll take what I can get. It'll never last, but that's okay because she keeps writing me these horrible Goth poems."

"Really?"

"Mm-hm. The last one was about us dying and sharing a coffin, our bodies becoming one as they decompose. Very hot."

"Searing!" Jason agreed. "Do your uncles know?"

"That I'm a lesbian? Yeah. They helped me figure it out. I started having feelings for a neighbor girl when I was thirteen, which freaked me out. She was my friend, and I couldn't stop thinking about—well, you probably don't want to know. I decided to get away from her to see if that helped. Uncle Ben and

Tim had just gotten this place and it was summer, so I asked if I could come stay. Seeing two dudes kissing when they thought I wasn't looking sort of tipped me off that maybe I wasn't so weird after all. When I finally confided in them, just being able to talk about it helped."

"Did you ever tell the neighbor girl?" Jason asked.

Emma rolled her eyes. "While I was away for the summer, she found herself an unbelievably hot boyfriend."

"Figures," Jason said. "Being gay isn't hard. I'm okay with that, but I wish it wasn't so impossible to meet someone."

"Tell me about it." Emma nudged him. "Let's make a pact, seeing as how we're already arranged to be married. If we make it to our thirties and still haven't met someone, we really will get hitched. That way we don't have to live alone."

Jason mulled it over. "I think there's some sort of tax break too."

"And if we want to have kids," Emma said, "we can do the turkey baster thing."

"Okay," Jason said, holding out a hand. "It's a deal. If we're still sad and single when we're thirty, you'll become Mrs. Grant."

"Or you could take my name," Emma said, but then she reconsidered. "Actually, Emma Grant doesn't sound bad. Makes a nice theater name. Way better than Emma Trout. You know what? It's a deal!"

They shook on it, Jason smiling broadly. Not only did he land himself a place to live today and make some new friends, but he'd also gotten engaged.

When they returned indoors, Ben was cooking an early dinner. Greg had been dragged away from the television by his wife. They all gathered around the breakfast bar, like the studio audience of a cooking show. Jason hopped up to help—being a deft hand at chopping produce, even if his meals rarely turned out right—and everyone talked and laughed as he and Ben worked together. Even Chinchilla was happily passed out on the cool stone floor. Jason could have joined her. He'd only been here an hour, and already he felt relaxed.

Foster home number seven. That one had been full of four biological kids and two adopted, plus the parents and a grandfather. On weekends the entire family would gather, playing games or just sitting around telling stories and laughing. The vibe had been wonderful and warm… except Jason couldn't figure out how he fit in. Instead he sat on the sidelines and watched with envy. This time he had no problem integrating. Jason had always liked Michelle, and not surprisingly, those good feelings extended to the rest of her family. After all these years, maybe he had finally found his own little piece of paradise.

"Tim! Hey!"

Jason's head rose at the sound of Ben's voice. He turned to see a man standing in the doorway. His hair was jet black, or at least it appeared that way since he was wet with exertion. His shirt was soaked with sweat too, sticking to a body every bit as muscular as Greg's, if not a bit leaner. Emma was right. Tim could easily compete with her father when it came to good looks. He was handsome enough that when he locked eyes with Jason, it was a struggle to hold his gaze.

"Hey," Tim said, nodding upward.

"Hi," Jason replied.

Those eyes! For once Jason's knowledge of precious stones failed him because he couldn't quite find the right one. Too much gray to be a diamond, but man, were they clear! Like someone had taken silver and somehow made it transparent.

"Dinner is almost ready," Ben said. "Care to join us?"

Tim looked away from Jason, which made it easier to breathe. "I have some work at the gallery. I was just about to head over there."

"Big surprise," Greg muttered. Then he winced, most likely due to the elbow Michelle jabbed in his ribs.

A shadow crossed Tim's features when he saw Greg. Then the sun came out in full force when he noticed Emma. "Hey! What are you sitting there for? Come give me some sugar!"

"But you're disgustingly sweaty," Emma complained.

Jason wouldn't describe it as disgusting by any means. He watched Tim curiously as he hugged Emma, squeezing her even closer when she made a face and complained. In that uninhibited moment, Tim allowed himself to smile, cranking up the sex appeal a notch higher than it had any right to go. But then his eyes returned to Jason and that light faded. Tim gave another little nod, followed by a reserved smile without showing teeth. Then he excused himself and left the room.

"Ow!" Greg said. "What? I didn't say anything that time!"

"You were going to," Michelle replied.

Jason glanced back toward the empty doorway, feeling a lot less certain about his new home than he had just a moment ago. Then again, he supposed every paradise had its serpent.

When night had fallen and Michelle and her family had gone home, Ben became anxious. Conversation was stilted, Jason having to repeat himself multiple times, occasionally stopping completely in midsentence without Ben noticing. He tried not to take this personally. Ben was obviously distraught, his attention repeatedly returning to the front door. It wasn't hard to guess who he was waiting for.

"I think I'll start getting settled in my room," Jason said. "Unpack a few things."

"Do you need help?" Ben asked.

"No, thanks."

Jason was eager to give him privacy. Maybe then Ben would call Tim and get it all sorted out. Then again, that wasn't likely to happen unless one thing changed. *Foster home number eleven.* The mother there had pampered Jason, treated him like a prince. The family had no other children, biological or otherwise, for him to compete with. Her husband was the only issue. He wasn't a gruff man by any means. In fact, he was soft-spoken, but it became painfully obvious that he didn't want children the way that his wife did. Lucky for him, Jason's resentment over someone trying to replace his mother bubbled up, and he solved the unwilling father's problem by breaking every single dinner dish before loading the shards in the dishwasher and running the machine.

If Tim was the same way—if he wasn't happy to have Jason here like Ben was—remained to be seen. Maybe Tim was only avoiding Greg. Perhaps, now that he had gone, Tim would be more friendly and welcoming.

Trying to put the issue out of mind, Jason slowly personalized his new room by unpacking. First was a framed photo of him and Steph taken during their road trip to Las Vegas. They had thought eighteen was the legal gambling age and were sadly mistaken, so most of their trip was spent walking the strip and looking at the lights. Or hanging out in their hotel room, giggling over the stupidest things. He set the photo on the nightstand and emptied a box of knickknacks: An alarm clock, which was the most useful. A book he'd been trying to finish for so long it was more of a decoration. A plush pig Steph had given him before leaving that she insisted he talk to and cuddle with, as needed.

At the bottom of this box was a white bandana. Jason wasn't shocked to see it, since he'd tossed it in there when packing. He put it in the same place he always did, between the mattress and box-spring, where it would remain until he was feeling melancholy some quiet evening. Probably a Sunday, he imagined. The past tended to catch up to people on Sunday nights.

Jason took a break to stare out the window at the backyard before unloading another box in the bathroom, choosing between the familiar and what Ben had bought him. He stored the rest beneath the cabinets. Then he returned to his room to set up his computer. He placed it on top of the dresser, not having anywhere else to put it. Maybe one of the gift certificates Ben had given him would be good for a small desk or table.

Finally he moved a potted plant out of one corner so he could lean his guitar there. That was about it. Home, sweet home. The rest of the boxes were full of things he thought he'd need or that would only be useful when he got his own place again. He stacked those against the wall for now.

Jason considered sitting on the bed with his guitar and strumming out a quick tune, but the hour was late enough that Ben might have already gone to sleep. Poking his head in the hallway to find out, Jason heard voices from downstairs. Was Tim home? Or was it just the television?

Old habits died hard. Some refused to die at all. Jason had spied on most of the foster families he had been placed with. Often this was dreadfully boring; other times he had gleaned information that made him bail out earlier than normal. Of course this wasn't a foster placement. Not exactly. So why should he bother spying? What did he have to gain? Then again, it couldn't do any harm.

Jason rolled his eyes at himself and crept into the hallway. He took the stairs one by one, simultaneously listening for the creak that would give him away while also trying to tune in to the conversation below. Tim was definitely home, but so far Ben was doing most of the talking.

"You can't avoid him every time they come to visit. Seriously.

He's a part of my family. I know Greg isn't blood, but that doesn't matter. Call a truce or something. For me."

"I don't get why you care," Tim said, but after a heavy pause he added. "I'll try."

In slow motion, Jason eased down a few more stairs so he could hear better and tried not to breathe.

"Where were you?" Ben asked. "They left more than two hours ago. Didn't you get my text?"

"At the gallery. And yeah, I did."

"So why didn't you come home sooner?" Silence. Then Ben's voice sounded less patient. "You *never* work late. It's not just Greg you were avoiding, is it?"

"This is your thing," Tim replied.

"We talked about this! You said we would do this together!"

"I know, but you can handle it. I thought about it today, and I think it's better for everyone if I stay out of the way. Hey! Where are you going?"

Jason tensed, wondering if he was about to have company in the stairwell, but relaxed when Ben spoke again.

"To get a drink. When I come back, you better have a damn good reason for what you just said. Or better yet, a change of heart."

Well well! Looks like Ben wears the pants in this relationship! Jason figured it would be the other way around. He wondered if this determined their roles in the bedroom too. Kind of a shame if it did, because Tim seemed like he'd make a good—

"My parents."

Jason leaned forward, puzzled by Tim's answer. He wasn't the only one.

"Your parents?"

"Yeah. Look what a great job they did with me." Tim's voice was dripping with sarcasm. "The thing is, I don't know how to do it right. I can't raise a kid."

"He's turning nineteen!" Ben said, sounding on the verge of laughter. "He's already grown up. He doesn't need a dad."

"Fine," Tim said. "What about Ryan?"

Ben was quiet a moment. "What does he have to do with any of this?"

"He was about Jason's age. Look what a great job I did with him. The kid ended up in the emergency room."

Unease crawled up Jason's spine and made the hair on his neck tingle. Tim had put someone in the emergency room? What did he do, beat the guy half to death?

"This is different," Ben insisted. "Jason is nothing like Ryan."

"You don't know that," Tim said. "Ryan was a perfect little angel when I first met him. By the time we separated… Well, you saw for yourself."

"It's not the same, and I doubt Ryan was that innocent when he met you." There was a sound like an aluminum can being set on a table, then the rustle of couch fabric. "So all of this is because you're worried about screwing up?"

"I'm not worried," Tim said. "I *know* I'll fuck this up. You won't though. You'll know exactly what to— Hey, I'm trying to talk here!"

"And I'm trying to kiss you."

"I thought I was in the dog house."

"You might be still," Ben replied. "But you being worried about doing a good job is sweet. Sweet enough that I'll give you something to smile about while in the dog house."

"Punishment accepted. Uh, where is he?"

"Upstairs. I think he's asleep."

"Okay."

Jason listened to the wet sound of lips mashing together and wondered if maybe he would hear more. He was leaning forward so far that he nearly toppled over when Chinchilla came around the corner, butt wagging when she saw him. She started panting loudly, which hopefully disguised the yelp that escaped his lips. Then he started crawling backwards, attention still on bottom of the stairs in case anyone was coming to investigate. Hopefully Ben and Tim were too involved with what they were doing to notice.

Once on the top stair, he stood just in time to avoid a kiss from Chinchilla and tiptoed back to his room. He was shutting the door when the dog waddled inside. Then she made herself comfortable and sat down.

"Have it your way," Jason whispered as he shut the door. "Honestly, if I were you, I'd probably stay down there and enjoy the show."

Chinchilla stopped panting and put her head on her paws.

"Then again, I guess you've seen it all before."

Jason crossed the room, grabbed his guitar, and flopped on the bed. As he plucked out a song, he did his best not to think about how long it had been since he'd had someone to argue with, and how fun making up could be.

Chapter Sixteen

When Jason woke the next morning, he noticed a strange scent in the air. After sniffing a few times, he made his best guess. Dog farts. His fault for helping Chinchilla into bed last night. He rolled over to check on her, the dog raising her head and looking at him accusingly.

"Nice try!" he laughed. "I know that wasn't me."

Stomachs grumbling, they both got out of bed, Chinchilla racing off down the hall as soon as the door was open. By the time Jason caught up with her in the living room, she was being let out the back door.

"She slept in your room the whole night?" Ben asked with a smile. "Wow. She probably thinks you're staying here just for her."

"Fine with me," Jason said. "I'll be her pet human."

"There are leftover waffles in the kitchen," Ben said, walking him in that direction. "And by leftover I mean those that turned out right. You're lucky you weren't down here earlier. I made Tim eat all the burnt ones."

Jason fought down a smile. "Is he home?"

Ben's face grew more solemn. "No, he's at work already. I took the day off. I figure we could go out shopping, blow through some of those gift certificates."

Ben kept him company during breakfast, mostly fretting over whether Jason drank coffee or tea, or if he should run to the store to buy Mountain Dew when Jason said he preferred it instead. He declined the offer, of course, but he appreciated getting the five-star treatment. While in the shower, Jason found himself rushing through his morning rituals, eager to return downstairs. He was beginning to see why Ben had been lucky enough to marry someone like Jace.

That topic hadn't come up again. Jason kept debating whether or not he should offer his condolences or if it was more respectful to not mention Jace at all. He felt relieved when Ben took the initiative. They were in the car together, nearing civilization.

"So, you met Jace?" Ben asked.

"Yeah. I was going through a hard time, and Michelle thought it would cheer me up."

Ben checked his blind spot, switched lanes, then looked at him. "Did it?"

"Definitely. Most adults try to offer solutions, but he was more about telling me he'd been there, gotten through it, and found his dream guy."

Ben grinned. "Really? He said that?"

"Yeah. He talked about you a lot."

Ben's grin grew wider. "Really really?"

Jason chuckled. "Really for real. Are you so surprised? I mean, the guy married you, right?"

"I know," Ben said demurely. "It's just nice to hear it again, like getting a message from him after all these years."

"I'm sorry," Jason said. "About what happened, I mean."

"It's fine," Ben said, before reconsidering. "Actually, it's not. Jace dying will never be okay, but accepting that has helped a lot. I've learned I can still feel happy along with the sorrow. And that I can love another without having to stop loving or missing him." Ben hesitated. "Listen, Michelle told me that Jace invited you to come live with us. I want you to know that he meant it. I don't remember him mentioning it to me, but at the time he was struggling with memory problems. He didn't forget people though, just details, and I don't want you to think he forgot about you. Or that he used an empty promise to make you feel better."

Jason shook his head. "I never thought that. The truth is, I turned him down. I'd gone through an ugly situation with my previous foster family and decided that I was done trying to fit in where I didn't belong. As much as I liked Jace—and I really did—I just wasn't ready. I told him that too. I'm guessing that's probably why he didn't mention the idea to you."

"Okay," Ben said. "That makes sense. I was constantly worried back then, and I'm sure he didn't want to add to that. Still, I'm surprised you were able to resist his charms."

"Only because I was shell-shocked," Jason said. "I ended up calling him eventually, didn't I?"

"True. If you don't mind me asking, what exactly happened with you and your last family?"

"It's a long story," Jason warned.

As they pulled into a mall parking lot, Ben shrugged. "I've got time."

Jason told his story, touching a little on his childhood but mostly focusing on his stay with the Hubbards. By the time he was through, they had just finished having lunch in the food court and his throat was dry from talking.

"How long ago was this?" Ben asked.

"About three years."

"And since then? Have any guys come close to competing with Caesar?"

Jason blinked. "There haven't been any other guys."

Ben's eyes went wide. "None?"

"Some unrequited crushes, but besides that, nada."

"Wow." Ben leaned back. "That's one hell of a dry spell!"

"I know. Meeting guys is easy. It's meeting guys who like guys that's tricky."

Ben laughed. "Even harder is meeting a guy who likes guys and who *you* like."

"And harder than that is finding one who likes you back."

"Wait," Ben said. "Let's add it all together. It's hard to find a guy who likes guys that you like who also likes you back. Somebody should put that on a bumper sticker."

"I'm getting it as a tattoo," Jason said. "Right across my forehead. It really is hard. I'm not old enough to go to bars, and what else is there? Every time I get a new job, I scope out everyone, hoping to meet the right guy."

"We know a lot of gay people," Ben said. "Most of them are too old for you, but a friend of ours has the occasional party and usually a younger crowd shows up there."

Jason nodded. "I'd be willing to give it a shot, although ideally, I would love to be out walking my dog and run into some cute guy walking *his* dog. Naturally that would lead to us talking. Then we'd start meeting in that same place every day, like little ten-minute dates. After weeks of this, maybe even months, we'd agree to meet without the dogs. Unchaperoned, so to speak. That would be romantic. Way more so than a party or a bar."

Ben smiled. "You've given this a lot of thought."

"Well, thinking about it is all I've got, so yeah." Jason gulped down the last of his soda and put the empty cup on the tray. "So how did you and Tim meet?"

"High school sweethearts," Ben said. "I just happened to… uh, run into him while out rollerblading one day and we started talking."

"Simple as that?"

Ben's cheeks flushed. "No, but the real version will only make me look bad. The important thing is that I pursued him. I listened to my heart, let it talk me into doing stupid things without putting up a fight. Tim, on the other hand, wasn't so good at doing the same."

"How so?"

Ben sighed. "He was a hopeless closet case, and I was ridiculously proud. Not the best combination. I'm tempted to say things were different back then, that being openly gay in the nineties wasn't easy or even heard of in some places. You and Caesar not being hampered by that issue is wonderful. But then again, I know that tons of teenagers still struggle and are probably living the same story Tim and I did. That makes me angry. Not only does it seem nearly impossible to find another gay guy, not to mention the right one for you, but on top of it all, so much internal fear and external hate keeps trying to get in the way of love."

"Yup," Jason agreed with a resigned sigh. "Finding someone is against the odds."

"Screw the odds. You can do it, but it's definitely a marathon instead of a race. Sometimes it takes years, if not decades, to get there."

"Like you and Tim?"

Ben nodded. "Exactly."

"That still confuses me. If you and Tim were high school sweethearts, how does Jace fit into it all?"

"Ah. Tim and I weren't always together. He had a long journey ahead of him, and I guess he had to take that trip on his own. At least I wasn't willing to accompany him, so we split up in high school. I honestly thought it was over. Eventually I met Jace and was happy, but when that story came to an end, Tim was right there waiting for me."

That sounded incredibly romantic, but also not very like the guy Jason had met. Tim hadn't stuck by Ben's side at all. At least not yesterday. Or today, for that matter. These thoughts must have been transparent, because Ben reacted to them.

"He just needs a little time, that's all. Tim can be… shy? No. Reserved isn't right either." Ben reconsidered. "Tim is like this really good-looking animal out in the woods, maybe a unicorn, and if you want to get near, you have to sneak up on him really quietly or he'll spook. Hell, you practically have to walk backwards so he doesn't know if you're coming or going. But once you ride that unicorn, he's yours for life."

Jason just stared in response, figuring it was better than laughing.

Ben's face turned red. "God, did I really just say that? Enough metaphors. Basically Tim has some very dumb and stubborn ideas, but once he spends some time with you, he'll get over it all. That's why I thought we could swing by the gallery later to see him."

"Okay," Jason agreed. He figured the kind of person who could win Ben's heart must be decent. First impressions weren't always the best, so Jason was totally open to giving it another shot.

They left the mall to shop stand-alone retail stores. Jason found a cheap desk for his computer, and after some extra reassurance from Ben, also chose plum-colored sheets and a chocolate-brown comforter for his bed. Best of all was the huge electronics store that had a selection of musical instruments. Jason had no intention of ever parting with his old guitar—no matter how worn out it was—but he nearly shouted for joy when he found a guitar stand on sale.

"Do you have the guitar to go with it?" Ben asked.

"Yeah," Jason said. "Upstairs in my room. I've had it ever since I was little."

"So you can play?"

"I don't keep it around just because it looks cool," Jason teased. "Do you play anything?"

"Just myself," Ben said before looking panicked. "That was supposed to sound clever, and *not* like a sex joke. I can sing. That's what I meant."

"Are you any good?"

Ben pretended to look offended. "Am I good? I do it for a living! Partially, anyway. I sing at a little dinner theater, depending on the play in season. I avoid the productions without music because I can't act, and the audience only forgives me when I make with the voice."

"Let's hear something," Jason said.

"Right now?" Ben cocked his head, tuning into the song on

the store speakers. "I can't rap. Sorry. I'm not big on singing *a cappella* either."

"Then at home," Jason said. "I'll provide the tunes and you sing."

Ben's smile was subtle. "All right."

They browsed further, but Jason was done shopping. He wasn't used to blowing through money and already felt overwhelmed by what he had chosen. Ben insisted they make one last stop at the bookstore for a copy of the local newspaper.

"Back in the dark ages, companies used to advertise for help in the back of non-electronic paper," Ben said. "You might find something in there that isn't listed online."

Jason humored him, rushing into the store and returning with not one, but two discoveries. "Classifieds for jobs," he said, holding up a copy of today's paper. Then he held up the free magazine he'd found called *Gay Austin!* "And classifieds for love. But don't worry, the hunt for employment takes top priority."

"You're really determined to find a job, aren't you?"

"Depends what kind of 'job' you mean," Jason said with a lewd wink. He felt like he was testing the boundaries of their relationship, but luckily his joke earned a laugh.

"You can take some time off," Ben said. "Figure out what you want to do with your life."

Jason shook his head. "I'm not here for a free ride. You're right that I don't know what I want to do, but it's definitely not mooching off you."

Ben reappraised him and nodded. "Okay. Let me know if there's anything I can do to help."

They drove downtown, getting stuck in traffic on the way. Jason kept playing with the radio, trying to find a song Ben would sing along to, but Ben kept refusing, swearing a single note wouldn't cross his lips until Jason played the guitar for him. Jason continued begging, tuning into increasingly terrible music and laughing at the horrified faces Ben made. He was still laughing when they parked in an older part of the city where the shops were one long row of smooshed-together buildings, partially hidden behind overgrown trees.

He noticed the art in the windows as he stepped out of the car—black and white paintings with copper mesh attached directly to the canvas. He examined a few, looking over at Ben, who shrugged like he didn't get it either. Jason supposed neither of them needed to understand it, not as long as Tim was a good salesman, and obviously he was, since they seemed to have a lot of money.

Ben led the way inside. Seated at a minimal desk in the center of the room was Tim, who smiled at Ben. Jason was once again struck by how Tim lit up when doing so. But then his presence was detected and that light retreated. He thought of what Ben had said and wondered if it wasn't true. Maybe Tim *was* something magical, like a unicorn, but to get close to that light would require tact.

Figuring Ben and Tim would want some time to speak alone, Jason stepped into one of the side rooms. He remained closest to the art near the doorway, so he could still listen in. First came the sound of a kiss—an unlikely greeting between generals about to go to war.

"What happened to the artists being here to represent their work?" Ben asked.

"They're college students," Tim replied. "They have to go to school."

"I know, but one of them is usually here. You don't usually put in this many hours."

"It's fine," Tim said dismissively. "So what have you been up to?"

"Jason and I went shopping."

"Have fun? Did you get anything for me?"

"Yes we did, and no, I didn't. Will you be home for dinner?"

There was an awkward silence that even Jason felt tempted to fill.

"I might have to stay late," Tim said finally.

"Are you kidding me?" Then, so quietly that Jason had to strain to hear, Ben whispered, "He's living under your roof. You can't keep avoiding him."

"I'm not," Tim mumbled.

"Then go talk to him!"

Jason quickly moved to the far wall, stopping before a painting of blue and purple squares, a stencil of a white bunny spray-painted in the middle. He grew tense as a single set of footsteps approached him, pausing once along the way. Then, accompanied by a whiff of cologne and aftershave, Tim was standing next to him.

"Hey," he said.

"Hey," Jason replied, glancing over at him and then quickly away again. Tim was even hotter up close. That was a bad thing, because looking directly at him became impossible.

"So… sleep okay?"

Jason nodded. "Yeah. Thanks."

Tim shifted his weight back and forth. "Chinchilla usually sleeps with me."

Jason waited for something to be added to this, some sign of Tim being amused or maybe surprised. Instead, it remained a cold hard fact.

"I'm sorry?" Jason tried.

From the corner of his eye, he could see Tim turn around, probably to seek guidance from Ben or to be spurred on. Feeling a little sorry for him, Jason decided to throw him a bone.

"This is an interesting painting," he said. "I like it, but I don't really get it." He snuck a peek and saw Tim's silver eyes moving over the canvas.

"It's a juxtaposition of old values versus the new. The checkered pattern was common in the fifties when conformity was valued over individual expression. The spray-painted rabbit represents the guerilla tactics artists use on the street today, still waging a war against repression almost sixty years later."

"Oh," Jason said, the corners of his mouth twitching. "I thought it might represent Easter."

"Easter?"

"Yeah, you know. Blue and purple are sort of Easter colors, and then there's the rabbit." He glanced over again to see a strong jaw clenching.

"What's this one make you think of?" Tim asked, leading them a few spaces over to a rough sketch of an old man. "Santa Claus?"

"Too skinny," Jason said, peering at the art. "And naked." He licked his lips, too nervous to check for a reaction to this statement. He was trying to be funny but had the feeling he was pissing Tim off. He supposed this was a very serious topic for him, since it was his livelihood, so Jason tried changing gears and showing more interest.

"This one here," Jason said, taking them to a canvas so tall it almost reached the ceiling. "How much does it cost? Does the size mean it's more expensive? I notice there aren't any prices."

"We keep them listed in a book," Tim said. "That way people don't judge the art by the price tag alone. If I remember right, this one goes for about five grand."

"Wow!" Jason said, not faking his awe. "And how much of that do you keep?"

"You mean the artist? They get all of it."

"Then how do you make money?" Jason asked.

"The gallery is funded by patrons," Tim explained. "Their donations pay the rent and utilities."

"Yeah, but how do *you* make money?" Jason pressed. "What's your commission? You're a salesman, right?"

In his confusion, Jason forgot his nervousness and looked at Tim directly. This gave him a nice view of the handsome brow getting all knotted up.

"You think I'm a salesman?" Tim spun around. "He thinks I'm a salesman!"

From across the room, Ben laughed, then hurried to them. "Tim doesn't get paid for being here," he explained. "He helps run the foundation that opened this gallery. Tim's an artist. He had his first exhibition here."

Jason didn't care. His face was burning because he felt a mixture of embarrassment and anger. How was he to know that Tim didn't work here? Or that he was an artist? Oh god! Maybe that bunny painting was his, and Jason had stood there making fun of it. But Tim could have said something, could have explained what he did here instead of making Jason feel awkward. Of course Tim was only talking to him at all because Ben was forcing him to.

"I think I need some fresh air," Jason said, heading for the door.

He was around the corner and in the main room when he heard Ben speak.

"Don't make that face! How is he supposed to know anything about you when you keep avoiding him?"

Rolling his eyes, Jason shoved his way outside. He waited by the car, leaning against the back of it so he wouldn't have to face the gallery. Tim was smoking hot. That had to be the only reason Ben liked him. All this stuff about him being a magical creature? Bullshit! Tim was a donkey. A mule. An ass.

A familiar feeling rose up in Jason. Time to get out of here, make an excuse and go back to the group home… Except he wasn't a kid anymore. He was too old for such things now, and he'd lost his apartment. He was stuck here. For the moment, at least.

Jason sighed. He'd have to make the best of it until he saved enough money to get his own place. Until then, Tim wouldn't have to avoid him because he wouldn't even know Jason was there. That's how little they would see of each other.

The scalloped potatoes were great. The big slab of steak that went with them was a little dry, but nothing a healthy dose of ketchup couldn't fix. The vibe at the table, *that* was the problem. Ben tried to be sociable and kept bringing up pleasant topics for Jason to latch on to. They even moved to the couch, bringing their plates with them, which was wonderfully casual. Not that it helped, since Ben's eyes kept returning to the front of the house, as if he would find Tim standing in the entryway. Jason didn't bother looking or even listening for his car. He knew the deal. Tim would do everything possible to avoid him, and Jason would do likewise.

He realized it wasn't fair to hog Ben like this, so tomorrow Jason would make himself scarce. He wasn't here to wreck their relationship. Nor was he here to fix it. *Foster home number fourteen*. That one had been a real nightmare; a childless couple just entering their forties who clearly didn't like each other. One of them decided a kid could salvage their broken marriage, maybe thinking that's what other couples had that they didn't. What Jason remembered most was the way they fixated on him, desperate to interact with anyone but each other. That's why Jason had found a way to lock them in the garage together. Eventually they dismantled the electric garage door just to get out. Hell, maybe them working together helped fix their relationship. Regardless, they sent him back to the care home.

Once dinner was over, Jason insisted on doing the dishes alone. When he returned to the living room, Ben was leaning against the back of the couch, petting Samson who napped there. Occasionally he still glanced toward the front door. He looked up when Jason entered, almost hopeful, like Tim had snuck in through the kitchen window or something. Then he must have realized his behavior, because he stood fully as if determined.

"You know what? Go get your guitar. What this house needs is some music!"

Jason didn't need more prompting than that. He raced up the stairs—Chinchilla chasing after him—and grabbed his guitar from its new stand. When he was back downstairs, he was happy to see Ben wearing the same grin he was. This was going to be fun!

"What can you play?" Ben asked him.

"What can you sing?" Jason challenged back.

"All right. I don't suppose you've ever heard of Roberta Flack."

"Nope. Know anything by Steely Dan?"

Ben shook his head. "Sorry. I really liked No Doubt's new album."

Jason grimaced. "How about Fleetwood Mac?"

"I've heard of them," Ben said. "But I can't really name one of their songs."

"Sure you can." Jason started strumming. "The Cranberries did a cover of *Go Your Own Way* that the radio stations played to death."

Ben perked up. "Oh yeah! I've sung that one a million times."

"There we go," Jason said, playing louder now.

Ben definitely knew the lyrics, probably finding significance in them. Jason nodded his head approvingly, loving the way the song didn't waste any time launching into the chorus. When it did, he nearly dropped the guitar because Ben positively belted out those lyrics, and not in a shouty amateur kind of way. His voice had power, and holy shit, was it beautiful! Jason had to force himself to concentrate on the chords, because most of him wanted to stop and listen. When the song came to an end, he simply let his jaw drop and shook his head.

"You're not so bad yourself," Ben said, laughing. "That thing sounds better than I expected it to, considering how beat up it is."

"Tell me about it," Jason said, looking down at his guitar. The poor thing was in worse shape than ever. Now, in addition to being cracked and peeling in places, it had a hole in the side of the body. That had happened during a moving accident when he and Steph had first gotten their apartment.

"So," Ben said. "What's next?"

"Paul Simon? Or maybe Carly?"

"*You're So Vain*?"

"Interesting choice," Jason said.

Yup, Tim was definitely in trouble when he got home, but that wasn't Jason's problem. He started playing, enjoying the casual strum that allowed him to relax and focus on listening to Ben's voice. It was beautiful. *He* was beautiful. For once, this realization didn't cause the stirring of a crush in Jason's chest, but he felt the beginnings of something like love there. Ben was cool, friendly, easy-going, and talented. No wonder he'd once been married to the nicest guy in the world, and there was no mystery as to why a smoking-hot guy like Tim would want him around. Thankfully, Ben was also older than Jason, which might be why he didn't feel like throwing his guitar aside and rushing over to kiss him. No, the feelings were something new, but he didn't have time to dwell on them. Not when the song was winding down.

Together they chose another. And another, neither of them wanting to stop. They were in the middle of Tracy Chapman's *Baby Can I Hold You* when he noticed Tim standing between the entryway and living room, leaning against the wall like he'd been there for some time. He met Jason's eye and smiled—really smiled—almost like he did for Ben. The force of that gesture made Jason's fingers falter for just one note, which was enough for Ben to look up. Then Tim was looking at his boyfriend instead, Ben's singing instantly more intense. It was all Jason could do to keep playing, because sitting there and witnessing firsthand how much they loved each other made him want to cry.

When the song ended, Jason stood. "My hand is cramping," he said. Keeping his head down, he hurried to the stairs and up to his bedroom. Once there he exhaled, heart racing from the intensity of the experience. To think he ever worried about coming between them! Or wondered if he was there to fix their relationship. What Ben and Tim had together—it was perfection. Sure they didn't always get along or understand each other, but the love between them would compensate, would always keep them together.

A knock on the door made him jump. No, not a knock, a thump. Jason stood and opened the door. Chinchilla pattered in with a huff, turning and sitting before she looked up at him.

Jason chuckled. "Are they going at it again?" He shut the door as quietly as possible and flopped on the bed with a sigh. What he'd just witnessed, what Ben and Tim shared, there was nothing in the world he wanted more.

Around midnight, Chinchilla hopped off the bed and pawed at the door. Jason was on the verge of falling asleep and felt disoriented as he got up. When he opened the door for her, Chinchilla walked into the hall and then grumbled at him.

"What?" he whispered. "Do you have to go potty?"

More grumbling. Hitching up his pajama bottoms, Jason followed her downstairs. The house was dark and quiet. He fumbled at the back door, trying to find the lock, and discovered the door was already cracked open. Maybe so Chinchilla could let herself out. Besides, no robbers were going to make the trip way out here. Jason stepped onto the back patio, walking to the edge where stones turned to grass. Then he looked up. Here, away from the city lights, the stars were free to shine. He'd never seen so many in his life. They swirled through the sky in countless numbers, making him feel a strange sort of yearning.

Chinchilla grumbled again. Now she was sitting right in front of him, looking expectant.

"Go potty!" Jason tried.

Grumble grumble.

"What?" Jason asked her. "I thought you had to go?"

Grumble grumble.

"If you're not going to potty, then I'm going back to bed."

"She likes company."

Jason tensed and spun around. To the side of the patio, lounging in a chair, was Tim. He wore jogging shorts and a tight tank top, and as he stood and came closer, Jason could see and smell the sweat in his hair.

"Sorry," Tim said. "Didn't mean to scare you. I was just cooling off after a run." Chinchilla danced happily around his legs, Tim reaching down to pet her. "She likes company when she's got business to make. I had a hard time house-training her, and I think she got used to the praise when she actually went outside. Now she expects us to stand there watching so we can applaud or whatever."

Jason continued to stare.

Tim stared back. "Want to be her cheerleader with me?"

"Okay," Jason managed.

They walked across the grass, Chinchilla taking the lead as she tried to choose the ultimate spot to pee.

"An artist came into the gallery today," Tim said. "The one who did the bunny painting. You remember that one?"

"Yeah," Jason said, his voice a little terse.

"I asked him what that painting was all about. You know what he said?"

Jason shook his head.

"That he was thinking of his childhood and how much he liked painting eggs at Easter. He even used egg dye to make the checkered background. Said he had an idea for a Halloween-themed painting using smooshed candy corn."

Jason laughed. He couldn't help it. To his surprise, Tim joined him.

"Maybe I am a salesman," Tim continued. "People expect art to have some deep meaning, when really it can be as simple as wanting to create something that looks nice or is fun. So I guess I've gotten used to putting a spin on everything in the gallery to convince people that our art has value. And it does, but not because of any convoluted symbolism. Art is art. Simple as that. So you were right. About me, I mean."

"I didn't mean it as an insult," Jason said. "I was impressed that you've managed all of this." He gestured to the yard, the house, the land. "Ben said that you're the one with the money, and I just figured you were one of the best salesmen out there."

"One of the best, huh?" Tim was quiet a second, the amused smile fading. "I'm a fuckup. I have been my entire life. I don't know what Ben told you about our past but... Anyway, I was about your age when I met this guy, Eric. He was much older than me and really cool. I loved hanging out with him. Eventually there came a time when I didn't have anywhere to go, and he took me in. Without a second thought, he invited me in like I was family. The money, it's all his. He gave it to me because he wanted to take care of me. Or maybe he wanted to save me, because it's hard to imagine where I'd be if he hadn't done that. Eric couldn't stay, but he still managed to find a way of caring for me."

Chinchilla finished peeing and trotted back, looking up at them hopefully. Then came a very odd moment when Jason and

Tim praised her, their voices full of superficial cheer, before the dog got bored and chased after a moth. Tim turned to face him, Jason doing the same because out here in the shadows, Tim's handsome face wasn't very visible. This made relaxing so much easier.

"Eric would like that you're here," Tim said, "that his generosity is benefitting someone else now. I'm glad too, but I can't be Eric. I can't help you in the way he helped me. I tried once for someone else, and it was a disaster. Ben, on the other hand, he's what you need."

"Maybe I don't need either of you," Jason said, trying to keep his tone neutral. "I'm not broken or something. I just…" He trailed off, unsure how he'd ended up here and if it was his fault.

"I didn't mean it like that," Tim said. "It's not that there's something wrong with you, but there are people in this world who, after you meet them, you walk away a better person. No matter how okay you were before, they have a way of making you even better. Eric was like that, and so is Ben. I hope you stay here long enough to find that out."

"Thanks," Jason said. "For inviting me in and letting me stay, I mean."

Tim looked taken aback, then nodded. "Yeah. No problem. I uh… I should probably hit the shower and get some sleep. Don't let Chinchilla keep you up all night."

"I won't," Jason said.

He watched Tim walk toward the house, chuckling quietly at the way he kept looking back, like even he was surprised that they had managed a civilized conversation. Then Jason turned and considered the stars again, wondering what other surprises they had in store for him.

Chapter Seventeen

Tim was at the breakfast table the next morning. He didn't leap up from the table to hug Jason or anything, but he did give an upward nod when he entered the kitchen. Jason returned the gesture.

"Just cereal this morning," Ben said. He was already dressed, unlike Tim who was still in his robe. "Oh, and some yogurt and cantaloupes. Hope that's okay."

"No complaints here," Jason said. "I usually skip breakfast, so the cereal alone sounds luxurious."

He helped himself before Ben could do it for him and took a seat across from them. Tim was flipping through one of the papers they had brought back yesterday while digging into his melon with a spoon. Ben seemed to be watching Jason, his body language a little antsy. Maybe he was worried about him and Tim getting along, which meant he didn't know about last night. They were at least on okay terms now, right?

"You're going to be late," Tim said.

"I know." Ben looked back at Jason. "I have to go to the hospital."

Jason nearly spit out a mouthful of cereal. "What? Why?"

"Sorry," Ben said. "I work there part-time as a speech therapist. It's not an emergency or anything. What are you doing today?"

"Job search," Jason said, nodding at the papers.

"Oh, okay." Ben looked at Tim. "And you?"

"I'm going to sit here and give him hell the entire time." Tim turned a deadpan expression on Ben. "We'll be fine. Don't worry. Go to work."

Ben glanced back and forth between them, settling on Tim. "The electrician is coming today, don't forget."

"I won't."

Ben reluctantly got to his feet. "Okay," he said. "All right. You've got my number, Jason? Come to think of it, I don't have yours."

"No phone," he replied. Monthly plans were expensive.

"Well, I'll put my number on the fridge, and you can use the home phone to call if—"

"—if I try to kill him or anything like that," Tim said. "What? I thought it was funny."

Jason did too, and while it probably wasn't fair to keep Ben out of the loop, he supposed them having this secret was a weird way of bonding. "I'll be fine," he said. "I'll probably still be at this table circling ads when you get back."

That was enough to send Ben on his way, but only after a bit more loitering. When he was finally gone, Tim started clearing the table and putting bowls and spoons in the dishwasher.

"What sort of job are you looking for?" he asked.

"Anything besides waiting tables or fast food."

Tim nodded. "Good luck. If you need anything, I'll be around."

That was it. Jason was on his own. He allowed himself to be lazy and flipped through the gay newspaper. Then he went upstairs, took a long shower, and got dressed. Afterwards he spent his time browsing ads and making calls. He expected the entire day to be full of this, but on his sixth call he got lucky. Hurrying through the house, he failed to find Tim anywhere, even the studio, which Jason peeked into briefly for the first time. He was overwhelmed by the number of canvases he saw inside, but didn't have time to examine them closer. He checked the backyard next, feeling despair before he looked out front and noticed the garage was open, a figure moving around inside. Perfect!

"I got a job interview!" Jason said after rushing out there.

"Congrats," Tim said. "Where at?"

"That stays a surprise," Jason said. "Besides, I don't want to jinx it. The interview is in an hour."

"Oh, wow!"

"Yeah. Short notice. I guess they're really understaffed. Uh, the only problem is, I need a ride."

"No problem," Tim said, before his face fell. "Actually, big problem. The electrician is supposed to be coming out here soon. Our bedroom lights keep flashing on and off in the middle of the night and it's creeping me out."

"Could I borrow the car?" Jason asked.

Tim turned to consider the vehicle in question, Jason noticing it for the first time. The car was silver and polished, like it had just rolled off a dealership floor. The details were subtle but still ornate, and from the vehicle's condition, it was obvious Tim loved it. His eyes were shining even now.

"You know what kind of car this is?" Tim asked in reverent tones.

"As long as it's an automatic, I'm good," Jason replied.

Tim's brow lowered. "It's a Bentley Continental GTC!"

"Awesome. So can I borrow it?"

Now Tim looked pained. "Are you a good driver? I mean, you're not like Benjamin, are you?"

Jason blinked. "I rode with Ben the other day and he did fine."

"Really?"

"Well, he accidentally cut a guy off when reaching for the radio. Oh, and he went over a curb when pulling into the mall parking lot. He doesn't seem to notice stop signs either." Jason reconsidered. "Okay, so he's a terrible driver."

"Exactly," Tim said. "That's why he never drives this car. I bought it one day when I was feeling sappy, since you know, it's a Bentley, just like his last name."

"Aaaw!"

Tim snorted. "Yeah, I know. Thing is, this little romantic gesture cost me a small fortune. I should probably sell it before the value depreciates any further, but..." He reached out and lovingly stroked the hood.

"Sorry to interrupt," Jason said, "but the clock is ticking."

Tim's jaw clenched a few times before he nodded reluctantly. "Okay. She's all yours, but drive slow. And bring her right back after the interview."

"I will," Jason promised.

"And if something does happen," Tim said, "come back here and put me out of my misery."

"I'll beat you over the head with a shovel, I swear."

Jason returned to the house to check his appearance and grab his résumé. When he was ready, he found the car pulled up in front of the house. Fully exposed, the sunlight glinting off of every sexified curve, the car was anything but average. This impression was driven home when he slid into an interior that was both traditional and futurist.

"Very steampunk," Jason said to Tim, who was bent over and watching him through the driver-side window, face alternating between pride and terror. "I'm going to be late!"

Jason started the car and pushed the button to roll up the

window, nearly trapping Tim's nose in the process. Then he drove carefully down the drive, keeping his speed at an absolute minimum. Only when he reached the main road did he grin, push the gas pedal down hard, and gun his way toward Austin.

By the time Jason returned, Ben was already back. Not too surprising since Jason had been gone for hours. After the job interview, he drove around Austin, trying to get a feel for the city. Parts of it could have been Houston. The same chain restaurants, the same major retailers, but downtown Austin was something completely different, full of weird little shops and diners he was eager to check out. He browsed a few stores, but without any money to spend, he tired of this and settled for people-watching in a park.

Now he was home again and standing in the living room, but Jason's lips would remain sealed until Tim came back inside.

"He's out front checking on the car, isn't he?" Ben asked from one of the cozy corner chairs. He shook his head and smiled. "So how'd it go? You can tell me that much at least."

"Nope!"

Ben made a pouty face before flipping through a few more pages of the magazine he was reading. Jason noticed it was the gay one. "I'm looking for Tim," Ben explained. "He did some modeling years ago, and occasionally he'll pop up in an ad for an escort service or something. Gets upset every time it happens, but it's not like he's nude."

Jason moved behind the chair to look over his shoulder until Tim came back inside.

Once he did, Tim exhaled as if disaster had been narrowly avoided and nodded. "She's okay."

"Thank goodness for that!" Ben said sarcastically. "Now then, tell us—"

"I got the job!" Jason blurted out.

"Already?" Tim asked. "Don't they usually call you back later?"

"They were desperate," Jason said. "I start tomorrow. The really good news is that I'm working at a pet store and get an employee discount. I can use it to help you save money until I start paying rent."

"Congrats, man!" Tim said.

"Yeah, congratulations," Ben said, "but you don't need to worry about rent."

"Of course I do," Jason said, plopping down in the chair next to his and throwing a leg over one arm. "I'm not here to mooch."

"No," Ben said, "but you *are* here to get back on your feet, and that includes planning your future."

"Uh-oh," Tim said, heading for the kitchen. "Benjamin's on the warpath! Better give in, kiddo, because he always knows what's best for everyone."

Ben grinned shamelessly. "The reason I don't want you paying rent or bills is so you can save money. Have you thought of going to college?"

"Oh. Actually I dropped out of high school."

"That's okay," Ben said. "Did you get your GED?"

Jason nodded.

"Well, there you go. Nothing's holding you back. What do you want to be when you grow up?"

"You mean like a real profession?" Jason said. "No idea. I've never known."

"Perfect!" Ben said, sounding satisfied. "College is *made* for people who don't know what they want to do."

Jason grimaced. "I really don't think college is for me."

"Okay," Ben said. "Just think about it a little, that's all I'm asking. Now, my other big idea is right here."

Ben opened the newspaper and pointed to an ad. Jason took the paper and read it.

Lonely, lost, and looking for fun? Gay youth meeting, every Sunday at All Souls Unitarian Church.

Jason looked up. "Gay youth? I'm eighteen."

"Which sounds awfully young to old people like me," Ben said. "I called the number and asked about that. The meetings are for anyone under twenty-one."

"Oh."

"Might be a way of meeting that dream guy. Unless you saw someone adorable and gay stocking the dog food aisle today."

Jason smiled. "I did just happen to scope out my coworkers, and they're mostly women."

"So what do you think?" Ben pressed. "Just imagine a whole room full of young gay people also looking to fall in love. You'll probably get mobbed when you show up."

"Can you go with me?" Jason asked.

"I'm a little older than twenty-one!"

"How much older?" Jason asked with a grin.

Ben squirmed in his seat. "I'm still in my twenties."

Tim chose that moment to return. "Keep saying that while you still can, Benjamin. The months are counting down!"

Ben slumped in his chair. "Thirty," he sighed. "It's all down hill from there."

"Not when you've got me getting old with you," Tim said, swooping in to kiss Ben on the neck.

From the floor, Chinchilla grumbled and met Jason's eye. Yup, time for them to make themselves scarce again!

"So what do you think?"

This was a big question to answer, which is probably why Emma remained uncharacteristically silent on the other end of the phone, allowing Jason to come up with a response.

"Ben is awesome, obviously. The house is great, although I wish it was closer to Austin. Let's see… Samson is cute, and I'm in love with Chinchilla. So, yeah. I'm happy."

"Hm," Emma replied.

"Hm?" Jason echoed.

"You didn't mention Tim," Emma said. "No breakthroughs there?"

"Tim is…" Jason paced his bedroom, trying to find the right word and came up with one that summed him up completely. "Complicated."

Emma laughed as if she understood, but then asked, "How so?"

"He's super-hot, so I get uncomfortable when I'm around him. I mean, I don't want to hook up with him or anything, but still. Half the time he seems self-centered, the other half it's like he lives solely for Ben. That's it, actually. Even when Tim is nice, I get the feeling that he only wants to be alone with Ben."

"That's because you've invaded their love nest," Emma said knowingly. "Why do you think they live in the middle of nowhere? They have this weird thing about being alone together. Tim tried to explain it once. I don't get it, but I still envy them."

"Yeah," Jason said. "Makes me eager to get my own place so I'm not bothering them anymore."

"No way!" Emma said this with such enthusiasm that Jason had to pull the phone away from his ear. "They *need* you there. They can't live their whole lives in solitude. Whenever I come to stay, they always say how much life I bring to the house. Ok, so maybe they don't actually say that, but I can tell it's good for them. Ben doesn't look happy when you're around?"

Jason switched the phone to his other ear. "I guess so. I think he likes me, so hopefully."

"I know he does," Emma said with her usual self-assuredness. "Tim just takes a while to warm up to new ideas. He used to look at me like I had three heads."

Jason laughed. "We'll see. I won't be moving out any time soon, even with the new job. Hey, speaking of which, Ben found an ad for a gay youth group. He thinks I should go."

"Do it!" Emma said instantly.

"I don't know," Jason said. "I hate that first-day-of-school feeling where everyone else is already friends with each other."

"Want me to go with you?"

"Yeah," Jason said without hesitation. "Too bad you're so far away."

"When is it?"

"This coming Sunday."

"Wow." Emma sighed. "A gay youth meeting… I so want to go! Maybe I can get Mom to drop me off on Saturday for a sleepover. Especially if Uncle Ben or Tim will drive me back the next day."

Jason sat up. "I could drive you back after the meeting. If they'll let me borrow a car."

"They will!" Emma said. "I'm totally sure! Hold on."

The phone on the other end rustled and went still. Jason strained to hear what was happening, tried to picture Michelle's home and what she was doing when not walking around with a manila folder in her hand, saving kids. He was wondering if he should hang up and let Emma call him back when he heard her voice in the distance.

"Yes!" A few seconds later and her voice was louder in the receiver. "They said yes! Sleepover!"

Jason felt he was too old for sleepovers, and probably too old to be friends with a fourteen-year-old, but he smiled anyway because he was happy Emma was coming to visit.

Chapter Eighteen

They stood in a parking lot, eyeing the church in front of them. Jason's stomach was full of so many butterflies that if he burped, multicolored wings would probably come flying out. He glanced over at Emma, whose eyebrows were raised like the building wasn't good enough for her. He resisted the urge to grab her hand, but only just.

Emma glanced over at him. "Nervous?"

"Yeah," he admitted.

Emma nodded. "Me too."

"Really? But you seem so—"

"Calm and collected? I'm an overweight junior high student who hasn't done anything more than kiss another girl on the cheek. I've never met another lesbian in my life, as far as I know, and I have absolutely no idea what to expect. The confidence thing? That's called attitude and it's my armor."

"Well, it works," Jason said. "You'll have to give me lessons later." He looked back at the church. "Should we go in? What's the worst that can happen, right?"

"They can point and call us names, crippling our self-esteem and ensuring we'll never try anything like this again. Then we'll die single and alone, the echo of their cruel laughter still ringing in our ears."

"Very encouraging," Jason said. "So glad I brought you along. And you're wrong, because we won't die single and alone. We made a promise, remember?"

This time he did take Emma's hand and led her forward. Once in the church, they wandered down halls, reading signs on doors to find the correct room. When they found one with the door open, Jason took one look inside and knew it was the right place. The age tipped him off more than anything else, since everyone seemed so normal.

Sure there were a number of girls with shorter hair, and a few of the guys seemed dressed more for a nightclub than church, but for the most part, it could have been any random classroom. To Jason's relief, he saw plenty of guys his age, if not a little older. Quite a few had turned to stare, eyes moving to the hand he was holding. Emma shook free first, striding into the room. All Jason could do was follow.

The room was drab with brown paneling and carpet that matched. Judging from the children's drawings on the walls, this space was probably used for daycare or Sunday school or something similar. Unless part of the meeting would involve coloring pictures.

Chairs and a few couches lined the room, except for the far end where a table was set with refreshments. Emma led him to this, eying the display but not taking anything.

"It's like an AA meeting in here," she mumbled.

A skinny guy standing not far away overheard, and in a loud lispy voice said, "You've got that right, honey, but it's not booze we're addicted to!"

There were a few laughs, but Jason tensed up. This wasn't what he wanted. He dreamed of meeting another guy in some romantic fashion. Not sitting in a circle and making jokes full of sexual innuendo. He turned to leave, hoping Emma would follow, and found his way blocked by an older man. His hair was thinning, and he wore outdated glasses and an unseasonal flannel shirt. One slightly hairy hand was extended outward.

"You must be new. I'm Keith, the group leader."

Jason took his hand unwillingly, the skin of his palm soft. He watched as Emma shook hands with him too.

"We were just about to get started. If you two want to grab a drink first and—"

"We're ready!" Emma said, grabbing Jason's arm and leading him toward some chairs. Once he was seated he understood why. Directly across from them sat a group of girls, one of whom was so handsome that even Jason did a double-take. She had a tight lean body, her hair was gelled into spikes, and she sported a number of facial piercings. Emma kept looking in her direction, which meant he was stuck here. One meeting. He supposed he could suffer that much for her.

Keith took a seat next to this girl. "Today we're going to talk about relationships," he said, shaking his head at the catcalls this summoned. "But first, let's do a round of introductions. Now, now!" he added after half the room groaned. "Some new faces are here today, and I could also use a reminder of who's who. Tell us your name and one thing about yourself."

As much as Jason was dreading his turn, this did give him an opportunity to check everyone out. A few guys were too young for him. Most of the others weren't his type or were already paired up and holding hands. The lesbians didn't interest him, of course, but Emma kept elbowing him every time she saw someone she liked.

"My name is Kelly," said an articulate voice. The speaker was beautiful in a way that transcended gender. Skin as dark as freshly brewed coffee, eyes almond in both shape and color, amazing cheekbones, and perfectly pouty lips. Despite being undeniably pretty, he was also masculine enough to get Jason's attention. "And I'm very disappointed Lisa didn't bring brownies this time, since I skipped breakfast."

"Sorry!" a mousy girl next to Jason replied.

Kelly smiled. "It's okay."

Jason nudged Emma in the ribs.

"I'm William," said a quiet voice, which was odd considering how big the guy was. He was a good head taller than Kelly and a complete contrast to him. Handsome rather than beautiful, and skin so creamy and pale it looked like milk. Blond hair was swept to one side, his green eyes twinkling as he made a joke. "And I'm glad there aren't any brownies since I ate way too much this morning." The goofy smile was insecure and quickly forced away, even though the lips quivered a moment longer in amusement. Jason's eyes darted down to a muscular body stuffed into tight clothes, but almost instantly returned to that face. He knew him. Or at least he felt he did, even though he honestly couldn't say from where, or if he'd ever seen him before. That didn't make sense, not logically, but Jason's pulse picked up anyway. *William.* Even the name sounded right. Jason felt like he should stand up, should draw attention to himself so William could confirm this feeling of familiarity. "Oh, hey!" he'd surely say. "I know you! I've always known you!"

Jason elbowed Emma so hard that she cried out.

"Oh, go ahead!" Keith said.

"Sorry," Emma said, managing somehow not to blush. "All this talk of food got me excited."

There were a few appreciative laughs, including one from the handsome girl she'd been checking out.

"My name is Emma, and I was born to love you. Unfortunately I can only love one of you, so let's keep things civil. No cat fights, please, but I do accept bribes."

The whole room laughed this time, Jason glancing over to catch sight of William's white teeth.

"And who did you bring with you?" Keith asked.

"Jason," he said, averting his eyes back to the group leader. "And I… uh…"

His throat made a wheezing noise like he'd taken his last breath, which was appropriate since he now felt like dying.

"That's okay," Keith said. "How about you, Lisa?"

Jason's face burned, and felt like it would catch fire when he glanced over to see Kelly staring at him with one eyebrow raised. Kelly didn't look away, either. Not at first. Eventually his eyes rolled over to the current speaker. Jason turned his attention to the carpet rather than discover what William's reaction was. God, he missed being able to hide behind his hair!

Jason alternated his attention between the ceiling and floor, taking quick peeks when he heard a male voice introducing himself, but he didn't see any other guys he was interested in. Mind-blowingly beautiful Kelly or deliciously sweet William were his only choices, and if he was honest, he didn't think he had a shot with either. Not unless he could somehow redeem himself during the meeting. The topic was relationships, something he at least had experience with. He paid close attention as Keith lectured them on the basics. Then Keith rolled a marker board out and made two columns, one labeled *Men*, the other *Women*.

"Psychologists and trashy magazines insist that men and women have different priorities in relationships. In other words, men and women want different things. But does that apply to gay men and gay women too? Let's find out. What do you look for in a potential partner?"

Emma's handsome lesbian raised her hand. "I want to be understood."

This caused a murmur of agreement.

"Okay," Keith wrote this on the board. "What else?"

"I want to feel appreciated," Emma said, looking directly at the object of her desire.

"Excellent," Keith said, still writing. "Let's hear from the boys too."

"He has to be hot!" someone called out.

"Goes without saying," one of the girls chimed in.

Keith nodded. "So both sides want someone they are attracted to. Everyone has their own definition of hot, so this can be anything. What else? Yes, William."

Jason latched on to this excuse to glance at him. After all, everyone else was looking too. Just like before, Jason felt that strange sense of familiarity.

"Commitment," William said. "Loyalty is important."

"Trust," Kelly chimed in immediately. "You should be able to trust the person you're with."

"Very good," Keith said.

The markerboard squeaked as these points were added, but Jason's focus remained on William, whose expression was now slightly pained. He reached over to take Kelly's hand, placing it over a balled-up fist that eventually relaxed to allow their fingers to intertwine.

Jason turned his attention back to Keith. He wasn't completely surprised. Two super-hot gay guys were sitting next to each other. Of course they were together! Maybe part of him hoped they weren't, but he wasn't distraught over this. Like seeing a Ferrari driving down the street, he felt a sense of awe and a desire to hop behind the wheel, but reality soon caught up. Things like Ferraris—those were for other people. Not him.

"Humility," Jason said out loud.

Keith stopped writing and glanced over at him. "Humility?"

"Yeah," Jason said. "I don't want some guy I have to impress or one who feels like he needs to show off. I just want someone who loves me that I can love back. Simple as that. That's all it takes. I don't really care about honesty or being totally understood or any of the other stuff, because being human is all about messing up and breaking trust and telling lies. I wouldn't want to be with someone perfect. Just some humble, totally normal guy will do."

The room was silent; Jason's eyes met countless other pairs. Few seemed to get what he was saying except the girl Emma was interested in, who nodded her head in understanding. Kelly didn't look pleased. Finally Jason made eye contact with William, and he swore he saw recognition there. So they really did know each other?

"Humility," Keith said at last, writing it on the board. Then he took a step back. "So as you can see, we all have a lot of emotional needs, despite gender or sexuality. It's important not to give in to gender stereotypes or keep perpetuating them. Now let's pair up, boy-girl, boy-girl, and do some role-playing. Come on now, everybody find a partner."

"You take mine," Emma whispered. "I've got yours."

To his horror, she hopped to her feet and made a beeline for William. Like witnessing an impending disaster, Jason was torn between shielding his eyes and staring. He didn't need to do either, since the girl Emma liked soon occupied his field of vision.

"Jason, right?" she asked.

"Yeah, and you're… Sorry."

"Bonnie. It's okay. It took me tons of meetings before I got half the names down. You want to be partners?"

"Sure."

Keith explained their assignment, which involved pretending to be the opposite gender, and then pretending to be that gender pretending to be the other. Most of the group didn't seem to get this—Jason included—and chose instead to socialize. Bonnie sat next to him, dark eyes twinkling.

"I like what you said back there."

"Thanks," Jason replied. "I was kind of winging it."

"Well, it makes sense," Bonnie said. "I've been in a lot of relationships, and I can deal with the lying, arguing, cheating and almost everything else because love feels so good, even with all the baggage. But some people won't come down to your level or let you up onto theirs, and those are always bad relationships."

"Yeah." That wasn't exactly what Jason meant, but he was glad she got so much out of his impromptu speech.

"There's one thing you weren't totally honest about," Bonnie continued. "We all want someone we find attractive."

"True," Jason said, "but that kind of goes along with the rest of it. Sure, you can find someone attractive when you first look at them, but even the hottest guy or girl can get ugly when they open their mouths and say something stupid. Likewise, some people are hotter when you get to know them."

"I guess so," Bonnie said. "Speaking of which, your friend is cute."

"You think so?" Jason asked.

"Yeah. Do you think I'm her type?

Jason decided to play this carefully. "I'm sure she wouldn't be offended that you find her attractive."

"Hmmm. There's just one thing. How old is she?"

"How old are you?"

"Seventeen."

"Oh, well, she just turned sixteen, so you're not so far apart." A lie, of course, but Jason wanted to give Emma a fighting chance. "She lives out of town though, and still hasn't gotten her license."

Bonnie shrugged. "I have a car."

The rest of their conversation focused mostly on Emma, but Jason did nod to a few random people and ask who they were. He didn't really need to know, but he didn't want to ask about William immediately. Eventually though, he nodded to him.

"Do you mean Kelly or William?" Bonnie asked before shaking her head. "Doesn't matter since they're inseparable. It's too bad they can't breed. I bet they'd have beautiful children. Kelly has been coming here since he was thirteen. He was here the first time I showed up. That was before the accident."

"Accident?"

"Yeah. You didn't notice? Tell him that. It'll make him happy."

Jason stole a few glances at Kelly, looking him up and down. He looked perfectly normal—aside from being exceptionally hot. He was on the verge of asking Bonnie what she meant when he noticed a leg of the dark pants he wore was deflated toward the end. Kelly sat with one leg crossed over the other, but from the knee down, only flat denim remained. Jason didn't feel sorry for him, because he felt that would somehow be insulting. He took note of it as he would any other trait and turned his attention back to Bonnie.

"What about his boyfriend? What was his name again?"

"William," Bonnie said, not at all convinced by his ruse. "I don't know him that well, but he's just as sugary sweet as he looks. And hopelessly loyal to his boyfriend."

"Message received," Jason said. "Loud and clear."

"Sorry," Bonnie said.

"It's fine. Story of my life!"

Role-play came to an end, and everyone returned to their seats. Keith's lecture on relationships didn't last much longer, officially ending the group meeting, although everyone hung around to socialize. After whispering in Emma's ear that she was now sixteen, Jason left her to have her fun. He hung out with some of the other guys—avoiding both Kelly and William—and tried to be friendly even though he mostly just wanted to leave. After twenty minutes of this, Emma came to free him from his misery.

"Didn't work out?" he asked.

"Worked out fine!" Emma countered. "She has to go to work or we'd still be talking. And who knows what else!"

Jason chuckled, guiding them to the hall. "Think she'll visit you in Houston?"

"Was there ever any doubt?" Emma said. "And since we both know there was, yes. Yes, she is. Next weekend."

"Emma's first date!" Jason said.

"With a real lesbian, anyway," Emma said with a sigh. "An honest-to-goodness lesbian." Then, in a quieter voice, she whispered, "There's yours!"

Jason looked ahead. Down the hall, he saw Kelly first. The missing leg was obvious now, since one pant leg was folded up and pinned to keep it from dragging. Two crutches gripped his forearms and helped him move forward. He seemed comfortable enough using them. William was just ahead, and having reached a door, he opened it and held it open.

"You know I don't need help," Kelly snapped, breezing past him and outside.

"Trouble in paradise," Emma said, perhaps a little too loudly because William noticed them and kept the door held open.

Then she whispered something about running interference before picking up the pace. William playfully moved to the opposite side of the door while still holding it open, his arm becoming a bridge she had to duck under, but only just, since he was fairly tall. His figure was a silhouette against the daylight. Jason, barely able to make out his features, paid attention instead to the shape of his body—the broad chest, the narrow waist, the curved muscles of the arm he was about to pass under. Jason breathed in as he did so, taking in a scent that was chemical and yet clean. He struggled to place it. Not cologne. Whatever it was, he liked it. Then again, he seemed to like everything about William without actually knowing anything about him.

He could see Emma in the parking lot, talking to Kelly and not-so-casually moving back and forth to block them from view. Jason might not get another chance to talk to William alone, so he stopped and turned around.

"Have we met before?"

William stared at him, then laughed. "That's an old line." A second later he looked taken aback. "Wait, you're serious?"

Jason nodded. "Yeah. I feel like… okay, this is *really* going to sound like a line, but I feel like I know you."

William smiled again briefly, but this time with less amusement. Then he looked at Jason. Not at his features or at his body, but right into his eyes, like he was reading his soul.

"Hey!" Kelly yelled from somewhere behind them. "Are we going or what?"

William blinked, looked over Jason's shoulder, then back into his eyes again. "Sorry," he said. "I'm pretty sure we've never met. But now we have. See you at the next meeting?"

"Yeah," Jason said, even though he had no intention of being there. "I'll see you then."

He turned and walked diagonally across the parking lot, waiting by the car until Emma caught up with him.

"Well?" she asked.

"He's with someone," Jason said, getting into the car.

"I know that," Emma said as she settled into the passenger seat. "But I thought that maybe, I don't know, he might bonk you over the head and drag you by the hair back to his cave. That's what guys do, right?"

"Exactly," Jason said with a wry smile. "Unfortunately, Kelly is gorgeous, so I don't think William is going to ask me to be his cavewoman anytime soon. Or ever."

"You never know," Emma said. "I sensed tension."

"I sensed chemistry," Jason perked up. "Unless William said something to you about wanting to break up with Kelly?"

"Afraid not. But he didn't talk much about him either. I do know where William works, that he's still a senior in high school, and that he likes to swim."

Chlorine! That was the scent on his skin. Jason always liked how clean it smelled, how it brought back memories of summer days spent by the pool. "I don't suppose he told you where he swims?" Jason asked. "Maybe I can hang out in the bushes with some binoculars."

Emma put her hand on the door handle. "Want me to go ask?"

"No!" he said quickly, starting the car to discourage her from trying. "Thanks, but there's no point."

Emma crossed her arms over her chest. "I think you should go for it."

Jason put the car in reverse and shook his head. "Someone got there ahead of me, and honestly, even if William was single, I don't think he'd spare me two glances."

Emma scoffed. "You need to spend more time checking yourself out. There's such a thing as too much humility."

Jason looked into the rearview mirror, considering the eyes William had stared at only moments before. Grayish-blue rather than any certain color, and thick eyelashes that he worried made people think he wore mascara. The eyebrows a darker hue than his brown hair didn't help either. Then again, when taken all together, he supposed they weren't too bad.

"Stop," Emma said calmly.

"Huh?"

"Stop!"

Jason hit the brakes, noticing the rearview mirror was now full of an older man wearing an expression of terror.

"You almost ran over Keith," Emma pointed out.

Just one more embarrassment to add to the day's list. Jason definitely wouldn't be coming back for another meeting.

When Jason returned home with Emma in tow, they found Ben and Tim sitting on the back patio. Samson was prowling the yard, occasionally pouncing on what he saw in the grass. Chinchilla followed along behind, head cocked with interest as she watched the cat hunt. As charming as the scene was, Jason dreaded reporting how the youth group had gone. When Ben turned around, face eager for news, Jason made an excuse to return inside and stood in the kitchen. When enough time had passed that he was sure Emma had told them everything, Jason went back outside.

"Maybe you'll have better luck next time," Ben said.

"I'm not planning on going back." Jason sat cross-legged on the concrete. Emma plopped down next to him. "There's no point."

"Could be different guys there next time," Tim said.

"Exactly," Ben agreed. "Someone new or maybe a person who doesn't attend every single meeting."

"Maybe," Jason said noncommittally.

"He doesn't need a new guy," Emma said. "He likes William.

Don't you think he should go for it, Uncle Ben? Surely you of all people think he should!"

Ben looked puzzled. "What do you mean?"

"I mean how you met Tim. Have you told him that story yet?"

Ben smiled. "I was out rollerblading after school one day, and I was never a good skater—"

"No, how you really met Tim. Like the first time you saw him."

"Oh." Ben said.

"In the hallway, right?" Tim asked. "At school."

"No," Emma said. "Way before then. Tim was out jogging—"

"It really doesn't matter," Ben said quickly.

Tim shifted in his seat to face Ben. "You saw me when I was out jogging? Like before we ever met?"

"Once or twice," Ben admitted.

"More like a million times!" Emma chimed in.

Now Tim grinned. "So you went out looking for me on purpose? How long did this go on for?"

"Not long." Ben sighed. "Just the last month or so of summer."

"Oh, *just* a month," Tim said with a wicked smile. "Wow. I had my own stalker without even knowing it. Come to think of it, I always wondered how you already knew where I lived."

Ben sat upright. "That was a coincidence! Allison and I were out driving around, and I saw you mowing the lawn. I didn't follow you home. I'm not that creepy!"

"And I bet you never walked by my house at night?" Tim challenged.

"Before we met?" Ben asked. Then he laughed like he'd been caught doing something naughty. "Maybe once or twice." He turned a theatrical glare on his niece. "What does this have to do with anything, young lady?"

"You told me to always listen to my heart and go after what I want." Emma jerked a thumb at Jason. "He should do the same."

"This is different," Jason said in his own defense. "William already has a boyfriend. Tim was single when Ben went after him."

"Not exactly," Tim murmured. "I had a girlfriend."

"Krista Norman!" Ben said, comically shaking his fist in the air. "God, I hated her!"

"She wasn't that bad," Tim replied. "Anyway, what do you expect him to do, Emma? Unless you know where William lives and he happens to go jogging every night. Then Jason can pull a Ben, hide in the bushes—"

"I never hid," Ben said. "You just never noticed me."

"That's not true."

"It is."

Tim shook his head. "I refuse to believe it. The first time I saw you was in school, and you got into my head. Right away. You never left again, either."

Ben looked like he was about to argue further, but ended up making doe eyes at Tim.

"Juicy James," Emma said, sounding impatient. "That's where William works. I think it's one of those fruit juice places at the mall. All Jason has to do is start picking up a smoothie every day."

"The mall *is* right across from my work," he admitted reluctantly.

"Couldn't hurt to swing by," Ben said. "At the very least, you might make a new friend."

Or get his hopes up, or worse, his heart broken. As far as Jason was concerned, William was a lost cause. The sooner he forgot about him, the better.

Chapter Nineteen

A day off, and for the first time since coming to Austin, Jason had complete privacy. In the morning he walked the house, finding it empty. After a leisurely breakfast and a shower, he ventured out front, but even the garages were empty and still. Aside from Chinchilla and Samson, he had the house all to himself. Jason wasn't sure what to do with this privacy. He browsed some illicit sites on his computer for sexual relief, stretching out in bed afterwards and basking in the euphoria. He was still daydreaming when he turned his head and noticed the stack of boxes along the wall. All his old things he didn't need, taking up space and smelling like musty cardboard.

He planned to find a place for them in the garage, and was carrying a box in the hallway when a small rope dangling down from the ceiling caught his eye. The attic door was just outside his room, much closer than the garage. If it was a finished attic, he might find space for his things there. Setting down the box, he leapt up, snagged the rope, and pulled. A cross between stairs and a ladder folded out for him. Jason climbed a few steps and peeked. Sure enough, the attic had a proper floor and everything. Boxes and old furniture were up there already, making it the perfect place to store his belongings.

Jason brought up the first box, setting it down in the middle of the space as he glanced around. He saw an old lamp, an electric fan, and nearest to him, a stack of boxes. Leaning against this was a canvas, which he turned so he could view the front. Jason still hadn't seen Tim's art. Not properly. If this was one of his paintings, he was impressed. Depicted was a man near his own age, but one so pretty he'd hold his own against Kelly. The young man's hair was blond, the eyes blue, his features fine and fair. He seemed to be wearing a pink bathrobe, of all things, and a mischievous smile. Jason wondered if it was meant to be Ben and if the likeness was off, but the rest of the painting was too skilled for this to be true. The style struck him just as much as the subject's beauty, colorful light playing along every surface as if the young man was surrounded by rainbow-casting prisms.

Jason stared long and hard at the painting before turning his attention to the stack of boxes. He knew he shouldn't pry, but that's what made the idea so appealing. He opened the first box, finding an old Halloween mask. A werewolf. He put this on, looking around for something to see his reflection in and not finding anything. He dug through the rest of the box while still wearing the mask, discovering only old clothes, before he turned himself human and put it all back as he'd found it.

The second box was full of books—biographies mostly. The third box too. The very last box was mostly crushed by all the weight that had been placed on top. This one was full of brushes and mostly empty tubes of paint, as well as sheets stained with colors. He dug around in this disinterestedly, noticing a black sketchbook at the very bottom. Jason took this out and began flipping through it.

Some of the pages were full of drawings, others filled with messy handwriting. He paid attention to the sketches first, seeing a familiar person over and over again. He was much younger, and Tim's drawings weren't nearly as skilled as his painting, but Ben's grinning face was unmistakable. In one drawing, Ben wasn't smiling. Instead he rested his head on a pillow, his expression dreamy as he must have laid there and watched Tim draw him. Jason hovered on this image for quite some time, a yearning making his chest ache. He turned the page to spare himself any more discomfort, finding a tight column of text. Sketched next to it were two butterflies, one fluttering in the air while the other remained on the ground.

He tried to read the first line, hesitating when he saw it was written in Spanish. He'd taken a few years in school, and while his language skills were rusty, he scanned the text, trying to pick out familiar words. He didn't have much luck, but this looked like a poem. Jason skipped down to the last line, stuttering over the words.

"Ensuhnahm… No, wait. *Enséñame volar me merry—"*

The floor behind him creaked, and Jason's head whipped around. Tim was standing at the top of the attic stairs, brow furrowed. *"Enséñame a volar, mi mariposa hermosa,"* he said, reciting the line with perfect pronunciation. Silver eyes took in the boxes around Jason. "What are you doing up here?"

Jason stood, grasping for an excuse before realizing the truth would do. "I was looking for a place to store some stuff I don't need."

"Okay," Tim said, coming closer, "that's what you came up here to do. Now what are you actually doing?"

"Oh." Jason held out the sketchbook. "I like your drawings. They're really nice."

"No, they aren't." Tim took the sketchbook. After scowling down at the open page a moment, his features softened somewhat. "*¿Hablas español?*"

"Not really," Jason admitted. "How was my pronunciation?"

"Terrible," Tim said. "Or maybe my bad poetry is to blame."

"What's it about?" Jason asked.

"The usual," Tim said dismissively, closing the sketchbook.

"Oh, okay." Jason looked around, spotting the painting. "Is this your work? It's really great!"

"Thanks," Tim said, expression conflicted as he considered the permanently smiling face.

"Seems a shame to keep it up here," Jason said.

"Think so?" Tim exhaled. "I should probably sell it. I keep it up here because I can't bear to look at it, and yet I can't bring myself to throw it away, either."

"Whoever he is, he's hot. I'm sure it would sell lightning-fast."

Tim glanced over at him, then back at the painting. "His name was Ryan. *Is* Ryan, I guess I should say. It's not like he's dead or anything."

But he had been in the emergency room. On Jason's first night here, he had overheard Tim talking about Ryan. Back then he'd wondered if Tim and Ryan had a violent history together. Now he wasn't so sure, but he was cautious when he pried. "I take it you don't see him anymore?"

Tim shook his head. "There was a long period when Ben and I weren't together. That's where Ryan fit in. He needed something I couldn't give him. Yeah. That's probably the least complicated way of explaining it."

"Didn't end well?" Jason pressed.

"No." Tim laughed bitterly. "No, it certainly didn't." He turned the painting around again so the front couldn't be seen. Then he noticed something else and quickly walked to it. "Hey, did you see these already?"

Jason joined him as he opened a shoebox. Inside was a pile of jumbled photos.

"We had them all digitized," Tim explained. "Otherwise they wouldn't be up here. There aren't a lot of us together, but..."

Jason watched as Tim shuffled through the photos, catching a glimpse of Ben with a pretty black girl and a photo of Jace sleeping in an old chair, Samson curled up on his lap. An entire history flashed before his eyes, stopping on one image that Tim held out to him. Jason took it. The four-by-six glossy paper was a gateway to another world, a teenager's room, full of outdated things like the rack of CDs off to one side. Dead center, two guys younger than Jason sat on the edge of a bed. Both were instantly recognizable. Tim's hair was longer, and he appeared much more boyish than he did now, despite having more muscle than the average teenager. Next to him, Ben's hair was much lighter, his features a little smoother. Tim was jerking a thumb at Ben while grinning cockily at the camera. Ben, however, was staring at Tim with an expression like he couldn't believe his luck. The funny thing was, Jason had seen Ben giving Tim that same look just the other day.

"Ben's best friend, Allison, she took this one." Tim sighed wistfully. "Back then I didn't realize how much this photo would mean, or else we would have taken more together. Actually, I probably would have been too scared, but whatever."

Jason glanced up to see Tim looking at him and shaking his head.

"What?"

Tim grunted. "You make me feel old. You know that?"

"Sorry," Jason said.

"Don't be. Just don't waste it. I could have had so many more years with Ben if I'd made him my top priority."

Jason considered the photo again before handing it back. "You guys are so lucky. I'd give anything to have what you've got."

Tim took the photo, put it with the rest, and closed the box again. "That poem," he said when he turned around. "It's about how Ben seemed so small and weak at first, but once I got to know him, I realized I had never met anyone stronger. I wanted so badly to be like that, but I couldn't be. Not back then. Ben did all the work, chased after me no matter how hard I kept running. If he hadn't—" Tim exhaled. "I can't even imagine what my life would have been like. I know it wouldn't have turned out so good. Ben saw that we were meant to be together. Way back then, he knew it, even when I didn't. So maybe the same thing is happening with you."

"What do you mean?" Jason asked.

"I mean maybe you should start drinking juice on your lunch break, find out if this William guy has that same potential."

"I don't really know anything about him," Jason said.

Tim nudged him playfully. "That's my point. Go find out, and if he's not the guy, then don't stop looking. Besides, Ben won't rest until he gets you paired up with someone. Do it on your own terms, or you'll probably come home to find blind dates waiting for you."

Jason laughed. "Will they be hot blind dates?"

"Nope. They'd have to be desperate to drive all the way out here on a whim. No, I'm pretty sure they will be old and ugly, just like me."

Jason pretended to be repulsed. "In that case, I promise to find someone on my own."

"Good," Tim said. "Now let's get your stuff up here so we can seal this vault of memories. I'm enjoying the present too much to dwell on the past."

After all the boxes were put away and Tim went to scrounge up something for lunch, Jason lay on his bed and thought about everything he'd learned. Then he reached for his guitar, his body eager for something to do while his mind wandered. Except the guitar stand was empty. That was odd, since he never failed to put the instrument back in its proper place. In fact, he was downright neurotic about doing so, but he supposed no one was perfect.

Then again, the more he got to know Ben and Tim, the more he wondered if that was true. They sure seemed perfect to him.

"Have you seen my guitar?"

This became Jason's mantra over the next few days. He'd already searched the house many times—even the backyard—and kept asking this question of Ben and Tim more often than was sane. Jason called Emma to ask her, just in case this was a prank, and asked Chinchilla on the off chance she would lead him to his missing treasure. No luck, no matter which way he turned. This was his worst nightmare come true.

Not that it hadn't happened before. *Foster home number nine*. Some parents love to spoil their foster kids, give them everything they had missed out on. Most kids considered this ideal, although material gifts often made Jason uncomfortable, like he was obligated to act a certain way in return. Rarely did he feel that gifts came without strings attached. One family did seem generous without cause, and that was when his guitar went missing in the morning, replaced by a brand new one when he returned home from school. Jason had been distraught, flying off the handle and demanding to know where his real guitar was—the one his mother had given him. He threw a fit until his foster parents took him to the Salvation Army where they had donated his guitar. Jason had brought along the new one to exchange for it. Similarly, his foster parents had returned him to the group home later that week, no doubt choosing someone who suited them better.

Ben and Tim were also very generous. That, combined with Jason's upcoming birthday, was enough to make him suspicious. When the big day finally rolled around, Jason felt more eager than ever to get his present, just to see if he was right. Part of him hoped he wasn't, because he didn't want a new guitar. But if he *was* right, at least they might be able to tell him where the old one was. If it wasn't lost to the trash. Walking downstairs to the kitchen, he heard words that made him both excited and apprehensive.

"We found your guitar!" Ben said, standing next to the table with Tim at his side.

Jason rushed over and groaned. On the table was a cake in the shape of a guitar, *Happy Birthday Jason!!!* written across it in red frosting. "Thanks," he said, trying to manage a smile.

Tim shook his head while looking at Ben. "You're really cruel, you know that? Just give the boy his present."

"Fine," Ben said. "Go get it."

Tim strode out of the room, Jason sitting at the table and watching the doorway for his return. His stomach sank when Tim strolled in, holding a guitar by the neck. The instrument was wrapped, obscuring it from view, but there was no mistaking that outline. Jason's hands felt numb when he reached out to take it. Instead of opening it, he placed the present across his lap and kept his head down.

"Listen," he said. "I really appreciate this. I do. But the old one has sentimental value, and as much I'm sure I'll like this new guitar, I need the old one back."

"Sentimental value, huh?" Tim said.

"Yeah. My mom gave it to me when I was a kid."

"Oh." Ben looked worried. "Um... Okay. Maybe you should open your present. Then we can talk."

Jason nodded, trying to muster some excitement as he peeled back the paper one tear at a time. The new guitar was a lot like the old one. They must have gone out of their way to choose a similar style because— No, not similar, but exactly the same! Had they managed to find a brand new version of the old guitar, one that had never been used? He looked up in confusion, Ben grimacing in worry.

"I thought having it restored would be a nice gesture, but now I—"

"Restored?" Jason looked back down, tore away the rest of the paper and looked closely. The wood finish was perfect and glossy, the body without holes that shouldn't be there. The strings were brand new, and yet the tuning pegs had familiar wear to them, certain frets darker with oil from where his fingers played his favorite chords. "Holy shit!" he said. "It's like magic!"

"Bad magic?" Ben asked uncertainly.

"Good magic!" Jason said, breaking out into a laugh. "This is amazing!"

"Okay," Ben said. "I was starting to think all those scratches represented memories you might miss."

"No," Jason said. "The memory is in the guitar itself. And all the music it's made."

And music is exactly what he was hungry for. Jason wanted nothing more than to feel the guitar against his chest, summon the deep vibrations to echo through him.

"Why is he taking off his shirt?" Tim murmured.

"Uh..." Ben replied.

Jason was too excited to be self-conscious. He pressed the body of the guitar against his bare skin, exhaling happily at the familiar sensation.

"You need some private time with that thing?" Tim asked.

"Maybe later," Jason said, grinning wildly.

He felt unbelievably happy, so he chose a song that was just as goofy and started playing *La Bamba*. He even tried singing, making up fake Spanish, to which Tim shook his head. Ben noticed this and nudged him.

"Go on," he said. "I can't sing in Spanish, but I'm sure you can."

"No way!" Tim said.

"Yes way," Jason said, playing louder. "It's my birthday wish!"

Tim rolled his eyes, but when the chorus came around again, he gave it his best. His voice was dry and nearly toneless, but at least he knew the lyrics. Jason nodded encouragingly, laughing when Ben started shaking his hips and dancing around Tim, doing a samba. This helped Tim loosen up even more, and when he started moving his shoulders and looking at Ben with half-lidded eyes, Jason brought the song to an end. Otherwise they would end up on the table and ruin his cake.

"Sorry about the head trip," Ben said when he was done laughing. "I thought it would be a nice surprise."

"It's cool," Jason said, beaming down at the instrument. "This is the best present I've ever gotten."

"Can we eat some cake now?" Tim asked.

"Nope," Ben said. "You know how we do things in my family. Presents come first, and we have one more for you."

"Fine." Tim handed Jason another box. "Welcome to the 21st century."

Jason clawed through the paper to reveal an image of a grinning woman with a cell phone pressed against her ear. "My own phone?" Jason asked. "Nice! Now all I need are some friends."

Ben shook his head. "You've got us, Emma, Michelle—"

"And I've been thinking about getting Chinchilla her own phone," Tim said. "That way she can call when I need to rush home and let her out to pee."

Jason smiled. "Thanks. For both presents. They're amazing. Thank you!"

"You're very welcome," Ben said. "Now let's light some candles and have cake for breakfast. Do you know what you're going to wish for?"

"He already used his wish," Tim complained, but Ben hushed him into silence.

Jason's mind raced to come up with an appropriate wish. As soon as the last candle was lit, he knew what he wanted. After he blew them out, he turned to Tim.

"So can I?"

"Can you what?" Tim asked.

"Borrow your car."

Tim raised an eyebrow. "That was your wish?"

"No," Jason said. "But I need your car to go find out if my wish will come true or not."

Tim shook his head before realization dawned. "Heading to the mall?"

"Yeah," Jason said. "I have a sudden craving for a smoothie."

Chapter Twenty

The mall wasn't very busy on a Wednesday, but with school over for the day and most work shifts coming to an end, the corridors were slowly starting to fill. Including the food court. The Juicy James vendor had a Western theme, a cartoon mascot painted on the wall behind the counter that held two bananas like they were guns. The employees were expected to wear red-and-white checkered shirts and giant cowboy hats. The outfit was ridiculous and embarrassing, and yet one employee in particular still looked fetching. Jason viewed all of this from a distance, watching William smile as he served customers, as if he genuinely enjoyed his job.

Jason walked the mall a few times, trying to work up his courage. Then he realized how silly he was being. He didn't plan to reach across the counter and kiss the guy! All he wanted was a smoothie or whatever it was they served. Heart pounding, he got in line, eyes fixed on the menu posted above. In this manner he managed to reach the counter while appearing oblivious to who worked there.

"Hey!" said a familiar voice. "Haven't we met before?"

Jason looked at William and managed an expression of surprise he felt worthy of an Oscar. He even added a touch of confusion at the end, like he needed time to recognize who this strange person was. Then he got the joke William had made.

"Met before?" Jason said. "No. Sorry, don't think so." He smiled to show he was only kidding.

William's smile widened in return. "Jason, right?"

"That is correct. And you are—" He read the nametag pinned to the checkered shirt. "Wild Wild Will?"

"Yeah." William's ivory skin turned a little pink. "They force us to choose ridiculous nicknames."

"I like it," Jason lied.

"Thanks. So, what can I get you?"

Jason blanked. Despite how long he'd stared at the menu, he actually hadn't read it. "Uh, what do you recommend?"

"I always get the protein power smoothie," William replied. "Actually, I'm about to go on lunch break. Want to keep me company?"

Behold the power of birthday wishes!

"Sure," Jason said casually enough.

"Great. Tell you what, your smoothie is on the house. Meet me over by the pizza place? That way I can grab something to eat."

"Okay," Jason agreed, getting out of line so the next customer could be served.

He casually reached up to check his hair as he walked to the pizza vendor. His breath was still minty fresh since he'd brushed his teeth before leaving and then chewed almost an entire pack of gum while walking the mall. Jason felt awkward waiting by the pizza place and hated the idea of standing in line with William, so he went ahead and ordered two of their giant slices. He had them in hand when William walked over.

"You got the drinks," Jason said. "I've got the food."

"Oh, great! Thanks!"

Jason glanced around at the tables, most of which were covered in crumbs and greasy smears. "So should we…"

"I usually eat outside," William said. "Escape the chaos for a little bit."

"Okay."

Jason followed him out the nearest door. Ahead of them was the parking lot, but to the side was a little bench and a few potted plants. William sat first, a leg on each side of the bench, like someone perching the wrong way on the end of a diving board. This made Jason happy, since it meant he could do the same and they would be facing each other. On the wooden space left between them, Jason laid out the pizza and William offered a smoothie in a Styrofoam cup.

"I hope Canadian bacon is okay," Jason said.

"It's my favorite! How'd you know?"

"I've been stalking you for weeks," Jason said, relieved when William laughed instead of looking terrified. As nervous as Jason had been, he felt oddly comfortable now. He remained on edge, sure, but also had no trouble being himself.

"Good choice," William said, taking a bite of the pizza. Normally the slices looked huge, but William had big hands, making it appear average at best. "I *love* Canadian bacon."

"It's delicious," Jason agreed. "I do wonder how they get the Canadian pigs all the way down here. Think there's a passenger train they all ride together?"

William's eyes twinkled at his humor. "Yeah. I bet the really fat pigs get to sit in the first-class wagon."

"And the poor skinny pigs have to ride with all the luggage."

William shook his head while smiling. "So what are you up to today? Out doing some shopping?"

That would have been an obvious cover, but Jason didn't have any bags with him. "Just stretching my legs," he said. "I actually work across the street at the pet store. I'm off today, but I always come here for lunch. I guess it's a habit."

"Then I'm surprised I've never seen you before," William said.

Probably because what Jason really did was sit in his car and eat the sandwich he made every morning. "This is my first smoothie," Jason said. "I'll be honest with you. I'm terrified."

"Don't be. I made it myself. You're perfectly safe."

Jason exhaled in exaggerated relief and took a sip. The smoothie tasted like bananas and… powder? He guessed that was the protein component. "So is this your secret?" he asked, nodding at William's chest. The buttons of the checkered shirt were struggling to hold the cloth together over his pecs.

"What do you mean?"

"Uh…" Jason wished he hadn't said anything. "You're in really good shape."

"Oh!" William's cheeks turned pink again. "Thanks. I actually just like how the protein powder tastes. Is it gross?"

"No!" Jason said. "I was just hoping I'd get great boobies like yours."

William chuckled. "In that case, all you have to do is go swimming every day."

"Every day?"

William nodded. "Every morning, actually. Before school. And sometimes after work if I'm not too tired."

That definitely explained the body, but not something else. "Don't take this the wrong way," Jason said, "but you don't look like a swimmer."

"Because I'm pale?" William asked. "Irish skin. Can't be helped. I'll get a little more tan in the summer, but not before burning a few times. Luckily, the YMCA has an indoor pool."

"That explains it," Jason said, forcing himself to pull his eyes away from William's body. This wasn't hard, because he loved his face. Jason could stare into those happy eyes all day long. And he liked how unselfconscious William seemed. Not in an exceedingly confident way, like Emma, but almost as if he didn't realize how hot he was or even how doofy the oversized cowboy hat looked. Any other guy would have ditched it before going on break, but not William. Then again, maybe he wasn't concerned with what Jason thought about his appearance.

"So what did you think of the youth group?" William asked.

"It was okay, I guess," Jason said. "I think I'd like it better if everyone just showed up to hang out."

William swallowed the last of his pizza and shook his head. "That's happened before when we were between group leaders. Everyone formed their little cliques and stopped talking to each other. The lesbians were on one side, the gay guys on another, and even those two camps split into smaller groups. Keith gets everyone interacting. I know his lectures can be a little tedious at times, but without him we're a mess. Are you coming to the next meeting?"

He looked genuinely eager for him to be there, so Jason nodded. "I'll give it another try."

"Good."

William's eyes darted to Jason's pizza, which hadn't been bitten into yet, so Jason offered it, insisting he wasn't really hungry. He sucked on his smoothie instead, watching in amusement as William practically inhaled the slice. A big guy like him probably went through a lot of food. Jason imagined himself as a housewife, cooking huge meals and creating elaborate table spreads for when William returned home from work. He came out of this fantasy to find William watching him too.

"Are you still in school?" he asked.

"No," Jason said. "I'm done with high school, and I'm not sure about college. Right now I'm working full time to save up some cash. What about you?"

"High school senior," William said. "After I graduate—" He checked his watch. "Well, it's too complicated to explain now. I have to get back to work soon."

"Oh." Jason felt panicked at the idea of their time together ending, mostly because he didn't see how this would happen again. Unless he showed up at this same time every day and kept buying pizza slices as bait. That wouldn't do at all. Jason wanted more than to be stuck with William at a loud and greasy food court. A breeze blew across the parking lot, the wind whirling around the area they were in, bringing with it a hint of chlorine and a little inspiration.

"Do you give swimming lessons?" Jason asked.

William sucked on his straw and shook his head, appearing puzzled.

"It's just that I never learned," Jason lied. "I've been meaning to take a class for years, but the idea of being with a group of little kids is embarrassing."

"You really don't know how?" William asked.

Jason shrugged innocently. "Just never got around to it."

"I guess I could try," William said. "You willing to get up early?"

Jason would happily sacrifice sleep if it meant getting to be around him. "Yeah." He whipped out his new phone. "Let's trade numbers. That way we can talk and set up a date."

William reached into a pocket to get his own phone, looking somewhat skeptical. "I hope I don't sound like a jerk for asking this," he said, "but you know I have a boyfriend, right?"

"Yeah," Jason said. "You and Kelly are together. That's totally cool. I have a boyfriend too."

"You do? What's his name?"

"Tim." It was the first name that came to mind, and Jason instantly wished he could take it back.

"Oh, okay. I didn't want there to be any mixed signals. Well, not mixed signals … I just don't want Kelly to get hurt."

Jason nodded. "Of course not." His cheeks started to flush, so he focused on programming William's name into his phone. Townson turned out to be his last name, and his number was equally as mundane. When they finished exchanging info, Jason stood. "I should probably go."

"Okay." William stood and wiped his hands on his jeans. "You'll call, right? To make plans?"

"Yup," Jason said. "I promise."

Hugging was out of the question and shaking hands seemed too formal, so Jason simply gave a little wave, turned, and walked into the parking lot. He kept walking all the way to the end of the lane, because his car was parked on the opposite side of the mall. When he was forced to turn around, he was relieved to see that William had gone back inside. He took a deep breath, asked himself what the hell he was doing, then decided he didn't have time to worry about it. What Jason really needed to do was practice flailing in the water, like he couldn't swim.

William strode across the parking lot toward the YMCA, a duffel bag slung over one shoulder, looking fresh and energized despite it being six in the morning. Jason slouched along behind, still trying to wake up completely.

"Ready for this?" William asked, flashing a smile.

"No," Jason admitted.

"Don't be nervous," William said. "You're in good hands."

That's what worried Jason. When he'd hatched this little scheme, he hadn't considered all the implications. A swimming pool meant swim suits. Jason wasn't exactly insecure about his body. Being tight on cash meant he ate sparingly, so he didn't have an ounce of fat on him. Seeing William in nothing but a swimsuit... *That* troubled him! Jason had gone shopping for a pair of swim trunks he hoped didn't reveal too much, just in case he lost control.

William led the way inside, flashing a membership ID and waiting patiently while Jason paid for admission. Then he led them to the locker room where they could change. Once William had chosen a locker, Jason moved an aisle over to find one for himself. Maybe this seemed weird. Hopefully it communicated he wasn't there to gawk at William getting undressed. Not that he was against the idea, but what Jason really wanted to figure out was if they had any romantic potential. Was this just another hormone-powered infatuation, or was William the kind of guy he could love?

Jason had just pulled up his swim trunks when William came around the corner, towel slung over one shoulder. Harnessing every ounce of willpower he possessed, Jason kept his attention fixed squarely on William's face.

"Ready for your first lesson?"

"I think so," Jason replied.

"Let's go!"

William led the way out of the locker room, allowing Jason to scope him out from behind. His shoulders were broad, his back muscles toned, but not to a hardened extreme. Even more of William's milky skin was exposed, Jason imagining it would feel soft as silk and be ideal to cuddle up against. Jason's thoughts weren't completely innocent, since the Speedos showed off an ass that looked bulletproof. And speaking of hard, Jason decided he'd better redirect his train of thought lest he suffer embarrassing consequences.

The indoor pool was large, the deeper side dedicated to swimming lanes. William led them around to the shallow end where steps descended into the water. He waded in, turning around once the water reached his waist to check on Jason. He was doing fine, of course. Normally by now he would have dunked himself under the water to get completely wet, but he supposed he should pretend to be apprehensive.

"Okay," William said. "The first thing you should learn is how to tread water. Do you think you can handle that? We'll go a little deeper, but your head will still be above the surface. Once there, you'll kick both your legs, sort of like you're running in place."

"Yeah," Jason said, feeling stupid. "I can handle that."

Together they waded into deeper water. Jason felt it would be silly if an adult couldn't handle this step, so he didn't pretend to be incapable.

"That was easy," William said. "Uh, let's see. I guess next it would helpful if you learned to float. If you start to panic, try to remain calm. Let yourself go perfectly still, allow your legs to drift forward as you recline, and you'll end up on your back. You won't need to kick or anything. You'll be safe."

"Okay," Jason said. "Let's try it."

"I'll support you."

William came close and put an arm around his shoulder, and as Jason's legs floated upward, put an arm beneath them too. This should have been a thrilling moment, William touching him for the first time, but Jason felt uncomfortable. Like when he got his hair washed before a cut, he was left staring awkwardly up at the ceiling. He supposed now was a good time to flail, like he was horribly uncomfortable.

He turned his head to the side, about to do just that, and found his face ridiculously close to William's, which wore an expression of encouragement.

"You're doing great!" he said.

Jason's stomach felt heavy with guilt, like he'd swallowed a fistful of lead. How far would he let this go? Was he really going to have William teach him the basics, and then accept his praise when Jason pretended to swim on his own for the first time?

"Listen," he said. "I have to confess something. I know how to swim."

The smile left William's face. "What?"

"I can swim. I'm not great, but—"

"You're serious?" William interrupted. "You can swim?"

"Yeah."

"In that case…" William removed the arms supporting Jason and used them to dunk him instead. Jason was so shocked that he swallowed a mouthful of water before he started kicking himself to the surface again. When he did, he saw William cutting a line through the pool with a strong stroke that took him to the deep end. He turned around once there, shook his head as if in disgust, and started doing laps down one of the lanes. Jason couldn't possibly keep up with him, so he got out of the pool and walked around to where William was swimming.

He didn't know how to get his attention or make him stop, so Jason jumped right into the lane. William was still plowing along and wasn't expecting someone to be in his way, so they collided. The collision was less painful than it would have been out of water, but a whole lot of muscle still slammed into Jason.

"What are you doing?" William spluttered.

"Just let me explain!"

William treaded in place, eyes distrusting. "Fine."

"Uh," Jason said, realizing his explanation was just as crazy as his actions. He didn't have time to come up with a good lie, so he settled for the truth. "There's something about you. When I saw you in the meeting the other day, it's not like I was all 'Oh, he's hot! I think I'll go after him!' I mean, you are, but that's not why I'm here exactly. It's hard to explain. When I saw you, something inside of me felt… drawn to you."

To his surprise, William's features relaxed somewhat. He didn't even look confused. "I have a boyfriend," he said.

"I know," Jason said. "You and Kelly make a gorgeous couple, and I'm not deluded enough to see myself replacing him. I didn't come here to try to hook up with you, I swear. But I do want to get to know you. That's all. Nothing creepy. At least, nothing beyond what I've already done. Asking for swimming lessons just seemed like a convenient excuse."

William snorted, but those gentle green eyes searched his. "You should have just said you want to hang out."

"I know," Jason said. "I'm not very good at making friends. I never have been."

William considered him a moment longer. "So now what?"

"Well," Jason said, "I *can* swim, but I don't really know any techniques. I just sort of kick while underwater, but aside from that and dog-paddling, I'm not real good. I can't swim across the surface like you do."

"So you *do* want lessons?" William asked incredulously.

Jason tried a smile. "That's what we're here for."

William shook his head but looked amused. "Okay. Time for the advanced course."

Jason was taught the front crawl stroke, which despite its name was the stroke William had been using to zip down the lanes. He didn't shy away from supporting Jason a second time so he could practice how to move his arms correctly. This made Jason feel his lie was forgiven. At least until William suggested they start doing laps. Then he became a drill sergeant. An adorably sweet and soft-spoken drill sergeant, maybe, but every time Jason said he was going to take a break, William denied him.

"One more lap." Jason soon lost count of how many times he was told "just one more" but he understood this was his penance and pushed himself like never before. Eventually, his choice became either to quit or die of exhaustion.

Jason climbed out of the pool, sitting on the edge and watching William complete more laps. When he noticed Jason had stopped, he swam over to him. "Hop back in," he said. "Just one more."

Jason shook his head. "If you want to kill me, there are easier ways than this."

William grinned, arms flexing as he pushed down against the pool's edge to lift himself upward, water coursing over his body. Then he turned around and sat next to Jason, chest muscles looking bigger than ever from exertion. "I suppose I can take it easy today."

Jason nearly gasped. "You're kidding, right?"

"Nope. I push myself every single day. I need to if I'm going to become a rescue swimmer."

"Is that like a lifeguard?" Jason asked.

William laughed. "Yeah, except instead of sitting in a chair by the pool, you get dropped from a helicopter into massive waves. If a plane crashes into the ocean, a boat goes down, or if people need rescuing during inland floods, that's when a rescue swimmer is called in. It's not easy to become one, but I figure I've got a shot if I keep training every day."

"Where do you go to learn something like that?" Jason asked. "Superhero school?"

"The Coast Guard," William said. "Or the Navy, but I don't want to go international. It won't be easy either way. Most people don't make it through the AST program, but I've been planning this for years. I really think I've got what it takes."

If the condition of his body and his determination had anything to do with it, William shouldn't have any trouble. "Not that you need a reason to help people, but what's your motivation? Following in the footsteps of your father?"

"Nope. My father is a roofer, so his only time spent in the water is when it rains. I've always liked to swim. Once I learned how, anyway." William's brow furrowed. "Maybe that's the real reason why. When I was a kid, I was visiting my cousins for the summer. They had a private pool. A great big one. That family had a lot of money at the time, and my cousins were always swimming. I didn't know how, so I'd remain on the sidelines, feeling embarrassed. They teased me unmercifully. When I'd had enough, I decided to teach myself. I knew they'd make fun of me for trying, so I waited until late at night and snuck out back."

"Not the best idea," Jason said.

"Definitely not." William's attention was beneath the water, where he was gently kicking his feet back and forth. "I'm sure you've heard people say the best way to teach a kid is to throw them in. I hope that's a joke, but at the time I took it seriously. So I went to the deep end and jumped right in."

"What happened?" Jason asked.

"I panicked. I hadn't even remembered to hold my breath before I jumped, so I got a nice drink of water on my way down. I actually touched bottom. Just the tips of my toes, but that scared me even more. I tried to— Don't laugh, but I tried to call for help, which obviously made things worse. My arms and legs were kicking and waving in every direction, and eventually I just accepted I was going to die. That's when I went still and felt my body rise. In a split second, I remembered all those TV shows where a body is found floating in the water. I figured that must be possible without having to die, so that's what I did. I floated on up, got myself turned over, and started coughing up water and choking in air."

"Which totally explains why you love swimming so much," Jason said.

William chuckled. "You want to know what I did next? I floated over to the shallow end of the pool, got out, caught my breath, and jumped right back in."

"Into the deep end?"

"Yeah. Right back to where I was. The second time all I did was stay calm and let myself bob back to the surface like a cork. I kept doing little things like that, figuring out how to swim piece by piece. To this day I've never taken a swimming lesson."

Jason leaned over, let their bare shoulders bump briefly. "You're kind of awesome."

William shook his head. "We'll see about that. AST school is going to kick my ass. If I make it through and become a rescue swimmer, then you can call me awesome. If you still want to."

"I'm pretty confident I will," Jason said.

For a moment, all that could be heard was the gentle lapping of the pool and echoes of voices elsewhere in the YMCA.

"It's nice to have company," William said, glancing over at him. "I've gotten used to swimming alone."

"So Kelly never… I mean, can he?"

"It's possible." William turned back to the water. "I've seen videos online of people swimming with just one leg. It takes determination, which Kelly has in spades, but he doesn't want to. He could at least keep me company, sit there like you are now."

This time when William looked over, his eyes ran up and down Jason's body. Was this a good thing? Or was William wishing he saw Kelly there instead?

"I don't know if I can handle this every morning," Jason said, "but I could definitely imagine doing it again."

William nodded. "Good. You've got my phone number. Or you can just show up. I'm here seven days a week, same time every morning. Speaking of which…"

"Yeah," Jason said, getting to his feet. "I have to be at work soon."

"And I have to go to school," William said without much enthusiasm. They were nearing the locker room when he spoke again. "What are you doing this weekend?"

"Nothing besides work on Saturday."

"Day shift?"

"Yeah."

William was silent for a moment. "A friend of mine is having a cello recital, and she's nervous about it, so she wants a big support group there."

"Really?" Jason said. "I'd want as few people to show up as possible."

William laughed. "Yeah, me too. Anyway, maybe you could come along."

"I'd love to," Jason said.

"Good. I'll be with Kelly. Maybe you could bring Tim."

"Tim?" Jason asked.

"Your boyfriend. That's his name, right?"

"Yeah! I'm just surprised you remembered."

William shrugged. "We can make a double date of it. Grab something to eat afterwards. Sound good?"

Jason shook his head subconsciously. "Sounds perfect!"

"I am *not* going on a date with a teenager!"

"Ahahaha!" Ben replied, which wasn't too surprising because he'd done nothing but laugh for the past five minutes.

Jason stood in front of the couch, looking back and forth between them and growing more frustrated by the minute. "I didn't say you have to. I was just explaining what happened." He glared at Tim. "But I can't show up there alone!"

"I'm ten years older than you!" Tim said, looking panicked. "Is that even legal?"

"How old was that Ryan guy?" Jason retorted. "In the painting he looks younger than me!"

"Ohohoho!" Ben said.

"Ryan *was* younger than you, and at the time, I wasn't so damn old!"

"Heeee!" Ben said, wiping his eyes and trying to pull himself together. "You know, this might just work!"

"Oh god," Tim said, sinking into the couch cushion behind him. "He thinks it's a good idea. I might as well give up now."

"Think about it," Ben said, trying to keep a straight face. "Remember when I got all upset about you and Krista Norman being together? What if I had shown up at school with a super-hot guy on my arm?"

"One ten years older than you?" Tim demanded. "He would have been arrested on sight. Besides, where would you find a guy hotter than me?"

"What makes you think you're hotter than William?" Jason asked.

Tim raised an eyebrow.

This sent Ben into another fit of giggles, leaving Tim and Jason staring each other down, arms crossed over their chests.

"You know what?" Jason said. "I'll take Ben with me. We'll just pretend his name is Tim."

"No," Ben said, shaking his head. "It needs to be Tim. Someone to really make them envious. I'm sure William is very handsome, but just look at my man!" Ben pinched one of Tim's cheeks and jiggled it, causing him to look vindicated.

"We'll take my car too," Tim said. "Just wait until they get a load of that!"

Jason fought down a smile. "You're so superficial."

"Oh yeah?" Tim said. "In that case, I'll load up the back seat with painting supplies and show off my deep and thoughtful artistic side. This William guy isn't going to know what hit him!"

Now Jason really did smile. "Then it's a date?"

"Damn straight," Tim said, glowering. "Just don't expect me to put out."

"Stop!" Ben pleaded. "I'm going to pee my pants!"

"See that?" Tim asked. "Hot, artistic, *and* funny!"

Jason pretended to be impressed. "I'm a lucky guy! Remember that when I break up with you. Just one date, and then we're through."

Chapter Twenty-one

The Bates Recital Hall was located on the University of Texas campus, which only added to Ben's insistence that this outing was a good idea. Tim drove them there early, walking the campus and playing tour guide. Occasionally he would smile at undisclosed memories or shake his head at others. The university was nice, but that had never been Jason's fear. He still didn't know what he wanted to do with his life, and creating a debt by studying a random subject for four years didn't seem smart.

"Let's head back to the car," Tim said, checking his watch.

"We can just walk to the recital hall," Jason replied.

"They need to see us pulling up in the Bentley," Tim insisted. "Tonight is all about making an impression."

Tim was definitely doing just that, looking absolutely stunning in a white dress shirt that contrasted nicely with his Latino skin. The fabric was thin and gauzy, providing a teasing glimpse of the body beneath. The tight gray slacks were revealing in their own way, although Jason was trying hard not to look in that direction. Tim's dark hair was swept at an angle across his forehead, the three-day beard carefully cultivated. That he looked gorgeous was no surprise, but now Jason worried he'd stand out even less than usual while next to him.

Not that he hadn't tried to look his best. Ben had helped him pick out a navy blue dress shirt and brown pants. His hair could still use a trim, which is just how he liked it. He'd felt pretty confident until he walked down the stairs and saw Tim, but he supposed that was what he'd asked for. William would see him with a super-hot guy and instantly decide Jason wasn't desperate. He might even wonder what Jason could offer a guy like Tim, adding a layer of mystique. Of course, right below that fabricated layer was the desperation he was trying to conceal, but whatever. Fake it until you make it.

"There won't be any parking by the recital hall," Tim murmured to himself as he drove. Then louder he said, "I'll drop you off out front. That's where we're meeting them, right?"

"Yeah," Jason said. "Right by the door. Actually, there they are."

William and Kelly were waiting by the curb. They flinched when Tim tapped on the horn and pulled over. Everyone else in the vicinity looked too. Jason's face was already turning red.

"I'll find a parking space and meet you by the front door," Tim said. "Don't try to kiss me or anything, all right?"

"I'm not going to kiss you!" Jason said, sounding like a temperamental child, which made the vibe in the car even weirder. Trying to play it off as a joke, he added, "Don't embarrass me in front of my friends."

Tim rolled his eyes. "I wouldn't dream of it!"

Jason opened the car door, his nervousness dissipating when he saw William. He was wearing… oh, something. Jason didn't care much about that because he loved his face, the goofy, slightly shy smile, the blond bangs that the wind had blown into disarray, and those emerald eyes which were shining just for him. Or maybe they shined for Kelly, decked out all in black and looking like a sexy panther ready to spring on anyone foolish enough to touch his property.

"Hi," Jason said, making sure to shake hands with Kelly first. "Nice to see you again."

"Yes," Kelly replied. "How unexpected too. We didn't really talk at all during the meeting, and yet, here you are."

"Yeah," Jason said, uncertain of how to respond. Instead he turned and shook hands with William, which seemed too impersonal. Sure they had only met a few times, but that feeling of familiarity remained.

"Should we wait here while your boyfriend parks?" William asked.

"No, we can head toward the entrance," Jason said. "He'll find us."

"That's quite the car he has," Kelly commented as they began walking. "Expensive too. Is your boyfriend Richie Rich or is he an older guy?"

"He's a little older than me, yeah." Jason felt amused. No doubt they were picturing a gray-haired sugar daddy.

"Have you been together long?" Kelly pressed.

"We live together," Jason said. "It's pretty serious."

Kelly's crutches hit the ground harder, as if he was trying to crack the concrete. "Now why should that concern me?"

Ah ha. So Kelly *was* feeling suspicious, despite thinking that Jason had a boyfriend. He felt bad about that, so he decided to make Kelly's relationship with William the topic, hoping that acknowledging it would show he respected it. "How long have you guys been together?"

"A few years now," William replied.

"Wow!" Jason didn't need to fake his awe. "High school sweethearts, huh?"

"That's right," Kelly said, voice sounding a little warmer. "It was love at first sight."

Jason shot a quick glance at William and saw his brow furrowed up, like he didn't quite agree. "So how did you two meet?"

"We were training for a triathlon," Kelly said. "William is the school's best swimmer, and at the time I was the best runner—believe it or not—so we decided to team up."

"Not quite," William said. "You cornered me in the hallway and said no matter how good I was at swimming, that I'd never keep up with you on foot."

Kelly smiled. "And then you showed up at the track that afternoon to really start training. So I started showing up at the pool..."

"Not exactly love at first sight," William said.

Kelly raised an eyebrow. "Speak for yourself. So Jason, how did you meet your man?"

"Oh. Our story isn't nearly as good as yours," he said, playing for time.

Luckily, one of the most ostentatious distractions possible showed up, placing a possessive arm around him.

"Hey, sweet cheeks," Tim said, beaming at him in a way normally reserved for Ben.

"Uh," Jason replied, legs feeling weak.

Tim's smile intensified as he brought his face close to Jason's. For one terrifying moment, he thought they really were going to kiss, but Tim's lips went for his ear instead.

"You don't look happy to see me," he whispered.

Jason recovered himself and put on a smile, which was good since it probably appeared he was reacting to something amorous Tim had said. He made hasty introductions, Tim pumping their hands and sizing up each of them before turning back to Jason.

"So, honey, where's that music you promised me?"

"Right this way," Jason said. And then, just for good measure he added, "darling."

They walked in pairs toward the entrance, William and Kelly in the lead, exchanging glances with each other. Tim seemed amused. Jason still felt nervous, even though their scheme was working. William looked back at Tim, eyeing him and the arm still firmly wrapped around Jason's shoulders. That arm felt good too—warm and muscular. Jason pretended it belonged to William instead.

"So, Tim," Kelly said as they took their place in line. "We were just asking Jason how you two met."

"Do you want to tell it?" Tim asked Jason.

He shook his head, hoping to communicate that he didn't have a good story.

"Okay," Tim said. "Well, it's a little embarrassing really. I was on my way downtown to do some shopping when I saw this handsome guy walking down the street." He squeezed Jason closer. "So I parked the car as quick as I could and headed to where I'd seen him last. Luckily he had stopped to look at a window display, and I walked up behind him, checking out his reflection in the glass. He saw me too, and when he turned around—" Tim shrugged helplessly. "We just hit it off!"

"Interesting," Kelly said. "Is that something you do a lot? Pulling over when you see a guy you find attractive?"

"Never before," Tim said. "Not once. But come on! Look at him! Aren't his eyes intense? They sort of burrow into your soul, don't they? Or the way he clenches his jaw when he feels embarrassed. Or his messy messy hair." Tim ruffled it affectionately. "But really, those eyes are his best feature. Or maybe his lips, because man, the first time I kissed him..." Tim made a face like he'd just eaten something spicy. "And if music is your thing, this boy can play the guitar! He's the one who should be up there on stage tonight. Then we'd be in for a treat!"

"Thanks," Jason said, and he meant it too, because he'd never expected Tim to put a positive spin on him like that. Even now, Kelly was openly reassessing him. William's expression wasn't as easy to read, but his lips were downturned. Was he unhappy? Unconvinced?

The line had moved forward enough for them to enter the recital hall. The person who took their tickets gave them each a program and asked them to proceed directly to their seats, since they were already behind schedule. The hall itself was elegant, with wood-paneled walls and low lighting that lent atmosphere. Directly ahead of them and above the stage was a huge organ bristling with silver and brass pipes. Theater seating descended from their high vantage point until reaching the ground floor.

"We're in the front row," Kelly said. "One of the perks of being handicapped, although they didn't tell me about all these damn stairs."

"I think there's an elevator," Jason said.

"It's fine," Kelly snapped.

He slowly made his way down each step, swearing a few times. Despite his head being held high, he avoided making eye contact while taking a seat. Jason wondered how new all of this was to him, if whatever had caused him to lose a leg was recent history.

Jason ended up seated between Kelly and Tim, which wasn't his preference but probably for the best, since it would be less distracting. Or so he thought. Jason kept watching the happy couple out of the corner of his eye. When William reached over to take Kelly's hand, he felt pressured to do the same. Tim's hand was on the arm rest. Jason reached for it, but when he got near, Tim grabbed the theater program, keeping both hands on it as he read. Or pretended to. The pages weren't turning, but he did casually elbow Jason's arm away.

Fair enough. Jason turned his attention to the stage where a piano and a number of other instruments waited. Above these was an artificially low ceiling that blocked the organ and the true ceiling of the hall from view, probably to improve acoustics. Playing here would be a thrill. Jason didn't crave an audience, but he would like to experience an environment optimized for sound. As the lights went down, he found himself genuinely excited.

The recital began with a female vocalist accompanied by piano, her voice effectively silencing the audience and leaving them rapt. She was obviously scheduled first to grab their attention, which was good because the subsequent dueling banjos followed by a painfully long accordion demonstration felt more suited to a high school talent show. Before Jason could lose faith, a violin and acoustic guitar duet swept him off his feet again. He was so dazzled by this performance that he didn't notice the next musician on stage until she started playing. The young woman wasn't dressed for the occasion, wearing instead a concert T-shirt and ripped jeans, which were a stark contrast to the elegant instrument held before her. This was the cellist William and Kelly had come to support, but what surprised Jason was that he knew her too.

As Bonnie coaxed a baleful tune out of the cello, he smiled to himself. Emma would be jealous when she found out he'd seen her crush performing on stage. He was tempted to use his cell phone to record footage for her. As the song reached a gentle lull, Bonnie cast her eyes over the front row, giving a little nod in their direction and smiling when she spotted someone else farther down from them. Family, maybe. The song demanded her attention again, Bonnie closing her eyes as she expertly stroked her instrument. Jason wondered how different the cello would be from a guitar. If given a day to play with the instrument, could he get such a beautiful sound out of it, even for one moment?

The song increased in pace, sounding like a chase through a dark forest or a coven of witches summoning bad magic up on a hilltop. Bonnie considered the audience again, eyes intense, but this time she looked to only one place. His curiosity getting the better of him, Jason leaned forward casually and glanced down the row. He practically fell out of his seat, because even beneath the pile of styled hair and carefully applied makeup, the face lit up like it was her wedding day was unmistakable. Emma!

Jason leaned back in his chair, eyes still wide. What was she doing here? But it wasn't hard to guess. Bonnie must have driven to Houston to pick her up, just so she could be here tonight. He doubted very much that Emma had done so with her parents' permission, or else they would have gotten Ben involved. Besides, Emma was still in the closet. Jason very carefully turned to Tim, making sure he hadn't seen the same thing. Tim's attention remained on the stage, a flicker of irritation manifesting when he caught Jason staring at him.

Okay. No crisis yet. As soon as the recital was over, he needed to get Tim out of here as quickly as possible. Bonnie left the stage to a round of applause, a series of performers taking her place. Most of them were exceptional, drawing Jason back into the show. When the lights came up again, he hopped to his feet, ready to go, but Kelly was in no hurry. Not only that, but he needed time to get up all those stairs. Jason could hardly rush him. The lobby was full when they got there, people mingling, having drinks, and burbling with excited conversation.

"We're supposed to meet Bonnie here," William said.

"Actually, I could use some fresh air," Jason said, taking hold of Tim's arm. "Coming?"

Tim shrugged him off, eyes on the bar. "I need a drink."

"You're the designated driver," Jason reminded him.

"Then I'll have a very small drink."

As Tim wandered off, Jason forced his gritted teeth to resemble a smile. William and Kelly weren't paying attention anyway, searching the crowd for their friend. When they perked up, Jason grew tense. Bonnie was approaching them, Emma trailing along beside her, their hands locked together. He felt a momentary burst of happiness for her before he spun around and saw Tim returning with two flutes of champagne. Like a disastrous cosmic event, multiple forces collided at the same time. Kelly was congratulating Bonnie, William giving Emma a hug, and Tim had put an arm around Jason's neck, holding one of the glasses near his lips. Then two of these people froze as their eyes met.

"Emma?" said one, sounding confused.

"Uncle Tim?" said the other, sounding panicked.

Then, simultaneously, they both said, "What are you doing here?"

The star of the hour stepped forward to break the tension. "You're Emma's uncle!" Bonnie said, offering a hand. Tim's were both occupied by champagne flutes, so he offered her one. "Oh, thanks." Bonnie turned to Jason next, observing the arm around his neck. "Hey! Sorry, I didn't recognize you at first. Wait, you're Emma's uncle? The one who can sing?"

"No," Emma said, looking puzzled herself. "You're thinking of Ben."

"And does Ben know you're here?" Tim asked. "Or your parents?"

Emma looked away. "They think I'm staying at a friend's house."

"Which she is," Bonnie said. "She's staying with me tonight."

"No," Tim said. "She's staying with us. I'll call Ben and tell him to come pick you up. He'll decide what to do."

"Uncle Tim," Emma pleaded. "Please don't! I'll be home tomorrow morning! It's not like it's a school night."

"You're fourteen years old," Tim said. "You're too young to be on your own in a different city."

"She's not on her own," Bonnie said before shaking her head. "Wait, what? Did you say fourteen?"

"You can't make me do anything!" Emma said, ignoring her. "You aren't *really* my uncle!"

"Then I'll call Ben," Tim said, digging in a pocket for his phone. "And we'll see what your *real uncle* thinks of all this."

"Hold up," Kelly said. "This is worse than reality TV. Who is related to whom?"

"You know I'm still in the closet," Emma said, still pleading with Tim. "How am I supposed to explain why I'm here? Think about when you and Ben used to secretly meet."

Tim hesitated, thumb jabbing his phone before he put it back in his pocket. Then he drank down the champagne in one gulp. "Okay," he said. "Let's all just calm down and talk about this."

"Over dinner?" Kelly said, sounding amused.

Jason thought of the tangle of lies that would slowly be pulled apart under scrutiny. "Maybe we should all just go home," he suggested.

"You can't go!" Bonnie said. "It's my big night!"

"And I'm starving," Kelly said. "No, I definitely think some food is in order. Followed by what I imagine will be a very enlightening conversation."

Six people sat at a table, an invisible line dividing them. On one side sat the prosecution—William, Kelly, and Bonnie. Across from them, past the barely-touched plates of Italian food, sat the accused. Jason and Emma were separated by Tim, who had traded his suit of seduction for the mantle of parenthood.

"So basically," Kelly was saying, "Emma told you, Bonnie, that she was sixteen, when in fact, she is only fourteen."

"Almost fifteen," Emma corrected. "Just a few more weeks."

"Congratulations," Kelly said dryly. "But 'almost fifteen' does not equal sixteen, which you claimed to be."

Bonnie frowned. "I don't think she told me her age at all."

"That was me," Jason said. "I told you she was sixteen because I thought you wouldn't give her a chance."

"Of course she wouldn't have," Tim chimed in. "Fourteen is too young to date."

"Oh, absolutely," Kelly agreed, smiling like a serpent. "But what I don't get is if you aren't her uncle—" He pointed at Tim and then Jason. "—and you aren't either, then where does this Ben guy fit in?"

"Ben and Tim are—" Emma began, but Tim raised a hand to silence her. "She has an uncle who lives here in Austin. I'm more of an honorary uncle."

Kelly nodded, not at all dissuaded. "But you and Ben meet in secrecy sometimes."

"Not anymore," Tim said. "We used to in high school when we were a couple. Then we broke up."

That much was true, even if he failed to mention they had gotten back together since. Tim was doing a very good job of not lying at all. Maybe they could still get away with this!

"How odd," Kelly said. "Bonnie clearly expected Ben to be with you. He's the one who sings, right? Or can you sing, Jason? That would surprise me because you've been very quiet recently."

Jason stared him right in the eye, jaw clenching. Kelly wanted him to squirm? Too bad. "Tim's not my boyfriend," he said.

Kelly rolled his eyes. "Obviously."

"Emma's uncle, Ben, is Tim's boyfriend," Jason continued. "They're an amazing couple and are nice enough to let me live with them. And go along with my stupid ideas, like this one."

Kelly gave William an I-told-you-so expression. "And why would you want to pretend to be with someone when you're not?"

"Haven't you ever been single?" Tim asked. "Haven't you been around other couples, ones you envy because what they share seems so incredibly wonderful that you want it for yourself? And, even though they might not intend to, don't those happy couples sometimes make you feel small and insignificant, like you aren't good enough to join their ranks? I know. I've been there before, and I didn't want Jason to feel the same way. He deserves to be loved. I meant what I said earlier about how handsome he is, but it's his personality that really shines. He's a survivor. He's been on his own since he was a kid, he's worked full-time since he was sixteen, and life *still* hasn't given him the good things he deserves. But he doesn't let that make him bitter. From what I can tell, he falls in love way too easily, but that's not a bad thing. I met a guy like him a long time ago, and I've been chasing him ever since. So maybe Jason is single now, but it won't be long before someone recognizes how special he is. *That's* not a lie. It's a prediction. Stick around and you'll see it come true."

The table sat in stunned silence at this speech. Kelly looked irritated, Bonnie and Emma were glowing with some sort of excitement. And William… Jason's stomach sank at the sight of him, because it was clear he wasn't happy at all.

"I don't care how old she is," Bonnie declared. "I was thirteen the first time I fell in love, and the woman wouldn't even look at me. I have to respectfully disagree with you, Tim. Fourteen is old enough to feel, and dating just means spending time with the person you love. Maybe she shouldn't be alone in Austin with me, but I'm not going to judge her by an arbitrary number. Emma, you're mature enough for me. That's all that matters."

Emma smiled at her and looked very much like she would like some privacy, which might have prompted her to turn to Tim. "Soooo. About tonight."

Tim shook his head. "Your father hates me enough as it is."

"Then it can't get any worse," Emma joked. "Besides, he'll never find out. I swear."

"Fine." Tim sighed. "But you're staying at our house. In the morning, we'll drive you back to Houston. Jason, you're the designated driver tonight, because I'm going to need a few beers before I have to face Ben."

"Deal!" Emma said. Then she leaned forward to look around Tim at him. "Right?"

"Right," Jason said, and although he was happy for her, he didn't feel like smiling because William's face remained troubled the rest of the meal. Luckily Emma had returned to her usual chatty self, Bonnie keeping up with her. This made the table appear lively, even though Kelly seemed bored now that the drama was over. Tim focused solely on his beer. William didn't say a word, not until they were all out in the parking lot.

"Need a lift to your car?" Tim asked him.

"I don't drive," William said. "Neither of us do."

"Then a ride home," Tim offered.

William shook his head, but Kelly nudged him. "It's better than the bus!"

"Bonnie can drive me," Emma said hopefully. "Ben's at home, right?"

"Yeah, okay," Tim said, the beer having mellowed him. He handed his keys to Jason. "Let's get this show on the road!"

Kelly sat up front with Jason, which was practical since he needed more room for his crutches, but it certainly didn't feel very comfortable. Kelly kept conversation to a minimum, only feeding Jason directions to where he lived, which turned out to be a large house in a conservative new subdivision on the other side of town. Tim was still enjoying his buzz, chatting to William about his plans to build a swimming pool on their property. They were talking so much that neither noticed when the car pulled over and parked.

"Time to go," Kelly said.

William glanced up. "I'm staying at my place tonight. I'm tired."

"You can be tired here," Kelly said.

"I want to be in my own bed." William said. "Besides, my mom misses me."

"Fine."

Kelly seethed quietly as he got out of the car. William also got out and walked him to the door. Jason watched as they stood on the front porch and talked. Or argued, since their body language appeared a little too animated.

"I can see why you like him," Tim said from the back seat. "Seems like a good guy."

"Yeah," Jason said, eyes still on the house. "I think I've pretty much blown it though."

When William returned to the car, his cheeks were red and his features tense. He seemed distracted when giving Jason directions to a much more humble neighborhood, Jason having to brake sharply a couple of times to avoid missing his turn. The street William lived on wasn't well lit, but the small house they pulled up to looked nice, from what Jason could see without a porch light on.

"Thanks for the ride," William said, before turning around to face the back seat. "And thanks for dinner. You didn't have to pay for us all."

"It was my pleasure," Tim said.

William nodded, turned to face Jason, and then wordlessly got out of the car. Jason watched him walk halfway across his lawn before he opened the car door and gave chase.

"Wait," he called, but didn't need to because William had already turned around. The neighborhood was quiet, except for the gentle chirping of insects. In the dark, William was much more intimidating. Without the gentle eyes or friendly face visible, he was just an outline of a large, muscular body. Jason came as close as he dared, hoping to see through the shadows. "I'm sorry," he said.

"I don't like liars," William replied.

"It's a nasty habit," Jason said, trying to make it sound humorous, but he knew it wasn't. "When I was growing up, I had to do certain things to get what I wanted. Or to get away from places I didn't want to be. I didn't lie exactly, not always, but I went to extremes to get my way."

"Were you abused?" William asked, sounding concerned.

"No," Jason said. "I lost my parents, so I was in and out of foster homes my whole life. That's not an excuse. I don't know what I'm trying to say, except that I know I'm messed up, and I'm sorry if I made things tense between you and Kelly."

"There's a reason I'm with him," William said.

"I know. I'm sure there are plenty of reasons, and anyone with eyes could—"

"Just one reason," William said, voice hard. "And I'm not sure it's a good one."

Jason hesitated, feeling lost. "What do you mean?"

William's silhouette shook its head. "I don't want to talk about him. Remember what you said to me at the pool? How you felt when you first saw me?"

"Yeah."

"Was that a lie?"

"No!" Jason said. "I swear it wasn't. I only lied about not being able to swim. And about having a boyfriend."

"That's two strikes," William said.

"Do I get a third?" Jason asked, not daring to feel hopeful. "I mean, I don't want another strike, but if I'm not out yet…"

"You're not," William said. "I felt it too. When we first met. But I don't know what it means. Maybe we're meant to be friends. Maybe, if things were different, we could have been more. Either way, I don't have room for a liar in my life."

The breath caught in Jason's throat, leaving him unable to respond.

"I'll see you at the pool," William said. "Monday morning."

"Monday," Jason managed. "I'll be there."

A breeze blew across the lawn, wind cutting between them and breaking the spell. William's dark form turned and walked the rest of the way to the house. Jason peered at the dark porch, saw William illuminated briefly as light shone out from the interior. With his back to the door as he pushed his way inside, William was looking at the exact spot where Jason stood. Then he was gone. Taking a deep breath, Jason returned to the car and got inside.

"How'd it go?" Tim asked.

Jason considered everything, weighing it carefully. "I honestly have no idea."

When they returned home, they found Emma and Ben in the backyard. Ben rose and went inside to have a word with Tim. Emma stayed where she was, lying on her back in the grass and staring up at the stars. The peaceful scene was slightly marred by Samson stalking Chinchilla, the dog tearing across the yard every time the cat got close. After watching this spectacle for a moment, Jason joined Emma on the ground, each of them taking turns sighing as they considered the sky.

"I'm never going to lie again," he said, letting the stars be witness to this most solemn of oaths.

"Speak for yourself," Emma said. "Personally I'm thrilled with the results. I don't think Bonnie would have given me a chance otherwise."

"I'm glad it worked out for you," Jason said.

"That it did." Emma sighed again. "She kissed me. When she dropped me off here, she walked me to the door just like in all those after school specials, and then she kissed me."

"Wow!" Jason said. "Congratulations. So I take it Ben didn't open the door at the exact wrong moment?"

"Nope," Emma said. "It was perfect. Absolute perfection."

They lay in silence together, Emma no doubt replaying that kiss in her mind, Jason fantasizing about his evening having ended in a similar fashion.

"Was Ben angry about you showing up out of the blue?" he asked eventually.

"No. Just surprised. Of course, now that Tim is back, who

knows what will happen. Ever notice how adults are cooler when on their own? Get them together and they start trying to out-responsible each other."

They waited in increasing anticipation, tensing up when they heard the back door open and close again. Footsteps too soft to be Tim's approached.

"Sit up," Ben said. "Both of you."

They did so, Ben taking a seat in the grass in front of them. He sat cross-legged with his back straight, looking like he meant business, which made his words so surprising.

"I'm sorry," he said. "I feel like I've failed you both."

"What?" Emma cried. "Why would you say that? You're awesome!"

"Thank you," Ben said solemnly, "but instead of behaving like an adult, I've let matters get out of hand. I cherish the story of how Tim and I met, perhaps a little too much, and I've allowed that to cloud my judgment. Looking back now, I should have done things very differently. I shouldn't have told the hospital that Tim's parents had hired a nurse. Without proper care, something very serious could have happened."

"Which is why you skipped school to take care of him," Emma said.

Ben grimaced. "Yes, but I had no professional training, so I wouldn't have known what to do in an emergency. What I'm trying to say is that I made a lot of stupid mistakes when I was younger, and they just happened to work out in the end. I got lucky. But Emma, running off to a different city with someone you barely know is extremely dangerous. And Jason, I shouldn't have encouraged you to lie or go through with this ridiculous charade tonight."

"Oh, totally," Emma said sarcastically. "We both should have stayed at home feeling lonely. That's way better than taking a few small risks."

"Sometimes small risks lead to serious consequences," Ben said. "Falling in love doesn't require behaving foolishly. There are other ways to accomplish the same goal."

"How?" Jason said, trying to remain respectful. "I'd like to know, because if I had played it safe before, I never would have fallen in love the first time. And tonight, even though it was a disaster, it got me somewhere. I know now that William feels something for me too. If I hadn't gone to the mall to see what would happen or to the recital tonight, I wouldn't have gotten closer to him."

"But that didn't require deception," Ben said. "And Emma, you could have asked this girl to meet your parents first, take you on a date somewhere in Houston."

"And you could have called Tim's parents and got him a nurse," Emma said. "But why didn't you? Or have you forgotten already? What's the one reason you did things the way you did?"

Ben's eyes drifted to the horizon for a moment, then he snorted and partially covered his face with his palm. "Because of how I felt about him." Ben dropped his hand. "I could have done things differently, and I knew that back then, but all I cared about was the way he made me feel. Ugh. You know what? I'm glad I'm not a parent, because I suck at this."

"You don't," Jason said, trying not to laugh. "At least you're honest with us."

"I'm not sure that's a good thing," Ben said, shaking his head. "Jason, it's better if you're honest from now on. Lying can push people away from you instead of drawing them closer."

"I'm learning that," Jason said, nodding his agreement.

"Emma," Ben continued, "this is the absolute final time I help you hide anything from your parents. I want you to be open and feel you can confide in me, but if you're doing something I feel is dangerous, I'll tell them because it's better than seeing you get hurt."

"Fair enough," Emma said, "but you won't tell them about tonight, right?"

"Right. But I think you should come out to them. You know they'll accept you. They accepted Jace, didn't they?"

Emma crossed her arms over her chest. "Having a lesbian daughter is different from having a gay brother."

"They loved Jace," Ben said. "And they love you. There is no difference. Just think about it, okay?"

"Fine."

"Good." Ben stood, brushing the grass off his butt. "Now if you'll excuse me, I have to go inside and give my boyfriend a lecture about being responsible."

"No!" Emma said. "Uncle Tim was so cool! Please let him off the hook."

"He tried his best," Jason said. "The first thing he said when he saw Emma was that he was going to call you."

"Exactly! We ganged up on him so he wouldn't," Emma chimed in. "Tim was outnumbered. You should have seen him when the others found out Jason was single. He sat there and lectured Kelly and William on how incredible Jason is and how it's their loss."

"Really?" Ben asked.

"Yeah," Jason said. "If he hadn't stood up for me, I'd probably be jumping off a bridge right about now."

A hint of a smile crossed Ben's lips. "Well, in that case, I'll go inside and tell him what a good job he's done."

"And we all know what that's code for," Emma said. "You've got half an hour. After that we're coming back inside, and I don't want to hear squeaking bed springs."

"Our bed doesn't squeak," Ben said, but he checked his watch anyway. Before he left, he had one more thing to say. "I didn't win Tim or even Jace through risky behavior. All I really did was squeeze my way into their lives. Once there, I was lucky enough that they wanted me to remain. The same will happen for you, because you're both wonderful. Keep showing up in the lives of the people you love, and I have no doubt that they'll want you to stay."

"He's so sweet," Emma said when Ben had gone.

"Totally," Jason agreed. "So, no more risky behavior? Just mature, carefully thought-out decisions from now on?"

They glanced at each other solemnly before they both started laughing.

Chapter Twenty-two

Integrating himself into William's life sounded like good advice. Jason just wished the process wasn't so physically painful. He showed up at the pool on Monday, William behaving as if nothing unusual had happened over the weekend. They were back to square one. At first Jason felt somewhat relieved by this. He trained alongside William the first two days, then skipped the third since his muscles hurt so much. His body might have been spared the pain, but the absence caused his heart to ache, so Jason decided to always show up, even if he didn't swim. On such days he would sit on the sidelines, admiring the graceful way William moved through water.

Every swimming session ended with them talking, sometimes in the hot tub or more often in the parking lot when they should be leaving. Jason always wanted to linger. Sometimes William didn't seem to want to part either. As nice as their daily tryst was, frustration began building. Jason chose to talk about his past, letting William discover piece by piece where he came from and who he was. William, on the other hand, only talked about the future—his plan to become a rescue swimmer and where he hoped the Coast Guard would send him. Anywhere but Austin seemed to be his destination, which hurt because Jason wanted him to stay, wanted to *be* the reason William wouldn't leave. That begged another question.

"What about Kelly?" Jason asked one day in the locker room. "What's he think about your plans?"

"He knows," William said, pulling on his shirt. "He's known for years."

That's all he said about it. Kelly was a forbidden subject, at least when it came to their history together. William was never cold with Jason. He remained just as friendly as before, but often he would shake his head at a Kelly-related question or change the subject completely. As much fun as they were having every morning, Jason couldn't help obsessing over the invisible barrier that stopped them from getting closer.

He did his best not to be the problem. Jason kept his promise to tell only the truth. This was especially challenging during the next gay youth group meeting. Jason was reluctant to go on his own, but William kept insisting he try it again. So he did. This time Keith lectured them on dealing with homophobia, insisting they would face such opposition the rest of their lives. Jason found the topic interesting and was happy when Bonnie approached him afterwards. Sure, she was mostly interested in talking about Emma, but he was grateful for her company. Talking to William when others were around—especially Kelly—seemed an awkward prospect.

Kelly didn't seem to share this reservation. While William was busy elsewhere, he approached Jason outside the church. Two other guys accompanied him, their faces eager for the show to come. For a second Jason wondered if they planned on jumping him, despite Bonnie being there. Instead, Kelly chose to fight with his favorite weapon: his venomous tongue.

"Enjoying your swimming lessons?"

"Yeah," Jason replied, keeping his tone neutral. "I am. I can't really keep up with William's routine, but I'm trying."

Kelly's eyes narrowed. "Must be hard to swim while drooling over William. I can only imagine how much water pours into your slack jaw every morning. Maybe that's why you look so bloated."

"Retract those claws," Bonnie said, trying to lighten the tone. "No need to be mean."

Kelly wasn't dissuaded. "It's the truth, isn't it, Jason? You're only there because you wish you could have him."

Jason wanted to lie, especially with four pairs of eyes awaiting his reaction. He'd like nothing better than to deny his own feelings, but William had no room for liars in his life. "Yeah, I like him. Of course I do. He's perfect. I'm sure I'm not the only one to fantasize about being with him."

The other two guys suddenly found it hard to make eye contact. Kelly noticed this, jaw clenching.

"I've never fantasized about William!" Bonnie said, waggling her hands comically. "No? Nobody is going to laugh at the lesbian?"

"The thing is," Jason said, "just because I wish William was mine doesn't mean I'll do anything to take him from you."

"So what's your plan?" Kelly asked. "You're just going to follow him around, hoping he and I break up? Pathetic!"

Jason shrugged. "Maybe it is. But that's not the only reason.

I like William for who he is, not what I wish he could be. He's my friend."

"That's right," Kelly said, turning to leave. "And that's all he'll ever be."

"Hey, at least I like the guy," Jason called after him. "You act like you can't stand your own boyfriend!"

Kelly shot a glare over his shoulder as he went, but for once he remained silent.

"Sorry," Bonnie said when they were alone again. "He's not usually like that. Kelly is a really great guy, believe me, but I think he feels threatened by you."

Jason wished he could take comfort in that, but on the drive home, Kelly's words kept bouncing around in his mind. Maybe he really was being pathetic by hanging around William so much and doing nothing about his feelings. What was the alternative? To destroy their relationship? William wouldn't respect him for doing so. The idea didn't sit well with Jason either, but he was beginning to feel trapped. He needed to do *something*. He just didn't know what.

When he parked Ben's car in the garage, he wasn't surprised to see Tim's car missing. He knew they would be out visiting friends. Jason was looking forward to having the house to himself since misery didn't always prefer company, but the car parked out front gave him pause. The vehicle was massive and looked even more expensive than Tim's car. This was confirmed when he bent over to inspect the hood ornament. Below a little silver fairy with her wings extended was a logo of a double R.

"Rolls Royce," Jason murmured to himself before whistling appreciatively.

Maybe Ben had decided to stay home and was having dinner delivered by an excessively wealthy pizza boy. Jason went inside but found the downstairs both empty and quiet. Puzzled by this, he went upstairs, walking down the hall and peeking into each room, ending with his own. The last thing he expected to find in his bedroom was a fat man stretched out on the bed, a large bottle in one hand, a glass in the other. The man was sitting with his back against the headboard, leisurely sipping champagne. When he spotted Jason, he froze momentarily. Then he moved the glass aside and smiled.

"There's nothing quite like a teenager's room," the man said in a husky voice. "The vague smell of socks and cologne, the buzz of sexual frustration in the air... Then there's the mess—not quite as careless as a child, and yet, not so boringly organized as an adult. I bet you know where everything is in this room, don't you?"

Jason glanced at the floor, at the few days' worth of clothing he'd meant to pick up and the scattering of half-read magazines. He didn't think it looked *that* bad. And who was this guy to judge? Who was he at all? His hair was short, gray on the sides and lighter on top where he was balding. The suit was tight against his body but finely tailored, if not slightly crinkled at the moment.

"My name is Marcello," the man said, grunting as he swung his legs over the side of the bed. He set the bottle of champagne on the side table, and after a moment's thought, picked it up again and set down the empty glass instead. "Now then, who are you and how long have they been keeping you secret?"

"Where are Ben and Tim?" Jason asked.

"I haven't the foggiest."

"Do they know you're here?"

Marcello chuckled. "Heavens, no!"

"I'm calling the police."

Marcello appeared shocked. "But I'm one of Tim's dearest friends! My goodness, you can't have lived here for long or surely they would have mentioned me by now. I've known Tim since he was your age. I daresay I'm rather like a father to him. Or like a big brother. Better yet, a younger brother. Ha ha!"

Jason just stared.

"Look, I have a business card here somewhere." Marcello dug in his wallet, mumbling to himself. "Hm. Fresh out, but I found this. Here."

A green bill was extended toward him, and even from the doorway, Jason could see the "100" printed in one corner. He stayed in the doorway, not daring to come closer. Then again, a hundred dollars was a hundred dollars. As quick as he could, he stepped forward and snatched it out of the man's hand.

"Like feeding a baby goat at a petting zoo." Marcello chuckled. "Very good. We've established trust. I used to bring slices of ham with me just so the dog wouldn't chase me around the house. Such a fierce little creature!"

"Where is she?" Jason asked.

"Chinchilla? She's outside, but I refuse to watch her do her business. I don't have the stomach for it, which is saying a lot considering all the things I've seen."

Jason felt a little better. Marcello knew the dog's name and her habits. That was a start.

"Thanks for the money," Jason said, pocketing it. "I'm still calling the police."

Marcello barked laughter. "As well you should! I've trespassed into Tim's home more times than I can count. Before you summon the authorities, tell me your name."

"Jason."

Marcello looked expectant.

"Grant."

"Nice to meet you, Jason Grant. And what are you doing in Ben and Tim's life? I assume the purpose isn't illicit, since I've been through their bedroom top to bottom and didn't find anything of interest. Hopelessly vanilla! I'm sure you know what I mean."

"Huh?"

"For such a delicious couple, they're lacking in shameful secrets. Especially in the bedroom. Are you telling me you haven't snooped since you've been here?"

Jason squirmed. "Maybe just a little."

"Excellent! So what *are* you doing here?"

He realized that Marcello had turned the questioning on him, but Jason lacked the energy to turn it back again. "I met Jace a long time ago, and he said if I ever needed help, I should call. By the time I did—"

"Very tragic occurrence," Marcello said gravely. "So Ben and Tim decided to take you in. I assume, then, that your family doesn't accept who you are?"

"I don't have any family," Jason said. "I'm on my own."

"Ah! A fellow orphan." Marcello patted the mattress next to him. "Come sit next to me."

Jason narrowed his eyes, but found himself doing what he was told. As soon as he was seated, Marcello offered him the bottle. When Jason shook his head, Marcello shrugged and took a swig directly from it.

Jason eyed him. "It's a little early to be drinking."

"That would be true," Marcello said, "if I had gone to sleep last night. As it stands, it's really quite late to be drinking."

"Oh. So how do you know Tim?"

"I'd like to think it's he who knows me," Marcello said. "Let's try an experiment. Usually when meeting someone new, we present our best side and try to make a good first impression. Instead of doing that, let's reveal the ugly truth. What's your Achilles' heel, the thorn in your lion's paw?"

"You're very confusing," Jason said.

"Yes, but we're having a moment here. Tell me your greatest weakness, your ugliest fear, the biggest problem plaguing you."

Instead of answering, he glanced between Marcello and the champagne a few times.

"Perhaps I have had a few too many." Marcello set the bottle next to the empty glass. "Very well, I shall go first. I deal in beautiful men. That's my livelihood. If it involves male beauty in any shape or form, I've found a way to profit from it. I'm most proud of my modeling agency. Much of what I dabble in is illicit at best, but my artistic integrity shines when it comes to my photography. We provide images of unparalleled quality to the finest fashion labels in the world and have catered events so illustrious that even I had trouble getting my name on the list."

"Sounds horrible," Jason said. "No wonder you couldn't sleep last night."

"Ah!" Marcello said. "But with success comes pressure. Technology has changed the world, and not in the way I had hoped. In the old days, the key was to find the most beautiful faces or steal them from your competitors. These days, even I could slip into a pair of bikini briefs and have a team of digital artists shape me into perfection. True beauty has become meaningless."

"So your business isn't doing well?" Jason asked.

"Business is fine financially, but we are losing prestige. Once my agency stood out from the rest. Now we are slowly becoming a face among the crowd. So I ask you, my newest friend, what would you do in my situation?"

Jason shrugged. "I probably wouldn't bother at all. I've never found models to be hot. At least not in magazines. They always look too perfect, almost inhuman. You might as well photograph shop mannequins if you don't want any flaws."

"So you are suggesting," Marcello said, "that models should have acne and eating habits as vivacious as my own?"

"Maybe. I just think guys in real life are hotter. Take someone like Tim. He's gorgeous, but if he was going to be in a magazine, I bet you'd cover him in makeup first, then photograph him in black and white, and then airbrush anything imperfect out of the final photo. That seems crazy to me because, well..." Jason dug out his cell phone and tapped at the keys. "Look."

The photo he brought up was of Ben pointing a garden hose at Tim. The water, frozen in time, was just inches away from splashing Tim in the face. His terrified expression was comedy gold and made Jason laugh every time. Marcello chuckled too, but also paused, noticing the same thing Jason had. Despite Tim's eyes bulging and his mouth hanging open at an angle, he looked great, because the photo had captured something endearingly vulnerable.

"I should have locked that man into a ten-year modeling contract," Marcello said wistfully.

"I don't know about that," Jason said, "but maybe you should try letting your models be human. That way people can actually relate to them."

Marcello nodded. "You might be on to something. The raw approach is hardly new, but with my expertise, maybe I can put a new twist on it. Send me that photo, would you?"

For his age, Marcello knew his way around a phone. Better than Jason, arguably. In short order, they had exchanged contact information and the photo had been transmitted, along with the next one in sequence that showed Tim getting a face full of water.

"Now then," Marcello said, "maybe I can be of equal assistance to you. What's his name?"

Jason's jaw dropped. "How did you know?"

Marcello raised an eyebrow. "At your age, trouble comes in two flavors. It's either money or love, and you weren't quite desperate enough for that one hundred dollar bill I offered you."

"I still took it," Jason said, but then he shook his head. "His name is William, and I think he likes me, but he already has a boyfriend."

"Simple enough," Marcello said. "You need only present what assets you have. For instance, I assume you can play the guitar sitting over there?"

Jason nodded. "Yeah."

"And have you played it for William yet?"

"No," Jason said. "Look, it's going to take more than a song. His boyfriend is really really pretty."

"You'd be surprised," Marcello said, "how quickly the eye adjusts to what is beautiful. I have the most wonderful view outside my bedroom window, but after living there for so long, I rarely notice it anymore. Likewise, I work around handsome men all day long, and despite how pretty any of them are, my eye is always looking for the next great find."

"Ben and Tim still look at each other."

"That is love," Marcello said, "and is quite different indeed. Does William love his boyfriend?"

Jason hadn't seen any moments between them like what Ben and Tim shared. Or even the way Caesar had been pained by the idea of cheating on Nathaniel, as if it was tearing his heart apart. At times, William seemed almost reluctant to be with Kelly. "He says he loves him, but for the wrong reasons."

Marcello took this in. "I can't think of a more succinct way to describe a dying relationship."

"You think so?"

"Yes. You're arrived early on the scene, that's all. I'm sure you'll do fine."

"I don't know," Jason said. "I feel like there's more to it. William never talks about his past. It feels like he's running from something."

"We all have our secrets," Marcello said, attention on his phone again. "Give me his last name."

"Townson. What are you doing?"

Marcello finished keying something in. "I'll poke around for you, see what I can find."

"About William? You really don't need—"

"What are you doing here?" Tim shouted as he rushed into the room. "Get away from him!"

"Hello to you too!" Marcello said, looking offended.

"Did he offer you money?" Tim said, looking Jason over for signs of injury. "Or worse, did he offer you advice?"

"Both," Jason said.

"Oh god!" Tim turned on Marcello. "What kind of work did you trick him into? It better not be anything less innocent than modeling."

"Consulting work," Marcello said, standing and brushing

off his suit. "One hundred dollars per session. He's already been paid in full."

Tim turned to Jason. "For real?"

"Yeah."

"Okay." Tim exhaled. "Forget his advice and you might come out of this encounter unscathed."

Marcello sniffed. "I feel like a criminal."

"And I bet part of you likes how that feels," Tim said, offering him a hand. Once Marcello took it, Tim's muscles flexed as the larger man was yanked toward him and trapped in a hug. Even after they separated, Tim kept an arm around his shoulders. "Did you tell Jason how you got a key to this house?"

"Ah!" Marcello clapped his hands together. "I called a locksmith and claimed I'd slowly lost every key to my house. I asked if he could come and replace all the locks with new ones, which meant a lot of money for him, and really, who would request such a thing for a house that didn't belong to them?"

"You, apparently," Tim said. "When Ben and I came home, our keys wouldn't work anymore. Then the door swings open and Marcello presents us with a brand new set."

"Very generous of me, I thought," Marcello said. "Now then, where's that lovely boyfriend of yours?"

"Downstairs," Tim said. Guiding Marcello toward the door, he glanced over his shoulder. "You coming too?"

"No," Jason said. "I've got some things to take care of."

"Just remember," Marcello purred on his way out. "When you get to be my age, you're either haunted by the things you should have done or nostalgic about the things you did do. Given enough time, right and wrong cease to have meaning."

"Don't listen to a word he says!" Tim said, forcefully dragging Marcello down the hall.

Jason smiled and turned to consider his guitar. Then, before he could overthink it, he swung out of bed, grabbed his phone, and called William.

"Speak of the devil," said the voice on the other end. "Give me a minute and I'll call you back."

The line went dead. Jason sat on the edge of the mattress, then grabbed the bottle Marcello had left behind and took a hearty swig. The second his phone made a noise, Jason hit the answer button and held it to his ear.

"I heard what happened," William said. "At the group meeting. Bonnie told me first, and I've been hearing about it from Kelly ever since."

"Sorry," Jason said. "I didn't mean to—"

"I know, and it's not you who should be sorry." William sighed. "Kelly wasn't always like this, you know. Lately he's been getting more and more bitter, but I guess I'm to blame. For all of this."

"What do you mean?" Jason asked.

"Nothing," William replied. Then he took a deep breath. "He doesn't want me to see you anymore. At least not alone. He can't stop you from coming to the group meetings, but no more swimming together."

Jason's jaw clenched. Kelly had it all—William's heart, affection, and years of history together, and that *still* wasn't enough for him. He knew Jason had feelings for William and had to settle for friendship, and now Kelly was taking even that away. Fuck him! If he wanted a fight, then he better be ready for a long hard war, because Jason didn't feel pathetic anymore. He felt angry.

"I think we should keep seeing each other," he said. "In fact, I want to see more of you."

"Jason," William said, but there was a smile in that voice.

"So I guess you're the tie breaker. Kelly wants us to stop seeing each other. I want you to come to my house, meet my friends, and then go on a picnic with me. So you tell me what you want, and whatever it is, I'll respect it. Just be honest with me, because I have no room for a liar in my life."

William chuckled before lapsing into thought. Jason listened intently to the silence, palms getting sweatier by the second. This was it, he promised himself. If William turned him down, Jason would move on. But if he accepted…

"I do love a picnic," William said. "When?"

Jason exhaled in relief. "Right now?"

William laughed like this was a joke. "How about Saturday? I'll bike to your place as my morning exercise instead of swimming."

"We live outside of Austin," he said warningly.

"Sounds like a good workout. Text me your address. Right now, I have an argument I have to get back to, but uh…

Swimming? Tomorrow morning?"

Jason grinned into the phone, his muscles already aching at the prospect. "Absolutely!"

War was beautiful, and war was liberating, because it meant Jason didn't have to hold back anymore. He complimented William whenever he felt like it, praising the way he swam, or smiling openly at his sparkling eyes when he heard all the ways Jason had gotten himself kicked out of foster homes. The worst-kept secret was out. Everyone knew how Jason felt, so he saw no sense in pretending otherwise. William was receptive to this, although at times he seemed puzzled, like it wasn't deserved. Jason did his best to prove him wrong, holding back only when it came to the physical.

They didn't touch. No hugs hello and goodbye, not even a handshake. Any swimming tips were purely verbal now because the tension between them was palpable. If they touched, even once, somehow that would make it cheating. To be overly fond of another person was one thing, but to reveal that affection with the simplest caress... There was no turning back from that.

William's feelings—whatever they were—he kept under wraps, although he did make more of an effort to see Jason, mentioning his work schedule or more specifically when he took his lunch break, indirectly inviting Jason to join him. Which of course he did.

William even showed up at Jason's workplace. Friday afternoon, as Jason was organizing boxes of bird food, someone skidded to a halt at the end of the aisle. He smiled when he saw it was William, but the gesture wasn't returned.

"You work here, right?"

"Yeah," Jason said, catching on and conducting himself more professionally. "What can I help you with?"

William rubbed his chin thoughtfully. "I'm visiting a friend tomorrow and want to bring along a few house-warming presents."

"How very considerate of you," Jason said. "And is this friend of yours a bird?"

"Huh?" William glanced around the aisle. "Oh! I see. No, he's human but crazy about animals, so I thought I'd bring something for his pets. Think he'd appreciate that?"

"Sounds like a nice gesture," Jason said. "What kind of animals are we talking about here? Snakes? A wombat? Or maybe a zebra?"

"Nothing so exotic. Just a dog and a cat."

"Dogs and cats," Jason said thoughtfully. "You know, I *think* we might have a few things for dogs and cats. Let's go look together, shall we?"

They dropped the act then, shopping for Chinchilla and Samson, but every time one of Jason's colleagues came by, they pretended to be customer and sales person again. They were in this mode when William asked him another question.

"The guy I'm visiting, what could I bring him? I want to make a good impression."

"You must like him quite a bit," Jason said, trying to be silly.

William nodded. "And I want him to know that."

"In that case," Jason said, "I'd recommend diamonds."

"Diamonds?"

"A bucket full should do."

William pulled a face. "Maybe I don't like him that much after all."

Jason fought back a smile. "If this person likes you as much as you like him, I'm sure you being there is all that's required."

"I hope you're right," William said, holding up the items they had picked out. "I don't suppose you can ring me up?"

Jason shook his head. "Sorry. One of my associates will have to take care of you."

"Okay," William said. "Nice knowing you, helpful pet store employee."

"The pleasure was all mine."

William walked backward down the aisle, smiling at him the whole way. Then he disappeared around the corner.

Tomorrow. Everything hinged on tomorrow. Jason felt sure of it.

Chapter Twenty-three

Jason stood in the bathroom in front of the mirror. Aside from the many times he ran downstairs to check on the picnic preparations, he had been here most of the morning, trying to find the perfect hairstyle to make him handsomer than he really was. He even tried slicking it back, hoping it would make him appear debonair. Instead, he looked like he needed a pocket protector and glasses held together by tape. Jason gave up, washed his hair again and was toweling it dry when Marcello strolled into the bathroom. Or at least his large figure blocked the doorway.

"I didn't hear the doorbell," Jason said sarcastically.

"I'll be sure to ring it on my way out," Marcello said. "I've brought you a present."

"More money?" Jason said hopefully.

"Alas, no, but I do have something infinitely more valuable."

In the mirror's reflection, Marcello held out a manila envelope. Jason let the towel rest on his shoulders and turned to take it.

"What's this?"

"Information. Your William does indeed have a tragic past," Marcello said. "All of his secrets—or at least a good number of them—are in there."

Jason stared down at the envelope, feeling like a snake had just offered him a juicy apple. "I didn't ask you to do this," he said, feeling defensive.

Marcello held up his hands innocently. "Consider it repayment for your sage advice the other day. You've given me much to think about. Have you ever considered a career in consulting? You'd be surprised how rare an honest and unfiltered voice is."

"He'll be here any minute," Jason said, holding up the envelope.

"How exciting! Do I get to meet him?"

"No. Uh, do you think I should read this now?"

"Understanding someone is part of loving them," Marcello said with a devil's smile. "Even if they don't want to be understood."

"Right. Okay. Thanks."

Marcello retreated back down the hall, leaving Jason staring at the manila envelope. It looked so innocent, really. Just a plain rectangle of brownish paper. His fingers moved to the lip of the envelope, found it unsealed, and reached inside. He felt cheap paper, thin and disposable. A newspaper? Why would William be in a newspaper? For winning some swimming medals maybe, but Marcello had said his past was tragic. Jason pulled his fingers out like they'd been burned, opened a vanity drawer, and tossed the envelope inside before slamming it shut. He felt like opening it right back up again, but instead he went to find more clothes to wear.

Any sort of dress shirt seemed too formal for a picnic, so Jason chose a comfortable navy blue T-shirt that he felt complimented his skin tone and went with the white shorts he already had on. He was wondering if he looked too much like a sailor when the doorbell rang. Jason practically flew to answer it, his feet only touching three steps on the way down. He paused briefly in the living room, where Ben, Tim, and Marcello were not-so-casually loitering.

He rolled his eyes at them before the bell rang again. He opened the door to find William covered in sweat, tank top sticking to his heaving chest. Jason felt pulled by sheer attraction onto the front porch, closing the door behind him for privacy.

"You weren't kidding about living far away," William panted, wiping the sweat from his brow. "Great workout, but I can't meet your family like this."

"My friends," Jason corrected, "and they won't care."

"I have a spare outfit with me." William unslung his backpack. "Maybe I could take a shower?"

"I can't sneak you past them," Jason said. "They're all in the living room, desperate to meet you."

"Oh." William's face lit up. "Is there a faucet out here? I could hose off real quick. I'd rather meet them soaked in water than in sweat."

Jason stared. "Are you sure?"

"Yeah!"

"Okay. We'll have to go around back."

That's exactly what they did. Jason could imagine Ben and the others, creeping to the front window for a peek and discovering nothing there except William's bike. The backyard was abandoned, Chinchilla napping inside to avoid the warm weather.

"Perfect!" William said, spotting the hose.

He stripped off his shirt, and although Jason had seen him in nothing but a swimsuit, he still felt an extra thrill at the way his pale skin glowed in the sunlight. The nylon shorts remained, sadly, as William motioned for Jason to turn on the hose. He did so, stepping back and admiring the view as William took an impromptu shower. He was grinning at Jason and blasting water under his pits when the back door opened and a jumble of gay men stumbled out.

Ben smiled, covering his mouth. Tim looked a little envious, and Marcello began to flail. Jason didn't understand why until he started shouting.

"Oh my goodness! Apollo has descended and here I am without my camera! This is exactly the sort of scene you can't fake!"

William spun around, looking bashful, before tossing aside the hose and holding out his hand. Ben was the first to step forward, introducing himself and laughing when their gripped hands made a squelching noise. Tim already knew him, of course, which left only Marcello.

"What a delightful way to make a first impression!" he raved. "The next time I meet a boy's family, I shall do exactly the same thing."

"I'm so embarrassed," William said, but he didn't need to, since the blush on his face was threatening to spread to the rest of his body.

Ben noticed this and ushered the others inside so Jason and William could be alone again. Once they were, William dug in his backpack, pulling out a shirt that he put on, this one white with navy lettering. Jason took this as a cosmic sign that they were meant to be together.

"I don't suppose we can make a run for it?" William said. "That was beyond humiliating."

"You compete wearing less than that," Jason pointed out. "If anything, you were over-dressed. Come inside and meet everyone properly."

This time things went smoother. William presented Chinchilla with a Kong, which was a big hit, and Samson came out of hiding when the container of catnip was opened. After some small talk, William excused himself to finish getting refreshed, and Ben helped Jason pack all of their picnic items.

"He's a hottie," Ben said, loading a backpack with potato salad, chips, and a few bottles of water. "I can see why you've been so motivated."

Jason grinned. "That's one way of putting it, but it's more than just his looks. He's kind of goofy. I mean, who thinks hosing off is a good idea? But I like that about him. William showed up at the pool one time wearing those inflatable armbands for kids and kept them on the whole hour, like it was completely normal. It's wild. He has his whole future planned out, but he can still act completely child-like."

"I can see the appeal of that," Ben said carefully.

Somehow, Jason didn't think he was referring to Tim.

He could hear William in the living room chatting with Marcello, which made him tense. Maybe because Marcello knew things about William that the rest of them didn't. Jason thanked Ben, grabbed the backpack, and asked William to join him outside. Tim had already rolled his bike out of the garage, loaning Jason wheels yet again, so they were ready to go.

The route to St. Edwards Park wasn't long, and they took it at a leisurely pace. William kept pulling up alongside Jason and pestering him about the contents of the backpack.

"What's in there? Some kind of salad?"

"Maybe," Jason replied.

"Tuna salad?"

"Nope."

"Hmmm. Egg salad?"

"Uh-uh."

"Must be potato salad," William said with a grin. "Did you make it yourself?"

"Depends on if you like it or not," Jason said. "If you do, then I made it."

"Is that a lie?" William asked, but he shot Jason a wink.

"Oh yeah, honesty," Jason said. "In that case, even if you don't like it, I still made it."

"Lucky for you I'm starving."

William spotted the park entrance and pedaled ahead. Jason had expected mowed lawns, playgrounds, a man-made lake, and maybe a patch of sand with a volleyball net. Instead he saw a dingy parking lot, a trail map carved and painted into a wooden sign, and an overflowing trashcan. That was all.

"This is excellent!" William said, and not sarcastically. He pulled his bike up to the trail map and studied it. "Let's find somewhere along the water to picnic."

"Lead the way," Jason said. They remained on their bikes, heading south. Once they were away from the parking lot, the environment improved considerably. They passed thick clusters of trees, leaves still waxy and fresh from spring's renewal. Then came grassy fields that Jason thought perfect for a picnic, but William didn't stop there. When he saw the water, he was glad they had ventured farther. The map had promised them a simple creek, one that widened temporarily in the middle, but it was surprisingly scenic. And more comfortable. Here the air was damp and cool, countering the day's heat. The path soon petered out, forcing them to walk along the water while pushing their bikes.

"Looks like a dam up ahead," William said. "A nice little waterfall too. We better not get too close or our voices will be drowned out by the roar."

He was kidding, since the water spilling over a rocky shelf was too tame to be loud, but it was pretty enough to look at. They chose this spot despite the hard ground, but the blankets Ben had packed would help.

"I've got one too," William said, opening his backpack. "We can double up."

They kept shooting glances at each other as they set up the picnic. Jason fantasized for a moment that they were making a bed together after having slept in each other's arms. The idea of something so simple, so domestic, made his chest ache. To share a bed with someone. Not in the sexual way, but to own it together, to lie down next to someone, night after night.

"You okay?" William asked.

"Yeah," Jason said. "Just a little hungry."

"Me too. Let's see what you've got."

William had already guessed it all but still acted excited when Jason heaped portions of potato salad onto two paper plates.

"It's heavy on the mayo," Jason said.

"Perfect." William shoved a plastic forkful into his mouth

and swallowed without much chewing. "The great thing about exercising so much is all the calories that get burned. I get to eat like a pig. Speaking of which, my mom made cookies."

William nudged a Tupperware container toward him. Jason opened it. Inside were a dozen peanut butter cookies, a crisscross pattern on the surface of each created by a fork pressing against the dough. He had a vague memory of his mother using the same method.

"These look awesome," Jason said, mouth watering.

"She made them especially for you."

"Really? She knows about me?"

"Mm-hm." William chewed and swallowed. "She kept asking if this was a date."

Jason didn't hide his puzzlement. "Doesn't she know about Kelly?"

"She knows all right! That's why she's hopeful that I'm moving on." William's expression was exasperated. "Kelly and my mom don't see eye to eye. They never have."

"Oh." Jason snacked on one of the cookies thoughtfully. "So… *is* this a date?"

William's face lit up, and he seemed about to say something, but then he shook his head and shoveled in more food. Jason watched the pile on the plate disappear like water evaporating off a hot stone. He took a few more bites himself, but didn't feel much like eating anymore. When William was done—for the time being, at least—Jason handed him a bottle of water and opened one of his own.

"This is probably none of my business," he said. "But do you and Kelly get along?"

"No," William said instantly. He took a swig of water, eyes locked with Jason's as he drank. "He probably feels otherwise, but then Kelly likes to argue."

Jason didn't know what to say, besides the obvious: Asking why they were still together seemed too direct, too aggressive. Then again, all was fair in love and war, especially when they shared the same battlefield. "The other night, when we all went out together… You told me that you love Kelly but for the wrong reasons."

William shook his head. "I said there's only one reason I'm with him."

"You don't love him?"

William pulled up his legs, studied the place where hard dirt met the soft blanket. "I like that you like me. I really do, and I hope it's obvious that you're not alone in your feelings."

Jason's heart thudded in his chest. "I wasn't sure—"

"You don't know me," William interrupted. Then he sighed. "I mean you do. This is the real me, but there are things you don't know, and if you did, I don't think you'd like me so much anymore."

"Try me," Jason said.

"You never ask about Kelly's leg. Why is that?"

Already fearing the implications, Jason's stomach sank. "I figured it was the sort of thing everyone asks about. That must get old. Besides, I don't want to feel sorry for him."

William looked puzzled. "Why not?"

Jason shrugged. "I guess because I wouldn't want people to feel sorry for me."

William huffed. "I don't think that's how Kelly feels at all."

"Sorry, I just—"

"No," William said quickly. "It's a good thing. You both have pride, but I don't think Kelly has dignity. Not anymore. Maybe that's why he's still punishing me, because I stole that from him. It's my fault Kelly lost his leg."

Jason struggled to find a response. "What do you mean?"

"We were arguing. We were always arguing back then. The first year we were together was good, but things kept deteriorating. Maybe we're both too competitive or… I don't know. But it reached a point where spending time with Kelly made me unhappy more than anything. And angry, because Kelly has a wicked tongue, and he's always known exactly what to say to hurt me. We were in the car—I was driving—and I wanted him to shut up. And I wanted to scare him, so I jerked the wheel and slammed on the brakes. I figured we'd end up parked on the side of the road, but the rain was pouring down and we started spinning. The vehicle behind us, a truck, slammed into Kelly's side of the car and— " William swallowed and shook his head, unable to continue.

"You didn't mean to," Jason said.

"I told you I wanted to scare him," William said, voice terse. "I could have calmly pulled over and told him he was walking to school. Instead I put him in the ICU. *That's* the kind of person I am. That's who you think you have feelings for, but I bet you're not so certain now."

Jason didn't respond. William wouldn't believe him even if he said otherwise, so he picked at the edge of a paper plate, searching for words that would help and coming up empty. "So what happened next?"

William looked surprised.

"I want to know everything," Jason said. "Tell it all to me. Then I'll decide how I feel."

After a moment, William nodded as if this made sense. "His recovery was difficult. I felt horrible, but I stayed by his side. His parents hated me and still do, so they glared at me every time I showed up at the hospital or said mean things that matched how I felt inside. Only Kelly was glad to see me, kept insisting I be there, and I was happy to be since it was the only way I could make up for what I'd done. These days I wonder if it was the painkillers. I know that sounds mean, but later things changed so much. When Kelly was home again, when he was weaned off the drugs and reality set in, that's when he became bitter. I don't blame him. His dream was to run in the Olympics. He was good—really good—so maybe he would have. He still acted like he needed me, kept saying that I made him happy, but I don't see it. All this time later and all I do is make him miserable, but he still wants me around."

"Do you love him?" Jason asked.

The question pained William. That much was obvious from his expression. His brow was knotted when he answered. "That argument in the car? I was breaking up with him. I didn't want to be with him anymore. If the accident hadn't happened, I wouldn't be."

"But you feel obligated," Jason said. "That's why you're still with him."

William's features were grim. "Please don't tell him that. I would hate for him to know. It would kill me to do him any more harm than I already have. So I won't leave him. Ever. I promised him as much when he was in the ICU, and even though he was jacked up to hell, he smiled. It's horrible, but now I wish I hadn't made that promise. Then again, it's the least I can do, considering all I've taken away from him. I can't expect him to forgive me, and I don't blame him for hurting me back in the little ways he does. But I wish he'd stop punishing himself."

Jason shook his head, trying to keep up. "How does he punish himself?"

"You asked if he could still swim? He won't even attempt it. Or run. There are prosthetics he could try. His family has money and can afford it, but he won't even go in for a consultation. I showed him this video online of an athlete missing a leg above the knee, just like him, and the guy still competes professionally. Kelly wouldn't even talk about it. He just looked at me like I was being ridiculous. He could be walking without the use of crutches. Did you know that?"

"You're upset."

"Well, yeah! It's one thing if he wants to make me miserable. Fine. I deserve it. But I still want him to have the best life possible! Why wouldn't I be upset?"

Jason took a deep breath. "I mean that you being upset is good. Yeah, you screwed up and something bad happened, but you obviously never wanted it to. You still care for Kelly, and you still want him to be happy because you're a good person. Do you really think me knowing all this is going to mess with how I feel about you?"

William didn't look relieved by this. Instead he stood and walked toward the waterfall, stopping halfway to lean against a tree. Jason gave him his space, distracted himself by rearranging their picnic gear without actually accomplishing anything. Then he rose and walked to join him.

"I want to be with you," William said without turning to face him. "You have no idea how bad I want to just… do the things we should be able to do. Even something small, like holding your hand. But now you know everything. You know it's impossible. Or would you really ask me to turn my back on Kelly and hurt him all over again?"

Doing so would hurt William, make him feel guilty and dreadful and ready for anything but Jason's affection. "Maybe we don't need to touch," Jason said. "Love is more than holding hands or kissing or sex. It's more than just the physical, right? If that's what this is, maybe we don't need those things."

William turned to him, and that's all it took to show Jason he was wrong. He wanted to reach out to him, to comfort him or simply feel their bodies pressing together. He knew that urge would never leave. They stood facing each other, unable to act, and Jason felt like crying or screaming or both. They had to find a way out of this.

The thing was, Jason had been here before. He kept finding these incredible guys, but he was always too late. He shouldn't be surprised, since why would someone like William or Caesar be single? And later, when trying to keep his distance from Caesar hadn't worked, he had made his move and pushed Caesar to be with him. Even without the disastrous morning when Peter had caught them, it wouldn't have worked. In the end, Caesar had still chosen Nathaniel.

"What are we going to do?" William asked.

Jason hesitated. "If I wasn't such an honest man these days, I'd suggest you stay in your loveless relationship with Kelly while secretly going elsewhere for what you really need."

"An affair?" William looked amused by the idea, which was progress. "No. You're too good to be the other woman. I won't do that to you."

"My feelings don't really hinge on you being so noble," Jason tried.

"There's got to be a better way."

There was, and he felt William already knew the answer. No matter what promises he had made, no matter how much Kelly thought he needed William, they were better off separate. But Jason wouldn't be the person to push William to make that decision, mostly because pushing Caesar hadn't helped. Besides, William had finally confided in him, and asking him to change his entire life wouldn't encourage him to remain open.

Jason decided to retreat. For now. "A picnic is a failure if any food is left over," he said. "Did you know that?"

"No," William said, "but I'm relieved, because I'm still starving."

Once they had decimated the potato salad, chips, and cookies, they got back on their bikes and explored the park. A few places could be reached only by foot, and at those locations they would leave their bikes leaning against each other, like the lovers they couldn't be. William showed off by climbing a tree, and Jason proved how cool he was with everything by not mentioning Kelly again. Later they shook out their picnic blankets over an empty field, lying on them side by side and soaking up the sun. When they grew tired of slapping bugs on their necks and picking brambles out of their shoelaces, they returned to Jason's home.

"I should go," William said, standing outside the front door. "I'm sure Kelly is getting more nervous by the hour."

"He knows we're together?" Jason asked, not hiding his surprise.

"Of course. Nothing like an early morning argument to start the day."

"Sorry."

"Nah." William waved a hand dismissively. "It was worth it."

"Hey!" Jason said. "Before you go, there's something I wanted to show you. Come up to my room real quick."

William raised a skeptical eyebrow but then smiled. "Yeah, okay."

Jason felt a little silly grabbing his guitar and sitting on the edge of the bed. Nothing had naturally led to this moment, but he wanted to share this part of himself, no matter how random it seemed. William sat next to him, expectantly looking at him and the guitar. Jason had planned to play something romantic, a song that somehow expressed how he felt, but he changed his mind at the last moment and went with a song by Paul Simon. *50 Ways to Leave Your Lover*, a playful tune about trying to talk someone into leaving the person they were with. Jason wasn't much of a singer, but luckily it wasn't a very demanding song. He plucked at the guitar, trying to put a funky twist on it, and felt relieved when William laughed during the chorus.

"Very interesting song," he said when Jason was done.

"Yeah, it's fun." Jason put the guitar back on its stand and leaned back.

"You're really good," William said.

"Thanks. Honestly, that's not the best song for me, but—"

"I thought it awesome," William said. "And it gives me something to think about on the long ride home."

"Yeah."

William was staring at him. Jason couldn't think of anything else to say. What he really wanted to do was lean over and kiss him, but that wasn't going to happen.

"I should go," William said, but he didn't stand. Instead he looked over at Jason's hand, which was splayed out on the mattress. Then William put his hand over it. He didn't grab hold of it, or intertwine their fingers. He simply rested his palm on top of Jason's hand, and as simple as this gesture was, it sent tingles racing over his skin. William left his hand there for the briefest of moments, eyes searching Jason's, before he squeezed once and stood.

"Fifty ways, huh?" he said.

"At least," Jason said. "I can make you a list if you want."

William smiled, shook his head, and sighed. "Thank you for a wonderful day."

"My pleasure," Jason said. "Want me to see you out?"

"That's about the last thing I want right now," William said. "Although, if that Marcello guy is still around, maybe you should."

Jason laughed. "I'm pretty sure he's harmless, but better safe than sorry."

Once William was gone, and Jason had deflected a million questions from Ben... Once the house had finally settled down, he found he couldn't sleep. Jason lay in bed, the sheets increasingly tangled as he tossed and turned. Then he rose, went to the bathroom, and took the manila envelope from the vanity drawer. He carried it back to his room, pulling out each piece of information, one by one.

The newspaper was first, and Jason was glad he hadn't looked at it earlier since it had a medium-sized photo of the car wreck, the passenger-side door completely caved in. Jason stared at the twisted metal, trying to imagine Kelly inside that mess before the paramedics had freed him. Then his eyes drifted up to the headline. *Star Athletes in Auto Collision!* The article itself was confusing, making it sound as if they were driving separate cars before crashing into each other. It also insinuated that drugs or alcohol might have been involved by stating it was uncertain if they had been. Another newspaper clipping had a shorter piece on the accident, getting the facts right and reporting that Kelly Phillips was in critical condition. Two small headshots were included, one of Kelly, one of William. Red ink surrounded Kelly's headshot, and next to it in handwriting, Marcello had scribbled: *Does he always look this good? Model material!*

The thing was, the photo didn't do Kelly justice. He was

way hotter in real life. Jason spent some time studying William's grinning face, wishing the picture was larger. He got his wish when he moved on to the next piece. This article was from the sports section. William stood with two other men in swimsuits, each of them holding up a medal won in a local competition. The grinning face matched the one from the previous article, meaning they must have cropped it. Jason carefully tore William free from this page, crumpling up and throwing away the two other guys. After a moment's thought, he trashed the rest of the information in the envelope. A quick glance revealed more articles from local papers or screenshots of online profiles and such. Marcello was quite the detective, but Jason had all he needed. If there was anything important he needed to know, he trusted William to tell him.

Jason took his flimsy black-and-white copy of William's photo and placed it on the pillow next to him. Then he got up and made sure the door was locked—because this really was embarrassing behavior—and got back into bed. When he lay back down, he adjusted the pillow so he could stare at William, still dripping with water as he held up his medallion with pride. Jason stared until this image was burned into his mind, until his eyes were too tired to stay open. William victorious and happy was the last thing he saw before falling asleep.

Chapter Twenty-four

Sunday brought an unwelcome surprise. When Jason showed up at the YMCA, still feeling bleary from a night of poor sleep, William wasn't waiting for him outside like he usually was. Jason waited ten minutes, then twenty, before going inside. Peeking through the door that opened onto the pool, he spotted William doing laps. Farther away, fully clothed and sitting on the edge of the diving board, was Kelly.

Jason retreated to the locker room, trying to decide what to do. Kelly knew they met almost every morning, so not showing up now—the day after their picnic—might seem suspicious. Deciding to pretend everything was normal, Jason changed into his swimsuit and walked out to the pool, acting pleasantly surprised when he saw Kelly there. Jason waved, and although the gesture wasn't returned, he happily dived into one of the lanes like he was eager to practice.

When William climbed out of the pool for a break, Jason did the same, flashing him a reassuring smile. Everything was okay. No need to panic. Naturally they couldn't talk freely with the third wheel around, and Kelly didn't respond to Jason's attempts to make small talk, so it was hardly a pleasant morning. Jason had to get to work anyway, and found himself eager to leave. That night he got a text message from William, which was rare.

Same weather tomorrow morning.

In other words, chilly. Monday brought a rerun of the previous morning, except this time Jason didn't pretend to be chipper. He swam a little, despite his muscles hurting too much to do so, but eventually climbed out of the pool and watched William, while Kelly watched Jason watching William. By the end of an hour, Jason's jaw wouldn't stop clenching and he had a headache. Part of him was impressed that Kelly had found another way of ruining their time together. Mostly he found himself hating the guy.

Jason stopped by Juicy James that day, but William was swarmed with customers. Buying a smoothie just to get a few seconds with him, Jason heard more news that didn't make him happy.

"I'm not going swimming tomorrow," William said. "You shouldn't either."

Obviously. What was the point if he wasn't going to be there? "When's your next break?"

William shook his head apologetically. "Kelly said something about shopping today. You should go. We'll figure something out, okay?"

Jason spent the next day trying to decide what that would be. Most of his plans revolved around strangling Kelly, or drowning him in the YMCA pool, or other violent fantasies that left him feeling sick to his stomach. The rest of Jason was filled with newly born love, and it felt wrong that hate was invading his heart as well. He tried to forgive Kelly, to imagine how it would feel to slowly lose the person you loved, but even this was difficult because he never saw Kelly being nice to William. If Kelly was so desperate to keep him, he could at least treat William right.

Jason was on the couch that evening, flipping through channels, when Tim returned from taking Chinchilla for a walk. Once free from her leash, Chinchilla hopped up on the couch with him. For some reason, Tim decided to stand right in front of the television. Jason glared and tried to angle the remote around him.

"There's someone out front," Tim said. "At the end of the drive. He's on a bike, and I can't be sure, but it might be your Apollo."

"William?" Jason asked.

"I think so. He didn't see me, and he's just standing there, so—"

Jason leaped to his feet and bolted out the front door. He ran all the way down the drive, wishing Ben and Tim had a short driveway like most people. Despite all the training he'd done with William the last few weeks, he was winded by the time he spotted a figure in the fading light—both feet on the ground and a bike between his legs.

"What are you doing here?" Jason panted, a wild grin on his face.

William swung his legs over his bike, letting it fall to the ground as he walked toward Jason. He caught him by the shoulders, hands gripping him firmly, and Jason found himself short of breath for another reason entirely.

"I told him I wanted to bike today instead of swim." William said. "I don't have long."

"Then why are you down here instead of at the house?"

William's eyes searched his. "I was trying to decide if I was going to do it or not."

"Do what?"

"This."

William's lips smashed into Jason's, and they were soft and salty with sweat and absolutely wonderful. Jason kissed him back, wrapping his arms around his back, the wet T-shirt chilly against his skin until replaced by the warmth of William's body. Jason ran his hand up William's spine to his neck, letting his fingers sweep through the short hair there. They were both huffing through their noses, breath short, but Jason didn't care. He could die this way, collapse from lack of oxygen rather than break the kiss he had been so hungry for.

William pulled away first, hands on each side of Jason's face as he smiled goofily at him. Then he came back for two short pecks, before Jason pulled him in for another real kiss.

"Okay!" William said, laughing as he took a step back. "Holy shit... That felt even better than in my fantasies."

"You've been fantasizing about me?" Jason asked with a sheepish smile.

William shook his head ruefully. "You have no idea!"

Jason hated to mention Kelly, but he had to know. "Did something happen?"

"Nothing has changed," William said. "I'm sorry. I guess I should have told you first, but I think maybe you're right. Until we figure something better out, we just... uh..."

"Have a sultry affair," Jason teased.

William grimaced. "I hate how that sounds."

"A sweet affair then," Jason said. "I'm okay with that. I hated the last few days—not being able to be alone with you."

"It's only going to get tougher to see each other," William said. "Like I said, I can't stay right now."

"Come back later," Jason said. "Or I'll sneak over to your place. You guys don't spend every night together, do you?"

William frowned.

"You do? Even on school nights?"

William sighed. "I never thought I'd say this, but unfortunately I have very liberal parents. He does too. I took care of him when he was recovering, and that meant us staying together, even at night. Somehow that became the norm."

"Lucky bastard," Jason said. "What are we going to do?"

William smiled. "You're a clever boy. I'm sure you'll figure something out."

Jason's mind had already begun racing, trying to find a solution. His brain shut down again when William kissed him goodbye, but when he had gone, Jason redirected the sexual frustration he felt into determination. He would find a way! No matter what he had to do.

The next week was a trial of emotional endurance, Jason's frustration growing with each passing day. Despite his determination, he was no closer to finding a way he and William could be together. Kelly was still showing up at the pool every morning, making it pointless for Jason to go anymore. Sure, swimming allowed him to see William, but Kelly had started making cutting remarks that remained with Jason and soured the rest of his day.

"William could say he has to work," Tim suggested once, "on a day he doesn't really have to. Unless Kelly checks up on him, he'll never know."

Except Kelly was showing up at William's workplace with more and more frequency. A few times, Jason had parked on the opposite side of the mall, and William had met him there during his break. This gave them ten minutes of privacy in the car. They would lower the seatbacks and talk or make out, but this felt more desperate than romantic.

"He needs to leave Kelly," Ben said, still determined to be a good role model. "You won't be happy until you can have William to yourself and out in the open."

Jason suspected this was true, and he tried broaching the subject during one parking lot session. William had admitted a breakup was inevitable, but then he started talking again about how he'd ruined Kelly's life. Before they could get anywhere in the conversation, William had to report back to work. Even phone calls were difficult, thanks to Kelly always being in the room with William, and text messages weren't at all satisfying.

"I need time!" Jason ranted after a Sunday lunch of grilled cheese sandwiches and tomato soup. "I'll never talk him into doing anything if we're constantly interrupted, or worse, chaperoned by Kelly."

Ben leaned back in his chair and studied the kitchen table. After a moment, he glanced sideways at Tim, who shook his head almost imperceptibly.

"What?" Jason said. "If you guys know a way and are holding back… I don't even know why you would do that to me."

Again they exchanged glances. "I had an idea—" Ben began.

"No," Tim interrupted, crossing his arms over his chest.

"He's not Ryan," Ben said patiently.

"What's that supposed to mean?" Jason asked, looking back and forth between them. "What's he got to do with anything?"

"Marcello is having a party," Ben said.

Tim sighed. "I love Marcello, I really do, but some of the people he associates with are trash. I don't want you getting exposed to that sort of element."

"That's when things turned sour with Ryan," Ben explained. "He and Tim were happy together, but then Ryan started running with a bad crowd—"

"Doing drugs," Tim said with a huff, "screwing around, stealing, partying and letting the rest of his life go to shit. I won't let you do that to yourself."

"Thanks for your concern," Jason said, holding back a smile, "but I'm only interested in spending time alone with the guy I lo— with the guy I really *really* like."

Ben looked amused. "So if someone comes up to you with a big fat blunt and USB stick full of hippie music, what are you going to say?"

"No," Jason said solemnly. "I'll say no."

"There," Ben said, looking at Tim. "He passed the test."

"You guys think you're so funny," Tim said, pulling out his cell phone, "but this is one genie you can't shove back in the bottle. Mostly because he's too damn fat."

"How's a party going to help me, anyway?" Jason asked. "Kelly will just tag along like he always does."

"How do you feel about being a topless waiter?" Tim asked. "And getting ogled by lots of old men."

"Huh?"

Ben rolled his eyes. "Marcello likes to staff his parties with handsome young men. It sounds horrible, but this one is a fundraiser, so it's for a good cause. You and William can work as waiters, allowing you to slip away for some private time."

"I appreciate the idea," Jason said, "but I need more than just ten minutes alone with him."

"That's the brilliant part," Ben said. "This charity supports the sick and shut-in. During one portion of the party, the waiters are all sent away while everyone else is locked in a room for the actual fund-raising."

"That sounds crazy," Jason said.

"It's to show people how it feels to be shut away without resources," Tim said. "And it only lasts half an hour, so it's worthless, really."

"Except," Ben said, "I'm sure Marcello would be willing to extend the time if we asked. I bet we could get an hour out of him."

"An hour?" Jason said, practically salivating at the prospect. "Sign me up!"

Ben nudged Tim. "Sign him up."

"Okay," Tim said, pushing a button on his cell phone. "Mark my words, getting Marcello involved in your love life is a terrible idea. You're all going to regret this."

"I should have seen this coming," Tim said, shaking his head. He was topless except for a metallic blue bow tie. Balanced in one hand was a tray full of champagne glasses. Even when he turned around to glare accusingly at Jason, the liquid in the glasses barely moved.

"You've done this before, huh?" Jason asked.

"Yes, I have!" Tim said. "And I swore years ago that I never would again."

"Thanks," William said. "We really appreciate it. You have no idea how special having time alone is to us."

"I can imagine." Tim's features softened as he looked them over. "Enjoy it. You guys make a cute couple."

Jason felt self-conscious as hell. Like Tim, he and William were wearing black slacks, uncomfortable polished shoes, and nothing above the waist except for their black bow ties. He had no idea where Tim had gotten the cool blue tie. Maybe from a previous party like this. Marcello was more than willing to help their crazy plan become a reality, but he required Tim to play waiter too, claiming that donations would skyrocket as a result. Seeing Tim's bare torso, Jason could understand why. The guy was absolutely cut, and even had a sexy scar running up one arm to his shoulder, a splash of pink against his naturally brown skin. Attractive as Tim was, Jason's attention kept returning to William, who looked like a Boy Scout trying his luck as a Chippendales dancer. Their impressive physiques made Jason feel insecure about his own body, especially since the other waiters were in good shape too. Soon Jason had other things to worry about, like making sure all the guests had stuffed mushrooms crammed in their mouths.

Marcello's home was palatial, and was perhaps just one hedge maze and swan-filled lake away from *being* an actual palace. Tonight's event took place in a ballroom on the first floor. On stage was a small orchestra that—oddly enough—played pop music for the delight of the guests, a female singer occasionally taking the microphone and crooning out lyrics, lending an edge of class, even when singing about being hungry like a wolf.

And the guests certainly seemed to be. After a mere five minutes, Jason darted back into the kitchen for more food. On his way back, he saw William standing next to where Kelly sat, smiling and chatting with him as a good boyfriend should. All part of the plan. Jason did his best to ignore them, focusing on the guests instead. Most were older gentlemen, wearing custom-tailored suits. They were often accompanied by younger guys who dressed more casually, although some of the older men walked the party, arm in arm. Jason envied them, hoping that he would one day be doing the same.

As the party went on, the younger guys convened, leaving their dates alone. This meant the older men became chatty. Jason had to keep excusing himself so he could continue serving *hors d'oeuvres*. Eventually Tim came up to him, a sea of heads turning to follow his progress.

"Less food, more talking," he whispered.

Jason scrunched his face up in confusion.

"These guys are more interested in talking to you than in eating," Tim explained. "That's why you're here. You don't have to give them lap dances or anything. Just smile and humor them."

"They want to talk to me?" Jason asked.

Now it was Tim's turn to appear puzzled. "You're a good-looking guy. You know that, right?"

Jason felt himself blushing. He looked away to find an older man checking them both out, smiling when he caught Jason's eye.

"See?" Tim said. "Just remember, it's for a good cause. And if any of them try to touch you, point me out and tell them I'll break their necks."

"Okay," Jason said, laughing nervously.

He started focusing on socializing more, taking the time to answer probing questions and feeling less and less taken aback each time someone laughed or seemed genuinely interested in what he had to say. By the end of another hour, his self-esteem was so inflated he worried he might float up to the ceiling. He didn't know why Tim complained about doing this. Maybe he didn't need the ego boost, but Jason would gladly volunteer again.

He was practically dancing across the room to fetch more food when someone placed a hand on his arm to stop him.

"The champagne is running a little dry. Better get another tray from the kitchen."

Jason looked up, because the guy who was speaking was tall. And huge and familiar in a way that made Jason feel like he was sixteen and insignificant again. For the first few seconds, he didn't understand why. But then a name came to his lips that he barely managed to keep himself from saying.

Nathaniel.

Caesar's one true love. Jason just stared at him, waiting for the recognition to be mirrored, but instead Nathaniel merely raised an eyebrow.

"Did you hear me? We need more champagne. Marcello will be asking for money in half an hour, and we want everyone feeling generous."

"I'm not old enough to serve alcohol," Jason stammered.

"Oh!" Nathaniel said. "Sorry. In that case just head to the kitchen and let them know. Tell any waiters on your way too, all right?"

"No problem."

Jason walked stiff-legged back to the kitchen, not daring to turn around until he was at the door. Had he been mistaken? But no, when he searched the crowd, he quickly found Nathaniel, smiling as he talked to a guest but also keeping an eye on the proceedings. What was he doing here? Jason glanced around, expecting to see Caesar walking through the crowd to join him.

Jason had made enough rounds that surely he would have spotted him by now. Then again, Nathaniel had been here all along, even if it took a moment for Jason to recognize him. He felt relieved that their reunion had been one-sided. The one time they met, Jason had spent longer watching Nathaniel from between shelves of books than their brief encounter had lasted. His hair had hidden his eyes back then too, so chances were, Nathaniel wouldn't recognize him unless Jason made a point of explaining who he was. Which he wouldn't.

"Half an hour until the shut-in," Marcello said from beside him. Jason jumped, making Marcello chuckle. "Feeling nervous? It's not your first time, is it?"

"No," Jason said, eyes returning to the crowd and one person in particular.

Marcello followed his gaze. "Don't tell me you're interested in someone new already?"

"No!" Jason said. "He just looks familiar. What's he doing here?"

"Nathaniel? He manages most of my projects. Very efficient. Very willful. Do you know him?"

"No," Jason said, pulling his attention away. "He said we need more champagne."

"The world always needs more champagne," Marcello said, hands on his tummy. "Don't worry. I already gave the order. Are you enjoying yourself?"

"Yes," Jason admitted. "Thanks for doing all this for me. I mean, I know it's not *all* for me, but I'm sorry my crazy relationship is messing with your plans."

"Don't be sorry," Marcello replied. "The only thing love needs to apologize for is being too difficult to understand and too easy to give in to."

"So true," Jason said with faux weariness.

"You still have my little map?" Marcello asked.

"Of course," Jason said, patting a pocket.

"Excellent. Be prepared to make good use of it soon. Now if you'll excuse me, I have my own affairs to attend to."

Marcello nodded cordially, a naughty smile on his face, before he slipped gracefully into the crowd. Jason fetched another tray of food, passing it out and resisting conversation again. Was Nathaniel being here a sign? Should he read into it? The situations were uncomfortably similar, but it wasn't too late. Not entirely. If he backed away now, maybe William and Kelly would be okay. He glanced over to where Kelly was sitting. William was crouched next to him, a miserable expression on his face as Kelly gave him an earful about something. Then again, they hadn't been okay before Jason came along. That was the difference. Caesar had loved Nathaniel, probably still did. William didn't love Kelly. Not anymore.

"Your attention please," Marcello said from on stage. "As you all know, the intent of this little soiree tonight is to benefit those who are unable to leave their homes, be it due to illness or other unfortunate circumstances. In order to understand how that feels, let's all bravely go an hour without food, drink, or charming company. I'm going to ask all my waiting staff to kindly leave the room. As they go, please place any remaining beverages on their trays."

Jason started making his way to the door, heart pounding. He forbade himself to look around for William, concentrating on not dropping the glasses piling up on his tray.

"Never fear!" Marcello continued. "One handsome face will remain, besides mine of course. The rather dashing fire marshal here will oversee our safety during the shut-in, and despite his good looks and charming outfit, I assure you he isn't a stripper. Now then, as the doors close—"

The rest of the speech was lost to Jason, since the kitchen was a rumble of noise. Already a group of waiters were sparking up a joint. One was draining glasses of the remaining champagne, while others looked on with abhorrence.

"That's one way of doing the dishes," William said in his ear.

Jason turned and nearly kissed him. Instead he pulled out the handwritten map.

"Where are we going?" William asked.

Jason followed the dotted line to an X and a description of the room. "To a love nest," he said with a grimace.

"Let's hurry," William said. "I want the entire hour alone with you."

Originally Marcello providing them with a map seemed silly, but Jason now realized more than ever that this wasn't a normal home. A staircase didn't lead up to a simple hallway and additional rooms. Instead the house had multiple staircases, multiple floors, and offered nothing straightforward at all. They entered a sitting room, leaving again through a door on the opposite side, and might as well have been in an additional house. They ducked through an open courtyard in a similar fashion. Finally, they entered a bathroom, and after a ninety-degree turn, discovered a bedroom.

"The love nest," Jason said with some reverence because it really was a magical place. The wallpaper was deep burgundy, incorporating an ornate pattern in gold leaf that reflected the light of candles placed randomly around the floor. There was little risk of a fire hazard, since the floor appeared to be dark marble. Striking, but not good for bare feet, which is why a lush carpet sat beneath a massive bed, a canopy of maroon fabric obscuring it from view.

"Think this champagne is for us?" William asked, fingers tracing the condensation on a bottle sitting in an ice bucket on an oak dresser.

Jason didn't answer. Instead he rushed to lock the bathroom door, then the bedroom door. Even if Kelly managed to navigate the maze of the house, he'd have to go through two doors to reach them. Marcello had chosen this location well. Jason wondered if he had lit the candles himself, or if that task had been delegated to his staff, maybe even Nathaniel. How ironic that would be!

"An hour," William said. "All for us."

Jason swallowed, feeling pressured to make the most of it, which made him unsure how he wanted to spend a single minute. "What do you want to do?"

William grabbed hold of him, wrapped his arms tight around Jason, and held him. They stood like that for a few silent minutes. Jason understood completely. He returned William's squeeze, reveling in simply being able to hug him without fear of being caught. Such a simple gesture, and yet one normally denied to them.

"I'm sorry," William said, pulling away. "We shouldn't have to resort to this. You're too good to have to sneak around. You deserve better."

"You deserve better than Kelly," Jason said.

"I ruined his life," William said. "I took his leg and ruined his dream. He's the one who deserves better. I know I'm not the right guy for him, but until that person comes along, he's not going to be lonely. At least not until I join the Coast Guard, but I have to. It's the only way I can make up for it."

"For what?" Jason asked.

William swallowed. "I ruined one life, but maybe if I save another, it'll kind of equal out. You know?"

Jason felt a lump in his throat. "I wish you wouldn't be so hard on yourself. And you're right that Kelly deserves to find someone who loves him, but if you're going to be out of his life eventually... Why not now?"

William considered him. "My parents are divorced. I hardly see my dad anymore, but I'll never forget what he put my mom through by leaving. I don't want to be that guy, so I'm hoping Kelly will leave me. I keep pushing for us to go to the youth group, hoping he'll meet someone. That way I won't have to break my promise."

Jason was tempted to argue that William was breaking an equally important promise now, but then again, all they had done so far was hug and talk. They could spend the entire hour talking, and part of Jason wanted to, in the hopes of walking out of the room together as a real couple. But if he didn't get anywhere with words, then all of this would feel like a waste.

William must have had similar thoughts, because he unclipped his bow tie before stepping forward to do the same for Jason. Their faces were close together, William smiling before he got down on his knees. Jason held his breath, but exhaled when he felt his shoes being untied. He watched as William loosened the laces, then lifted his feet so the shoes could be taken off one by one. Jason wiggled his toes in relief. Then William rolled onto his rump and made short work of his own shoes. When he stood again, he took a few steps back and placed a hand on his belt.

"At the same time?" he asked.

"Sure," Jason said casually, despite the pounding in his chest. Was he having a heart attack? Wasn't there something about one arm tingling? Thankfully both arms felt normal as he copied William's movements. It felt like getting undressed in front of a mirror, except he didn't recognize the body as his own.

Then William pulled down his pants and underwear in one smooth motion. He was already hard. His cock matched the rest of him—thick and pale and smooth. Jason stared, barely aware that he'd pulled down his own pants.

"You're not hard," William said, nodding at his crotch. "Are you sure you're really gay?"

"Shut up," Jason said with a chuckle. "I'm a little nervous."

William raised an eyebrow. "We've spent weeks around each other in nothing but swimwear, and you're nervous about the last skimpy piece of clothing being gone?"

Jason shook his head as he pulled his feet free from the pants bundled up around his ankles. "I wish we had more time. I want to spend the entire night with you, but the clock is ticking, and there's so much pressure."

"There isn't any pressure," William said gently. He shook off his pants the rest of the way and offered his hand.

Jason accepted it and allowed himself to be led to the bed. William got in first, lying on his back, switching hands so he wouldn't have to let go for long. Then he pulled Jason in and on top of him.

"Lay on me," William said. "All of your weight."

This Jason understood. He pressed their waists together, placed his legs alongside William's, let their socked feet nudge against each other. Their stomachs came next, then their chests as Jason tucked his arms beneath William's pits. They kissed momentarily before Jason lay his head against William's neck. The heat from his body, the slight smell of the food they'd been serving on his skin, the way William's arms pulled him closer—this was paradise.

"Breathe with me," William said.

Jason held his breath for a second, timing his so that when William exhaled, he was inhaling. When William's chest rose, filling with air, Jason's chest constricted. Not only were they pressed together now, but they were moving in perfect harmony, flawless and inseparable, like the way the ocean touched the sky.

"Not so nervous now," William pointed out.

That was true. Jason was aroused and ready for anything. William chose what this would be, flexing his muscles and rolling Jason over onto his back. William lay next to him, propped up on one elbow as he slid his palm over Jason's chest—fingers brushing against his ribs. Then William scooted down and bent over him. Jason gasped as William took him in his mouth, pumping and slurping. Then he laughed because it felt too damn good.

"Hey!" William said, squeezing Jason's cock with his fist. "This is serious stuff!"

"Totally," Jason said before laughing again.

William sat up on his knees, shaking his head as if he disapproved. "I see there's only one way to shut you up."

"Oh yeah?" Jason asked, pushing himself up on his elbows. His grin faded slowly as William swung a leg over him and brought his crotch close to Jason's face. He stared a moment at the pink cock head, the thick meat bouncing and flexing in anticipation before he looked up at its owner.

"That's got to be the most beautiful dick I've ever seen," he said with rapt admiration.

William looked smug—a surprisingly naughty expression from someone so nice. This only turned Jason on more. When he opened his mouth again, it wasn't to speak. Soon William started thrusting in him, growling and groaning as if working out his frustrations. He reached a hand down and placed it against Jason's cheek, which bulged sometimes when William changed angles and positions. Then he pulled out, scooting down so their tongues could twirl together. When William moved like he wanted to go down on him again, Jason grabbed him by the arm.

"Keep kissing me," he said.

"But how—" William glanced around, spotted a bottle of lube and condoms on the side table and grabbed at them.

Or just the lube actually, which made Jason nervous. He wasn't ready to do something like that, and really didn't know which role he was expected to play. Besides, he felt they should be safe. He was about to express this concern when William squirted cold liquid on him, making Jason suck in air and then moan as William began stroking. He started kissing Jason again, chasing the worries from his mind. As it turned out, he had nothing to be concerned about. William lubed himself, then rolled over onto Jason, pressing their hips together.

One of William's hands had a grip on them, but he was so thick that a single hand was barely enough, so Jason reached down to help out. Hands partially covering each other, they thrust and moaned, the sounds they were making silenced when they began kissing again. Then William stopped suddenly, pulled away, and stared at Jason with a look of surprise.

"You okay?" Jason asked.

"Yeah," William said. "Great. Are you close?"

"I was getting there," Jason said.

"Sorry," William said, hand moving again. He placed his forehead against Jason's, staring him in the eye. Jason stared back, trying to read what was going on, but soon pleasure overtook them both. Their huffing increased, Jason's eyes shutting as he bit his lip, not wanting this moment to end, but William was pumping harder. He pressed his lips against Jason's and held them there when he came. Jason only lasted a second longer.

William's body relaxed onto him. All that muscle was heavy, and Jason had a difficult time breathing, but he didn't want him to move. Eventually William rolled off. Propped up on one elbow, he traced a finger around one of Jason's nipples, then down to his bellybutton, which was full of liquid.

"Like a little hot tub," William said.

"Ew," Jason replied. "How can sex be so appealing one second and so totally gross the next?"

"It's not gross," William said, but he laughed anyway. "We better get cleaned up. It'll be obvious if we return to the party all sweaty."

Jason sighed. "I guess so. How much time do we have?"

Twenty minutes, they discovered. They hopped into the shower together, playfully washing each other. Once they were dressed and about to leave the room, William became solemn. He had that shell-shocked expression again, and as they walked down the halls, he almost seemed haunted. Jason thought he could imagine why, and as much as it hurt to ask, he had to know. He stopped walking, causing William to do the same.

"Do you regret it?"

William shook his head. "I just forgot what sex feels like when it's with someone you love." He said the word so casually, without any hesitation. He didn't even seem concerned about Jason's possible response. Instead he placed a hand on Jason's back, urging him forward. "Come on. We're running late."

Jason's head was spinning as they made their way to the kitchen. Waiters were already heading back into the ballroom, carrying trays. Before they could enter the commotion, William spoke words from Jason's past that made his stomach sink.

"This is the last time."

Jason spun around, not understanding. "Why?" he croaked.

"Because you deserve better," William said. "The next time we're together, we won't be sneaking around. I'll figure something out. Okay?"

Jason nodded, relieved but still unsure what any of this meant. Was William finally ready to end things with Kelly, or was he still hoping to find some hidden place where they could be together without being caught? They couldn't talk about it now. William hurried into the kitchen to grab a tray of miniature sandwiches and disappeared into the ballroom. Jason lagged behind, not wanting to make an appearance at the same time. He was almost the last person in the kitchen.

"Why are you just standing there?" a voice demanded. Nathaniel! Again! He walked up to Jason before his expression changed to one of surprise. "Oh, I didn't recognize you before!"

Jason's mouth went dry. "You didn't?"

"No, sorry. Marcello said two waiters would be sneaking around his house. You're one of them, right?"

"Yeah," Jason said after a moment. Nathaniel still didn't have a clue who he really was.

"How did everything go?"

"Good," Jason said. "Better than I expected, actually."

"So lucky," Nathaniel said, eyes shining. "There's nothing like young love. If I can offer some advice…"

Could this night get any weirder? Jason nodded numbly.

"Don't let it stay hidden. Love is like a flower. It needs to be out in the open where it can get fresh air and sunlight. Secrets can be fun, but eventually they'll smother what you have together." Nathaniel paused and then winced. "Did I really just compare love to a flower?"

Jason chuckled. "Yeah, you did."

Nathaniel shook his head as if disappointed in himself. "Anyway, you get my point, right? If you like this guy, you'll both have to come out or whatever the issue is. That's the only way you'll make it."

"I'll keep that in mind," Jason said. Then he licked his lips. "So what about you? Anyone special in your life?"

"No." Nathaniel said this firmly. "No, I think I'm done with all of that. I have better things to do with my time. If love is a flower, then someone ran over mine with a lawn mower a long time ago."

Did he mean Caesar? Regardless, Jason felt strangely relieved to know they weren't involved anymore, mostly because it meant Caesar wasn't here.

"Not that I'm bitter," Nathaniel said, adjusting the his suit jacket. "I'm just more interested in my career right now. Speaking of which, Marcello didn't say anything about you slacking off. Grab a tray of cocktail wieners and be sure to laugh when these guys make all the obvious jokes."

"Yes, sir," Jason said.

He did as he was told, but found he was tired of flirting, even if it was for a good cause. Besides, the interest and compliments the men paid him weren't so meaningful. Not when someone like William cared about him. No words could top the one he'd let slip so casually. *Love*. Jason sought out William in the crowd, found him doing the same, and as their eyes locked, he wondered if it could be true.

Chapter Twenty-five

Jason walked the pet store aisles, trying to look busy when really he hadn't done much the entire day. If his boss caught him slacking, Jason decided he'd claim a serious bout of love sickness and ask to be sent home. As magical as Marcello's party had been, the next day had brought unhappy news in the form of a text message.

Better steer clear the next couple of days. Sorry.

That's all William had to say. Maybe the shut-in had made Kelly more suspicious than usual, or perhaps William's conscience had finally gotten to him. Jason began to regret it all. He had helped William cheat. Sweet innocent William, the guy who wanted so badly not to hurt anyone's feelings. The person who had no room in his life for liars. Thanks to Jason, William had both deceived and no doubt hurt Kelly. Not that Jason blamed himself entirely. It took two to tango, but he worried William would resent him for what they had done. Now, three days later, things were looking dire indeed.

Jason found himself in the pet adoption area—a wall of cages sometimes occupied by animals from the local shelter. Normally Jason avoided this side of the store because he wanted to adopt them all. Today he hoped that seeing the plight of these poor animals would make him feel less sorry for himself. He browsed the cats, some of whom considered him with disinterest. Others rubbed up against the cage, desperate for attention. He poked a finger in, petting a few, before moving on to the dogs. He liked all animals, but dogs really pulled his heartstrings.

"Don't suppose you have room for one at home?" asked the woman from the animal shelter. "We're overcrowded at the moment."

Jason had spoken with her before. Her name was Barbara, and she had strawberry-blonde hair that was slowly turning white. Maybe from stress. Her clothes were always wrinkled, her hair frazzled.

"We've already got two pets at home," he said.

"Two is nothing," Barbara said. "I have six. Two cats, four dogs."

"Wow. I guess when you work around them so much, it's hard not to take them home."

"You have no idea." Barbara brightened up. "You ever think about volunteering? We're always short-staffed."

Jason squirmed a little. "I don't know if I can handle it. Emotionally, I mean. That's why I never come over here."

"I understand that," Barbara said, "but you soon get used to it. I feel better doing what I can, rather than turning away. Not that I'm trying to make you feel guilty."

Too late! Jason returned his attention to the dogs. One cocked its head, ears perked up, as if hoping they were about to play together. Maybe they did have room for just one more at home. Now that Jason had been around a few months, he had become old news, meaning Chinchilla had gone back to being Tim's dog.

"That one wouldn't take up much space at all," Barbara said, pointing at a small scruffy mutt. "She's smaller than a house plant."

Jason turned away reluctantly. "I'm living with friends right now, so it's not my choice."

"I'm sure they wouldn't mind, especially since they have pets of their own."

"I can't. I swear."

"Okay, okay," Barbara said, holding up her hands. "If you ever want to take her for a walk or have a second look, here's the address of the shelter."

She thrust a business card into his hand. Jason pocketed it and retreated before Barbara hit him with another sales pitch.

He was nearing the end of his shift when he got another text message. His heart leapt when he saw it was from William, but it quickly did a nosedive when he read what it said.

At work. Almost break time. 20 min.

Same ol' same ol' then. At least William hadn't written him off completely, but Jason wasn't in the mood for another hurried make-out session in Ben's car. After their last meeting, how could it be remotely satisfying? Then again, he was desperate to see William and gauge how he was feeling. Jason clocked out early, hoping no one would notice, and drove over to the mall.

As usual, he stood some distance away from the Juicy James booth, staring hard at William until he noticed. Then Jason nodded and started walking to where he always parked the car. He didn't make it far before someone grabbed his arm and swung him around. William was beaming at him, his grin just as doofy as the cowboy hat and checkered shirt. Jason felt like melting, but then he glanced around nervously. "What if Kelly—"

William gently took hold of his chin to get his attention. Jason froze, eyes wide as William leaned forward and kissed him. Shoppers swarmed around them, a few stopping to gawk, but after a flash of self-consciousness, Jason relaxed and decided he didn't care. He leaned into that kiss, putting an arm around William's waist to draw him in. Let the world stare! Let one of the most artificial places on earth be filled with something rare and daring. And let that group of snorting and giggling teenagers keep on walking, because this was too damn good to stop. Jason knew the truth even before the kiss ended. Only one thing could allow them to be so careless and free.

"We broke up," William said after he'd pulled away.

"Really?" Jason said, feigning innocence. "I didn't know we were dating."

William pushed him playfully. "Not you and me, dummy! Kelly and I broke up."

Jason grew serious. "How did that go?"

William's expression mirrored his own. "There's a reason I asked you to stay away."

"So he knows about us?"

"Kind of," William said. "I started with how I don't make him happy anymore, and after some arguing, he admitted it was true. I told him I felt obligated to stay because of my promise, but it didn't take him long to bring you up. Then I admitted my feelings for you, but there's one last secret I'd like to keep. He doesn't know that we've slept together already. I don't want him to. It would only hurt him more, and now that he and I are over, it doesn't matter. Cheating was wrong, Jason. I shouldn't have done that to him. Or to you."

"We did it to each other."

They both laughed at the double meaning before calming down.

"I won't betray anyone like that again," William said solemnly. "Not you or anyone else. It's better to hurt someone with honesty than to hurt them with lies."

"Okay," Jason said, ready to focus on the future instead. "So we finally have time together?"

"Nope, because I have to go back to work, and afterwards, I'm picking up my things from Kelly's house. He and I have actually been talking lately. Before all we did was argue and—" William noticed the face Jason was making. "Tomorrow," he said. "After school. We'll go on a real date together, and if you're lucky, I might just come home with you."

"To spend the night?" Jason asked a little too hopefully.

William smiled. "Wait and see."

"Isn't it wonderful when love emerges victorious!" Marcello said, pushing his way into the bathroom. "Primping yourself for your big date, I see."

"Mmr-wrph brrrf," Jason replied, toothbrush still in his mouth.

Marcello clapped his hands together. "No need to thank me. Playing cupid is such a delight!"

Jason spat into the sink. "I owe you big time. The party really made the difference. Both William and I liked being waiters. We'd do it again. For charity, at least."

"I'll keep that in mind," Marcello said. "You can never have enough handsome faces around, especially when asking gay men to part with their money. Speaking of which, your friend is quite the beauty."

"William?" Jason smiled. "Yeah, he's gorgeous. Maybe the hottest guy on the planet."

Marcello's smile faltered for a moment. "Yes, he is quite handsome. Very boy next door. The problem is, everyone seems to have a boy living next door. I'm afraid handsome has become passé. I found myself nodding off while browsing an Abercrombie and Fitch catalog the other day. Can you believe that? No, I was referring to the friend you and William brought along."

"Kelly?" Jason stammered. He shouldn't be surprised. Kelly was definitely beautiful. Jason just hadn't seen him that way recently.

"You were saying that no one can relate to models. What about a model we feel sympathy for? Better yet, one we admire, for not letting his disability hold him back." Marcello peered at him. "Do you find this offensive?"

Jason considered it. "No. Just because he lost his leg doesn't mean he can't do what everyone else can. Or at least what other pretty people can. If he wants to be a model, then more power to him."

"Precisely," Marcello said. "Maybe you could bring up the idea next time you speak."

"That's William's boyfriend," Jason said. Then he corrected himself. "*Ex*-boyfriend. I don't think he'll be in the mood to chat with me any time soon."

"Then perhaps you have some contact info—"

"I'm not sure he'd be up for it," Jason said, surprised by how resentful he still felt. But hey, Kelly had been in the way, had been a crappy boyfriend to William, and had been so damn mean in general.

"I see," Marcello said, looking crestfallen. "Well, the hunt goes on. Have fun tonight. Don't do anything I would do."

This gave Jason pause, but after thinking about it, he decided Marcello probably hadn't misspoken. When he was finished getting ready, he went downstairs and found Ben and Tim in the kitchen. Ben was standing over a steaming pot while Tim leaned against a counter, watching him cook.

"Where's Marcello?" Jason said.

"Was he here?" Tim asked.

"Yeah, just a second ago. In my bathroom."

"The man is a ninja," Ben said, not sounding at all surprised. "What did he want?"

"Nothing," Jason said. "Uh, I'm about ready to go."

Ben glanced over and smiled. "Very sharp! I knew that shirt would look good on you."

"Thanks," Jason said. The shirt in question was pale green and made of soft fabric—thankfully, since it was nearly skin tight. He hoped William would like it, even though he'd already seen the bare skin beneath it plenty of times.

"Anything you need?" Ben asked. "Have enough cash?"

"Yeah, I just got paid. Uh..." He glanced over at Tim, who smirked.

"I can't be your date again, kiddo."

Jason rolled his eyes. "It's not that. I was wondering—"

"I know what you want," Tim said, digging in his pocket and pulling out a set of keys. He tossed them to Jason. "You know the rules. Be insanely careful. Not one scratch, okay?"

"Okay," Jason said with a relieved grin. "Thanks! I'm on my way."

"Have fun!" Ben said.

"And bring it back with a full tank!" Tim called after him.

Unlike last time, Jason drove carefully all the way into Austin—partially because of what had happened to Kelly, but also because he didn't want anything getting in the way of this night. Finally, *finally*, they would have all the time together they needed. It almost seemed too good to be true. He worried he'd pull up to William's house to find Kelly waiting on the front porch. Or William wearing an apologetic expression for whatever else had gotten in the way. But when he reached the house and the door opened, a familiar smile greeted him. Oddly enough, it belonged to a woman, the family resemblance unmistakable.

In addition to having the same smile and the same nose, her hair was also blonde and just as light as her son's. Only her eyes were different, a dark brown instead of green.

"Come in, come in," she said, waving her hand as if the wind would sweep him up and into her home. It didn't, so Jason willingly stepped inside.

He often found himself uncomfortable around other people's mothers. Odd, since he'd had more than twenty foster mothers himself, but they always felt fake. Mothers like William's were the real deal, almost sacred in his eyes, and they inevitably made him think of his own.

"Willy has told me so much about you!" Ms. Townson was saying, looking him over like something she was considering purchasing. Produce, maybe, since she reached out and squeezed his arm. "Oh look! Your cheeks are turning red!"

"Mom, that's enough," William said, rushing into the room.

"This one is sweet!" she said. "Just look at him!"

"I have," William said testily, "and I'd like to keep looking at him, but not while you're around."

"Such a smart mouth," Ms. Townson said, swatting William's arm.

"Thanks for the cookies," Jason said, managing to speak at last. "They were incredible."

This delighted her, of course. "Willy said they were all you ate during the picnic."

"And he refused to share," William added.

Jason held up his hands and shrugged. "Guilty as charged!"

"Keep making my son happy and there will be more cookies in your future. Brownies too, but only if you marry him."

After a moment of shocked silence, she laughed, causing Jason to do the same. William appeared more exasperated than anything and ushered Jason outside again.

"She wasn't kidding about the cookies," William said on the way to the car. "She'll make you more, even if we don't get hitched. Just you wait."

Jason grinned. "I hope you like fat boys."

"I might. Oh, wow! Your boyfriend Tim let you borrow his car!"

Jason rolled his eyes. "Yeah, yeah. Laugh it up… Willy."

"I'll show you a willy!"

Jason wasn't sure if that was a promise or a threat but he was fine either way.

William was a nervous passenger. He fiddled with the glove box or acted preoccupied with the bells and whistles that such a fancy car provided, but Jason noticed he didn't look at the road much. He supposed that was understandable, considering what he'd been through, but Jason still felt relieved when they reached the art museum. The location had been William's suggestion. The museum appeared fairly small, the parking spots equally so. Jason had to squeeze between a minivan and a beat-up old truck. It was a tight fit, even after reversing and trying again a few times. Once the car was parked, William had to crawl over and exit through the driver-side door.

"I didn't know you were into art," Jason said after he had paid their entrance fee.

"I'm not," William said. "I just want to be somewhere we can talk. I love going to the movies, but you know."

"Two hours of silence," Jason agreed. "Or getting kicked out because we couldn't keep our mouths shut."

William grinned. "Yeah. So let's see what kind of deep conversation all this art provokes."

The museum was a square building, split into two levels with a small courtyard in its center. The paintings on the first floor were very traditional—landscapes, religious scenes, or portraits of long-dead people who had been rich enough to commission an artist.

"This one looks kind of like Stephen Fry," William said.

"Reminds me of Oscar Wilde for some reason," Jason responded.

"I think he played Oscar Wilde in a movie."

"And then he traveled back in time to have his portrait painted."

William acted amazed. "Is there anything that man can't do?"

They tried finding other celebrity look-alikes, discovering portraits of Cher, Bill Clinton, Kathy Bates, and about four who looked like Jesus with various styles of facial hair.

"Oh, I like this one!" William said, standing in front of a huge landscape painting. Pioneers were hauling their wagons against the backdrop of the most ridiculously beautiful sunset ever.

"Have you been here before?" Jason asked.

"No. Kelly wasn't much for art. Except for photography, but he dropped that hobby when... You know." William kept his eye on the painting and frowned. "Do you think it's possible to be friends with someone you loved?"

Jason exhaled. "I don't know. The only guy I was ever with—it definitely wasn't possible."

"Caesar?"

"Yeah."

William turned to him. "So besides him, there wasn't anyone else?"

"Nope," Jason said. "Just him and this other guy."

"Other guy?"

"Yeah, can't remember his name. Blond, nice swimmer's build, couldn't tell when I was joking."

William grinned. "Ah. So I'm your second?"

"Yup."

"You're my second too," William said, taking his hand. "Kelly was my first everything, so when you and I were together the other night—"

"It felt weird because it was different," Jason said, understanding. "But not weird in a bad way, I hope."

"No! Just different. Exciting too, like it was the first time all over again."

William kept hold of his hand, dragging him out to the courtyard where a number of sculptures waited with infinite patience. One made of wood was shaped like a giant walnut. A handful were metal two-dimensional silhouettes of people. They paused before a more traditional stone sculpture, this one a man with the legs and horns of a goat.

"Think that's supposed to be the devil?" William asked.

"Pan," Jason said, reading from the plaque. "He's a satyr, isn't he?"

"A god too, I think," William said, stepping closer. He stared at the statue with rapt fascination. "Do you think I can touch it?"

Jason glanced around. Staff members weren't on patrol here, and no ropes surrounded anything. The cobblestones went right up to each sculpture, the sky darkening above them.

"Go for it," he said.

William ran his hand along one of the furry legs, reached up to let his fingers fondle the wild beard, the pointed ears, the goat horns. Jason watched him do all of this, marveling that the same attention had been paid to him a few nights before. He was lucky. Once again he had shown up too late, the person he desired already belonging to another, but William's heart hadn't been claimed. Not completely. Maybe it still hadn't been. Jason intended to do everything in his power to change that.

"So cool," William was saying. "It's like actually meeting a god and being able to feel him." He laughed at his own comment before becoming thoughtful again. "Think I'd look good with a beard?"

"One like that?" Jason asked. "Maybe when you're older. Besides, it would get waterlogged and slow you down when you swim."

"Good point," William conceded.

Next they went upstairs where the art was more modern. This got conversation going as they made fun of works that seemed too simple and plain, and debated which pieces were actually worthy of praise.

"Hey, check this one out!" Jason said, waving William over.

The painting was of two figures, unmistakably male, despite being shaped with basic geometry. The figures were twisted around each other in a way both affectionate and impossible. This was interesting enough, but what really caught Jason's eye was the familiar play of light and color.

"*All Twisted Up*," William said, reading the sign next to the painting. "Local artist Tim Wyman. Hey, that's your foster dad, isn't it?"

Jason smiled. "Yeah, but I don't actually call him that. They're more like friends. Well, the sort of friends you call family, if that makes sense."

"Totally. You mentioned he paints, but I didn't know he was into abstract. Now I feel bad for making fun of the others."

"He doesn't always paint like this," Jason said. "In our attic there's one of a really hot guy, and it's practically like seeing a photo. The few hanging in the house are more realistic too. Maybe he likes to play around with style occasionally." He peered closer at the painting. "I wonder if this is supposed to be him and Ben?"

"I don't know," William said, "but they seem like a cool couple. I wouldn't mind hanging out with them some time."

"Like a double date?" Jason chuckled at the idea. "Yeah, why not?"

One corner of the museum got really weird, with art that didn't involve painting or drawing. Here packs of gum were glued together to form a mouth full of teeth. On the floor in one corner, a pile of action figures had all been painted army green. Jason's favorite was a high school letter jacket. Aside from being torn, burned, and marred with tire tracks, the jacket was also splattered with what he hoped was fake blood.

"I love it," he said. "I think it represents the hell that high school puts us through."

"Or maybe it's what the artist fantasized about doing to the popular kids," William said. "Either way, three more weeks and school is finally over for me. Did you feel relieved when you graduated?"

"Sort of. I actually dropped out when I was sixteen."

"Oh. Seriously?"

Jason bit his lip. "Yeah. I had given up on foster homes and was eager to start my own life, get a job, all that stuff. I have my GED."

William was quiet for a moment. "So what are you going to do?"

"That's the million-dollar question," Jason said. "Until now, I couldn't afford to do anything but work. Ben keeps talking about me going to college, but I'm not crazy about the idea. He and Tim would be paying for it, which feels wrong. I don't know what I'd study anyway."

"Well, what makes you happy?"

"You," Jason said, laughing nervously. "I don't know. Horror movies, but I'm not interested in acting or anything like that. Movies are just an escape for me and nothing else. I like animals a lot. That's what prompted me to get a job at the pet store, but I don't see that going anywhere."

"You could be a vet," William said. "I assume you like animals enough to want to help them. And if you like horror movies so much, you probably wouldn't get squeamish over a little blood or whatever."

"Yeah," Jason said. "I've never really thought of it, but that could be cool. Would I get to call myself doctor?"

"Doctor Grant," William said. "Sounds hot. You should think about it."

"Maybe I will," Jason said. "So what about you?"

"Undecided," William said as they strolled farther into the gallery. "It's possible to make a career of the Coast Guard, but I'm not sure I want to. I guess I could be a lifeguard. Or I could teach swimming, this time to people who actually need lessons."

Jason grinned shamelessly. "Hey, my little ruse got me this far."

"That it did." William stopped as if something had suddenly occurred to him. "If you dropped out of high school, then you must have missed out on some big things."

"Like what?" Jason said. "Running up on stage to get my diploma?"

"That," William said, "and prom."

Jason laughed. "I never cared about some stupid dance."

"Oh."

He glanced over to find William looking pensive. "Wait, is that something important to you?"

William shrugged. "It's romantic, isn't it?"

"For straight people maybe," Jason said.

"There's no rule saying we couldn't go."

"You and me?"

William nodded. "Yeah. So I guess I'm asking you. Wanna be my date to the prom?"

When Jason considered it, he was surprised to discover just how much he did want that. He grinned broadly, and instead of answering with words, he pulled William close and nuzzled his nose.

When they returned to the parking lot, the minivan was still there but the old pickup truck had gone. This was good, since it allowed William to enter the car through the passenger-side door. Strange, then, that he was still standing outside while Jason waited behind the wheel. He rolled down the window and leaned over.

"What's up?"

"Uh…" William replied.

Jason's blood ran cold. He was out of the car and standing next to William in one second flat, staring down in horror at an angry scratch across the door. It wasn't just a simple thin line, but a fan-shaped section where the paint had been scraped away.

"That's not good," William said.

"He's going to kill me!" Jason moaned. "Seriously, you have no idea! If Tim had to choose between this car and Ben …" He shook his head, the contest too close to call.

"Okay," William said, rubbing his chin and maybe wishing he had Pan's beard. "All right. No need to panic. This happened to my brother's car once, and he got a little vial of paint from an auto store."

"Did it work?" Jason asked.

William shrugged. "I was little and wasn't paying much attention. I only remember because later I used it to paint my nails."

Jason stared. "You painted your nails? With car paint?"

"I was little! Anyway, I don't think the body is dented. All it needs is a little cosmetic repair. We can get some paint now and fix it up. By the time we're back from eating, it'll be like it never happened."

What alternative did they have? They drove to an auto supply store, and Jason could see why little William had mistaken the paint for nail polish. The vials weren't so different, each having an applicator built into the lid. The labels listed the color and auto manufacturer. Since the store didn't carry any paint for Bentleys, they settled on one made for Hondas they felt was close.

In the parking lot, they painted over the scratch, squabbling like they'd already been together for decades.

"Stroke in one direction only," William insisted. "This isn't finger paint!"

"I'm trying to blend it in!" Jason insisted. "It doesn't match around the edges."

"That's because it's still wet. It'll get lighter. Or darker. I don't remember which."

"Maybe we should have sanded it down first," Jason fretted.

"Nah, the paint was already scraped off. Sanding would only make it worse."

After ten minutes of work and twice as long spent arguing about the best way to go about this, they stood back and considered their work.

"Shit," Jason said, shoulders slumping.

The damaged spot looked like it had been hit by a water balloon full of paint.

"It'll be fine," William said. "It just has to sink in. That's all."

"Sink in?" Jason demanded. "Paint doesn't sink in. At least not on metal!"

"It might," William said, still optimistic. "Give it time."

Jason shook his head and groaned. "Okay. Let's go get something to eat."

Unfortunately, when they were finished, the hasty repair job appeared even worse. The paint was too glossy, and they had used too much, the once-flush surface now bulging outward.

"You're dead," William said. "I'm sorry, but I'm glad we were able to share this final evening together."

Jason glared at him. "You're coming home with me to share my fate." Then he perked up. "You're pretty big. Think you can take Tim in a fight?"

William shook his head. "My muscles are only for show. Sorry. Should we head back? Face the music?"

Jason nodded reluctantly. The drive home felt like a death march. Tim could be cool, but he wasn't as laid-back as Ben. At the very least, Jason wouldn't be allowed to borrow either car again. At worst, they might ask him to move out. Jason was reminded of all the stunts he had pulled, how he had done exactly this sort of thing on purpose to get kicked out of foster homes before. Maybe this was karma. This time he didn't want to leave, and he honestly hadn't meant to do what he'd done.

Jason parked the car in the garage, happy that Tim wasn't already there with a magnifying glass. His relief was short-lived. They had just reached the front door when it swung open.

"How was your date?" Tim asked, but he was already looking over their shoulders at the garage.

"There was a slight problem with the car," Jason said carefully.

"But don't worry," William said, sounding chipper. "We fixed it!"

"Fixed it?" Tim asked. "You mean like a fan belt or…"

"Nothing so serious," Jason said. "Just a little cosmetic damage."

Tim groaned, making a face like he was in physical pain. Then he pushed past them, rushing to the garage. They followed behind, exchanging worried glances. Once in the garage, Tim circled his car, spotting their handiwork immediately.

"What is this?" he cried.

"It wasn't Jason's fault," William said. "We parked the car at the museum, and when we came back out, it was all scratched up."

"And you decided to fix it with what?" Tim asked, gesturing at the door. "A paintball gun?"

"Professional grade auto paint," Jason mumbled. "Listen, I'll pay to get it fixed."

Tim's face managed to get even more incredulous. "Just how much money do you have?"

"Not a lot," Jason said, "but last time I checked my savings, it was—"

"The question was rhetorical."

"Sorry," Jason said. "I understand if you want me to leave."

Tim's features scrunched up. "Leave? Like move out?"

"Yeah."

Tim snorted. "All you did was scratch my car. It's not like you ran over my dog. Did you?" He bent over to check the tires at about the same time Ben showed up.

"What's going on here?"

"See for yourself!" Tim said, pointing at the mound of silver paint.

Ben's hand shot up to his mouth, but not in shock. Instead he was trying to disguise his laughter.

"Oh, it's *real* funny," Tim said, grinning a little himself. "What if this had happened to your car instead?"

"My car is a piece of junk," Ben said. "Painting any part of it would be an improvement."

"What are we going to do?" Tim asked, shaking his head. "Can we ground him? Is that within our rights?"

"It's not a big deal," Ben said. "You love me, right?"

"Yeah," Tim admitted.

"And I'm not perfect, am I?"

Tim hesitated. "This is one of those trick questions, isn't it?"

Ben tapped a foot expectantly.

"You're perfect to me?" Tim tried.

Ben looked surprised. "Hey, that's the right answer!"

"I'm learning." Tim jerked a head in Jason's direction. "He thought we were going to kick him out."

"Or at least be angry," Jason said sheepishly.

"Nah," Tim said. "It's not like it's your fault. Unless you parked too close to the other car."

"He parked totally fine," William said quickly.

"There you go," Tim said. "If you'd been driving recklessly or something, I'd have you in a headlock right now. I gotta say though, being a professional myself, that you suck at painting."

"I'll stick to music," Jason said, finally allowing himself to relax.

Ben took Tim by the arm and started tugging him away. "Let them have their night together."

"Fine," Tim said. "Sympathy nookie?"

Ben rolled his eyes. "Maybe."

"They're so cool," William said once they'd headed toward the house. "Hey, can I ask them?"

It took Jason a moment to figure out what he meant. "Sure."

They left the garage, William calling after them. "Hey, you guys want to go on a double date sometime?"

"Again?" Tim called back. "Ow!"

After a moment Ben answered for them both. "Just tell us when!"

William spun around and grinned. "You *so* need them to adopt you!"

"Jason Wyman?" he replied, cocking his head. "Or Jason Bentley. Neither sounds right."

"Not as good as Jason Townson, anyway." William said with a wink.

Chapter Twenty-six

Tim crossed his arms over his chest, staring across the restaurant at the other diners instead of the fork in front of his face. "Mushrooms are disgusting," he said.

"You've never tried a portobello," Ben said, jabbing the fork at him.

Jason and William exchanged amused looks. So far, this dinner had been like a private soap opera as Ben and Tim flirted or got into little arguments. Mostly they got along, but moments like these cracked Jason up.

"Portobello is still a mushroom," Tim said, "and mushrooms are disgusting. This one is just bigger and slimier. Looking at it turns my stomach."

"Then close your eyes," Ben said. When Tim didn't comply, he sighed. "If you love me, you'll close your eyes."

There was no getting out of that. Tim closed his eyes. He was obviously peeking though, so Ben made him cover his eyes with his hands. Their waiter, who was approaching the table, stopped, stared, and turned around again. Meanwhile, Ben had replaced the mushroom on his fork with a slice of fried goat cheese from his salad. He popped this into Tim's mouth, and they all watched as he chewed thoughtfully and grimaced.

"Tastes just like any other mushroom," he said.

Ben pulled Tim's hands away, uncovering his eyes. "That wasn't a mushroom!"

Tim smirked. "I know. It was goat cheese. You really thought I wouldn't notice?"

"That was the plan," Ben said. "Now try some portobello for real."

Tim did what he was told, and even though it was obvious he didn't enjoy the taste, he made sure to tell Ben otherwise.

William chuckled and shook his head. "How long have you guys been together?"

Ben and Tim glanced at each other as they mentally tallied it up.

"About two years," Ben said.

"Two?" Tim looked incredulous. "More like thirteen!"

"Thirteen years since we met, but he asked how long we've been together."

Tim frowned. "Two years? Is that all?"

"Quality over quantity," Ben said. "We've made up for lost time since we got back together."

As comforting as the words were intended to be, it was clear that Tim still felt unhappy.

"You never stopped loving each other," Jason said. "When you were apart, you still felt the same way, right? So you could say you've been in love for thirteen years."

"There you go," Ben said.

"Not as cool as actually being together," Tim said, "but I'll take it. Besides, being apart was for the best."

"What do you mean?" William asked.

"If we had stayed together," Tim explained, "I'm not so sure I would have changed. At least not as much. I had to be on my own to become the person I needed to be."

Ben nodded. "You hear about high school sweethearts getting back together, and I used to think it was just nostalgia or people trying to recapture their youth. Now I know that people sometimes meet when they're young and see potential in each other, but then discover they aren't ready yet."

"That's right," Tim said. "People need time to get ripe. Like fruit. We're a couple of ripe bananas."

Ben laughed. "This probably sounds crazy to you both."

"No, I get what you mean," William said. "Sometimes you have to be on your own to become who you were meant to be. I feel that way too."

Jason glanced over at him, wondering what he meant.

"So," Tim said, "what movie are we seeing tonight?"

"Friday the 13th," Jason said distractedly, before giving Tim his full attention. "It's a remake, and if they've screwed up the franchise, I'll be the next Jason to get creative with a machete."

"Jason Takes Hollywood," William said.

"Exactly. Wait, was that a *Jason Takes Manhattan* reference?"

William looked proud. "I've seen my share of horror movies."

Jason was so impressed that he forgot about William's strange comment. At least until the subject came up again later that night. They were alone in the backyard, Ben and Tim giving them their privacy. Jason had fetched his guitar, stripped off his shirt, and settled down into a chair. William had adjusted a piece of lawn furniture so it was almost flat and was lying on his side, fist resting against his lips as he watched Jason play. Between songs, he moved away his hand and spoke.

"I'm excited about prom," he said. "Are you?"

"Honestly?" Jason continued to strum the guitar lightly. "I'm a little nervous. I take it you're out at school?"

"Yeah," William said, propping himself up on an elbow. "Since forever."

"And nobody gives you shit for it?"

"People have called me names..." William flexed an arm and grinned. "But for some reason, no one's tried to pick a fight."

"In that case I hope your muscles are still visible beneath your tuxedo."

"Did you rent yours already?"

Jason nodded. "Ben wanted to buy me one, but I insisted I could handle it on my own."

William rolled over onto his back and considered the stars. "This dance will be our grand finale. For now, at least."

Jason stopped playing. "What's that supposed to mean?"

"My enlistment in the Coast Guard," William said.

"So? That's still months away." Jason swallowed. "Isn't it? I figured it was like school. You get the summer off and..."

William sat up and swung his legs around. "I ship out to Cape May the week after I graduate."

"I don't even know where that is," Jason said, feeling lost.

"New Jersey."

"And how long will you be gone?"

William studied his face and must have seen the emotion there because he hesitated. "You've known about this since the beginning."

"How long?" Jason said, his throat feeling tight.

"Four years."

Jason set aside the guitar and stared. "You'll come back though, right? You'll have—I don't know—shore leave or whatever."

"I'll be back for holidays and such, but this is a full-time commitment. I don't get weekends off like a normal job. Joining the Coast Guard takes dedication."

"Can't it wait?" Jason asked. "At least until the end of summer?"

William shook his head. "I'm sorry. I enlisted last year so I wouldn't have to wait. At the time I was eager to get away from here. Now it's not so easy, especially since you came along. I know four years is a long time, Jason. Too long for me to expect you to wait."

"I don't care. I'll wait."

William smiled sadly. "I won't let you."

Jason clenched his jaw. "You don't have a say in it!"

"I do. Becoming a rescue swimmer is going to be the hardest thing I've ever done. It's going to take absolutely all of my willpower and attention and frankly..." William's face twisted up. "After all that time with Kelly, of trying to make someone else happy instead of taking care of myself, I need a break. I can't go to the Coast Guard and think about how sad you are, sitting here for years and years while waiting for me. What if you meet someone or just want to screw around? I can't worry about any of that. Not if I'm going to do what I need to do."

What Jason said next was selfish, and he knew it was, but he didn't care. "So don't join the Coast Guard. If it's a choice between me and leaving, then stay here."

William eyed him. "This is my dream we're talking about. You know that, right?"

"Yeah."

William chewed his lip, then nodded. "Okay. If you want me to give that up for you, I will. That's how much I love you."

"Good," Jason said, but he already felt terrible and knew he'd never forgive himself. "I'll remember that when you're gone." His voice cracked. "When it hurts the most, I'll remember that you would have stayed for me."

William hopped up, yanked Jason to his feet, and held him. "I'm sorry," he said.

Jason shook his head. "Don't be. You just become the best rescue swimmer they've ever had."

"I'll try," William said. "I promise."

"Four years!"

"I know. Of course, you could join too. Be my bunkmate."

Jason pulled away and laughed bitterly. "I've never done well with authority, and I doubt I'd even pass the physical. I don't think I'd make it."

"We will though," William said. "Just like Ben and Tim. All those years went by and they still found each other again. And if some hot guy sweeps you off your feet in the meantime, I'll be happy, because I'll know that you're loved. But someday, even if we're both in an old folks' home and have lost our husbands, I bet we'll find our way back to each other again."

Jason put on a brave smile, even though he didn't feel so certain. He knew that not all stories had happy endings and the chances of a guy like William staying single were slim to none. But Jason couldn't force him to stay, and he couldn't go with him, so there didn't seem to be any other choice. "So what now?"

William considered the question and exhaled. "Now we make the best of the time we have left."

Prom wasn't what Jason had expected. He thought it would be held at the school, maybe in the gymnasium, like in *Carrie*. A hotel ballroom had been booked instead, and yet that feeling of returning to high school remained. Had he not dropped out, Jason would have only been in his first year of college, but still, the vibe was much much... younger. Maybe he felt this way because he'd been on his own and working for the last few years, or maybe he was just being silly.

As the night wore on, the dance floor became a manic stage for drama. He overheard two breakups, saw more than one crying girl being comforted by friends, and had a lovely confrontation with drunk jocks who called him a faggot. Jason had swung—and missed—but before anyone could retaliate, William had stepped in front of him. After sizing him up, the jocks had wandered away to get wasted or laid or whatever mindless cattle did for entertainment. Not that Jason could judge. He would rather be in bed with William right now, or getting trashed so he could stop thinking about him leaving soon.

The last few weeks had been intense, Jason spending every moment he could with William. Any hour outside of work or school was spent together, and rarely did a night go by that they weren't sleeping side by side. And tonight—which really did feel like the end because William had graduation and so much to prepare for before leaving—had been mostly frustrating when it was meant to be special.

Jason tried to focus on William as they danced. He was so handsome, cutting a perfect figure in his conservative tuxedo, like a version of James Bond that was more sweet than suave.

Jason had done his best to find something that didn't conform, renting a tux with tails and borrowing Tim's metallic blue bow tie. And he'd let his hair remain shaggy and untamed. William had reached out, touching it more than once to the delight of the girls building up around them. The eyes of their audience shone more with every affectionate gesture. This helped ease Jason's anger at the jocks. If only women ruled the world. He was certain it would be a better place.

Jason caught sight of a school chaperone shouting at the DJ and pointing to the dance floor as if Godzilla had been spotted there. The DJ nodded, ended the song early, and replaced it with a ballad. The rowdy vibe died down as people either sought a partner or fled the scene. The lights grew dimmer, artificial starlight spinning around the room, but Jason stopped paying attention to their surroundings. He let William take him in his arms. Or vice versa, since William rested his arms on Jason's shoulders, just as so many girls around them were doing to their guys.

The next song was also a ballad, William pulling him closer, hugging Jason as they leisurely spun in place. Jason willed time to slow to a crawl, wanting this moment to last forever. William might have been wishing the same. When they kissed, a few girls around them squealed. William smiled against Jason's lips before really giving them a show. The outside world was forgotten again during the third song. Then, perhaps because the vibe had become tense in another sort of way, a dance song started pumping through the speakers.

Jason stepped back, asking with his expression if William really wanted to keep dancing. After a shake of the head, Jason led him by the hand out of the ballroom. Tim had rented a limo, which was a nice gesture. Or a way of preventing the Bentley from being loaned out again. The biggest present was the house being all theirs tonight. Ben and Tim were at a bed and breakfast. Jason hadn't thought to ask where, but the phone number was on the kitchen table.

He asked the limo driver to take them home and stared off into space. William fiddled with the mini-bar, making comments about the contents. Before long, he sighed and shook Jason as if he were asleep.

"You're thinking about it again," William said.

"Sorry." This happened a lot recently. How could Jason not think of the future and how empty it would be without William? He tried to plan ahead, searching desperately for something to occupy his time, like a second job or school. "I researched becoming a veterinarian. Did I mention that already?"

"No," William said. "Is there a special school for that?"

"Yeah, and you need four years of college to get into it."

William shrugged as if this wasn't a daunting task.

"Then another four years at *that* school to become a vet."

Now William looked surprised. "Eight years of school to become a vet?"

"Yup."

"Oh. Are you going to do it?"

Jason laughed. "I didn't have the patience to finish high school. I'm not going to sign up for almost a decade of education."

"Maybe you could be a veterinary assistant instead."

"Maybe," Jason said noncommittally.

"Doesn't matter," William declared. "There is no past or future right now. There's only tonight, which I'm very much looking forward to."

Jason smiled when William gave an exaggeratedly lewd wink. "It's hardly our first time together."

"Yes and no," William said coyly.

"Ah. How could I forget?"

The topic of anal sex had come up once before, and William had insisted he was saving himself for prom night. Jason had laughed at the time, thinking it was a joke, but apparently it wasn't. This made Jason a little nervous, because although he had bottomed for Caesar the last time they had ever slept together—and while that had felt good in its own way—he'd also decided it really wasn't for him. One look at his date, tuxedo stuffed full of muscles, was all he needed to determine William was also a top.

"I'm hungry," William said, rubbing his stomach.

"Again? We ate before the dance!"

"And then we burned a lot of calories."

Jason snorted. "What are you hungry for?"

A few moments later, they did the ridiculous and pulled into the McDonald's drive-thru. In a limo. The driver seemed happy with this decision, since he was hungry too. William suggested they park while they ate, the divider staying down as William chatted with the driver. Jason wasn't hungry. Instead he watched them sharing a meal, realizing again just how much he was going to miss having this happy, kind, all-too-generous person in his life. He tried to tell himself that it was for the greater benefit of the world, that countless people were going to meet William and benefit from the experience, but Jason was sure no one would love him quite as much.

The house was silent when they entered, but soon Chinchilla's panting and grumbling filled the air. They let her out and Samson in. Later, when both were fed and had settled down, the house grew quiet again. They were on the couch together, and Jason was pretty sure William had asked him a question, but he had no idea what about.

"Jason!" William complained.

"I'm sorry!"

William made a sympathetic expression. "You're breaking my heart."

"You broke mine first," Jason said, but he smiled to show he wasn't trying to make William feel bad. As much as he didn't like what was going to happen, he understood why it had to.

"I know what'll cheer you up," William said, kissing his neck. "Do you want to do it in Ben and Tim's bed?"

"What?" Jason pulled away. "Why?"

"They're so hot! We can pretend we *are* them."

Jason laughed. "You're way too into them."

"I don't care," William said proudly. "They're an awesome couple. I envy them."

"Yeah, me too. The answer is no, by the way, but if I had said yes, who would you pretend to be?"

"Ben," William said instantly. "I figure he's the—you know. I mean, Tim has that aggressive side to him, so he must be the top."

Jason replayed the conversation in his mind to be sure he understood. "So you would want to be the bottom?"

"Yeah," William said.

"But you're huge!" Jason retorted.

"So?" William smirked. "Oh, I see. Bottoms have to be slight and feminine, is that it? Don't judge a book by its cover."

"But it's such a pretty cover," Jason said, coming in for a kiss, but his stupid brain distracted him. "So Kelly is a top?"

"No!" William said, laughing. "No no no. That's just one

more thing I did to make him happy."

"So you've never actually..."

"No."

Jason shook his head. "Then how do you know you're a bottom?"

"Because the whole time I was topping Kelly, I was thinking how bad I wanted someone to do that to me. Maybe not Kelly. Maybe someone like you." William winced. "Wait, are you a bottom?"

Jason didn't answer the question directly. "So there's still a first for you."

"I told you I was saving myself for prom," William said with a grin.

"I guess I was too."

William's eyebrows shot up. "No! Seriously? Oh my god! This is so momentous. I mean, if that's something you want to do."

"Yeah!" Jason said. "Desperately. Uh, but not in Ben and Tim's bed. In my room. I want it to happen there."

William didn't ask for an explanation. He kissed Jason, stood, and offered his hand. Once upstairs, Jason slipped into the bathroom. Condoms and lube had mysteriously appeared there around the time of his first gay youth meeting. He'd found the presumption annoying when first discovering them, but now he felt grateful.

When he returned to his room, he found William with the guitar on his lap, pretending to strum the strings without touching them. His goofy face made Jason laugh, but William's complete lack of clothes soon sobered him up.

"I normally just take off my shirt," Jason said.

"Maybe you should take it a step further."

Jason took this as his cue, slowly undressing in front of William, who grinned appreciatively. Then things proceeded as they often did. They kissed, stroked each other's skin, took turns going down on each other, or paused just to hold each other tight.

"I'm ready," William whispered.

"Okay. Um."

William kissed him and smiled. "I've got a lot of experience you can learn from."

"I'll need all the help I can get."

"Get on your back. It's always easier if you let the bottom,

I mean me, be in control. That way I can set the pace. At the beginning, anyway."

Jason rolled onto his back and held up the condom. "Want to do the honors?"

"Sure." William swung a leg over Jason, bouncing up and down on his crotch a few times and causing them both to laugh. Then he opened the condom and twisted his neck around, working with his hands behind his back. Jason took this moment to admire his body, to trace a finger around the outline of his abdominal muscles or the defined lines that led from his hips to his crotch.

"Okay," William said after fiddling with the lube, and himself, a little. "Let's find out if this is something I really want or not."

For once he didn't look so certain. He kept his eyes trained on Jason's, his mouth open slightly as he concentrated. He bit his lip when the head of Jason's cock popped inside, looking a little panicked.

"Should we stop?" Jason asked.

William shook his head. "Play with me."

Jason took hold of William's dick, sliding his hand up and down it and summoning a moan. William made a face that said, *"Oh yeah, more of that!"* Jason was happy to comply, because the more pleasure he gave William, the more his body moved, allowing him to slip deeper inside. The sensation was warm and wonderful and made the love in his chest come pouring out. William must have felt the same way because he pawed at Jason, pressing a hand to his cheek before bending over to kiss him.

"Let's roll over," William said, "but try to stay inside, because that was trickier than I thought it would be."

William sat as far down on Jason as possible before—very carefully—they embraced and rolled over. Then Jason was on top, and William appeared to be in very tentative ecstasy. Jason moved his hips in and out once experimentally.

"Is that okay?" he asked.

William nodded. "Yeah. Oh, man… Go to town!"

Jason brought one of William's legs up and over his shoulder. He held back at first, but William's continued moans told him it was okay, so he gave all of himself that he could. Not just physically, because he felt like he was giving *everything* to

William—his thoughts, his energy, his soul. William's eyes were half-lidded, his face flushed and contorted with pleasure. He nodded encouragingly when Jason's breaths became shorter. They finished at the same time, which wasn't surprising because they might as well have been one person. That sensation slowly began to fade along with the euphoria, which could be why William clung to him and pulled him close.

"I love you," he whispered.

"I know," Jason said. "I could feel it. I love you too."

They held each other afterwards, not needing to speak because everything was so clear. Almost everything.

"I can't go," William said. His back was pressed to Jason, so his face couldn't be seen, but the sniffling implied he might be crying. "Not after that. There's no way. I can't."

Jason swallowed. "You have to. It's your dream."

"That's not my only dream," William said. "I've been waiting for you without even knowing it."

Jason smiled at the thought, but his heart still ached. "I'm not going anywhere," he said. "I'll still be around when you need me. You'll see."

After a moment of silence, William spoke again. "This isn't goodbye."

Jason didn't reply because he knew it was. Graduation was just around the corner, and William's family would surely all be there. Jason could picture William at the airport, ready to fly away, his mother crying. At least he hoped she did, because if Jason needed to comfort her, maybe it would distract him from the pain. They might have a few small private moments left together, but nothing like tonight. As much as Jason hated to admit it, this was goodbye.

Jason sat on the front porch, feeling the same way he had since William briefly turned around at the airport to wave. After aching for a day, Jason had woken up the next morning feeling like his insides had been hollowed out. He was no longer complete. Might not ever be again. He honestly didn't know. All he could do was take it one day at a time.

At least help had arrived. A Porsche pulled up to the house, and Emma hopped out of the passenger door and rushed to hug him. Now that summer was here, she would be coming to stay for weeks at a time, maybe longer if she had her way. Tim had already started building an addition to the garage so he could move his studio there, giving Emma her own room. Her father got out of the car with a much more reserved expression.

"Is Tim here?" he asked.

"Nope," Jason said. "He had some errands to run."

Greg visibly relaxed. "Oh. Okay. Michelle says 'hi.' She's having an emergency with one of the kids in her care, or she'd be here."

"It's cool," Jason said. "I'll give her a call sometime."

"Okay." Greg pointed to the house. "Is Ben inside?"

"Yeah. Go on in."

Once they were alone, Jason shook his head. "What is it with your dad and Tim? Shouldn't they be eager to talk cars or something boring like that?"

Emma rolled her eyes. "When Jace died, Dad took it hard. He and Jace were best friends their entire lives. Even though years went by before Ben got back with Tim, it was like Dad finally found someone to blame. It's ridiculous, and he mostly kept it to himself until there was a grill party here and he and Tim were both drinking. Alcohol makes dumb people dumber, so before you know it, they were fist-fighting."

"No shit?" Jason said. "That's horrible!"

"Yeah."

"So, uh… Who won?"

Emma raised an eyebrow. "Ben. He shoved himself between them and stopped them dead in their tracks with a stare. The only time Tim wears the pants in their relationship is when Ben lets him borrow them."

Jason laughed and shook his head. "I hope they get over it someday. Tim and Greg have a lot in common."

"I know." Emma peered at him. "How are you doing?"

"Ever see that Indiana Jones movie with the Voodoo priest who rips out people's hearts?"

"No," Emma said, "but I get the picture. Do you hate William now?"

"No!" Jason said. "I'm in love with him."

Emma scrunched up her face. "He left you to go build a life for himself and wouldn't give a long-distance relationship a try."

"That's right."

"And you still love him?"

"More than ever."

"Wow." Emma looked taken aback as she exhaled. "I hope Bonnie never leaves me. Speaking of which, youth group meeting tomorrow."

Jason groaned. "I'm not going."

"You have to! Dad says I'm here to see family, not run around with some girl. I'm *so* not happy I came out of the closet."

Jason smiled. "Yes you are."

"Anyway, he's in there right now, telling Ben I'm supposed to stay close to home. I just know it. But if you want to go to group, and I also want to, then that's spending time with family, right?"

Jason shook his head, but he understood. He'd give just about anything to see William right now, or even to hear from him. He hadn't received any text messages since the one saying he'd arrived. Maybe William wasn't allowed to have his phone, or perhaps he just didn't have time. Regardless, Jason hoped that William thought of him sometimes. Maybe just before he fell asleep or when he woke up in the morning. Just for a moment every day. That would be enough.

"Please?" Emma prompted.

Jason smiled. "Okay."

"Understanding where another person is coming from," Keith said, "can resolve almost any conflict. Or it can help you form friendships, make connections, get a job, close sales—anything, really. It's a powerful tool, so I want you to partner up with someone you don't know very well and change that."

Emma hopped to her feet, running across the church meeting room to Bonnie. Keith didn't seem to know about their relationship, so this went unchallenged. Jason had the same instinct. He'd rather hang out with a friend, but Emma and Bonnie being together eliminated the two people he knew. Not counting Kelly, of course. Jason had been surprised to see him in attendance, and not pleasantly so, since Kelly had spent most of the meeting staring at him. He was doing so right now, in fact, as he moved toward Jason with purpose. People got out of his way as his crutches helped bring him near.

"Want to be partners?" Kelly asked, sitting down next to Jason instead of waiting for an answer. He glanced around the room as everyone else paired up. "Although I think I know where you're coming from already."

"Do you?" Jason asked, waiting for the inevitable insult.

"Yes. After all, we both loved the same man, and he left us to go become a hero or whatever. I'm guessing you still love him as much as I do."

"Guilty as charged," Jason said.

Kelly nodded, looking him up and down and no doubt seeing how tense he was. "I'm not mad at you. Not anymore. William and me breaking up was the right thing to do. We didn't make each other happy. All we did was fight. Did you two ever argue?"

"Not really," Jason said, "but then we weren't together that long."

Kelly's smile was sly. "The first time William and I met was an argument. That should have been a warning sign."

"I didn't want you to get hurt," Jason blurted out. "I'm not saying I didn't think some evil thoughts about you, but I was only following my heart. Ideally you wouldn't have been in the picture at all, if that makes sense."

Kelly considered him and nodded. "Ideally he and I would have broken up that day instead of us getting in a car crash. I assume he told you about that?"

"Yeah," Jason said. He resisted saying he was sorry, feeling Kelly wouldn't want his pity. Perhaps he was wrong, since Kelly seemed to be waiting for those very words. When they didn't come, he nodded appreciatively and spoke again.

"I don't know about you, but I haven't got a clue what to do with myself anymore. There's an entire summer before college, and without William, the world feels empty. *I* feel empty. When I lost my leg, I needed a long time to get over missing a piece of myself. How I feel right now isn't so different."

"I couldn't have put it better myself," Jason said. "I keep wishing I had some of William saved up somehow. Maybe videos where all he does is look at the camera and talk. That way I could pretend we were having a conversation. I don't even have photos. I think the ones from prom got lost in the mail." Even the newspaper clippings were gone, Jason deciding to throw them away rather than risk William discovering them by accident.

"Here," Kelly said, taking out his phone. "Give me your number and I'll hook you up."

Jason did, tensing up again because he didn't want to see photos of Kelly and William sharing happy moments. Jason's heart wasn't that open. Perhaps Kelly understood this, because every photo he sent was of one person alone: William concentrating at the edge of a pool, about to dive. William laughing in front of a birthday cake. William in bed, still asleep in the early morning light.

Jason wiped at the tears in his eyes. "Thanks," he managed to croak.

Kelly nodded. "These are just the ones from my phone. I used to take real photos all the time. Sort of a hobby of mine. Give me your email address and I'll send you some."

Jason recited it so Kelly could type it in. Afterwards, he set the phone aside and took a deep breath. "Like I said, it's a long summer. I know I've been a bitch to you, but maybe we can hang out sometime. That way I can prove I'm not so bad after all."

Jason was so surprised by the offer that he nodded. They talked then, for a while, mostly about William. Jason got to see a side of Kelly that was softer, the person William had probably fallen in love with so long ago. Too bad it took them falling apart for it to resurface.

The group meeting was coming to an end. Jason was looking at the photos of William on his phone again when he decided to give something back. "You ever think about turning that camera on yourself?"

"Me?" Kelly asked.

"Yeah," Jason said. "Professionally."

Kelly didn't have any false humility about his appearance so he wasn't shocked by the suggestion, but something was holding him back. "I'm pretty sure having a full set of limbs is required if you want to be a model."

Jason shook his head, summoning up Marcello's number on his phone. "Talk to this guy for a minute, and he'll happily prove you wrong."

That his friends were succeeding was a good thing. Wasn't it? Jason thought so most of the time, but their happiness meant he felt even more alone. Emma and Bonnie's romance was its own rollercoaster, one both girls kept eagerly returning to ride. For most of the summer, Emma found excuses or schemes so that she and Bonnie could be together. Jason didn't blame her in the slightest, wanting nothing more than to be tangled up in a love affair again, but he only really wanted to be with one person, and that person was gone.

As for Kelly, modeling was a new lease on life for him, and a mixed blessing for Marcello, who was thrilled with the reaction to Kelly's photos but less than enamored by what a handful his new star model could be. Jason hung out with Kelly on occasion, but that happened less and less frequently. The only thing they really had in common was William, and Kelly was starting to put that relationship behind him.

Ben and Tim were always there, at least. Jason wasn't abandoned by any means, but the world still felt a lonelier place without William. Time crawled by. At this rate, four years would be an eternity. So it was by no accident that Jason found himself, on a slow day at work, heading over to the pet adoptions area. Barbara was looking frazzled as usual as she sized him up to see if he had a particular weakness for any of the animals.

"Still can't take any home," Jason said. "But this dog looks like he could use a walk. And maybe we could do a meet-and-greet event out in the parking lot where kids can interact with the dogs. Sort of like a petting zoo. The dogs will love it, and maybe it'll help form some bonds."

"I'm too busy scooping litter boxes to worry about such things," Barbara said with a gleam in her eye.

Jason smiled. "I can help with that too."

"Have any experience?" Barbara teased.

"Shoveling shit?" Jason asked. "A little. How much does this job pay?"

"Not a dime. Might turn your hair gray. Just look at me."

Jason did and saw a person too busy to worry about lost loves—someone who probably wished time would slow down so she could do everything that needed doing. Maybe time machines didn't exist, but he knew of one way to get the days to zoom by, bringing the future closer in the blink of an eye: hard work, and lots of it. Jason rubbed his chin, as if deep in thought, and then nodded. "Sign me up!"

Part Three:
Austin, Texas
2011

Chapter Twenty-seven

Two years. Not the happiest anniversary to celebrate, but Jason took it in stride, marking it on his mental calendar. Two years since William left to join the Coast Guard. At times Jason seriously considered doing something similar. Anything was better than waiting, sitting in the eye of the storm while the world around him changed. Volunteering at the animal shelter had been a wise decision and helped Jason lose himself in the maelstrom of a hectic life. At first he found it taxing emotionally, since so many animals lacked a home or a human companion. But as Barbara always said, he could either turn his back on them or turn himself into what they needed. That meant walking dogs, playing with cats, cleaning, grooming, feeding, and loving. He did so gladly, feeling a sense of kinship with these animals. After all, he was an orphan too.

The day job wasn't nearly as satisfying, nor were the long nights without William. Brief reprieves to this loneliness came when William returned home for the holidays or other special occasions. Then they would be together again, and Jason would feel at peace. William was happy too, having become a rescue swimmer. Jason wasn't surprised by this achievement, but when he heard that William was one of only three graduates in a class of twenty-five, he finally understood how difficult it must have been. William positively glowed. Proud, but not in an arrogant way. A serenity settled about him that must come from living one's dream. Jason adored seeing him that way, loved him even more than before, and at times like these, never regretted letting him go.

Then William would return to active duty, and Jason would ache all over again. But the pain was always worth it. Sometimes Jason would look at maps, trying to figure out how to make the thirty-hour drive to Cape Cod where William was stationed. He never did. William would probably be too busy to see him anyway. Perhaps that was why he never suggested the idea or asked if Jason could move there, find a civilian life not far from his world full of strange abbreviations and ranks and rules. Or maybe William was still enjoying his freedom. That would explain the most recent visit.

February, when William's mother celebrated her birthday. Normally William would show up on his bike, grinning and asking if he could stay the night. When meeting these days, all they wanted was to be alone together. This time when William called, he suggested they meet somewhere for lunch, but not a romantic picnic or a secluded meal of fast food in the car. They met in a very public place, William hesitating instead of sweeping Jason into his arms for a kiss. When they did hug, William had kept his body angled away from Jason, as if he was just a friend or a relative. Whatever intimacy they had was gone. Jason didn't bother asking why, or what the guy's name was. Part of him knew he'd been lucky to have William to himself for two extra years. That someone else had discovered this wonderful man was only natural.

Regardless, Jason was shaken by the experience. He found himself questioning his life and yearning for change. Maybe he'd seek out some of the light that made William shine, grab a piece of that for himself. On one such introspective day, Jason was in his room, sitting on his bed and considering his possessions. He was marveling that he'd lived in the same place for so long, something made evident by how personal this room had become. The desktop computer had been replaced by a laptop that usually sat on a table next to the cozy reading chair he'd bought. He had his own flat-screen TV across from the bed, since Tim and Ben were only willing to suffer so many horror movies. Next to this were small stacks of Blu-rays, DVDs, and even VHS tapes for the really obscure movies. Jason enjoyed them more than ever, especially since love was rarely a part of such films, and in such cases, a machete usually put an end to any happy relationship.

When the television was off, Jason's room was a much less gory place. After he'd expressed interest, Tim allowed a few of his paintings to be displayed in the room. Jason's favorite was of Chinchilla, bounding across a field full of rainbow light. Framed photos also hung on the wall, one from when he and William had gone to prom, which had arrived in the mail months after his departure. Next to it was a newer photo from Emma and Bonnie's prom night together. Hanging above them all, like the beginning of a family tree, was the photo of Ben and Tim from when they were young. Jason had dug it out of the attic, matted it, and framed it as carefully as possible. He'd meant for it to be a present, but loved it too much and put it on his own wall instead. Ben and Tim seemed to appreciate it too, and would always look at it when they entered his room.

Like now. After knocking—despite the door being open—Tim strolled into his room. Usually he'd only glance at the photo in passing, but this time he stopped and stared. When he turned to face Jason, he seemed a little flustered.

"Benjamin and I are going out to eat," he said. "Wanna tag along?"

"Where to?" Jason asked.

Tim made a face. "Some new Indian place."

Jason mirrored his expression. "Nah, I think I'll hang out here, maybe order a pizza."

"Save me some," Tim murmured, briefly glancing back at the photo.

"You all right?" Jason asked.

"Yeah," Tim said, pulling himself together. "How about you?"

Jason shrugged. "I've been doing a lot of thinking lately."

"You and me both." Tim sat on the edge of his bed. "What's been haunting you?"

"I'm thinking about moving out," Jason said. "Getting my own place."

"For real?" Tim looked aghast. "I knew we shouldn't have given you Ben's old car. Too much freedom. We'd rather have you trapped here with us."

Jason smiled. "Thanks, but I can't live here forever. I love it, don't get me wrong, but I'm twenty-one and still living at home."

"Yeah," Tim said grudgingly. "I get that. But I thought you were going to wait and get a place with Emma when she moves to Austin for college. That's still two years away."

"I know," Jason said. "I just… Something needs to change. You ever have that feeling?"

"Yeah, a fresh start and all that, but change isn't always for the better. Are you sure about this? Ben's going to take it hard. He's still getting over Samson passing away."

"I know," Jason said, "but I'd stay in Austin and keep coming by to mooch free food off you guys. I swear."

"Just think about it a little longer," Tim said. "Don't make any hasty decisions. And maybe don't mention it to Benjamin until you're sure."

Jason nodded. "I can do that."

"Good." Tim bit his lip. "Can you keep a secret?"

Jason smirked. "Only one way to find out."

"Actually, it's more like advice I need."

"From me?" Jason said, not hiding his surprise.

"Yeah. I'll be right back."

When Tim returned, he double-checked the hall and then shut the door. Jason's jaw dropped when he saw what Tim was holding: a little black jewelry box, the kind with a hinged lid. He rubbed at it, grumbling about lint, cheeks burning red as he failed to make eye contact.

"Is that what I think it is?" Jason asked.

Tim glanced up. "This is crazy, right? Do you think… Ugh. I don't know what I'm doing."

Jason suppressed a smile. "Show me the ring."

Tim opened the box, tossing it carelessly aside on Jason's dresser. He held the ring pinched between index finger and thumb, studying it a moment before handing it to Jason. "I wanted something basic," Tim said. "No diamonds or any precious stones. I don't want to present him with a million-dollar bribe or whatever. If he wants that stuff later, he can have it, so I just went with a simple platinum band."

"*Just* platinum?" Jason said with a chuckle. "It's nice! Very classy."

"Yeah." Tim sounded anything but certain. "I did have some words inscribed on the inside."

Jason tilted the ring to see. The words were in Spanish, but he had a good idea what they meant. "This is from that poem, right?"

Tim nodded. "Just the first part. I figured the second would go on the actual wedding ring, which will say 'my beautiful butterfly' because that's what he is to me."

Jason glanced up, eyebrows raised.

"You think I'm doing the right thing?" Tim asked.

Jason hesitated. "You're not sure if you want to marry him?"

Tim's eyes bulged. "That's not what I meant!" he said, laughing manically. "Oh man, I want to marry him so freaking hard! Ha! Oh my god…"

"Take a deep breath," Jason said patiently.

"Right," Tim said. "Okay. Whew."

"If it's what you want, you should go for it. The ring is perfect." Jason handed it back. "Is that what you were worried about?"

Tim studied the ring and swallowed. "Do you think he'll say yes? He was married before, you know. To Jace. I'm not trying to be his replacement, but maybe asking will bring back all the pain Benjamin went through—"

"Or maybe it will feel good," Jason interrupted. "It'll mean two different guys have wanted to spend their entire lives with him. That seems pretty lucky to me, and Ben is the kind of guy who doesn't take things for granted. Besides, have you seen the way he looks at you? And I don't mean when you guys are in the mood. Sometimes you ask him to pass the salt, and I practically expect to hear music swell."

Tim grinned. "I love when he gets all melty."

"And a million other nauseating things, I'm sure," Jason said. "Ben's list of what he likes about you is probably twice as long. So yeah, I think you should follow your heart on this one."

Tim was visibly relieved. "Maybe you're right. Now I just have to find the right time."

"Dinner tonight?" Jason suggested.

"No. I want to do it here. That might not sound romantic, but he and I have always been hiding away from the world together. Something important like this should be private. Hell, we might even have the wedding here. His dad will walk him down the hallway instead of the aisle."

Jason laughed. "Now *that* you might want to rethink."

"I will." Tim pocketed the ring. "If you promise to rethink moving out. There's no rush. We like having you here."

"Okay," Jason conceded.

"Just make yourself scarce when I give the signal," Tim said, practically giddy as he left the room. Jason smiled after him, and when he was sure the coast was clear, allowed himself a dreamy sigh.

Then he stood, walked to the dresser, and picked up the black box Tim had discarded. It was probably good that he had. The velvet surface really was covered in lint, probably from where Tim had been hiding it. The box was empty, of course, the inside fitted with black silk and a slit where the ring had been. Now the ring was gone. He tried not to view this as sad. The box hadn't been emptied. It was waiting to be filled. Jason closed the lid and stowed the box in a drawer, just in case Tim asked for it back.

A week passed without Tim popping the question. Jason began to feel just as nervous as Tim had acted. Every morning when he went downstairs for breakfast, Jason searched for signs that it had happened in the night. This morning in particular had a surprise waiting for him, one that represented the antithesis of marriage. Marcello was in the kitchen. Judging from the still-full bottle on the table, he hadn't been there long.

"Champagne for breakfast!" Marcello declared happily, toasting Jason. "What a wonderful way to greet the day. Have a glass with me. You're old enough, aren't you?"

"No," Tim answered for him, moodily adjusting his bathrobe. Next to him, Ben was sipping a cup of green tea like it was the only thing keeping him sane. Marcello gestured to the empty seat next to him, so Jason plopped down.

"What's up?" he asked. "Time for me to break out the bow tie again?"

"Not until the Eric Conroy fundraiser in October," Marcello said, eyes sparkling. "But speaking of scantily dressed men, with hurricane season winding down, it won't be long until we see your handsome young friend again, will it?"

"We've still got a couple months," Jason said. "Hurricane season runs until the end of November."

"Does it?" Marcello asked, looking surprised. "Well, you'll have to bring him to the Christmas party. He was such a delight last year, with all his swashbuckling stories of the high seas."

Jason shook his head. "I'll probably be showing up alone this year, but feel free to invite him anyway."

"Ah." Marcello nodded his understanding. "Well, I'm sure many young suitors will be excited to see you on your own, for once."

Tim huffed impatiently. "A social call? This early? For real?"

"Always such a grump in the morning," Marcello tsked. Then his face became serious. "I'm afraid I heard some rather disturbing news last night. As you know, the people who bought Eric's house—your old house—are friends of mine."

"Do you show up unannounced there too?" Tim asked.

"Only when they aren't at home. They're terrible bores, but

you know I love that house. You should come with me sometime. It's such a trip down memory lane."

Tim's features brightened somewhat. "Are you serious? You still have a key?"

"Oh yes. The new owners work during the day. We could have the house all to ourselves."

Tim blinked a few times. "Count me in!"

"Then I look forward to breaking the law with you," Marcello said happily. He cleared his throat. "As I was saying, I happened to run into the current owners, and they mentioned someone showing up at their house in the middle of the night. Someone who was asking about you."

Tim looked baffled. "Bill collector? Unless there's something I forgot to pay—"

"Ryan," Ben guessed.

Marcello nodded grimly. "The description matched, and even if it didn't, he gave his name. Unfortunately, my friends don't have any skeletons in their closet and thus don't value discretion as much as we do. They told Ryan about your work at the gallery."

Tim placed a hand over his forehead and leaned back. "Oh man. Someone came by last week when I wasn't there. He didn't leave any info, but the person on duty said the guy was acting weird. I figured it was an artist wanting his work exhibited, but it could have been Ryan."

"It most likely was," Marcello said. "Well, that should be the end of the trail for him. We'll institute a policy at the gallery that no personal information shall be given to anyone and—"

"Sorry," Jason interrupted, holding up his phone. The screen displayed a satellite map pointing to the house they were all sitting in. "If Ryan knows your first and last name, and that you're still in Austin, he can find where you live."

"Call the phone company," Ben said to Tim. "They can get us unlisted."

"And off the Internet?" Jason asked.

Tim held up a hand. "It'll be fine. He's probably just looking for a handout. If he shows up when I'm not here, don't answer the door."

"Precisely," Marcello said. "I didn't want to alarm anyone, but it would be wise to take preventive measures now. I'll have my administrator take care of the Internet listings. Tim, if you want to talk to the phone company and gallery staff, then I feel we can confidently say we've covered all bases."

"And if not," Ben said, clenching his jaw. "I've sent Ryan packing once before. If it comes down to it, I can do so again."

"What are you doing?" Tim asked, barging into the kitchen and looking at the loaf of bread in Jason's hands as if it were hard drugs.

Jason held up a slice. "Lunch time. Want a sandwich?"

"No." Tim glanced over his shoulder and back again. "Uh, I thought you had to work today."

"Nope." Jason reached for the mayo before doing a double-take. "Wait, you're asking him *now*?"

"Yeah." Tim grinned. "The weather is nice, and my parents' backyard was where I first figured out— Never mind. Here." He pulled out his wallet. "Go out and get yourself something to eat, okay?"

Tim shoved some cash at him. Jason took it, fanning out the bills. "There's almost two hundred dollars here!"

"So don't go to McDonald's." Tim was hopping back and forth on his feet like a little kid desperate to use the restroom. "If I don't do this now..."

"Okay," Jason said, understanding. "I'll throw on my shoes and be out of here in three minutes flat, I swear."

"Thanks," Tim said. "How do I look?"

"Stunning," Jason said. "As always."

Tim smiled and clapped him on the shoulder. "Maybe treat yourself to a movie too, or do some shopping, okay?"

"Don't worry, I won't be back until late." He glanced at his half-made sandwich. "Should I clean up?"

"No, don't worry about it," Tim said, starting to do his pee-pee dance again.

Jason took the hint and sprinted out of the kitchen and upstairs, laughing once he was in his bedroom. He put on his shoes as quickly as possible and grabbed his phone, noticing a text message from Emma.

Im dropping out of school.

Jason stared in shock and sat on the corner of the bed, texting her back.

Ha ha?

A second later, Emma responded.

I mean it. Im so sick of it here!

Oh boy. Jason hit the button to call her, and she picked up right where she'd left off.

"I'm never going to patch things up with Bonnie while I'm stuck in this stupid city."

"I thought you were over that?" Jason asked.

"Hope springs eternal," Emma replied. "You understand that better than anyone."

"Yeah," Jason said, knowing this wasn't an insult. He'd called Emma plenty of times to whine about still wanting William. "I was hoping you wouldn't make the same mistakes as me, emotionally or academically."

"Do you regret dropping out?" Emma asked.

Not really, since he still didn't want to go to college and didn't have big career aspirations, but he didn't want to encourage Emma to do the same. "Listen, if you drop out, then you won't get into college and you won't have an excuse to move to Austin. Ben is big on school. He's not going to reward you for quitting by letting you live here."

"I can get a job and we'll still get our own place," Emma said.

"Being a sixteen-year-old drop-out and finding a good job isn't easy, believe me. I don't think Bonnie's going to be very impressed by it either."

Emma sighed. "Maybe not. I could meet someone else though."

"Austin isn't the only city with a gay youth group."

"Fine," Emma said. "I wouldn't have texted you if I knew you were going to be so damn reasonable."

Jason chuckled. "You're welcome. I'm just glad I could talk you down for once. Usually I'm the one having a meltdown."

"Could you imagine if we both had one at the same time?" Emma asked. "Pity party!"

"Nuclear meltdown pity party."

Emma sighed again. "So how are things in paradise?"

"Fine, I was just—" Jason shot to his feet. He was supposed to be gone by now! "Oh shit!"

"Oh shit?"

"I really gotta jet! Like right now. I'll call you later."

He hung up the phone without waiting for a response and walked to the window, standing to one side so he couldn't be seen. Ben was on his back in a lawn chair he'd dragged out onto the grass so he'd get more sun, a paperback book in his hand creating shadow on his face. Tim had the garden hose out and was pretending he was going to spray Chinchilla, the dog running back and forth to avoid being hit. Jason wondered if Tim had chickened out, or if Ben had already given his answer. Surely the aftermath wouldn't be as casual as this!

Next Tim filled a watering can and walked to the corner of the yard where a flower bed marked Samson's grave. Chinchilla followed, much more solemn in this duty. Ben raised his head to watch them a moment before shutting the book, laying it on his chest, and closing his eyes. The scene was mundane, and yet so idyllic. Jason wondered if they realized what they had, if they still remembered how loneliness felt and were grateful for all these little boring moments together, because seen by a lonely person like him, it sure looked like heaven.

Tim approached the house again, Jason stepping away from the window. He could hear the sound of the garden hose slapping the outer wall as Tim looped it on its mount. When silence followed, Jason returned to the window.

Tim was standing over Ben and watching him, maybe dreaming of waking him with a kiss. Or maybe he said something, because Ben turned his head in Tim's direction. Their bodies were still as they exchanged a few words. Jason wondered if Tim was reciting poetry or had found the perfect words to say. Or maybe he was just trying to find air, because even Jason's chest was tight with nervousness. He practically squealed with excitement when Ben sat up and Tim dropped to one knee.

A look of surprise, a ring held up, then one of the longest moments in history. The sun caught the platinum band, shining like Ben's smile. After wiping his eyes, Ben held out a hand, his fingers splayed. For some reason Tim reached for the other hand instead, slid the ring on, and was practically knocked backwards when Ben kissed him. Those muscles came in handy as Tim lifted Ben up and held him tight in his arms.

Jason stepped back, wiping at the tears on his cheeks. *That's* what he wanted. His yearning for change had nothing to do with leaving this wonderful place. He wanted a love like that—one that could thrive and grow or even settle down and become routine. No more waiting and wanting. Just being together. Jason didn't need to move on. His heart did. And it was time.

In more than one way! Remembering his promise to not be around and not wanting to ruin this special moment, he crept down the stairs to the living room, stealing one last glance out at the backyard where Tim was grinning, thumb brushing affectionately along Ben's cheek. Resisting the urge to blubber again, Jason hurried out the front door, hopped in his car, and left Ben and Tim to enjoy their private little paradise.

Few things made Jason feel so conflicted, he was discovering, than being at a gay bar. On one hand, every guy he saw there was homosexual or bi-sexual or at least very open-minded. That was true in the youth group too, but rarely did more than thirty people attend. At least a hundred men were here, all of them touching, flirting, or checking each other out shamelessly. Which was the downside, because Jason caught quite a few people staring at him, but he honestly didn't know if they were interested, especially with so much competition around. The guy tearing up the dance floor for instance—lithe torso bare and glistening with sweat.

Or the older man with a George Clooney vibe, decked out in a designer suit and enough jewelry to signify wealth. Jason should be used to his type from the parties Marcello threw, but so many of those men were couples. Flirtatious, sure, but mostly settled down and not so... on the prowl. Jason sucked on his beer, taking it all in and missing the days when he'd been young enough to attend a humble youth group in a church classroom.

"Why did you want me here with you?" Ben said, voice raised to be heard over the dance music.

"You're my wing man!" Jason replied.

Ben grinned. "Yeah, but why didn't you want Tim to come too?"

"Don't take this the wrong way," Jason said, "but if Tim was sitting next to me right now, no one would have even noticed me yet."

Ben didn't look offended. Instead he seemed to understand perfectly. Of course it also didn't hurt that the George Clooney look-alike strolled over and asked Ben if he wanted to dance. Ben held up his hand, showing off the engagement ring and shook his head. Then George Clooney glanced over at Jason before retreating.

"Ouch," Jason said. "I'm not even second choice."

"He doesn't think he can get with you," Ben said. "Guys like that are insecure. Otherwise they wouldn't flaunt their wealth so much."

"Or maybe I didn't meet his standards," Jason replied.

Ben waved away this thought, as if it were impossible. Then he wiggled his ring finger again. "He probably thought we were together."

"I'm so glad Tim finally asked!"

"Me too. I never expected him to. I've always been the one to push our relationship further, and I figured eventually I'd be down on one knee. I wasn't ready quite yet—"

"You weren't?"

Ben shrugged. "I felt content. Everything has been so perfect that I didn't think I needed more. But when he asked…" Ben looked overwhelmed for a moment. "I guess it made me realize just how badly I did want it."

Jason nudged him. "Do you think I'm doing the right thing by being here? Sometimes I try to figure out what you would do in my shoes, and I think you would have waited for Tim if he went off to the Coast Guard. Or you would have moved up there without asking."

Ben shook his head. "I didn't always chase after Tim. I did until we were together, but afterwards, when he broke up with me, that was it. All those years I could have looked him up and chased him down, but at a certain point, you want a guy to be with you because he's willing, not because you're giving him the hard sell."

Jason considered this. "So you didn't wait for him to come back?"

"I waited. I told myself I would move on and even tried dating another guy, but I soon realized I couldn't feel the same about anyone else. Not at that point. So yeah, I did sit around and hope. For the rest of high school, I was waiting. Then, when I went off to college, I decided to try again. If I hadn't, I might not have met Jace or at least been willing to go on a date with him."

Jason glanced around, wondering if love could really be

found in a place like this or if he was open to it yet. "I feel guilty just being here," he said. "Did you feel that way at first?"

"After Tim?" Ben asked. "No. Not exactly. I felt horrible the first time I was with another guy, but that had more to do with him not being Tim or someone I loved."

"And after Jace?" Jason asked. Then he worried he was being insensitive.

"It's fine," Ben reassured him. "When Tim came back into my life, I'd been dealing with Jace's death for years. I'd had time to come to terms with it and was so happy to see Tim and experience all those wonderful emotions again." Ben grinned goofily before growing serious. "Later it became a little confusing. I'd wake up in the middle of the night, thinking Jace was next to me. Or I wondered if I was doing the right thing. When Jace and I got married, I made a promise. There was no ''til death do us part' in our vows. In fact, I didn't have any vows at all."

"Huh?"

Ben looked bashful. "I kind of blanked during the ceremony, but in my mind, I was making a promise. Jace and I were going to be together forever. In a way, we still are." Ben held up his left hand, the ring there different from the one Tim had given him. Then he held up the other hand with the engagement ring on it. "*This* makes it better. Tim and I are getting married, and I feel like it shows Jace that I'm not just messing around because he's no longer here. The love I feel for Tim is serious. Sure, part of me will always feel like I should live my life alone until Jace and I can be together again, but the rest of me wants to be happy and feel loved and to give that back. I'm pretty sure Jace would be okay with that."

"I'm envious," Jason said, "but I'm also not sure if I'm ready for a new relationship."

"There's only one way to find out," Ben said. "See anyone you want to dance with?"

Jason didn't have to search far. He stood and offered Ben his hand. "Can I have this dance?"

Ben pretended to fan himself, then accepted his hand, hopped off the stool, and walked with him to the dance floor. That was the end of their physical contact. They danced together, sometimes acting silly and other times seriously shaking their rumps to the rhythm, but they didn't gyrate against each other like some couples did. Maybe this is what communicated they were available. A guy with dark hair and even darker eyes casually danced his way between them until he was facing Jason. He gave a smile and an upward nod of his head, so Jason returned the gesture. Their dance became a lot more intimate. The guy kept putting his hands on Jason—on his hips, his neck, his chest, even ran his fingers across Jason's lips like he was trying to rub off lipstick.

As mildly erotic as this was, the guy wasn't Jason's type, which was weird since he was young and good-looking and definitely sexy… but he wasn't William. After dancing some more, Jason managed to shoot Ben a panicked expression without the guy noticing. Ben came to his rescue, grabbing Jason's hand and pulling him off the dance floor like a jealous boyfriend.

"Another drink?" Ben asked.

Jason considered all the faces that had caught his eye, all the people he'd scoped out the first hour he and Ben had sat and drank. He couldn't imagine any of them coming up, asking him to dance or offering their phone number, and him feeling happy about it. At times he longed for his younger days when a pretty face was all it took to make him feel infatuated, a couple of kind words enough to make him fall in love. William had cured him of his careless heart, Jason no longer able to fall as quickly or hard as he once had. He knew Ben was right. Eventually he'd have to shove aside his fears and at the very least give someone else a shot. But not quite yet.

"We can go," Jason said. "That's enough for my first bar experience."

"Too bad," Ben said, leading the way toward the front door. "I can't remember the last time I danced like that."

"Tim doesn't like to?"

"He's good for a slow dance, but besides that, I always tell him, 'Honey, you might be Latino, but you're no Ricky Martin.'"

Jason laughed, feeling relieved when they were outside and he could breathe in the cool autumn air. As they headed for the car, Ben was talking about the time he'd goaded Tim into taking a Samba class, which was probably why he didn't hear the person calling after them.

"Hey!"

Jason spun around. By the door of the bar, a figure leaned

against the wall. His features were lost in the hoodie he wore, but what Jason could see looked rough. The man took a few steps forward, gestured for Jason to come over to him. A breeze picked up in the parking lot, cooling the sweat on Jason's skin and making him shiver. He shook his head, not understanding if it was sex, drugs, or well-meaning advice being offered, but instinctually knowing he wasn't interested. Jason turned and hurried to catch up with Ben. As they were pulling out of the parking lot, he craned his neck to look at the bar entrance, but the man was no longer there.

Was it awesome? Emma texted.

Jason kicked off his shoes and flopped into bed.

Sure.

Were there lots of hot lezzies?

Jason thought about it. He'd noticed a few women at the bar, and presumably some of them were hot. *Oodles,* he texted back.

OMG!!! Wait! Was Bonnie there?

He laughed, thumbs flying across the keys. *No or I would have said so. I danced with a really hot guy.*

And?

I'm not ready to settle down yet. Still playing the field.

So easy to act badass while texting. He waited for Emma's response, puzzled when it came.

I saved a life tonight.

Jason scrutinized the screen, sitting upright when he saw the message was actually from William. He reread it again, this time hearing it in William's voice.

I saved a life tonight.

And it hurt. The last thing Jason needed was for William to remind him how awesome he was, how no one else could ever compare. Jason thought long and hard about what his response should be, and he wasn't proud of it exactly, but he needed to push back a little, just to see what would happen.

Wow. All I did tonight was go to a gay bar.

Then came a five-minute wait. Emma texted a few more times, but he ignored these. Finally, William's response appeared on his screen.

I want you to be happy.

Jason groaned, feeling horrible for having told William, for changing good news into something complex and awkward.

I'm proud of you. Jason texted back, as quickly as he could. *So crazy hugely proud of you! You're my hero. You always will be.*

After this was sent, Jason tossed aside the phone, buried his head under a pillow, and willed the world to disappear.

Chapter Twenty-eight

Bleary-eyed, Jason crawled out of bed, reached for his phone, and found nothing of interest on the screen. No texts from William, just as there hadn't been for the last three days. Jason wasn't sending any either, meaning they were back to not talking to each other. Or maybe William was just busy, or felt betrayed by Jason's visit to the gay bar, or any number of things. Their relationship—be it friends or something more—had become a guessing game. Jason relieved his bladder in the bathroom, and then went back to his phone to check the time and his work schedule. He was up early this morning. At least that meant he wouldn't have to rush.

He found Ben downstairs in the kitchen, having his usual tea, but nothing else was on the table.

"Tim went to get donuts," he explained.

In that case, Jason would get his sugar rush started right. He grabbed a soda from the refrigerator and sat down across from Ben. Coke can and tea cup clinked together, as if they were champagne glasses, before carbonated bliss poured down Jason's throat. After a satisfied gasp worthy of a commercial, Jason smacked his lips and asked, "You guys set a date for the wedding yet?"

"No," Ben said. "The idea of getting married is way more romantic than the endless preparations, as Tim is discovering. He's already stressing about certain family members being there—on both sides—and if we should go to a state where it's legal, what season it should take place in, what we should wear…"

"Poor guy."

"Mm-hm." Ben took a sip of his tea. "Right now I'm letting him stress about it. Eventually I'll step in and take care of it all."

Jason shook his head. "You're so mean!"

Ben grinned over the cup. "Sometimes."

"You guys can afford to hire a wedding planner, right?"

Ben shrugged. "Just because we have money, doesn't mean we should spend it. Sounds like Tim is back already. He's been speeding again."

To Jason, the car sounded like it needed a tune-up. They

yawned and blinked, waiting for their delivery of sugar-fried fat, and looking puzzled at each other when they heard Chinchilla barking in the backyard. Ben expressed what they were both wondering.

"Why didn't he come in the front—"

A snarl of thunder interrupted him, a numb silence following. Even Chinchilla's barks had ceased. No, not thunder! Jason stood up when he recognized the sound. He'd heard it over and over again when he and Caesar had practiced on the firing range. And a few dark times during his one and only hunting trip.

The backdoor opened and closed. Jason was looking around for any sort of weapon he could find when Ben also stood, face in shock when he noticed the stranger in the kitchen doorway.

Except he wasn't a stranger. Not completely. The guy outside the bar, the one who had tried to call Jason over the other night. When the man pulled back his hoodie with his free hand—the other holding a shaking gun—Jason recognized who he was. The painting in the attic, the one so handsome that Jason had snuck up there occasionally just to admire it, now stood there in the flesh, living and breathing. The name came to his lips, the one Ben, Tim, and even Marcello said with grave solemnity.

"Ryan."

The gun raised, pointed directly at him, and Jason knew what it felt like to be helpless, to be so close to death and absolutely powerless to escape.

"Who are you?" Ryan asked, eyes narrowing. They were practically slits when they turned to Ben. His mouth became a sneer, making him look more like a monster than a man. Odd, since just seconds ago, he had still been handsome. Sure he looked like he needed a bath, a shave, and a few weeks' worth of sleep, but beneath all that grime and wear, Jason had seen the beauty Tim had captured in the portrait. Except now it had been replaced by hate that turned Jason's spine to ice.

"You," Ryan said, gun hand trembling as he focused on Ben. "I knew it! You didn't see me the other night, did you? I guess I'm beneath your notice now. But your little friend saw me." The gun moved back and forth between them, like Ryan couldn't decide who to shoot first. Finally, it settled on Jason. "Who is he?"

"Just put the gun down," Ben said, taking a step forward.

The barrel of the gun instantly moved to stop him, Ryan

trembling as he rubbed the sweat from his eyes with his free hand. Was he scared? Or were these the shakes of a desperate junkie?

"Who is he?" Ryan shouted.

"He's nobody," Ben said, sounding phenomenally calm. "Just a guy who rents a room."

"Just a guy who rents a room," Ryan parroted sarcastically. "Does Tim know you were out with him at the bar? Does he know you're fucking around, just like you accused me of doing?"

"I didn't accuse you of anything," Ben said, showing his open palms. "Tim left you for his own reasons."

"That's right, he left me for you!" Ryan jabbed the gun in Ben's direction. Then he started walking forward, as if he was ready to end this, but he stopped halfway into the room. "Where is he? Where's Tim?"

"At the gallery," Jason said. "He'll be gone the whole day."

Ryan glared at him. "Who the fuck is this guy?"

"Nobody," Ben repeated.

"Tell me or I put a fucking bullet in his head! Then he really will be nobody!"

Ben didn't react. Not until Ryan pointed the gun at Jason. Then Ben's voice cracked as he answered.

"He's my son."

Ryan considered Ben disbelievingly, looking back and forth between them. Then he laughed. "I don't know what sort of sick game you're playing here. I bet Tim doesn't know either. When he comes home and finds your bodies on the floor together, he'll understand what was going on here."

"And what, take you back?" Ben said, sounding angry. "Do you really want that, Ryan? Or would you rather have so much money that you don't need Tim—that you don't need to rely on anybody. Because we can give you that. We have more money than we'll ever need. I'll pay you to leave us alone. Right now. Cash. No police, no drama. You get your money, and you get out of here."

Ryan's face had gone slack as he listened to this offer. He looked almost serene, like a boy who was desperate to lie down and rest, just for a few moments, just for a few centuries. Then his tired features twisted up again. "All of this *is* mine! You took it from me!" The gun kept jabbing in Ben's direction. It going off was only a matter of time, whether on accident or on purpose. Jason moved his eyes to the kitchen table, hoping to find a knife. The only items there were a can of Coke, a tea cup, and a basket of oranges. None of them had much potential, but if he could throw the tea cup, hit Ryan in the eyes…

"If you hadn't come along," Ryan continued ranting, "Tim and I would still be together."

"You really believe that?" Ben asked, taking a few steps forward. He stopped when Ryan's gun arm tensed, but he had made it past the edge of the kitchen table. "Tim would have left you eventually, if only to save you."

"Save me?" Ryan demanded incredulously. "Oh, so he was doing me a favor!"

Ben raised his hands again, to show they were open. Jason braced himself, feeling Ben had a plan but not knowing what it was. "You overdosed in the hospital. Tim agonized over that. He blamed himself."

"And he felt so bad that he threw me out on the street? You're going tell to me *that* was for my own good?" Ryan pointed at himself with the gun.

Ben moved, but he didn't rush Ryan like Jason expected. Instead he moved sideways. Jason didn't notice at first, since he had lunged for the tea cup. When he looked back up again, Ben was blocking the way. Standing in his path. That had been his plan all along. Not to attack Ryan somehow, but to protect Jason.

Ryan recognized this and laughed. "Is that really your kid? What did you do, knock up some girl when you were twelve? You can't protect him. I'll put a bullet through both your heads. Bang bang!"

"You want the money or not?" Ben asked. "You'll never get into the safe if we're dead."

"I told you what I want," Ryan hissed.

As if on cue, the front door squeaked open. "Lucy, I'm home!" Tim said, doing his best Ricky Ricardo impersonation. "Whose car is out front?"

Ryan moved back against the breakfast bar. "Don't you fucking move," he whispered, standing sideways and keeping the gun trained on them while he watched the kitchen door.

Tim was grinning at his own joke as he strolled into the kitchen. He saw them first—Ben with an arm held out to keep

Jason back, like a parent stopping his child from running into a busy street. Jason tried to tell Tim the whole story with one panicked expression. Tim responded with one of confusion, then fear as he took in the gun.

The box he was holding clattered to the ground, a cheerful rainbow-sprinkled donut rolling across the floor. It seemed too optimistic to exist here, too simple and happy, because Jason could no longer see this ending without one of them getting shot. Not unless Ryan broke down into tears and threw himself into Tim's arms.

"There he is," Ryan said, sounding bitter. "Mr. I'm-so-fucking-perfect. I like your family. Did you know about that one over there? Do you pretend he's your son too?"

Tim spared them a glance, one that clearly said 'let me deal with this.'

"I'm glad you're here, Ryan," he said. "Marcello told me you were in town. I've been worried about you. Why didn't you come here sooner?"

Ryan's eyes narrowed suspiciously. "You know, I thought about leaving you alone. I tried to find you at first, but then I figured maybe I'd find someone better. Then I saw your little bitch at the bar, and I remembered just how much I hate you."

"Then point the gun at me," Tim said. "If that's what you came here to do, point the gun at me."

"You ruined my life!" Ryan said, gun arm trembling. "My whole life turned to shit after you threw me out. I fucking hate you!"

"Then point the gun at me!" Tim shouted.

Ryan shrugged, as if it wasn't a bad idea, and swung the gun around. This wasn't a threat. Jason could see the fingers tighten on the gun, the tendons on Ryan's hand tense as he prepared to fire. Jason shoved Ben aside, rushed Ryan with the ridiculous tea cup raised like it was a broadsword. But he was too late. He heard the explosion just seconds before reaching Ryan. Jason smashed the teacup into his ear regardless, tried to throw his weight into him and knock him over, but a stool was in his way. All Jason ended up doing was falling over it, but still he grabbed at Ryan's wrist, trying to snatch away the gun and failing.

Ryan stepped back, disoriented at first, before he raised the gun and pointed it in Jason's face. Then his eyes moved, his mouth twitched, and he aimed at something to the left of Jason's head.

Ben. He was going to shoot Ben first.

A fist slammed into Ryan's cheek from behind. The gun went off again, this time close enough that Jason's world became clenched shut eyes and ringing ears. He blinked madly, trying to shrug off the panic jolting through his body. When he did, Ryan was on the floor, Tim on top of him and slamming fist after fist into his face. Ryan's arms were flailing, striking Tim randomly. The gun was still in one hand, and it was only a matter of time before Ryan remembered to use it. Jason rushed forward, grabbing Ryan's wrist and slamming it against the floor. The gun was flung from Ryan's grasp. Jason scurried after it, kicking it by accident and wincing because he was sure it would go off. When it didn't, he picked it up and swung around.

The scene had changed. Ryan was on his side, moaning and clutching at his face. Tim was on his knees, Ben standing over him before crouching. Tim remained kneeling, shaking his head at something Ben was saying over and over again.

Jason kept the gun on Ryan and stepped forward, not understanding what had happened.

"You've been shot!" he heard Ben say through the ringing in his ears.

Tim shook his head again. "I haven't." He forced himself to his feet, looked like he wanted to kick Ryan in the side, but instead fell over.

That's when Jason saw the blood, crimson and wet and turning Tim's light blue shirt maroon. Ryan got to his feet, forcing Jason to tear his attention away. Ryan pawed at his own eyes, at the blood soaking his face. Then he ran. Jason raised the gun to shoot just as Ben cried out, a horrible panicked scream. Tim was on his back, Ben pressing two bloody hands against a spot near his neck, a pool of blood continuing to spread across the floor.

An artery. Jason set aside the gun. Ryan had fled the room anyway, and more barking was coming from the backyard, meaning he wasn't sticking around. Jason rushed to Tim's side, trying to remember what he'd learned in the first-aid course Mr. Hubbard had made him take before the hunting trip.

"I can't stop the bleeding!" Ben raised trembling hands.

"Let me see," Jason said, pushing him away. He wasn't doing much good anyway.

The bullet had gone straight through the meat above Tim's collar bone. This wouldn't be so bad—at least not as far as gunshots went—but he was bleeding far too much. Jason didn't know where all the arteries were, but the bullet had to have passed through one of them. He closed a hand over the two holes and squeezed. Tim moaned in pain, eyes wide and unfocused. The scene was disturbingly familiar—the hunting trip buck, Jason's hands slipping on the red-stained fur, the animal growing still, the life draining from it. Tim moaned again before his head lolled and he stopped moving. Passed out from the pain, or dead?

"Call an ambulance!" Jason said, but when he looked up he saw Ben already on the phone, stammering out their address.

"They'll take forever," Ben said when he hung up. "We're so far away!"

"He'll be fine," Jason said, not knowing if it was true.

"We should drive him," Ben said. "You pick him up, put him in the car, and I'll drive."

Jason shook his head. "It'll kill him. We can't move him. He'll lose too much blood."

"Is he alive?" Ben whispered, dropping to his knees. "Tim?"

Ben reached for one of Tim's hands, eyes wide in panic.

"Check his wrist," Jason said, trying not to crumble under his own sorrow.

Ben's fingers trembled as they moved up Tim's arm. His whole body was shaking, his breath shuddering, before he looked up in shock.

"I felt something!"

"Of course you did," Jason said. "He'll be fine."

He focused on keeping the wound from bleeding. Jason wanted to remove his hand and use a shirt or something else instead, but worried about the blood loss this would cause. He had a pretty good seal on the wound now, or so he thought. There was so much blood that it was hard to tell. Tim's normally dark skin was unnaturally pale. Ben was right. The paramedics were taking forever. Jason wished he could slit his own wrist, let Tim gulp down the blood he had lost if that would save him.

Ben was whispering to Tim, saying things Jason felt he didn't have a right to hear, but that were impossible to ignore. *You promised not to leave me. You promised I would die first. Don't do this to me. Please stay. Please. I can't go through this again.*

Jason clenched his jaw, forcing himself not to cry. When he

heard the sirens come near and then stop, he started shouting to summon help. Ben pulled himself away and ran to the front door. Jason looked at the gun on the tile, praying that Ryan really had left. Surely the sirens had scared him away. Chinchilla was howling now, one long mournful sound.

A police officer entered the room first, gun drawn. Jason screamed at him to let the paramedics through. When they were allowed in, they had to pry his hands off the wound and shove Jason aside. He scurried backward across the floor, trying not to be in the way. He felt relief when they put a specialized bandage on the wound, then felt confused as they placed a collar around Tim's neck, as if it had been broken. Then Tim was loaded onto a stretcher and rushed from the room. Ben followed after him, and Jason tried to do the same before an officer blocked his path.

"We need to ask you a few questions," the man said.

"I need to go with them!" Jason responded, trying to push past.

"There isn't room," the officer insisted. "Help us catch the person who did this."

Jason felt deflated as the ambulance doors closed and the vehicle started down the long drive. He nodded his agreement. Then he tried to explain what had happened, but couldn't stop thinking of the ambulance, and of Ben, who would be all alone with no one to comfort him if Tim died.

Jason stared at the scene from the kitchen doorway, scarcely believing it could be real. A pool of blood on the blue tile, smeared to one side where Tim had been laying. Shards of a broken tea cup, the liquid that had once filled it splattered near the table. Messy footprints everywhere, misshapen maroon ovals, marring what had been one of Jason's favorite rooms. Now it was a mess, a ridiculous crime scene where a photographer tiptoed around in plastic-covered shoes, camera flashing like a tourist desperate to document his dwindling holiday.

"Son?" The officer standing next to Jason moved the digital recorder closer, hoping it would prompt Jason to speak. Officer Flynn was middle-aged, heavyset, and perhaps a little too young to call anyone son. At least not anyone Jason's age. "Are you feeling all right?"

"Yes," Jason said, even though it couldn't be further from

the truth. His heart hadn't stopped pounding, his every breath feeling forced, as if the normally ignored function now required constant vigilance, lest he forget to breathe entirely. "What was the question?"

"When did you first notice the perpetrator enter the house?"

"We were waiting for Tim to come back when we heard the dog— Chinchilla!"

Jason turned to the backyard where a constant noise finally got his attention. Chinchilla stood just outside, clawing repeatedly at the glass to signal she wanted in. Jason rushed to open the door, a hand on his shoulder stopping him just as he was reaching for it.

"You'd better let me," Flynn said, nodding at Jason's hands.

He noticed them for the first time, how they were covered in dried blood, his skin feeling tight and dry beneath the grime. Smears ran up his arm, and his T-shirt made it look as though Jason had also been shot. The knees of his jeans were still damp from where he had knelt in Tim's blood.

"Do you have a leash for the dog?" the officer asked. "We can't have her running through the crime scene."

He told Flynn where to find it, and while the officer went to fetch it, Jason stared through the glass, locking eyes with Chinchilla. She had stopped clawing now that she had his attention and had begun whining instead. Jason felt she was asking him one question. How was Tim? Was he going to be all right? Chinchilla continued to stare, Jason wishing more than anything that he could answer her truthfully and say that everything was going to be fine.

Motion farther away in the yard caught Jason's attention—a person creeping around—causing him to yelp.

"It's okay," Flynn said, returning. "It's just one of my colleagues securing the area."

The officer stepped outside to fetch Chinchilla before she noticed this other person, Flynn holding on to the leash when he returned inside with her.

"She looks fine," the officer said. "Just a little shaken up."

"Ryan fired at her," Jason said. "He was trying to sneak in through the back, Chinchilla started barking, and then we heard a gunshot."

Flynn nodded encouragingly, lifting the digital recorder again. "Then what happened? Tell me everything."

The facts became Jason's top priority. Whatever was happening inside the ambulance, whatever happened at the hospital, all of it was outside his control. Nothing Jason could say or do would change a thing. But he could ensure that the police had all the evidence they needed to bring Ryan to justice.

Jason began rambling, Flynn interrupting with the occasional question. The officer even returned to the kitchen doorway, eyes searching the scene for anything important, any little piece of information that was missing. While it was clear from his lack of abhorrence that Flynn had seen worse, he seemed eager to do his job and do it right. Jason felt thankful for that, trying his best to put his fear aside and be helpful. He allowed himself to be photographed, only second-guessing the police when they wanted his bloody clothing.

"As evidence," Flynn explained.

"But this is Tim's blood, not Ryan's," Jason said.

Flynn nodded his understanding. "Yes, but when this Ryan person is in court and starts lying, you'll want every shred of truth possible backing you up."

"Okay," Jason said, already stripping off his shirt, "but that's it. I need to get to the hospital now and—"

"You need to get yourself cleaned up or you're liable to scare someone," Flynn said.

"Fine." Jason took one step toward the stairs and froze.

"The entire house has been searched," Flynn told him.

"Okay." Jason didn't move. What if the police had missed something? What if Ryan was hiding up there, maybe in the attic, crouching behind the smiling portrait of himself. Nowhere seemed safe anymore. He turned back to Flynn and swallowed. "Do you think you could come with me? Just in case."

The officer glanced up at him, seemingly unsurprised by the request, and nodded. How often did he see this? Every day? Were people in various states of shock and terror so often? The world normally seemed so sane, but this wasn't the first time someone had been attacked in their own home. Not by far. Jason felt like he'd gone through life in blissful ignorance up to this point, believing such violence an invention of television to get viewers watching through the commercial breaks.

Flynn escorted him to the upstairs bathroom, giving Jason plastic bags to put his stained clothing in. He allowed Jason to take Chinchilla into the bathroom with him before the door was closed, Jason washing his hands off in the sink before looking up to see a thick smudge of blood on his cheek. He required more than just a quick rinsing of the hands. This time Caesar wasn't there to lovingly dab at his face with a washcloth, but at least Jason wasn't alone. He looked down at Chinchilla who continued to whine.

"I know," Jason said. "I'm worried too. I'll hurry. Just a quick shower, and I'll take you to see Tim. I promise. "

When Jason was clean and the police were finished questioning him, he loaded Chinchilla into his car. A rushed shower and fresh clothes did little to make him feel better. His pulse was still racing too fast, matched by the frantic fear coursing through his system. Jason felt paranoid as he drove, almost expecting Ryan to leap into the street and clamber over his windshield like something out of a horror movie. Chinchilla wasn't faring much better. She kept climbing over the center console to lick Jason's face, still whimpering and whining.

As they reached civilization, Jason obsessed over what had happened in his absence. Had Tim made it to the hospital, or had he… So much blood had been lost. On the long drive into Austin, despite the best efforts of the paramedics, maybe he had… Jason shook his head and tried to imagine his home, the perfect paradise he'd been invited into, without Tim. Doing so was impossible. That happy place would be ruined forever. The sun would never shine again.

As they neared the hospital, Jason tried to picture what he'd find when he entered the emergency room. Ben wailing in uncontrolled grief, the staff trying to subdue him? Or maybe he would just be sitting there motionless and pale, the shock making him numb. Each of these visions tore at Jason's heart. No matter what happened, he didn't want Ben to be alone.

Finally having reached their destination, Jason parked hastily. He whispered a quick apology to Chinchilla that he had to leave her behind before sprinting across the parking lot to the emergency room entrance. He found Ben sitting there pale and wide-eyed, just as Jason had feared, but at least he wasn't alone. Allison, an attractive black woman and Ben's best friend, had one arm wrapped protectively around him. Jason felt somewhat relieved, because he knew she would take care of him, even glare at anyone who dared look in Ben's direction. Literally, because she did exactly that before she recognized Jason and opened her other arm to him.

Before he went to her, before he accepted any sort of comfort, he had to know. "Tim?" It was all Jason managed to say, but he was instantly understood. And answered.

"They're operating on him now," Allison said. "The bullet nipped an artery, which they're trying to repair."

Jason nearly cried out in relief, because at least there was hope. Tim was still a part of this world, so everything wasn't over. Not quite yet. He hugged Allison when she stood, then grabbed hold of Ben. They clutched at each other, Ben crying and mumbling incoherent words.

Ben was wearing hospital scrubs, his hands washed clean, like he intended to perform the surgery himself. Luckily, Officer Flynn had prepared Jason for this, suggesting he bring along a change of clothes for Ben and anything he'd need for an overnight stay. When this was all over, and if Jason was still sane, he planned on sending that man a ridiculously huge basket of fruit.

"You're okay?" Ben kept asking. "You didn't get hurt?"

Jason had to reassure him over and over before he would let go again. When Allison made them all sit, Jason made sure Ben was in the middle, still feeling the need to keep him safe.

"The police left just before you got here," Allison said, "but they didn't have any news. Did they catch Ryan?"

"I don't know," Jason said. "I don't think so. They found a bloody handprint on the fence gate, so there's evidence. The whole house is a crime scene. I don't think any of us should go back there. Not alone."

"Chinchilla?" Ben asked, already braced for bad news.

"She's fine." Jason said. "She's in the car, but it's hot out there."

"You can take her to my place," Allison said. "I can clear out the office tonight, make it into a spare bedroom again."

Jason shook his head. "We'll stay at Marcello's house. He has plenty of guest rooms and the best security money can buy."

Ben nodded his agreement, his hands shaking, even though they were resting in his lap. "Maybe you should go there now. I want you to be safe."

"We're perfectly safe right here," Jason said, settling back, but he kept his eyes on the emergency room door. The rules of the game had changed. If they could be sitting at the kitchen table and be attacked, then surely nowhere was safe. Not completely. Jason kept clenching his jaw and shaking his head. None of this made sense. They hadn't done anything to deserve this.

They sat in silence for a few minutes, listening to a news reporter rattle off other tragedies in the world, all of them bigger than their own. He wondered if emergency rooms did this on purpose. *Keep calm. At least you don't live in a war zone.* Except now Jason felt as if he did.

"Seeing him lying there on the kitchen floor," Ben spluttered, "waiting for the paramedics to show up again…"

Allison hugged Ben tight, kissing his hair and murmuring comforting words. Her affection for him made Jason think of Emma, even though she'd be more likely to slug his arm and tell him to get over it. She'd want to know about this. Jason pulled out his phone to text her, but it was all too complex for one hundred and sixty characters. He excused himself, stepped outside, and called.

Emma had barely said hello before it all came pouring out. Halfway through the story, Jason started crying, and he was glad Ben couldn't see because he wanted to be strong for him. After he was done talking to Emma, he checked on Chinchilla and brought the clothes and toiletries he'd collected for Ben back to the emergency room. There still wasn't any news on Tim, and after sitting there another half hour, he decided he needed to take Chinchilla somewhere cool.

"Call me," Jason said. "The second anything happens, call me."

Allison promised she would. When he returned to the car, Chinchilla was desperate to see him. Jason wondered if she could sense that something was wrong. Maybe Tim wasn't doing so well. That idea alone nudged Jason's fear toward a different emotion. He hoped Ryan was lying in a ditch somewhere, bleeding to death.

This anger was shared by Marcello as Jason sat in his living room and explained everything. Marcello was normally so chipper, like a big happy hippo without a care in the world. Now his face was grim and dark. He barraged Jason with questions, becoming more furious with each answer. When he was finally satisfied, he looked like the devil incarnate, eager to claim a soul.

Marcello swept from the room without a word, leaving Jason sitting alone. He was happy for the silence, petting Chinchilla as she tried to settle down next to him. Eventually she did. Jason hoped this was a good sign, that she knew somehow that everything was going to be okay.

When Marcello returned, he was somewhat calmer, although still nowhere near his usual jovial self. "I've made some calls," he said, pacing the room. "Ryan was picked up by the police half an hour ago. I don't know the details yet, but they don't matter. Ryan is going away to prison, where I imagine he'll be very popular with the other inmates, whether he likes it or not."

"He's really going to prison?" Jason asked. "Doesn't there have to be a trial or—"

"There will be," Marcello said, sweeping around, "and I'll have every goddamned lawyer in the state prosecuting his pathetic ass! Not that it will be necessary because I'll make sure the right judge is on the case. One in particular regularly attends my fundraisers, and he's always been fond of Tim. Rest assured, Ryan *will* go to prison, and I daresay the little bastard won't survive the experience."

For a moment, Jason wondered if Marcello was powerful enough to have Ryan killed, but hopefully he only meant that Ryan would meet some random misfortune while behind bars. He sat in silence as Marcello continued to rant, happy for an excuse to look away when his phone chimed. A text message. Jason read it, and for the first time since everything happened, he felt hopeful.

"It's Allison. She says they've got Tim stabilized. Do you think that means he's okay?"

"I don't know." Marcello took a deep shuddering breath and exhaled again. "Well then, let's go see him, shall we?"

Ben was no longer in the waiting room when they arrived, having gone to Tim's bedside. Only one person was allowed to visit at a time, and even Marcello's influence couldn't budge the stubborn nurses. Eventually, their little group grew in number when Emma showed up with her parents. Greg took turns bear-hugging them all, one by one, even Marcello, who he didn't seem to know. Michelle held Jason. He supposed it might have resembled a hug from the outside, but she placed her arms around him so gently, like he was fragile and she was afraid of breaking him. Ben's parents arrived next, a laid-back couple who Jason had met on many occasions. Not too long after them, a stern-faced, white-haired man showed up with a beautiful Hispanic woman clinging to his arm. From the desperate fear in her eyes, she had to be Tim's mother. Allison seemed best equipped to deal with them, taking the couple aside for a hushed conversation, but soon Mrs. Wyman was among them, clutching their hands.

"So many people are here for my baby," she said, wiping at her eyes. "So many friends."

When Ben returned to the emergency room seating area, that was what he found waiting for him. So much family. So many friends. He nodded at them and managed a smile.

Tim was going to be all right.

Another day passed before Jason was permitted to see Tim. With only one visitor allowed at a time, Ben monopolized this privilege by spending the night at the hospital. He was the only person aside from Allison not to roost at Marcello's house that night. The Bentleys—and especially the Wymans—might have preferred to get a hotel room, but Marcello was insistent. Emma was thrilled by it all, but everyone else had to slowly get comfortable around each other. By breakfast the next day, the place was starting to feel like a resort full of the glummest tourists ever.

The Wymans left first to see their son. An hour later, everyone else gathered at the hospital to take their turn. Marcello asked Jason for permission to go next, which he could hardly deny. Then Emma did the same. Afterwards it seemed only natural to allow Michelle and Greg go next. Jason waited not-so-patiently through all of this, desperate by the time he was finally allowed to enter Tim's room.

After some wandering down hospital corridors and glancing into many bleak rooms, Jason finally saw Tim sitting up with a bandage wrapped over his shoulder and under his armpit. He was staring off into space when Jason knocked. Then Tim looked apprehensive. At first, anyway.

"Oh good, it's you," Tim said. "I thought Greg was coming back for another hug. They practically had to rush me back into surgery."

"For real?" Jason asked, moving to the chair by the bed.

"Yeah, he kept apologizing. Said I was a hero." Tim grinned. "I barely remember a thing, but whatever. I'll let him call me a hero if he wants."

"You saved Ben's life," Jason said, his throat tight. "Ryan was about to shoot him and—"

"I'm sure you had it all under control," Tim said dismissively. "If I hadn't gotten in the way, you would have headbutted Ryan or something awesome like that."

"I love you," Jason said. He swallowed against the tears. "I love both of you so much."

Tim considered him and nodded. "Believe me, we love you too. Are you okay? Besides the obvious, I mean. There's not something you guys aren't telling me, is there?"

"No," Jason said. "We're all fine. They caught Ryan, so you don't have to worry about that."

"I heard." Tim leaned back and winced. "I think this is going to leave a nasty bruise."

"Probably a little worse than that."

"Yeah, maybe you're right. Funny how all the guys I love leave their mark on me. This one over here?" Tim pointed to the scar on his opposite arm. "That one is called Travis. The new one will be named Ryan. Let that be a lesson to you. As awesome as love is, it can leave you scarred for life."

Jason laughed. "At least Ben hasn't scarred you."

"Are you kidding?" Tim said. "The first time I met the guy he nearly broke my ankle!"

"Really?"

"Really," Tim said. "Ask him next time, see if he'll tell you the truth. I guess I should have known back then. All the guys after him only left flesh wounds. Benjamin managed to get into my bones on day one."

"Sounds like true love," Jason said.

"Yeah. Speaking of which…" Tim gestured for Jason to come closer. "Next time you visit, think you can sneak Chinchilla in with you? She's family too, right? Me, you, Ben, and the dog. We're one big happy family now."

"Is that the morphine speaking?" Jason teased.

Tim was dead serious when he replied. "No. I've known for a while now. I definitely didn't need some guy putting a bullet through me to figure it out."

"Yeah," Jason said. "Me neither." Then he took a deep breath. "Does this mean I have to call you Dad?"

"It's either that or Mom," Tim said with a chuckle. Then he glared. "*That* was a joke. You better not call me Mom!" His features softened somewhat. "At least not in public."

Chapter Twenty-nine

Four years. Jason hated that he was counting down, because the more time that went by, the more pathetic he felt by doing so. Besides, he had more exciting things to focus on, such as a brand new summer and all it would bring. His world was changing. Jason was now the assistant manager at the pet store. During the job interview, he was told his passion for his work set him apart. In truth, all Jason really cared about was the increased pay. The extra money would come in handy because he and Emma were getting a place together.

She was on her way from Houston this very day. They would stay with Ben and Tim while apartment hunting, which shouldn't take long. Once they had their own place, *viva la freedom*! Not that Ben and Tim were at all oppressive, but Jason needed his own place so he could feel like an adult. One who would be living with an eighteen-year-old college student. Jason smiled at the thought. They were going to have so much fun!

Four whole years, and now they were finally over. Not that it mattered anymore, because the dreams and promises made back then had all faded away. Regardless, after his morning routine, Jason carried his laptop outside to the backyard, intending to get a head start on the apartment search. He checked his email first, just in case William had sent him any hint of his plans. Jason was dying to know if he'd be returning to Austin, but William never gave a clear answer. "We'll see," was the standard response. Jason had even visited Ms. Townson, as he did occasionally when wanting to talk about William. Unfortunately, she didn't seem to know what her son's plans were either.

"Willy could make a career out of it," she had said, not sounding too happy about the prospect. "He could remain stationed where he is or anywhere else on the coast. I might have to pack up and move. Maybe I could take up surfing."

Jason had laughed, but inside he wondered if there was another reason, another person, that made William want to stay where he was. Regardless, he checked his email every day and his phone every hour, hoping for news. He was even tempted to call Kelly, even though they had mostly lost touch, to see if he knew anything.

The laptop finished its work. No email from William. Instead he found advertisements from various stores, a spam message from someone in Africa who had bequeathed him twenty-three million dollars, and a Facebook friend invite from— Jason's mouth went dry. He shielded the laptop screen from the sun to be sure.

Caesar Hubbard.

He stared at the name, at the little letters that—when placed in that exact combination—made him think of sneaking into a bedroom at night, playing his guitar with a head on his lap, or riding a bicycle down a major highway in the middle of the night. Caesar-freaking-Hubbard! After taking a deep breath, Jason clicked a link in the email. Not the one that accepted the request, but the one leading to the profile instead.

Caesar's information wasn't set to private. Jason clicked the little profile photo first, eager for a fresh look at his first real love. Maybe Caesar was overweight or had gone bald prematurely, or maybe... Jason sighed. Caesar looked better than ever. His face was more mature now, the cheekbones more defined. His hair had grown out a little, and he was rocking a three-day beard.

Jason studied the image, comparing it to what he used to know, before he started flipping through others. Caesar on a golf course, clothes tight on an all-too-familiar frame. Caesar shaking hands with someone old and important. Caesar at a bar, smiling with friends both male and female. Jason paused and couldn't help wondering if any of them were the person who had replaced Nathaniel. He closed the photos and clicked on the tab for more information. New Haven, Connecticut. So still in Yale territory. Maybe Caesar was going for his doctorate or something. What Jason really wanted to know...

Relationship Status: Single

Okay. Good to know. Not that it could possibly matter, but whatever. Jason pored over the profile, not learning much else. He was reading and trying to interpret status updates when Tim strolled out into the backyard. Shirtless, of course.

"Naked again?" Jason rolled his eyes. "You're doing it on purpose."

"What?" Tim asked, flopping into a deck chair. "I'm wearing shorts."

"You know what I mean. Every time Greg comes to visit, your shirt mysteriously disappears."

Tim grinned. "He thinks my scars look cool. Besides, I like it when he calls me the Terminator."

Jason shook his head, glancing at the pinkish-white circle between his neck and shoulder. To him it was an unhappy reminder, but naturally Tim found a way to make it work, like getting shot was the sexy thing to do these days. Jason returned his attention to the computer, hungrily devouring anything and everything on Caesar's profile. He was still doing so when Greg and Emma entered the backyard.

"Hey, there he is!" Greg said, boxing the air. "Tim the Terminator!"

"You two get a room," Emma said, brushing the hair from her eyes. She was just as big as before and twice as beautiful, but the real change had come from the inside. Emma was calmer now, not quite as excitable, the air of confidence real. No longer a girl, but a woman. Emma was in complete control of herself, all grown up, a lady in every sense—

"My ass feels like a thousand dentists have been jabbing it with novocaine," she declared, "and they didn't bother taking me to dinner first. I'm so glad I won't have to make that trip again."

"Except when we move the rest of your things here," Greg said. "You'll have to come home for that."

Emma batted her eyelashes at him. "But Daddy, I thought you would take care of it all for me!"

Greg shook his head, then offered a hand to help Tim up. "Come on. I'll show you the new car. You show me the new swimming pool."

"I'm so glad they found each other," Emma said, taking the deck chair when Tim and Greg had disappeared. She leaned back and sighed contentedly. "My new life begins right now."

"Welcome to Austin," Jason said. They eyed each other a moment before squealing excitedly. "This is going to be so cool!"

"I know!" Emma nodded at the laptop. "Apartment hunting already?"

"I was going to," Jason said. "But then..." He clicked on Caesar's profile photo again, stood up, and handed her the laptop. "Take a look."

"Not bad," Emma said. "I'm not into sausage, but if I was, I'd be nibbling on his."

Jason grinned. "Look at the name."

"Caesar Hubbard," Emma said in a snooty British accent. Then surprise registered. "Wait, is this *the* Caesar? *Your* Caesar?"

"I'm not sure I can say he was ever really mine, but yeah, that's him."

"Huh." She perused a few more photos, Jason looking over her shoulder. "He looks like the lead singer from that old music video."

"Could you be less specific?"

"Give me a second." Emma hummed for a moment. "Incubus, I think?"

"Oh yeah!" Jason said. "You're right. That guy was hot."

"*This* guy is hot," Emma said, closing the photos. "So you got nostalgic and decided to do a little online stalking?"

"Nope. That's the weird thing. He sent me a friend request. I haven't heard a peep from him since the day his parents kicked me out of the house. When was that, a million years ago?"

"At least," Emma said.

"Yeah. And now he wants to be virtual pals."

Emma looked up at him. "Did you accept?"

"No."

"Why not? Where's he live?" Emma clicked a few times. "Connecticut? It's not like he can just pop by. You might as well friend him, if only to get his life story. He's probably hounded by regret and will end up drunk-texting you."

"I don't know if that's a good idea," Jason said.

"Didn't say it was a good idea," Emma replied, clicking some more.

"Wait, what are you doing?" Jason grabbed the laptop from her and glanced at the screen.

You are now friends with Caesar Hubbard.

"Oh, great." Jason said, pursing his lips, but he only did so to keep from smiling. "I could have waited a day before accepting. Now I'll appear desperate."

"Who needs him anyway?" Emma said. "You and I are going to hit the scene, find some fresh hot love to pave over the holes in our hearts."

Jason sat back down. "There's a gay youth group meeting tomorrow, I think. You'll have to go solo because I'm too old now."

Emma was shaking her head. She made sure they were alone before leaning forward. "Fake ID."

"I don't know where to—"

"I've got one already. You and I are hitting the bars together. How about tonight?"

"Or how about we wait until we're on our own so you don't get caught?"

Emma considered this. "Nah. Tonight. You and me."

Jason was about to agree when the laptop chirped at him. He pushed a button to wake the screen and read the message. "Oh god! It's Caesar. He says hi. What should I say back?"

"Hello," Emma suggested helpfully.

"Do you think I should?"

She shrugged. "He's a million miles away. You could send him a naked photo and it wouldn't make a difference."

True enough. *Fancy meeting you here,* Jason typed back, trying to sound confident.

Caesar's response came instantly. *I know. Can't stand the drapes though. Let's go somewhere else instead. Meet me for dinner tonight?*

Sure, I'll just pop right up to Connecticut. Be there in five.

I'm in Austin.

"Fucking great!" Jason said, glaring at Emma accusingly. "A million miles away, huh?"

"What?"

"He wants to meet for dinner."

"He's in Austin?" Emma said, looking shocked. Then she laughed. "Tell him you've got plans already. Because you do. With me."

Jason had something else he'd rather say. He did some counting on his fingers, feeling more worked up when he was sure about the number. *It's been seven years since I've heard from you. Seven! And you expect me to be at your beck and call?*

"Are you telling him off?" Emma asked. "You've got your angry face on."

"Hell yeah, I am!" Jason said.

Caesar's response came slower, enough time passing that Jason thought he had scared him off completely. But he hadn't.

I drove all the way to Austin just to surprise you, so yes, I figured dinner wouldn't be too much to ask.

Jason glared at the screen, tried to find some way of being offended by the words. *You should have called ahead because you're wasting your time,* was probably the right response. But he liked that Caesar had traveled so far just for him.

He nibbled on his lip a moment and then looked up at Emma. "About tonight…"

"You suck," she said. "When you get back tonight—or tomorrow morning—I want details. The juicier the better!"

Jason waited outside the Japanese restaurant, the kind where chefs grilled right in front of the customers, flipping shrimp into open mouths or performing other culinary tricks. Such distractions would be useful if the evening turned awkward. He sat on the trunk of Ben's old car, staring down at his shoes and wondering if he should take them off. If he did, his feet probably already smelled bad since these shoes were ancient.

The rubber was cracked, the star logo label peeling off one and missing on the other. Jason kept poking his toe through a hole in one of the soles. Regardless, the once-neon green fabric still appeared somewhat optimistic beneath all the grime. Jason couldn't believe he'd held on to the shoes for so long. Well, actually he could. That he'd been sentimental enough to wear them tonight—that was a little crazy.

A familiar car pulled up next to his. Caesar's silver spaceship looked like it had been through one too many asteroid showers. The metal was dented and dinged, and the windshield was cracked, but all of this was forgotten when the driver stepped out. The car must have taken the brunt of time's wear and tear, because Caesar looked fantastic. Just like his Facebook profile photo, in fact, which must have been recent. Casually brushing at the plum-colored dress shirt he wore, Caesar glanced up, as if surprised to see Jason there. Then he grinned.

"Look at you!" he said.

Jason was having similar thoughts, but he tried to play it cool. "Still driving the same car?"

"You know how nostalgic I am," Caesar said, walking around the vehicle. He looked Jason over, noticing the shoes. "And I see I'm not alone."

"These old things?" Jason said. "Are they somehow special? I don't remember."

"Right."

Caesar walked up to him and offered a hand. When Jason took it—goose bumps racing over his skin—Caesar pulled him off the car and into his arms.

"It's good to see you again," he murmured into Jason's neck. "You still smell the same."

"Like I haven't bathed after all this time?" Jason asked, forcibly pulling himself free. "Gee, thanks."

"You always smelled good." Caesar's amber eyes were shining. "Even in the morning."

Hot damn, he was irresistible! Sometimes Jason looked back on their relationship and felt embarrassed, thinking it had been hormones and bad decision-making that had driven him to sneak into Caesar's room. Seeing him now, Jason was willing to forgive himself for any previous poor judgment.

"Hungry?" Caesar asked.

"Not in the slightest," Jason replied.

"Me neither. I'd rather just hang out with you. Catch up on everything. Is there somewhere we can go?"

Jason shrugged and hopped back onto his car. "Why not here? It's a lovely parking lot."

Caesar glanced around. "Suit yourself. So what has Jason Grant been up to all these years? Your profile is lacking when it comes to details."

The last thing Jason wanted to talk about was himself, so he made it quick. "Moved in with a family out here and dedicated my life to animals. What about you?"

"Wait," Caesar asked. "You got adopted?"

"Nothing that formal," Jason said. "But I have a family of sorts, yeah."

"I'm really glad to hear it," Caesar said. "So—"

"My turn," Jason interrupted. He had decided earlier what his first question would be because it would determine whether or not Caesar intended to be honest. "How are you and Nathaniel doing?"

"Oh." For a moment, Caesar didn't look so sure of himself. "It's a long story, but basically he dumped me."

"But you went to Yale together," Jason said.

"Yeah, we did. Things got a little weird there. Too much had changed. I was older, obviously, and the vibe between us... Nathaniel can be so domineering, and I guess that was okay for the big brother role he once played. But as an adult in college, I didn't want someone telling me how to live my life or trying to guide me. I had enough of that from my parents."

"So you broke up with him?" Jason asked.

Caesar glanced off into the distance. "He broke up with me. We argued a lot, so…"

"Sorry to hear that," Jason said.

Caesar looked surprised. "Are you?"

"Yeah, because if we couldn't be together, then at least there should have been a good reason. If you two were still a couple, us splitting up would have been justified."

Caesar considered him carefully. "So you're saying, since it didn't work out with Nathaniel, that you and I should have stayed together instead."

Jason felt surprisingly vulnerable, so he changed topics. "Just a random observation. How's the Hubbard family? Any new members?"

Caesar chuckled. "No. After you, my parents weren't so keen on adopting anymore."

Jason grinned. "I do make an impression, don't I?"

"Us making an impression together was the real issue," Caesar replied.

That certainly brought back memories. Rather than dwell on them, Jason moved on to the next burning question. "How's Amy doing?"

Caesar beamed. "She's discovered boys. I'm afraid she takes after me in that regard."

"Meaning?"

"That she's already breaking hearts at fifteen."

"So many boys, so little time?"

"Exactly, although her most recent boyfriend knows how to keep her attention. Real smart guy, honor student, runs clubs instead of just joining them. He's highly political too, and not that it matters, but he's black. I only mention that because—"

"Your parents," Jason said, nodding his understanding.

"Yeah. They're less than thrilled, but these days Amy isn't concerned with pleasing them." Caesar looked proud. "She's got a good head on her shoulders."

Jason smiled. "I'm glad to hear that."

"Yeah." Caesar said. "The others haven't changed so much. Carrie dropped out of college and does data entry, probably so she can listen to music while she works. Peter still worships my father and follows in his every footstep."

"And you're the perfect son, running the family business, just like daddy always wanted."

Caesar's face grew dark. "You know what? Maybe we should go inside. I could use a drink."

Jason was taken aback by this, but agreed. They managed to get a table away from the grills, one next to a giant fish tank that—while pretty—ensured that Jason wouldn't be ordering any seafood. He decided to stay sober too, sticking with cola. Caesar ordered a saké at room temperature.

"It's the only way to drink it," he insisted. "So how's your love life?"

"Mine?" Jason asked. "Great! Yeah. It's really good. … Actually maybe it's just average. At best. Does that sound right?"

Caesar chuckled. "You tell me. Is there anyone special?"

Jason gave the question thought. "There is, but we're sort of estranged. He had just come out of a long ugly relationship and was heading to the Coast Guard, so we put everything on hold."

"And never picked things up again?" Caesar cocked his head. "Well, maybe that's your answer. If you were meant to be together, one of you would have done something drastic by now. Like showing up out of the blue."

"Cute," Jason said, but he didn't mean it sarcastically. "So what about you? Any secret lovers texting you obsessively?"

"Nope," Caesar said. "This time I'm all clear."

In the condensation on his glass, Jason drew spirals and considered Caesar. Is that what this was? Another time? A new beginning? He tried to picture being with Caesar again, but not having to sneak around or compete with anyone. Would they start a life together? Would this lead to a wedding, Jason finally becoming a Hubbard after all? The idea of seeing Caesar's parents again made his stomach turn.

"So where do you live?" he asked. "You're done with school, right?"

"Yeah," Caesar said. "No more school. As for where I live, I'm still trying to figure that out."

Jason shook his head, not understanding. "Is working for your dad that flexible? I always imagined you moving back to Houston after college."

Caesar emptied his little cup of saké and refilled it from the jug. "I kept my apartment in Connecticut. The same one I had through college. Work required me to fly a lot, so it didn't really matter where I lived, or the car I owned, because I was rarely ever home."

"Past tense," Jason pointed out.

Caesar met his eye and nodded. "That's right. Two months ago, my father fired me."

"Geez," Jason said. "I'm sorry to hear that. What was the reason?"

"The reason?" His laugh was bitter. "Well, the biggest one is Peter. The little shit always wanted my life, and now he's got it." Caesar exhaled. "You know what? That's not even fair. My father groomed me to be someone I'm not. Unlike Peter, who was born to be a cut-throat businessman. Eventually, my dad figured that out. The son he always wanted was under his nose this whole time. Good for them. They deserve each other."

"But for your own dad to fire you like that," Jason said. "That's cold!"

Caesar read his face before his eyes twinkled. "Well, there might have been a small incident with a client."

"Ah," Jason said. "Let me guess. Did your dad walk in on you and this client sleeping together?"

"No." Caesar laughed. "I know history repeats itself, but thankfully, no. I didn't sleep with the client. His wife, on the other hand…"

"Check please!" Jason said, but not loud enough for the waiter to actually hear him.

"It's not as sleazy as it sounds," Caesar said. "We weren't just boning. We really cared about each other. Besides, this was in Switzerland. I figured marriages were a little more open over there."

"So the client walked in on you?"

Caesar sighed. "No, his wife told him. They had a pretty messed-up relationship, and in the heat of an argument one night, she wanted to hurt him. So she revealed it all."

"Ouch."

"Yeah. This was a very big contract—a lot of money, so Dad was furious. By that time, I think he'd already figured out Peter was the better man for the job, so he cut me loose. I mean that more than financially. Neither of my parents is real keen to talk to me right now."

Caesar didn't sound too sorry about this. Jason wasn't either. That Caesar no longer lived according to his parents' wishes was great. And yet, it didn't change the past. Or what had happened between them.

"So your life fell apart," Jason said, "and the first thing you do is track me down?"

"Not the first thing," Caesar said. "I have a little money saved up, so I took some time out for me. Just to relax and finally take a break from years of trying so hard. I couldn't sit around my apartment forever though."

"And so you decided to come see me?"

Caesar set down his drink and leaned back. "You sound surprised."

"Yeah, of course I am, because I was always your second choice. Third or fourth, depending on how many there have been after you and Nathaniel broke up."

"What's that supposed to mean?"

"The first time you were single again, you could have come back for me. Or at least called."

"Would you have wanted me to?"

"Yes!" Jason said, feeling exasperated. "You have no idea how lonely I've been. Most of the years we've been apart, I haven't had anyone, so yeah, I totally would have welcomed a call from you. Or anything else."

"I thought about it," Caesar said. "I phoned Steph sometimes. When you were living together. Did you know that?"

Jason shook his head.

"I made her promise not to tell, but I was never sure… Anyway, I always asked her if you were okay, and she said you were, that you were getting back on your feet. I didn't want to ruin that by showing up in your life again."

"And now you do?"

Caesar eyed him. "Now I hoped enough time had gone by for you to forgive me. You were a boy back then, Jason. Now you're a man, and the whole world can see that beautiful face of yours. When did you cut your hair?"

Jason didn't answer. Instead he tried to decide if this was worth it. Revisiting old wounds and feeling hurt all over again. Was that worth being able to reach across the table and touch the scruff on Caesar's cheek? Or feel it prickle against his lips when they kissed. Was it worth it?

He decided it was. Even for just one more night with Caesar, he was willing to pay that price.

"Yes," he said out loud. Then his face flushed.

Caesar studied him for a moment before smiling. "If I'm able to guess the question you just answered, do I get a prize?"

Jason raised an eyebrow. "Play your cards right, and you'll get one no matter what."

The rest of the meal was more relaxed. They laughed over old memories and pumped each other for more information about people they had once known. When they were finished eating and had returned to the parking lot, Caesar began to stumble and weave dramatically.

"Guess I drank too much!" he said.

"After all that food, I doubt you're drunk at all."

"Oh, I am," Caesar insisted. "I shouldn't drive in this condition. Can you give me a lift back to my hotel?"

Well played indeed. Jason was a willing victim to this con. He drove Caesar across town to his hotel, even pulled into a parking space, but when he stepped out of the car, he left the engine running.

"You're not coming inside?" Caesar asked. "I've got photos of Amy's first homecoming."

"Using photos of your little sister to get laid?" Jason tsked disapprovingly. "That's low. Even for you."

Caesar walked around the car, stepping dangerously close to Jason. "I have other things I can offer instead."

Jason dodged a kiss. "Not on the first date."

"This isn't our first date," Caesar said. "Think how much history we have. Sometimes it feels like we were together for years and years because I never stopped thinking about you. Do you have any idea how often I looked you up, have nearly contacted you? I've dreamt of this day so many times, but I thought you'd never agree to see me again."

"Lucky for you, I have terrible judgment." Jason leaned forward and kissed him. Caesar reciprocated and pressed him up against the car. Their surroundings were almost forgotten until a child started laughing before being hushed by his parents.

"Turn off the engine," Caesar said, "and come to my room. We have seven years to make up for."

*****

Jason had barely stepped into the hotel room before Caesar spun him around, shoved him against the wall, and started kissing him again. Opening one eye, Jason saw he'd had the decency to shut the door. Their privacy assured, his fingers went for the buttons of Caesar's shirt but were pushed away.

"Nuh-uh," Caesar said. "I'm in control."

"How could I forget?" Jason said before his mouth was covered by another kiss.

He allowed himself be dragged farther into the hotel room, their lips never parting, and felt the edge of a bed against the back of his legs. This didn't seem to be Caesar's goal though, since instead of pushing Jason onto it, he took a step back.

"Can I get a 'Hail Caesar'?" he asked.

"Oh, very funny."

Caesar held up his hands. "Hey, it used to work."

"When we were teenagers," Jason said. "You'll have to come up with a better line than that."

"Okay," Caesar said. "How's this for a line? You weren't my second choice. You were the *right* choice. I should have picked you instead. I was wrong."

Jason stared at him. "That one works," he breathed. "Whatever you want. Hail Caesar or anything else. You got it!"

Caesar smiled. "Let me undress you."

Jason braced himself to have his clothes ripped off, but instead Caesar approached him slowly, gently rubbing his palms up his torso and along his ribs to pull off his shirt. Then Caesar's hands went to Jason's jeans, honey-sweet eyes on his as he unbuttoned and unzipped them. Jason sat on the edge of the bed so his pants could be taken off completely, Caesar tickling his feet before pulling off his socks. Soon Jason was left wearing only his underwear. Caesar offered a hand, helping him to stand again. Still gripping his palm, Caesar walked a circle around Jason, raising an arm and making him spin around like a ballerina.

"Just as beautiful as I remembered," Caesar said. "Unless... No, that can't be possible."

"What?" Jason asked.

"Unless you've become even more handsome since we last met."

Jason laughed. "You're really laying it on thick, aren't you?"

"It's working," Caesar said, nodding at the bulge in Jason's underwear.

"That?" Jason said. "That's just a sock I shove in my pants before every date. You're going to be very disappointed."

"I don't think I will," Caesar said, getting to his knees.

The last remaining item of clothing he removed with his teeth. Now Jason was nude while Caesar was still fully dressed. This made him feel vulnerable, like this was a prank and photographers would come barging into the room any second. Of course if they did, Caesar would be incriminated too, considering what he was doing with his mouth. Jason ran his fingers through Caesar's hair, moaning gently as he closed his eyes.

The hair wasn't right. William's had never grown so long, and always felt a little dry and fluffy from all the chlorine. Jason's brow furrowed. He opened his eyes and forced himself to look down. He wasn't with William. He knew that. He was with someone else he loved, or had loved, and that was good enough—had to be or he'd never move on. William was gone and had been for years. Caesar was here, right now, and he needed to accept that, enjoy it, embrace it. No more longing for the hero who had ridden off into the sunset so long ago. Time to move on.

Jason reached down, grabbed Caesar's wrist and pulled upward. Caesar took the cue and stood. Jason wasn't as patient with him, or as gentle. After fumbling too long with the first button of the dress shirt, he tore the shirt open. That chest was familiar. The hair was thicker, the muscles a little softer than they once were, but Caesar's body was still comfortably the same. Jason had tried dating occasionally in the last two years and had slept with even fewer guys. Those he did have sex with weren't comfortable like this. Instead they were strangers in their appearance and habits and how they tasted and smelled. Usually Jason went home afterwards wishing for William. Maybe he should have been thinking of Caesar instead, since he was equally familiar.

Jason pressed his lips against the warm skin of Caesar's neck while fumbling at his pants, licking and kissing his way down once he had them open. Caesar had obviously missed him just as much. He still talked all the time too, a million wishes and desires on his breath.

"With your hand, yeah. No, slide it. A little bit of teeth. Ungh.

Exactly! Reach your free hand up here, touch my chest."

Caesar had always been this way, but now Jason could barely keep up. "Do you want me to cook you dinner while I'm at it?"

"That would be nice," Caesar said, filling Jason's mouth again.

Eventually, he had another request, but this one Caesar didn't verbalize. After helping Jason to his feet and then onto the bed, he reached for the side table and pulled out a condom and a bottle of lube. The arrogant grin on his face was almost enough to make Jason hold his tongue, but when Caesar started putting the condom on himself, he felt the need to speak up.

"I think you're forgetting something," Jason said pointedly. "We were never very compatible in that way."

"That's not what I remember," Caesar said. "The hunting cabin?"

Jason swallowed. "That was a special occasion." More like one of the most emotionally raw moments of his life.

"And this isn't?"

Jason shook his head. "I don't know what this is."

Caesar studied him for a moment. Then he laughed. "I forgot how complicated you are." He made like he was going to take off the condom before hesitating. "Can I at least stick it in your ear?"

"It's about the right size," Jason teased.

Caesar feigned offense as he pulled the condom off. "You are *so* lucky you won't feel just how big my dick is! I wasn't planning on being gentle."

"That's exactly why I chickened out," Jason lied.

Caesar crawled on top of Jason, rubbing his cock against his stomach. Jason reached down and took hold of it. Caesar brought his face near, looking him deep in the eye, even when they kissed. Jason began to believe that maybe Caesar did regret the choice he made all those years ago, that when Nathaniel broke his heart, Caesar had looked to the past and known he'd chosen the wrong guy. He certainly seemed desperate to prove himself. Caesar scooted down, did things with his mouth that Jason had nearly forgotten about.

Thirty minutes of his kisses, his stares, his pumping hand, exploring tongue, and welcoming mouth, was all it took for Jason to forgive him. Seven years paid off in half an hour. Hail Caesar!

Chapter Thirty

If emotions were something tangible—a part of the physical world—they would constantly change color and size and shape, never recognizable from one moment to the next. Jason returned home the next morning surrounded not by violet-tinged clouds of love from the night before. Instead shadows seemed to hound him, slipping into his mouth and down his throat, filling his stomach with dread.

"What have I done?" he asked himself rhetorically. He got an answer anyway.

"Murdered someone?" Emma guessed. "Held up a convenience store? Or gee, maybe you slept with an ex and are having second thoughts."

He made a pouty face, so Emma grabbed a pillow from behind Tim's head and used it to thwack Jason.

"Don't you two have rooms of your own?" Tim asked, rubbing the back of his noggin where it had hit the headboard. "Or beds of your own, for that matter."

They did, but on a lazy Sunday morning like this when Ben and Tim themselves couldn't be bothered to leave their room, the social activity of breakfast usually reconvened in their bed, which was certainly large enough to fit them all. Ben was sitting up where he usually slept, a pair of dark-framed glasses on his nose that had no prescription strength or magnification. Ben simply thought they looked cool. As he lazily thumbed through a magazine, Jason had to admit they did. Next to him, Tim sketched out rough ideas on an iPad, using his finger instead of a stylus or paint brush. Chinchilla lay against his side. Jason—at the end of the bed—would sometimes reach out to stroke her. The last available space on Ben's side was occupied by Emma, sitting cross-legged as she happily thwacked Jason again with the pillow.

He supposed it was an odd sight, an unusual family gathering at a strange place, all of them dressed in pajamas. Well, except for Chinchilla, of course. And maybe Tim, since his Terminator scars were in full view, but presumably he had something on beneath the blanket.

"No pillow fights this morning," Ben said, raising an eyebrow until Emma returned Tim's pillow. Then Ben gave his attention to

Jason. "Whatever it was that happened between you and Caesar last night, why would you regret it?"

"I don't know," Jason admitted. "It felt really good—being around him again, I mean—and also very wrong."

"Guilty sex is the best sex," Tim said with a smirk.

"I didn't feel guilty at the time," Jason said. "I'm not even sure why I do now. Maybe I'm betraying myself by going back to him. Does that make sense?"

"Nope," Emma said. "Uncle Ben, did you feel that way when you got back together with Tim?"

"Which time?" Ben asked with a chuckle. "I suppose the one most similar to your situation happened when I was in college. I was definitely excited to see Tim again, and a little horrified, and then really really happy. The guilt came afterwards. But I was with Jace at the time. If I hadn't been, I don't think I would have felt any remorse. I still would have felt hurt about the way we originally broke up, but we talked through it."

"Did you try that?" Tim asked. "You've got to tackle any unresolved issues."

Jason nodded. "Yeah. We covered the important things."

"Then you shouldn't feel guilty," Ben said. "Or is there someone else you like?"

William. Jason tugged at a loose thread on the comforter. Admitting he still liked someone who had said goodbye to him four years ago was too embarrassing. Instead he mentioned the other issue at hand. "I'm worried about making the same mistakes. Or more like, I'm worried Caesar will make the same mistakes with me."

"Ah," Ben said.

Tim glanced over at him. "What do you mean *ah*? I don't like the way that sounds."

Ben set aside his magazine. "Caesar broke his heart once before, and it takes a long time to get over something like that. Naturally Jason is worried about you, I mean him—"

"Freudian slip!" Tim said, looking aghast. "You're worried I'll break your heart again?"

"No, not *now*," Ben said. "But when we first met again in college, yes. Past all the confusion of still having feelings for you and loving Jace at the same time, I was scared of getting hurt again."

Tim frowned. "Now I feel like shit."

"You shouldn't," Ben said. "After all this time, you really shouldn't."

"So what's the verdict?" Emma asked. "Should Jason keep seeing the guy with one strike against him, or should he look for someone with a clean record?"

"That's something he has to decide," Ben said. "We don't know Caesar, so it isn't fair for us to debate his worth."

"I wish you guys could meet him," Jason said. "He wants to see me again today."

Emma perked up. "Then let's take him to the gay youth group," she said. "The one taking place *tonight*."

"Meetings aren't on a Sunday afternoon anymore?" Ben asked.

"Not these days," Emma lied.

"Aren't Jason and this other guy too old to go?" Tim asked.

"They can go as my legal guardians," Emma said.

"Right." Ben picked up his magazine. "If you get caught using your fake ID, I know nothing about it."

"And no drinking," Tim said. "If you come home drunk, Emma, I'll drive you straight home to Houston and hand you over to your father."

"I liked it better when you and my dad were enemies," Emma pouted.

"Be safe," Ben said. "Both of you."

Jason promised they would, although when it came to his heart, he knew there was no guarantee.

Jason waited outside the bar with Emma, both of them feeling nervous for very different reasons. Emma kept glancing down at her fake ID, insisting on seeing his so she could compare them. Jason had other issues on his mind. He felt strange standing here, just a few yards away from where he had first seen Ryan that night. Jason half expected to see him there now, even though he knew Ryan was behind bars and would remain there for a very long time.

The more pressing concern was Caesar. Jason kept wondering if yesterday had been a nostalgia-powered fluke and nothing more. Maybe he wouldn't find Caesar alluring at all. That would conveniently end his heart's confusion. But when Caesar arrived wearing a suit the same dark hue as his hair, the light material hugging his frame, Jason practically sighed. If this was the sort of clothing Caesar wore on business, small wonder he'd landed in an affair.

"Wow," Emma said when Jason pointed him out. "Good idea or not, I think you're going to have fun."

"Maybe." The nice thing about living with Tim was how routine a good-looking guy had become. Jason liked to think he'd built up an immunity. He proved this to himself when Caesar tried to kiss him and Jason pretended not to notice, making quick introductions. Then he turned and headed for the bar door.

"Let me go first," Emma whispered. "If you guys get in and I don't, I'll be all by myself out here."

"Fake ID," Jason whispered for Caesar's benefit.

"Ah."

The bouncer at the door didn't seem too interested in them. He glanced at Emma's ID and was about to hand it back when he did a double-take and began to scrutinize it. "Do you have a driver's license I can see?" he asked.

"No," Emma said. "I have a fear of driving. Got run over by a taxi when I was a kid. Barely survived. Left me traumatized."

The bouncer handed back the ID and started to shake his head when Caesar shoved his identification under the man's nose, a fifty dollar bill not-so-casually sticking out from beneath it.

"Here's mine," Caesar said with a smile.

The bouncer took the ID and the money, glanced around before pocketing the fifty, and nodded for them to enter. Before they could, he offered Emma some words of wisdom. "Better not try your luck with the bartender. He has a lot more to lose."

"No problem!" Emma said. As soon as they were inside, she grabbed Caesar's arm. "Oh, I like you! Care to dance?"

"I'd be honored," Caesar said as he was dragged away. "You coming, Jason?"

"Nah, I'll find us a table."

All of this had been planned, of course. Emma felt she could get a better read on Caesar if they were alone, and that the answers to her questions might be more honest or direct without Jason there. Feeling mildly uncomfortable as he always did in this environment, Jason navigated his way past groups of giggling guys and more serious soloists on the prowl, not making eye contact with any of them until he found a table. Then he waited, feeling more awkward without a drink to make himself look busy. A guy came up to him and made small talk, Jason responding with just enough not to be rude but also little enough to communicate his lack of interest.

Finally, Emma returned with a happy expression. Caesar followed behind her, jacket over one shoulder.

"Thumbs up from me," she murmured. Then she spun around. "I'm going to get us all drinks. By which I mean I'm going to where all those fine lesbians are sitting and will probably remain there until you two drag me kicking and screaming from this place."

Jason waved a hand as if dismissing her, but Emma didn't notice, already on her way to a world full of new possibilities.

"Want me to get us some drinks?" Caesar asked.

"No, I'm fine. Unless you need to rehydrate."

"Not just yet." Caesar sat at the table across from him. "That girl sure can dance!"

"Yes," Jason said. "Yes, she can."

"And talk. She was gabbing the whole time. Must have a real set of lungs on her." Caesar grabbed a cocktail napkin and patted his forehead dry. "She wants me to be honest with you."

"Really?" Jason replied. "What an unusual request."

Caesar laughed. "Let me finish. She wanted to know what I'm doing here, what I hope to get out of showing up in your life again. Have you thought about that? Everything would be different this time. No parents, no restrictions—"

"No Nathaniel," Jason said.

"That's right." Caesar reached across the table, hand stopping an inch away from Jason's. "This relationship you were in, the one that was put on hold, is that something we need to take into consideration? I don't want either of us to be put in an awkward situation again."

Jason swallowed, then shook his head. "There's nothing on hold. Sometimes I think of it that way. The truth is it mostly ended four years ago, and died completely two years ago. I just felt like it was on hold because I never moved on."

Caesar put his hand over Jason's. "You can move on now. We can do so together, finally go places we couldn't before. What we had as teenagers—the potential we both felt—that can finally be explored. That's what I told Emma. If you're willing to try again, I'd relocate to Austin so we can be together."

"That's a big step," Jason said.

"I don't care," Caesar replied. "I'm not afraid to risk everything. Hell, that's what I should have done seven years ago. I should have disowned my parents and moved into the orphanage with you."

Jason laughed, knowing that Caesar was familiar with the proper terms and was just being silly. In fact, he knew a lot more about Caesar than that. Glancing around at all the strangers, he took solace in the idea of being with someone who knew him, who had come back after all this time just to be with him again. Jason turned his hand over so their palms were touching.

"Is that a yes?" Caesar asked.

Jason smiled. "More like a 'let's take things slowly.'"

"I can handle slow." Caesar nodded. "As long as we get there eventually, slow is okay by me."

When Jason and Emma returned home, they found another bouncer waiting for them. That's how it felt, anyway. As soon as they opened the door, Tim was in the entryway, looking them over.

"Step forward for a breathalyzer test," he said, pointing at his nose.

"You're kidding," Emma said. She sighed when it was clear that Tim was not. "Next time I'm eating raw garlic on the way home."

"Just as long as you aren't drinking," Tim said.

Emma huffed in his face, and once he was satisfied, he motioned for Jason to step forward.

"I'm old enough to drink!" he protested.

"But not drink and drive," Tim said.

"Don't you trust me?" he complained.

"Not in the slightest."

"Have *you* been drinking?" Jason countered.

Emma rolled her eyes. "Have fun smelling each other. I'm going upstairs to my room to sort through all the phone numbers I picked up tonight."

They waited patiently until she was gone. As soon as she was,

Tim clapped an arm around Jason's shoulder. "Wanna have a beer out back with me?"

"I thought you'd never ask."

Soon they were seated in the backyard, Chinchilla leaping and nipping at the first fireflies of the year. Jason clinked bottle necks with Tim, and after taking a sip, rolled the sweating glass across his forehead.

"How'd it go?" Tim asked.

"Fine. Emma had a great time. Didn't touch a drop. Just flirted her pretty little heart out."

"That's good, but I mean with you and Caesar. Are you guys still on?"

"Yeah," Jason said. "At least I think so. He seems serious."

"I'm sure he is," Tim said, sounding certain in his declaration. "People can change. I was thinking about the conversation we had this morning, and I was worried you got the wrong idea. All you heard was Ben talk about being nervous, but I didn't tell you how ready I was to be with him again, how badly I wanted to be. I had changed. That's the thing. Maybe not as much as I needed to, but I've always been a slow learner. Caesar's probably going through the same thing. He's a different man and wants to make up for the past—earn another chance."

"You think so?" Jason asked.

"Yeah, I do. You'll have to give him time to prove himself, but you guys have better odds than Benjamin and I did back then. You're both single. You don't have to worry about Jace being in the way." Tim's eyes went wide and he looked up to the heavens. "Nothing personal, big guy, but at the time it was frustrating as hell. For us both, I bet. Ha ha! Am I right?"

Jason took a swig of beer. "Are you seriously talking to Ben's dearly departed husband?"

"You mean you don't?" Tim asked in deadpan tones. "Maybe you should give it a try. He probably gives better advice than I do."

"Nah," Jason said. "I think you're right. I should at least give Caesar a chance."

"Or two or three chances, if he needs them," Tim said. "I'm heavily biased though."

Jason grinned. "How many chances has Ben given you?"

"Three, and that's only counting today."

Jason laughed. They clinked bottles again, and after turning them upside-down a few times, gasped in satisfaction.

"So when are you two finally getting married?" Jason asked. "It's been ages since you asked him. I'm beginning to think it's never going to happen."

Tim nodded slowly, as if confirming this possibility. "We have some reservations."

Jason sat upright. "About getting married? What's there to think about?"

"We're okay," Tim said. "Right now, I mean. Ben and I are happy. We get along, the sex is great, we can talk for hours on end or sit together in comfortable silence. I love him more than I ever have before. From what I can tell, he's just as happy with me."

"So seal the deal!"

"We're good as we are," Tim said. "Why tempt fate?"

Jason shook his head in confusion. "Like if you guys get married, it'll somehow make bad things happen? Are you that superstitious?"

Tim looked embarrassed and shrugged. "I asked the guy to marry me and shortly afterwards, my psychotic ex-boyfriend showed up to gun us down."

"You're silly," Jason said. "Does Ben feel this way too?"

"A little, yeah. Almost losing me brought back some bad memories for him, so I feel like we're waiting for the dust to settle. Make sure the coast is clear."

"I would have thought nearly dying would make you even more desperate to tie the knot," Jason said. "Do it before it's too late, that sort of thing."

Tim laughed. "Maybe that's how we should be looking at it. Or maybe we're just too damn happy with the way things are. Speaking of which, are you really going apartment-hunting tomorrow?"

"Yeah," Jason said, "and this time I won't let you talk me out of it."

"It's just that I had this idea about turning the garage into a guest house and—"

"No," Jason said. "If it were up to you guys, I'd still be here when you're old and gray."

"Hey, someone has to change our diapers." Then more seriously, Tim added, "I like a big family. I didn't have one growing up, so it's nice."

"It is," Jason admitted. "Maybe you and Ben should adopt."

"Believe me," Tim said. "We've been talking about it a lot lately."

Jason's head whipped up. "Really? Like a little kid?"

"Michelle suggested something along those lines." Tim shrugged and finished his beer. "You want another one?"

"No," Jason said. "I think I'll call it a night."

He went upstairs to his room, head spinning with all they had spoken about. A little brother or sister? Ben and Tim never marrying? Caesar being desperate for another chance? Jason checked his phone, as he so often did, and for once there was a text message waiting for him. Not from William, of course, but from Caesar.

Some guy came up to my car and tried to put the moves on me.

Jason snorted and texted him back. *Are you with him now?*

A minute later, Caesar responded. *No. I told him that I already have a guy from my past who wants to take it really slow. Took forever to explain. If only there were some sort of convenient title...*

Jason sat on the edge of his bed. *What would you suggest?*

The phone rang a second later, Jason answering it right away.

"Boyfriend," Caesar said on the other line. "I want to be your boyfriend."

Jason glanced out the back window where Tim was reclining, hands behind his head. Maybe he was thinking of a time when he had wanted nothing more than another chance to prove how amazing he and Ben could be together.

"Boyfriend," Jason said, as if trying the word on for size. "Has a nice ring to it."

"Yeah?" Caesar asked, sounding excited.

Jason smiled. "Yeah."

The last cardboard box having been shoved into the moving truck, Jason took a step back, wiped the sweat from his brow, and allowed himself a moment of satisfaction. One life, all nicely packed up and ready to go. Part of him felt like a thief, since the truck was full of Ben and Tim's furniture, but that hadn't been his idea. Ben had walked around the house earlier in the week, making excuses to give him everything he could possibly need.

"Oh, we were going to buy a new couch anyway. You'll be doing us a favor if you take this one." Or "We need a kitchen table that seats more than four. We can't always have dinner parties in the backyard." Soon Jason had to start coordinating with Emma, who was going through a similar process in Houston. Otherwise they would have ended up with two of everything.

Jason hopped up on the truck bed and was trying to get the rear door closed when a voice called out.

"You forgot one!"

Jason poked his head around the side of the truck and noticed a box near the rear tire, but it was soon forgotten when a bike pulled up and skidded to a halt. On it, grinning and covered in sweat, was the most beautiful man he'd ever seen. Sure, maybe Marcello had never offered him a modeling contract and maybe heads didn't turn when he walked down the street, but Jason's body reacted to his appearance in countless ways. Increased pulse, weak legs, dry mouth, and most of all, a yearning that almost brought him to tears.

William swung off his bike, placed it on the ground, and hurried to pick up the wayward box. Then he held it up to him. Jason stared a second longer before he put his hands on it, but he didn't pull it away. Nor did William let go. In this way they were connected, which was more than they had allowed themselves in the past two years.

"Moving?" William asked.

"Very," Jason said. Then he blinked. "I mean, yes." He adjusted his grip on the box, taking it from William's hands and placing it on top of a stack. Then he turned back around. "Home for a visit?"

William shook his head, still smiling up at him. "Home for good."

Jason almost fell out of the truck. Before that could happen, he sat down, legs hanging over the edge. "You're moving home?"

William nodded. Then reconsidered. "More accurately, I moved home already. I'm back."

"No more Coast Guard?" Jason asked. He didn't mean for his voice to sound so rusty or for his stupid eyes to water, but he felt like a man who had been given his freedom after years of false imprisonment.

"I'm considering my options," William said, "but no more active duty. I decide what I want to do now. Please tell me you aren't moving away from Austin."

"No!" Jason said. "I finally got my own place in town. With Emma, actually."

"Emma?" William took a step back. "Wow. Is she—"

"Eighteen," Jason said, nodding his understanding. "Time flies by. She's starting college in the fall."

"Wow," William said again. "How long was I gone?"

"Four years!" Jason said with a mad chuckle. "I can't believe you're back!"

"Feels like a dream, doesn't it?"

They looked at each other for a moment. William was still fit, his muscles appearing much harder than they used to. This, along with his buzzed hair, made Jason wonder if he would still feel soft in bed, if holding him would feel as good as it once had.

"So," William said. "What's going on in your life?"

Jason understood the question. At least he thought he did. William wanted to know if he was single. Jason struggled to answer. How could he explain that he had waited, that his heart had been loyal for years, even though William never asked him to be? Then the past had returned, and the last three weeks hadn't been lonely. Well, the last few days had been, since Caesar had returned to Connecticut to pack up his own life.

"Ready to go?" Tim asked, appearing from the house. "Oh, hey! Look who's here!"

William tore his eyes from Jason and smiled at Tim, who asked him all the obvious questions, like if he was done with service and what he planned on doing next. The commotion eventually attracted Ben, and the happy greetings happened all over again. Jason remained passive during all of this, watching one of his biggest dreams come true, but being unable to reap the benefits. That was okay, because Caesar was great. Jason was really happy. Besides, William probably had someone, so everything was fine. Really.

William offered to help with the move, and soon Jason was smooshed in between him and Tim as they drove across town. Tim kept asking questions about his service, William answering with stories. They were entertaining too, at least the ones Jason managed to concentrate on when he wasn't overwhelmed by racing thoughts and confused feelings. Once they arrived, he gave a surreal tour of his new home, a two-bedroom apartment on the top floor of a completely average complex. Nothing fancy, but it had a balcony and a nice kitchen. The two bedrooms were on opposite sides, allowing privacy, and each had a private bathroom. He was looking forward to living there.

Then they started moving in. Sometimes Jason and William would pass each other on trips to and from the truck. When they needed to bring in heavier furniture, Tim and William teamed up, since they were the strongest. By evening when they were finished and sitting exhausted on the living room floor, it felt like the most normal thing in the world that William should be there. Jason could almost imagine that they had just moved in together, gotten a place of their own after so many years of dating and seeing each other regularly. But that wasn't the case.

"I'm starving," Tim said. "Let's order a pizza."

"Better call Ben first," Jason said. "He might have fixed something for us."

"Good idea." Tim got to his feet, wincing and groaning a few times before stepping outside to make a call.

William and Jason eyed each other a moment before laughing. Jason had no idea why. Maybe they did it to relieve tension.

"I wish we were at your old place," William said. "I'd like to hose off out back again."

Jason grinned. "They have these new things called showers, you know. Very cutting edge. There's one here. Two, in fact."

"Sounds amazing," William said. "We should try it out." When he saw the panicked response this caused, he added. "Not together, of course. That is unless… We have a lot of catching up to do, verbally, because I don't even know what your situation is."

"My situation?"

William nodded. "I noticed you're not moving in with another guy."

"Oh." Jason swallowed. "There is someone, actually."

"That's great!" William said with a smile. "That's what I wanted for you."

"What you wanted?" Jason repeated.

Tim opened the front door. "Everyone, into the truck! There's lasagna waiting for us! I just hope he made two, because I swear I could eat one all by myself." He looked puzzled when neither of them moved. Then he seemed to figure it out. "Oh. Sorry, boys, but Benjamin is going to have hurt feelings if we don't show.

Especially since this is your last night with us, Jason."

He nodded his understanding. "We'll catch up later."

"Right," William said. "Of course."

The mood was more somber on the way back. Once they were home again, William asked to take a quick shower. Tim went to do the same in the master bedroom. Jason waited upstairs for his turn, leaning against the hallway wall and listening to the muted sound of artificial rain. If nothing stood in their way, would he be in there with William now, giggling as they soaped each other up? Frustrated, Jason went to his old room and checked his phone. Caesar had written again.

How's the move going?

All done, Jason wrote. *Went fine. You?*

Should be there late tomorrow. Miss you. Can't wait to rumble in the jungle.

Jason laughed, his body reacting. Maybe he was just sexually frustrated. *Hurry hurry,* he texted back.

I will. Love you.

Jason hesitated. Then he responded with the push of two buttons. *:)* A lame smiley. Hopefully that would buy him some time, because despite his body knowing what he wanted, right now his heart felt like it was rocking back and forth in a padded cell. He distracted himself next by answering Emma's texts. She was packed and ready to make the drive tomorrow. That meant more unloading, the thought alone causing Jason's back to ache.

"Shower's all yours," Tim said, cruising down the hallway toward dinner.

Tossing aside the phone, Jason exhaled, then got cleaned up. He was the last one at the table. Tim was already eating, offering a shrug of apology. The others had waited for Jason. Ben had shiny eyes, like he couldn't believe how grown up Jason was or something. Putting on a brave smile for him, Jason focused on the food, praising it and making excited conversation about his new place. Inside, he began to seethe. Why had William shown up, gotten flirtatious, then acted like Jason being with another man was all part of his plan? Was he masking hurt feelings? Or did he really want Jason to move on emotionally? Maybe William had only been hoping for a hookup and was relieved that Jason didn't expect a relationship. If so…

"What the hell!" Jason said, letting his fork clatter to the plate.

He looked up at William, who sat across from him. "You *wanted* me to be with another guy? How could you even say that?"

William glanced self-consciously at Ben and Tim, but he answered anyway. "I didn't want you waiting for me. I wanted you to have your freedom."

"Why?" Jason asked. "What's the use? Did you really think that would stop me from loving you?"

"Eventually," William said.

"Really?" Jason asked in disbelief. "Simple as that? Well, I don't work that way. Maybe you do. Took you about two years to stop caring about me, didn't it? That's when it really ended."

William looked away instead of responding.

"Maybe we should give them some privacy," Ben said, standing up.

"I'm not done eating!" Tim protested.

"It's okay," William said. "I should head back home. My mom will be getting worried. She hates it when I ride my bike at night."

"We can give you a ride," Ben offered.

"No, really. It's fine. Thank you for dinner. It was wonderful seeing you again. All of you."

Jason glanced up. William was looking at him, of course, his face as gentle as it always was. This took some of the steam from his hissing emotions, but he still didn't say anything as William left. The table was quiet when he had gone, except for a squelching sound coming from the pan as Tim helped himself to another piece of lasagna as silently as possible.

"Sorry," he whispered, slopping it onto his plate.

"It's fine," Jason said. "Everyone should keep eating. I didn't mean to ruin dinner."

"You didn't ruin anything," Ben said. "At least not yet. It's not too late."

Jason eyed him a second longer before hopping to his feet and rushing out of the room. He ran down the front drive, catching up with William just before he reached the main road.

"Wait," he panted. "Please! I'm sorry."

William stopped and stood, fists gripping the handlebars. "I'm the one who should be sorry."

"No," Jason said. "Let's just forget everything, okay? That was no way to welcome you back. Let's just move on."

William was quiet for a moment. "I really do have to get home."

Jason didn't want him to leave, especially without knowing when he'd see him again. "We're having a housewarming party," he said. "This Saturday. We can make it a homecoming party too."

"Do I have to wear a corsage?" William asked, some humor returning to his voice.

Jason grinned. "Not that sort of homecoming. It'll be a welcome home party for you. Saturday. Seven o'clock. Please."

William nodded. "I'll be there."

Jason watched him pedal away into the dark before he turned around and slowly began walking to the house. William was back. He should be happy right now, but instead his heart ached. Is this what moving on felt like?

Chapter Thirty-one

Between his day job and volunteering at the shelter, Jason didn't have much time for unpacking. The apartment would have been a disaster if not for Emma, who not only tore through cardboard boxes, but was revealing a natural talent for home improvement.

"I'm a lesbian," she said proudly one night as she cobbled together her bed frame. "I'll probably graduate from college just to become a plumber."

Every night when Jason returned to the apartment, he found the place feeling more and more like home. He and Emma were having a great time too, staying up late and talking. Maybe the apartment was fairly average, but to him it felt like a slice of paradise. Mostly.

Just a little past midnight on Wednesday, the doorbell rang. Emma was busy in the kitchen, trying to fix a broken cabinet, so Jason went to answer the door. Caesar stood there, holding the last thing in the world that Jason wanted to see—another cardboard box.

"Did you get my texts?" Caesar asked.

"No," Jason said.

Caesar lifted the box to make sure he could see it. "Can I come in? This thing is heavy."

"Yeah, of course." Jason stepped aside, confused by what was going on.

"I got kicked out of the hotel," Caesar said.

"What?"

"I know. It's terrible. My car is a total mess. I had to throw everything in there at the last minute. I didn't want to leave any electronics out there, so…" Caesar set down the box. Then he strode over to Jason and kissed him. "What would I do without you?"

"I have no idea," Jason said. "Why did they kick you out?"

Caesar sighed, sat on the couch, and rubbed his forehead. "I told you I had a little money saved up?"

Jason nodded. "Yeah. So?"

"Well, when I said little, I meant it. I'm bone dry."

Jason shook his head. "But you've been looking for an apartment."

"Because I expected to get the deposit back from the old place by now. That would be enough for two months rent and then some. They couldn't cut me a check when I moved out, but they said I'd have it within a week. Meanwhile, the storage unit I rented maxed out my credit card… I just need a place to stay until I get my deposit back."

"Okay," Jason said. "No big deal."

Caesar grinned and held out his arms. "Come here, baby."

Jason rolled his eyes and smiled. "I need to get to bed. I have work first thing in the morning."

"Bed is exactly what I had in mind," Caesar said.

"I need to sleep," Jason said. "Every minute counts. Trust me."

Caesar frowned. "Are we okay?"

"Yeah, of course!"

"It's just that ever since I got back into town… Or ever since Mr. Coast Guard showed up, things have been a little chilly."

Jason snorted. "Are you jealous? The almighty Caesar is worried he can't compete?"

"You tell me."

"It has nothing to do with William. Seriously." Jason offered his hand. "Come on, you big baby. I'll prove it to you."

Caesar's eyes lit up. "In the bedroom?"

Jason nodded. "In the bedroom."

Jason wrapped two strips of leather around one hand, then two more around the other, feeling like a primitive warrior getting ready for a fight. And in a way, he was going into battle, but he already knew that he was greatly overpowered.

"Okay, you little brats," he said. "I don't have much time tonight, so we're doing this as a group. You want to run. You want to poop. I want to go home and relax. Are we agreed?"

Four heads turned toward him, tails wagging. Jason sighed, already knowing the battle was lost. The second he opened the door, his arms were nearly yanked from their sockets. Jason stumbled around the yard of the animal shelter, being pulled this way and that. Leashes got tangled, a small fight broke out between two of the dogs, and Jason stepped in a fresh pile of crap. For all his trouble, in the end he probably only saved ten minutes.

"Told you it wouldn't work," Barbara said when he returned.

"Oh, it worked," Jason said, still trying to untangle the leashes.

Barbara raised an eyebrow. "So you'd do it again?"

"Never," Jason admitted. "Nope. Absolutely not."

"Here." Barbara reached for the leashes. "Let me get those sorted out. I think someone is here to see you."

"Really?"

"Well, he asked if you were working tonight."

Jason resisted grimacing. He had avoided going home after work, simply because he needed a break from Caesar. Living together, even temporarily, felt very premature. Ironic since they had lived together on the first day they had met. Regardless, Jason wanted a little space, so he had turned off his phone, grabbed fast food for dinner, and gone straight to the shelter. In contrast, Caesar had nothing but free time and had probably come looking for him. Jason returned to the public area, where a few people were browsing the animals.

"I'm looking for a housewarming present," a voice said.

Jason spun around and smiled. William stood just a foot away, smelling like cologne and—Jason sniffed—yes, a hint of chlorine. Sometimes, after Tim had installed the pool, Jason would sit out there and breathe in the smell, just because it always brought him right back to William. He wasn't the only one sniffing right now. William made a face.

"Oh!" Jason said, lifting his shoe. "I had a little accident. A dog, I mean. Not me. Ha ha! So what are you doing here?"

"Like I said, I'm looking for a housewarming present."

Jason shook his head. "But how did you know I'd be here?"

William winked. "Just because we've been apart four years, doesn't mean we haven't spoken. We kept in touch a fair amount, didn't we?"

"Yeah, of course. It's just that there's more than one animal shelter in Austin and—"

"All those text messages you sent me? Every email and letter? I read them all. Multiple times. I never stopped caring about you. My leaving wasn't about that."

Jason hesitated. Was he meant to read between the lines? Were they picking up the conversation where dinner had left off?

"So anyway," William said, "what sort of pet do you think my friend would like? He's about your age, your size. Just got himself a rockin' two-bedroom apartment."

"Hm." Jason pretended to be thoughtful as they began to stroll. "I'd imagine he likes big dogs. Not really into puppies because they take more effort and they get adopted easily. He's probably the kind who likes ugly mutts with problems, because he knows they'll have a hard time finding a home."

"So something big, ugly, and weird," William said. "Have anything like that here at the moment?"

Jason stopped. "Honestly, I bet your friend is a little too overwhelmed with all the changes in his life to take on a pet right now." Besides, Jason already felt like he had a puppy waiting at home, one who definitely needed a lot of care and attention. "It's a nice idea," he added. "I'm sure your friend will appreciate the thought."

"I hope so," William said. "Hey, I called Kelly the other day."

Jason felt a pang of jealousy. "Really? How did that go?"

"Fine. He said you guys had lost touch."

"Yeah," Jason said. "Sad but true. We actually got along pretty well after you were gone."

"I heard. Anyway, his photography has really taken off. He has his first exhibition next week, and look—" William pulled out a folded brochure, turned it over, and pointed at the address. He didn't need to. Jason already recognized the space from the photos. "That's Tim's gallery, right?"

"Yeah," Jason said.

"So do you want to go with me?"

"To the opening?" Jason hesitated. "Is that a good idea? If you're trying to get back with Kelly..."

William laughed. "No. And even though that bridge has been thoroughly and completely burned, I still want to show my support."

"Yeah," Jason said. "Okay. It'll be good to see him again."

"I wonder why Tim didn't mention it to you," William said.

"Probably didn't make the connection," Jason said. "You'd be surprised how many artists try to get their stuff shown at the gallery. It's getting national attention."

"Cool. Hey, did he and Ben tie the knot yet?"

"Nope. They haven't even set a date. They're too happy or superstitious or who knows what. I think they're being silly and should get it over with."

"Hm," William replied. "Maybe we should have a preacher meet us there one morning, march up to their room, and make them go through with it before they can even get out of bed."

Jason laughed at the idea. "Yeah, we should! Maybe that would start a new trend. People can get married in bed and consummate the marriage right then and there."

"Would make being a preacher a lot more interesting."

Talking to William felt so… good. Such a simple small word, but also precise. Just moments ago, Jason had been exhausted and had dreamed of going home to veg out in front of the television. But now he was reenergized, felt like he could spend the entire evening with William, chatting about whatever came to mind. Jason invited him to walk a few dogs, and as they did so, they left the past where it belonged. Eventually, though, it was time to go.

"You'll be at the party, right?" Jason asked him.

William nodded. "I'll be there."

Jason practically felt high on the drive home. When he strolled into his apartment and saw Caesar sitting on the couch, guitar on his legs as he fumbled at the strings, all Jason could think of was the time William had sat on the corner of his bed, naked except for the instrument in his lap. What had followed had been one of the best nights of Jason's life.

"I'm still trying to learn," Caesar said, handing the guitar to him. "Those lessons you gave me years ago are pretty much useless."

"Oh sure, blame the teacher," Jason said, strumming a few quick chords.

Caesar's eyes lit up. "You look good. Had a nice day at work?"

"Something like that," Jason said, setting down the guitar and plopping on the couch. "What about you?"

"Still no deposit check," Caesar said.

"So what did you do?"

"Helped Emma around the house a little. Moved more of my stuff in from the car—"

"Hey, don't be getting too comfortable!"

"I know, but my suits were getting all crinkled out there."

"Suits that you'll be wearing to job interviews?" Jason hinted. "That deposit check won't last long."

"I know, I know."

Caesar toppled over, putting his head on Jason's lap so he could be petted. Yup, just like having a puppy.

"What are you going to do?" Jason asked. "You have a fresh start now. You can finally chase after your dream."

Caesar scrunched up his face. "Become a paramedic?"

"Yeah, why not? You'd be helping people, and it's about time you started living for yourself."

"I have a master's degree in Business Administration," Caesar said. "From Yale. I'm a little over-qualified to be a paramedic."

"Geez, fine. So you're going to do something business-related?"

"That's where the money is."

"Okay." Jason thought about it while he played with Caesar's hair. "I have a friend, Marcello, who owns a small empire. I'm sure he could find a position for you."

"Marcello who?" Caesar asked.

"Maltese. Owns a company of the same name. They do all sorts of things. Photography, video, multimedia production. There's got to be a job there for you."

Caesar sat up, body tense. "I'd rather find something on my own."

"Why?" Jason said. "I understand pride and all that, but you could have a job within days. You'll need the money if—"

"I'll figure it out," Caesar said. "Trust me."

Jason shrugged. "Okay. Fine."

Caesar made an apologetic face. "I didn't mean to ruin your good mood," he said, coming in for a kiss so aggressive that Jason was forced to lie back. This suited Caesar just fine, since he crawled on top of him while still kissing him. A moment later, he wiggled his way between Jason's legs, putting them over his shoulders.

"I'm not a gymnast," Jason said, as Caesar pressed down on him.

"But you have other talents," came the response as Caesar began moving his hips suggestively. "I want to feel close to you."

Jason held back a sigh. What Caesar wanted was to fuck him. Jason pushed against him with his palms. "Let me up. I feel like I'm being crushed."

Caesar didn't move. "Do you love me?"

"This has nothing to do with me loving you or not," Jason said.

"Just answer the question."

Jason smiled, trying to lighten the mood. "What happened to taking it slow?"

"Seriously?" said a new voice. "You two are going to gay it up on the couch instead of doing the decent thing and going to your room?"

"Sorry, Emma," Jason said, pushing Caesar again. This time he finally rolled off.

"It's fine," Emma said, walking to the kitchen. "Just don't complain when you walk in on me eating out some supermodel."

"Gross," Jason said.

"Oh, I don't know," Caesar replied. "Sounds kind of hot."

Emma clinked around in the kitchen long enough that the mood was thoroughly killed, which was fine with Jason because he felt more troubled than he did horny. When he got into bed later that night, one question kept repeating in his mind, spoken in Caesar's voice.

Do you love me?

Handsome women. Pretty women. Thin women, fat women, shy women, loud women. Jason's apartment was full of women. Emma had apparently invited every woman she had met since moving to Austin, and considering how short a period that was, the results were impressive. Jason's invite list was much more humble. Barbara from the shelter, Ben and Tim, naturally, and Marcello, who was too busy with a party of his own to attend but had a fruit basket delivered as a housewarming present… along with a big screen TV. Caesar had insisted on setting up the television before the guests arrived, Emma helping him wall-mount it. Right now it was playing a steady stream of music videos in such high definition that it almost bested reality. Jason could probably change the channel to a real estate show, switch on the 3D conversion, and invite drunken guests to step through to the rest of his home.

And then there was William, who stayed discreetly on the opposite side of the room from Jason. Always in plain sight, no matter who he was talking to, but never at Jason's side or even within earshot. Just as well, since Caesar seemed intent on staying close. Only halfway through the party did Jason find any sort of privacy.

"Beer is running low," Ben said. "I'll run to the store to pick some up."

"Get something good," Caesar said.

"Of course," Ben replied. "Miller Lite is still popular, right?"

"Seriously?" Caesar asked. "Microbrewed is better. There are a few local—"

"Come with me," Ben invited. "I'll never remember otherwise."

"Oh. Well, actually—"

"And I'll need help carrying it all."

"I'm too drunk to help!" Tim declared.

"And I'm so proud of you," Ben said, patting his arm. "Come on, Caesar. This party could turn ugly if the lesbians find out the beer is running low."

"Thank you," Jason said. "Both of you."

Caesar grudgingly followed Ben out of the apartment. As soon as they were gone, Tim threw an arm around his shoulder and spoke in perfectly sober tones. "Ben is going to get lost on purpose, so you have a decent amount of time."

"What?" Jason asked.

"You know how he is. Personally, I like Caesar and still think you should give him a shot, but Ben wants you to talk to William. And why shouldn't you? It's your party."

"Okay," Jason said. "Thanks."

Feeling jittery, he made his way across to where William stood. By chance, he wasn't too far from the bedroom, and after a quick hello, Jason found what he really wanted was seclusion.

"This brings back memories," William said once they were inside the bedroom and the door was shut. "Although last time we were playing waiter."

"That's right," Jason said with a grin. "Uh, but I didn't bring you in here—"

"I know," William assured him. "Those days are behind us. No more cheating." He sat down on the edge of the bed, Jason joining him. "I'm glad we have a chance to talk. There are things I want to set straight."

"Okay," Jason said, feeling nervous.

"Two years ago, when we stopped sleeping together or being affectionate, that wasn't because I stopped loving you."

"Then why?" Jason managed.

William kept his gaze forward. "Because I felt like I was holding you back. I was never okay with making you wait four years, but every time I returned to Austin, all I wanted to do was see you and be with you, and I knew that kept you hanging on. So I made the decision to let you go. Properly. And it worked. I knew it would hurt you, but you finally moved on."

"No, I didn't," Jason said. "I didn't stop loving you. Ever."

William glanced over and smiled. "That's different than moving on. We'll always love each other. That's how it works. But there's more I want to say because I'm not a saint. I'm human, and I've been with other guys. There were situations I found too tempting, or that I simply wanted. So two years ago, that wasn't an act of self-sacrifice. I needed that freedom, and I needed you to have it too."

"I've also been with other guys," Jason said. "After you and before Caesar. Guys who didn't mean anything to me, and a few who I thought could be something special. But none of them even came close to what you are to me. None of them changed how I feel."

William nodded as if this made sense. "The guy out there, he's the one from your past, right? There aren't too many people named Caesar, so I figured…"

"Yeah. It's him."

"Knowing that makes it easier," William said. "And harder."

"What do you mean?"

William shook his head. "I'm thinking of leaving Austin."

"What?" Jason stood and turned around. "Why would you even say that?"

"I need to figure out what I want to do with my life. Coming home felt good, but I guess that old saying is true. You can never go home again."

"Is this because of me?"

"No," William said. "This isn't a childish ultimatum. I get that you and Caesar have a history together. It's a blessing and a curse, because if he was some guy you'd only been with for a few weeks, I'd chase him off in a heartbeat. But he actually means something to you. And you're happy. I want to be happy too, so I'm exploring my options. That's all. The Coast Guard was great, and I'm not sure I'm ready to leave it."

"And Austin doesn't have a coast that needs guarding," Jason said numbly.

"That's right," William said. "So it's not your fault. Even if we were together, I'd still have to decide what my future will be."

Jason sat on the edge of the bed again and sighed. "I don't want you to go."

"I know."

"Isn't there some sort of civilian job you can take? Ultra-lifeguard or something."

William laughed. "There are a lot of possibilities. I'd like to keep saving lives, so originally I was thinking of working as an EMT."

"What, like a paramedic?"

"Yeah. I am one already, technically. I had to get my certification as part of training."

"For real?" Jason started laughing. "You're a paramedic?"

"Yes. There's more to rescuing someone than dragging them out of the water. Why is this funny?"

"It's not," Jason said, wiping at his eyes. "I used to know a guy who wanted to be a paramedic, that's all. You should do it."

"Think so?"

"Yeah! You won't always be young enough to jump out of helicopters, right? Sounds like a good choice." Jason nudged against him. "And by the way, I love how casually you say 'I'd like to keep saving lives.'"

"Just doing my duty," William said with an exaggerated Southern accent. Then, more seriously, he added. "When I saved the first guy… You remember that? I texted you."

"Of course I remember."

William beamed proudly. "That was such a high. I felt so good, like I had paid back a debt. I don't know if that makes sense, but anyway, when it was clear the guy was going to make it, I thought of you. If you hadn't told me to go, that guy might have died. Sure, maybe someone else would have been there in my place, but then again, maybe not. Either way, you made it possible. By letting me chase after my dream, you saved his life too."

Jason couldn't help feeling flattered, and a little embarrassed. "Cool as it sounds, I can't take credit for that."

"Sure you can," William said. "Him and all the others."

"How many?" Jason asked.

"It's hard to say, since some of them could have survived on their own, maybe been picked up by boaters eventually, or—"

"How many?"

"Five," William said.

Jason felt like swooning. "You're a freaking superhero, you know that?"

William smiled. "So are we good now? You understand what the last few years were about and absolve me of all my sins?"

Jason nodded. "We're good."

There was a knock on the door, then they heard Tim coughing loudly.

"Times up," Jason said. "Caesar probably jumped out of the car and ran back to—"

Whatever else he was going to say was silenced by William's lips on his. Jason tensed up, then started to melt, just as the kiss came to an end.

"For old times' sake," William said. Then he stood and headed for the door. "From now on, I promise that you're all his."

"That's for me to decide," Jason murmured to himself. Then he flopped onto his back and sighed.

Chapter Thirty-Two

All around them, people dodged each other while trying to keep trays balanced. Sounds of talking and hissing and slurping filled the air, as did scents from many of the world's cuisines, combined into what smelled like a stir-fried pizza on a bed of freshly baked cookies. Ben glanced around the mall food court, not hiding his puzzlement.

"When you said we needed to talk privately, I was picturing something more… private."

"I know," Jason said. "I meant away from Caesar and Tim. I need advice, and I don't want either of them to overhear."

"Okay," Ben said, leaning back in his chair. "Are you sure you don't want something to eat? It is your lunch break."

Jason shook his head. Lately his stomach had been too twisted up for food. "You understand what it's like to love two men at the same time, right?"

"Yes," Ben answered instantly. "I definitely know that feeling."

"Okay, this might sound weird, but it occurred to me that Caesar is a little like Tim, and William is sort of like Jace."

Ben thought about it for a moment, then he laughed. "I can see that. Caesar didn't struggle with his sexuality though, and William is more the athletic type. Jace never was, but they're both kind-hearted so… It's not a perfect parallel, but I think I see what you're getting at."

"Yeah," Jason said. "What I need to know is, how did you decide? How did you choose which one was right for you?"

"That's complicated. When Tim and I were teenagers, the choice was between getting hurt again or moving on. That was hard, but much more clear-cut. After I'd met Jace and Tim showed back up…" Ben bit his lip. "He still hadn't really accepted who he was, but what it came down to was that Tim had hurt me before. Jace hadn't."

Jason considered this. "Problem is, Caesar hurt me by choosing another guy. William hurt me by choosing the Coast Guard. I don't really blame either of them, considering the circumstances, but they're neck and neck right now. What about when Tim showed up later in your life?"

"By then Jace and I were married," Ben said. "I'd made a promise to stay committed and faithful, which meant having to say goodbye to Tim, because I still loved him."

Jason sighed. "I guess I made a promise to Caesar when I agreed to be his boyfriend. So I should say goodbye to William?"

"Maybe." Ben hesitated. "Our circumstances aren't exactly the same. Jace wasn't the only issue keeping Tim and me apart. The Tim you know today is a different person from who he was back then."

"So who would you pick today?" Jason asked.

"If Jace were still alive?" Ben asked.

"Yeah. Say in some alternate reality, you never got married, and both guys came up to you and proposed. The Tim from today, and Jace as he always was. Which guy would you choose?"

Ben thought about the question. "Jace was so gentle, so kind. I'd give anything to bring him back. I would. Even if he wasn't with me, he should be a part of this world again. Tim has always been such a damn mess, but he also fought the hardest. He went from being the guy who would rather leave me than tell his parents, to one who would willingly take a bullet for me. So if Jace came back today, I honestly don't know who I would pick. They're both so damn wonderful that I'd probably tell them both to get in bed with me and snuggle up, whether they liked it or not. " Ben thought about it a moment longer. Then his cheeks flushed and he wiped at his eyes.

"I'm sorry," Jason said. "It wasn't a fair question."

"Are you kidding?" Ben said. "That might be the most beautiful fantasy I've ever had! Besides, putting me on the spot should show you how difficult a decision like this is for anyone. Even me, after all these years."

Jason sighed. "Maybe I should flip a coin."

"Don't do that," Ben said. "Tell me instead what you like about each of them."

"Okay. Well, I always admired Caesar's confidence. He's sexy and charming, and he used to live up to his name. When I was younger, he felt like the emperor of his own little world. Maybe not so much now, but I'm sure he'll get back there eventually. He can be very sympathetic. Smooth and sensitive at the same time. That's pretty cool."

"Okay," Ben said. "Now what do you like about William?"

Jason glanced up at the Juicy James booth, the boy in the goofy cowboy uniform now a skinny redhead, but he still caused pangs of nostalgia. "Everything," Jason said. "His face, his smile, the way he smells, the way it feels to hold him. I love how high-pitched his laugh gets when he's really cracking up and the way he looks ashamed after he farts." Jason chuckled to himself. "That he eats like a total pig, bikes everywhere, and is always pushing himself to be a better person when he's already perfect. I even love that he left me to follow his dream. With Caesar, if I could turn back time and stop him from choosing Nathaniel, I would. But not William. I'd let him go a million times over again because I've seen how happy it makes him, how the world is a better place because of him. Most of all, he makes me feel special. Even though we've both been with other guys and had bigger priorities, I know that he loves me, and with William, I don't think that happens too often. Caesar can fall in love with anyone, and I admire that too, but as generous as William is, he doesn't give his heart away so carelessly."

Ben's eyes were wide. "Wow. After that, do you really need me to point out the obvious?"

Jason's shoulders slumped. "I know, but Caesar's world has fallen apart. He's finally free from his parents, but he's also broke and completely on his own. I'm his safety net. I never saw that coming. Part of me feels good that he needs me, but the rest—"

"Feels like snipping that net and letting him fall?"

"That's one way of putting it," Jason said. "Anyway, dumping him now seems cruel. William doesn't need me like that."

"I'd wager he needs you in much healthier ways," Ben said. "Don't stay with someone because you feel sorry for them. That's not doing Caesar any favors."

"It's not just that," Jason said.

"Because you love him?" Ben asked. "Go ahead and say it. Convince me."

Jason smiled. "I love Caesar."

"Like you mean it!" Ben said. "You could have been talking about a good friend there. Now say you love William."

Jason took a deep breath. "I love William." He sighed the words more than he said them, goose bumps covering his skin. Even the hair on the back of his neck stood up.

"*That* was electric," Ben said. "Even I could feel the difference!"

"You're right," Jason said. "You're so totally right." He thought about going home early, telling Caesar as gently as possible that it wasn't working out. And then what? Caesar sleeping in a car already stuffed with his possessions? Or on the couch, which would be awkward for them all. "He'll be moving out soon," Jason said. "I can't dump him now. It would be cruel. As soon as he has his own place, I'll cut him loose."

Ben raised his eyebrows. "Okay. Just be careful that William doesn't fly the coop before the nest is empty."

"Did the check come? Get your deposit back yet? Hear anything from the landlord?" Jason asked these questions or variations of them every day, usually disappointed with the answer. Time was running out. He knew William was staying in town at least until the weekend when Kelly had his exhibition. After that was anyone's guess, since Jason rarely found time alone to call, text, or anything else. If he wasn't working, he was usually out somewhere with Caesar. Going to movies, go-kart racing, bar hopping, anything but being home where they could potentially sleep together. The prospect wasn't tempting to Jason in the slightest, but Caesar was becoming increasingly amorous as the week wore on.

"Did the check—"

"I got the money," Caesar said, cutting him off. "It's in the bank."

Jason set down his keys and took off his nametag from work. "That's great! Is the apartment you looked at still available?"

"It is," Caesar said, standing to kiss him.

Jason made sure it was only a peck. Then he went to the kitchen to grab a drink, so his lips would be otherwise occupied.

"I thought we'd go out to celebrate," Caesar said.

"There's the gallery opening tonight," Jason said. "I can't."

"Then I'll come with you."

Jason had been prepared for this. "I have to help Tim behind the scenes," he lied. "Plus a lot of old friends will be there—"

"Like William?"

"Yeah," Jason said. "It's probably the last time I'll get to see him before he leaves town again, so I was hoping catch up with him and Kelly. That's his other ex-boyfriend, if that tells you anything. Besides, I'll be with Emma the whole time."

Caesar shrugged. "I'm not worried. I know who you come home to every night."

Not for long, Jason hoped. He felt obligated to reward Caesar for trusting him and spent some time snuggling with him on the couch, which made him feel guilty for several reasons. Luckily Emma came home from a job hunt shortly afterwards and kept "inconveniently" popping into the room, even when Jason was getting showered and dressed for the evening.

"Break up with him now," she suggested in a rare moment of privacy.

"He still doesn't have a place to stay. I'll go with him tomorrow to get the apartment. I'll help him move in. And then..." Jason dragged one finger across his neck.

"You're going to murder him?" Emma asked, pretending to be horrified.

Jason rolled his eyes and finished getting ready. Then he and Emma drove to William's old house. His mother opened the door, beaming at Jason like it was prom night all over again.

"Willy came home because of you," she whispered. "I owe you some homemade cookies."

"Peanut butter," Jason whispered back. "I'd also accept oatmeal cookies, but only if they have raisins in them."

"I hope you're not dieting!" Ms. Townson said with a giggle.

William walked into the room wearing a navy blue suit jacket, which accentuated his strong shoulders. "Too formal?" he asked. "I figured the jeans would balance it out."

"You look stunning," Jason said.

William smiled at the compliment, kissed his mother on the cheek, and led the way outside. Emma called shotgun, which was mean, but then took the back seat anyway. The mood in the car was buzzing on the way over to the gallery.

"I can't wait to see Kelly again," William said.

"Don't be too glad," Jason said, pretending to be jealous.

"I can't help it," William said, playing along. "The second I see him, I'll probably sweep him into my arms and give him a kiss."

"No!"

"With lots of tongue."

"Nooooo!"

Although William was joking, they were all taken aback when

they entered the gallery and saw the man of the hour. He was in the middle of the room, talking to an older man. As if sensing them, Kelly turned around and walked toward them. He *walked*. Smiling and waving and not having to depend on crutches at all. Aside from a slight limp, he seemed just as whole as anyone else.

"Surprise!" he said, laughing at their shocked expressions.

William grabbed Kelly, holding him tight. They murmured a few words to each other, and when William stepped back, he was wiping tears from his eyes. Kelly was struggling with his emotions too.

"Prosthetic leg," he said, addressing Jason and Emma. "It's amazing what they can do these days. When Marcello found out I was looking into them, he insisted on flying me to Europe, where they have the very best prosthetics in the world. All paid for by the company."

"I love that man," William said. "I love you!"

Kelly rolled his eyes. "Someone fetch William a drink. He gets so emo!"

They all laughed. After catching up a little longer, Kelly insisted they browse his photos. Emma and Jason went to do so. William stayed next to Kelly, but Jason wasn't worried. He understood how William was feeling. Seeing an ex could be a wonderful feeling at first, especially when the ex in question was doing so well. Jason had been happy to see Caesar. Part of him wished they had shared that meal and maybe the night in the hotel room and left it at that.

Kelly's photography was extensive. Landscapes, children, animals, architecture, and quite a few handsome men. None of the photos were of Kelly himself, implying he had moved on from his modeling days or at least wasn't into self-portraits.

"Oh shit!" Emma said while they were looking at a photo of rain clouds reflected in skyscraper glass. At least that's what Jason was looking at. Emma was staring across the room. "Bonnie is here!"

"Ah," Jason said, hiding a smile. "Hey, isn't this gallery where Ben and Tim finally got back together?"

"What are you saying?" Emma asked, cheeks flushing.

"That maybe it's a magical place. Worth a shot, right?"

Emma seemed terrified by the prospect, but then her confidence took over again. She strode across the room, perhaps a little stiff-legged, to test his theory.

Chuckling, Jason turned back to the portraits, stopping when he came to one of William. He was much younger in the photo, his eyes smiling at the camera. Jason recognized the look of adoration. The photo must have been taken when he and Kelly were still fond of each other, before the relationship turned sour. Jason stood in front of the photo and pretended William was looking at him that way again. With any luck, he would return to doing so soon. For now, Jason could only bask in the memory.

"Such a handsome young man!" Marcello said, placing a hand on Jason's shoulder. "And you've managed to bring him home again from his fire-fighting duties!"

"He was in the Coast Guard," Jason said, turning to Marcello and scrutinizing him. "Too much champagne again?"

"No such thing," Marcello said, shaking his jowls. "And besides, I'm sure the ocean catches fire occasionally. I'm certain I saw it do so in a movie once."

"Of course," Jason said, offering him a hug. "Thank you for the housewarming present."

"You're very welcome," Marcello said, patting him on the back. "Did you like the pears? They're deliciously juicy. It isn't always easy to find a juicy pear."

"They were great," Jason said, taking a step back. "I was mostly referring to the television."

"A trinket," Marcello said dismissively. "I hope you and William have many happy hours ignoring it while on the couch together. You always made such a pretty pair."

Jason laughed. "We're not back together yet. But between you and me, I'm working on it."

"I'm sure you'll do fine. Where there's a William, there's a way." Marcello appeared pleased with himself. "Oh, I wished I'd saved that one for the wedding day toast! No matter, I'm sure I'll think of something appropriately clever before then."

Jason humored him with a smile. Once Marcello had gone to find himself another drink, Jason returned to staring at William's photo. When a couple of other people started to do the same, he forced himself to move on. Kelly's photos were beautiful. He had a way of capturing life on film, even in portraits of inanimate objects, like the rusty old car that seemed to be smiling because of the way the bumper sank in the middle.

Soon Jason started strolling around the room and watching people instead. Emma deep in conversation with Bonnie in one corner. Marcello holding court with a group of people. Kelly leading William from photo to photo, probably explaining the story behind each or sharing memories. He watched them a moment longer, worried for a second about old flames finding new fuel, but he decided to trust in William's love. Even if he didn't know Jason's plan, surely he would wait. Forcing himself to turn away, Jason noticed that someone was watching him.

His heart skipped a beat when he saw who, but only out of nervousness. Nathaniel was decked out in a suit, holding a full glass of champagne, and wearing a sober expression as he stared at Jason. His being here wasn't a complete surprise. Marcello owned the gallery—or at least the foundation that owned it—and as one of his employees, Nathaniel could be here on an official basis.

Jason tried a tentative smile. The gesture wasn't returned. Instead Nathaniel strode across the room to him, a few people having to move out of his way. Jason froze. He felt like a bouncer was about to throw him out of the place.

"I remember you," Nathaniel said, stopping just before him.

Jason nodded. "I've been a waiter for a few of Marcello's parties. We talked once, when, uh—"

"Marcello let you borrow one of his rooms," Nathaniel finished for him. "I remembered you back then too."

Jason's eyes widened. "What do you mean?"

Now Nathaniel smiled, as if amused. "I knew who you were. And I'm pretty damn sure you remembered me too." He held out a hand. "We both survived the Hubbards and their son. That much we have in common."

Jason took his hand and shook it, not apologizing for his own being so sweaty. "Why didn't you say anything back then?"

Nathaniel cocked his head. "And ruin your fairytale night with your lover?" He nodded in William's direction. "It's nice to see you two still together. Gives me renewed faith in love."

"Yeah," Jason said. "Thanks. This might be a weird question, but do you hate me?"

Nathaniel frowned. "Why, just because you almost ruined my chances of getting back together with Caesar? Or because you were instrumental in him getting caught by his parents again, making it harder for us to see each other? Or maybe because you slept with him, even when you knew he and I were together?"

Jason swallowed. "That about sums it up."

Nathaniel clapped him on the shoulder, nearly knocking Jason over in the process. "All water under the bridge. In fact, what you did made it easier to finally leave the guy. I even thought of you when Caesar showed up last month."

"Last month?" Jason asked. "Wait, you've seen him recently?"

Nathaniel nodded. "He rolled into town four or five weeks ago. Had a big sob story about his parents cutting him off and that he needed a place to stay. I was dumb enough to let him, but after a few weeks of him trying to get back in my pants, I decided I'd had enough. Nothing he could say or do would ever make me take him back. Not after what happened in college."

Jason suspected more than just arguing had caused them to break up, but that was the least of his concerns. "Wasn't Caesar living on the East Coast?"

"Yeah," Nathaniel said. "He said he came all the way to Austin just to be with me. Said the same thing on my voicemail the other night. I don't think I deleted it." Nathaniel pulled out his phone and held it up. "Want to hear his voice again?"

Jason nodded numbly, listened as Caesar desperately asked Nathaniel to see him again. *I came all this way just to be with you. I'm still here, and it's not working out, but I can't bring myself to leave. Please. Just call me back. Talk to me. I know we can make this work.*

Nathaniel studied his face while he listened, but Jason was too shocked to hide anything. When the message came to an end, Nathaniel pushed a button and returned the phone to a pocket inside his suit.

"You've seen him too, haven't you?"

Jason scowled. "Where do you think he's been staying?"

"Oh," Nathaniel said. "I didn't realize—"

Jason spun around, heading for the gallery exit. He spotted Tim on his way and made a detour. "Can you give Emma and William a ride home?" he asked.

"Yeah," Tim said, looking concerned. "Is everything okay?"

"I finally made my decision. Tell Ben that. He'll understand."

Jason stomped out of the gallery, gathering his anger around him like a thick coat to keep himself hot. He'd harness this rage to do what needed to be done. He hopped into his car and tried to make himself drive safely, but he was too furious. Enough so that he went through a red light, a car honking and swerving to avoid him. Jason took a series of deep breaths, focusing on the speedometer and the road ahead. If he got killed now, he would be cheating himself of William.

Jason arrived back at the apartment in one piece. When he burst inside, he halted instantly in his tracks. The place had changed. A tasteful statue stood next to the couch. A candelabra on the coffee table provided candlelight. A quilt had been draped across Emma's favorite chair. He stared at these things in puzzlement before he heard hammering coming from the bedroom. Jason crept in that direction, feeling like he was in the wrong home. In his room he found Caesar lifting a large painting, trying to get the mounting wire to catch on a nail in the wall.

"What are you doing?" Jason asked.

Caesar finished hanging the painting and stepped back. "Tah-dah!"

Jason didn't even look at it. "What the hell are you doing?"

Caesar's smile faltered. "I thought I'd bring in a few of my things. Show you how nice it could be if we lived together.

"Lived together?" Jason demanded. "Are you kidding me?"

Caesar looked vulnerable. "What's wrong? What happened?"

"When did you first come to Austin? Honestly. Tell me!"

"You know when."

"Yeah, I do," Jason said, "so cut the crap. Why did you come back to Texas? The truth."

Caesar clenched his jaw and sat on the edge of the bed. "I didn't lie. I wanted to see you too. I was having a hard night, and I was looking up people I missed. When I saw both of you were in the same city, it felt like a sign."

"But who did you go to first?" Jason demanded. "Let me rephrase that. Who was your first choice?"

Caesar licked his lips. "You know how I feel about him. Nathaniel was my first love. He got in deep. That's hard to shake."

Jason snorted. "You were my first love, and you know what? You're not my first choice."

"I know," Caesar said quietly. "But I thought I could be. When I found out you were single, I figured I could be that guy for you. I thought about how much I wanted Nathaniel, even though I couldn't have him, and I wanted to give that dream to you, be the incomparable first love that you yearned for. And *I* wanted to be with you. I still do."

"Right. Obviously. That's why you called Nathaniel and begged for him to take you back."

Caesar shook his head wearily. "I called him because, ever since William showed up, it's been obvious that what you really need is him. There's no room left in your life for me. I'm not blind."

He wished Caesar had shouted this, had fought back instead of speaking in the resigned honesty that stole the wind from Jason's sails. He tried his best to claw his way back up to anger anyway. "You called Nathaniel. From under my roof. As my boyfriend."

"I know," Caesar said, turning to face him. "Can you honestly say nothing has happened between you and William under this roof? As my boyfriend."

Jason thought of when William kissed him, and although it wasn't exactly his doing, he certainly had enjoyed it.

Caesar exhaled. "You don't have to answer. I don't blame you if anything happened. And I know calling Nathaniel was wrong, but just think how you would feel if William didn't want you. Think about how much you love him, and then pretend he won't even answer your calls. I got desperate, and frankly, a little scared, because no one seems to want me anymore. Not my family, not Nathaniel, not even you."

Jason sighed and sat on the bed next to Caesar. "You're supposed to lie, or worse, say that you're sorry, which would make me even angrier. Then I'd kick you out and this whole mess would be over with."

"I'm sorry," Caesar said.

"Get the hell out of my apartment," Jason deadpanned. When Caesar stood, Jason grabbed his arm and pulled him back down. "There's not much point in arguing about this, is there? Not when we both want to be with other people."

"I could imagine being very happy with you," Caesar said. "But no, I don't want to fight. Not when the battle is already lost."

Jason looked over at him and swallowed. "You were the best thing that happened to me when I was a teenager. You know that? Even though it ended badly, you gave me hope that I could find love again someday. And I really did love you. So much that it hurt. I still love you. But not in the same way. Not anymore."

"You grew up," Caesar said, biting his lip. His eyes were wet as he turned to Jason. "You have no idea how amazing you've become. You used to be this angry little guy who hated the very thing he needed. Now you've got a family and a home and friends, and you're incredible. It's good to see you like this, but I've lost all of those things, and I don't think either one of us wants to reverse roles. I can't be the same person to you I once was, and I don't want you to take care of me. It doesn't feel right. And I love you too, but not like I love him."

Jason put an arm around Caesar. "You're wrong about one thing. I do want to take care of you. I can be your family, I can be your friend, and you've got a home here for as long as you need it. But that's it."

"That's it?" Caesar said, managing a laugh. "Sounds like a lot!"

Jason shrugged. "It's all fairly standard. Welcome to foster care. You'll be going to church every Sunday, and doing lots of chores, but don't worry, we have chore rewards."

"Oh boy!" Caesar said. He rested his elbows on his knees and considered the carpet. "I'll sign a lease on that apartment," he said. "Doing so will force me to get a job. I don't want you taking care of me, but maybe after a little time, we can give friendship a shot."

"Or family," Jason said. "You started out as my big brother, don't forget."

Caesar grimaced. "Still sounds creepy after all these years."

"Yeah," Jason admitted. "It does. Friends it is."

Caesar nodded. "Are you and William together already?"

"No. Why?"

Caesar grinned. "Breakup sex? It was so awesome last time."

Jason laughed and shoved him away. "Not on your life!"

William showed up at the door holding two large Tupperware containers and looking puzzled. Once Jason showed him into the apartment, William walked into the kitchen and set the containers on the counter.

"You might want to be careful when eating these," he said. "Mom kept giggling the whole time she packed them. I think she may have discovered hashish."

Jason peeled back a plastic lid to discover oatmeal cookies. Complete with raisins. In the other he found peanut butter cookies. These brought back a happy memory, and despite having the apartment all to himself—Caesar had moved out and Emma was busy with her own personal dramas—Jason suddenly felt like getting outside to the warm weather.

"Let's go for a picnic," he suggested.

"Sure." Then William leaned close and whispered. "Where's Caesar?"

Jason kept a serious face. "I don't think he'll mind."

William still didn't know. Jason had taken the past week off, just for himself. He didn't want to hop from one relationship to another. He also wanted Caesar to be out of the apartment, to avoid any awkward situations or hurt feelings. Mostly, Jason just needed the extra time to calm down, to not feel so emotionally torn. He still felt plenty of emotions now, but one dominated the others, sweet and pure.

Just in case, he had asked Ms. Townson to call him if William talked about leaving town. He hadn't, obviously, making it possible now for him and William to dig through the refrigerator and stand at the counter making sandwiches together, all of which felt delightfully domestic. This would be their life together. Spreading margarine on white bread and debating if Swiss or American cheese was better. With any luck, they would be spending countless days this way, doing little mundane tasks that were so much better with someone to share them with.

They were in agreement as to where the picnic would take place. The choice was obvious. Jason drove them outside of Austin, past where he used to live with Ben and Tim, stopping only when they got to St. Edwards Park. They grinned at each other over the car when they parked, then squabbled over which way they had originally gone. Eventually, they found it. A little spot by the creek, a miniature waterfall in the distance. William started wolfing down the sandwiches. Jason contented himself with cookies. Then they chugged down bottled water and stretched out next to each other, taking in the blissful scenery.

"Ironic, isn't it?" William said.

"What?"

"Us being here. Last time you were single and I was in a bad relationship. Now I'm single and you're..."

"What are you trying to say?" Jason asked. "Are you saying I'm in a bad relationship?"

"No!" William said quickly. "I'm sure he's really nice. I just meant it feels the same."

"Oh, you mean you wish I was free to lean over, just like this, and kiss you."

William pulled away. "And then we had a discussion about not putting each other in awkward positions."

"Did we?" Jason said with a grin, casually brushing his arm up against him. "I don't remember that at all."

William studied him, wearing an almost pained expression. "Don't tease me."

Jason forced his smile away. "You're right, and you're wrong. I shouldn't tease you. You're totally right about that. But this picnic is nothing like the last one, because this time we're both free to do whatever we want."

"Meaning?" William said. "I don't want to have an affair. I don't want to share you."

"Caesar and I broke up," Jason said. "That's why I stormed out of the gallery that night. I decided I couldn't handle it anymore, so I went home, and we agreed to end it."

"You're serious?" William said.

"Scout's honor."

"You're not a Boy Scout."

Jason smiled. "True, but I'm being honest with you. I swear."

"Wow." William considered the implications. And hopefully the possibilities. "Is Caesar doing okay?"

Jason groaned. "You're so nice! Yes, the other guy is doing fine. He moved out already and look." He dug out his phone, pulled up the last text message Caesar had sent him.

Just had a job interview and my future boss is smoking hot! Can't wait for a debriefing. ;)

"Wow," William repeated.

"Yeah. His parents should have named him Casanova instead. Anyway, I think he's going to be fine."

"That's good," William said solemnly. "We need to talk."

"We do?" Jason furrowed his brow. Talking should be the last thing they were doing right now.

"Yeah," William said. "I contacted the Coast Guard. They have a position for me. I'd work as a technician. The pay is great, my room and board would be covered by them, and the benefits are amazing. I don't think I can turn it down."

Jason swallowed. "You're serious."

"Yeah."

"Where?"

William glanced over at him with an apologetic expression. "Alaska. I fly out tomorrow."

Jason's face started to crumple just about the time that William started laughing.

"You were kidding?" Jason demanded. "You seriously think that's funny?"

"About as funny as you keeping me in the dark all week," William retorted. "You have no idea how lovesick I've been. All I do is listen to The Cure and pace my old bedroom. It's pathetic."

"Geez."

"I know." William leaned closer. "I'm miserable without you."

"How come?" Jason asked.

"Because I love you."

Jason dodged a kiss. "Say it again."

"I love you," William said. Then he turned his face to the sky and shouted it. "Jason Grant, I love you!"

Jason tackled him, flattening William with an "oof!" and kissing him before he could catch his breath. "I love you too," he said. "I always will." Then, in a terrible imitation of Robert Smith's voice, he started crooning The Cure's *Love Song*.

"Stop," William pleaded, pretending to cover his ears. "I'm done with feeling sad. From now on, it's just you, me, and a whole bunch of happy days."

"How many happy days?" Jason asked.

William smiled. "More than you can possibly imagine."

Epilogue

What began as a joke was now nearing reality. William mentioned the idea every time Jason complained that the Big Day would never come. Eventually the suggestion was taken seriously. Ben and Tim wanted to get married. All they needed was the right set of circumstances. To celebrate the anniversary of when Ben and Tim had met again at the little art gallery, Jason made reservations for them at a bed and breakfast. The day they returned was the actual date of that fateful reunion. Jason had felt that was a nice touch, although now, in the midst of so much stress, he wasn't so sure if this was a good idea after all.

The guests were a challenge. There were so many to contact! He started with Michelle, which was smart, because she and Greg were willing to help. They took care of setting the scene, transforming Ben and Tim's backyard. A small stage with an arch was built, providing enough room for two people to stand and take their vows. White flowers were planted in the ground around the stage, butterflies and bees naturally attracted to them, colorful wings fluttering in the summer sun. In front of this were seats for the guests, large tables off to one side already filled with food from the caterers. Decorative glass jars that held thick candles added ambience, as did the chains of light strung along the fence. Everything would be perfect, assuming the two grooms weren't upset by what they found when they returned home.

Jason surveyed the guests, amazed that he'd managed to bring them all together, especially since some lived far away. Tim had a grandmother in Mexico City, for instance. When Jason had called her to reveal his plan, the old woman had shrieked in excitement and spent five minutes chattering in Spanish, forgetting to speak English. Jason had picked her up from the airport earlier in the day. She kept shoving little pieces of candy into his hand, insisting he call her Nana and patting him on the head, even though she practically had to jump to do so.

Tim's parents, when Jason contacted them, asked how long they had to make a decision. That seemed cold, but in the end they had agreed. When they showed up at the house, Mr. Wyman seemed none too pleased.

"I can't believe we have to sit here and watch this," he grumbled.

"You either watch your son get married and be happy," Mrs. Wyman replied, "or watch your wife get a divorce."

Mr. Wyman had been grinning like a zombie ever since.

Ben's relatives were easier, since Jason had been around them plenty of times. The only trick was making sure they had enough seats. In addition to Ben's parents and his perpetually sour sister, Ben had grandparents, aunts, uncles, cousins, and more. The Bentley family easily filled up their side of the aisle. Only Tim's side continued to be a ragtag bunch.

Allison sat there with her husband, perhaps because more space was available. She needed it now—or the baby that Allison cradled in her arms did, since a huge array of gear was required to keep the child happy. Tim's grandmother sat next to them, making conversation. Jason caught a snippet as he walked past.

"He have beautiful skin. Like cinnamon! I take him back to Mexico with me, yes?"

Next to Nana sat her daughter and son-in-law—Tim's parents—and behind them a row of empty chairs were reserved for Marcello and his guests, but he was too busy directing an army of topless waiters. And fretting over details Jason never would have considered. Like now, when Marcello was having a small table and chair set up on stage. Jason watched in puzzlement, feeling even more confused when a middle-aged man with graying hair went there and started arranging papers. When Marcello saw Jason coming, he met him halfway.

"Who's he?" Jason asked, nodding at the man. "And why does the altar now look like a classroom for one?"

"The man is Adrien York," Marcello said, "and he's here to make all of this legal."

"He's a lawyer?" Jason asked. "But gay marriage isn't legal in Texas."

"No, but there are possible concessions. Adrien has been quite clever about this. He offers wedding packages to gay couples. During the ceremony, they sign papers that guarantee they will inherit each other's estates, have power of attorney in medical emergencies, rights of visitation and that sort of thing. So while we gay Texans still can't marry legally, Adrien has dug up every useful law to get us as close as possible. He actually came up with the idea when helping Ben and Jace some years back. Normally he doesn't preside over such matters personally, but he and this family have some history together."

"Okay," Jason said. "I thought there would be a priest or something here instead."

"What does a priest know about marriage?" Marcello asked. "Would you buy a car from a man who had never driven one? Lawyers see marriages begin, and they certainly see them end. In this particular case, our lawyer understands everything in between, because he is a married man himself."

Marcello pointed to the black sheep side where an Asian man built like a stack of tanks was already weeping emotionally.

"In that case," Jason said, "he seems qualified. As long as I don't have to stand up there in front of everyone."

Marcello's attention focused elsewhere, eyes narrowing. "Why are those waiters unpacking the caviar from the ice? What are they going to do next, microwave it?"

Marcello stomped off to correct this gravest of errors, Jason turning his attention to the guests again. Greg was trying to get his two teenage sons to settle down and stop fighting, Michelle sitting next to them and ignoring the commotion with practiced patience. She patted an empty chair next to her, signifying she was saving it for him. He smiled in appreciation, but pointed at his watch. Emma had just arrived with her date and would probably sit with them. Of course there was still someone missing who Jason was seriously starting to stress about. Where was—

A flash went off, causing him to blink. Kelly walked over, a camera hanging around his neck. "Wait until you see your face. Stress City."

"That's because I thought you were going to be late," Jason said, breathing a sigh of relief.

"It's not a wedding without a photographer," Kelly agreed. "I was late because William needed a ride. He *still* refuses to drive. The man knows how to fly a helicopter, but he won't drive a car."

Jason groaned. "I was supposed to pick him up!"

"Don't worry about it. He knows you have way too much going on. That's why we also went to pick up the cake."

"Oh my god!" Jason cried, spinning around. William, along with a few of the waiters, was carrying the cake to an empty spot reserved for it. "How could I forget that?"

"Weddings are insane," Kelly said. "When my time comes, I'm eloping. Or hopefully someone sweet like you will take care of the preparations. The lucky couple is going to be so happy you did all this."

"You think so?"

Kelly glanced at his watch. "We'll find out any minute. I better get into position."

Jason thanked him, stomach burbling with nerves. He did one final check, ignoring the fact that Chinchilla was peeing next to their makeshift altar or that William was licking frosting off his finger that could only have come from one place. Then Caesar rushed into the backyard, clapping his hands.

That was the signal. Everyone hurried to take their seats, all but Jason, who went inside to greet them. He was supposed to be house-sitting and taking care of Chinchilla, and he had been, when not stressing about getting everything else ready. He waited by the front door, listening as the voices grew louder. Then he opened it and—

They were wearing tuxedos. Ben was dressed in white, hair freshly cut, face cleanly shaved. Tim looked stunning in black, his hair slicked back. Were those diamond cufflinks?

"Why are you dressed like that?" Jason stammered.

"We could ask the same of you," Tim said with a grin. "How many people wear a suit while house-sitting?"

"The gray brings out your eyes," Ben said. "You look very handsome. Will you be walking me down the aisle?"

"*You know*?" Jason said, not hiding his disappointment.

"You contacted everyone ever," Tim said. "One of them was bound to snitch."

"But we were still surprised," Ben said. "And flattered. So are we allowed to come inside yet, or…"

"Of course," Jason said, stepping out of their way and leading them through the house. "Who told you?"

"My lips are sealed," Ben said. Then he caught sight of the backyard, all the people waiting there, and the many decorations which had transformed it into a wonderland. And he stopped.

For one split second, Jason thought they wouldn't go through with it. But then Ben grabbed Tim's hand, glanced over at him and grinned like an excited child. Tim matched his smile.

Breathing out in relief, Jason rushed to open the door for

them. Then he grabbed his guitar that he had waiting there. As Ben and Tim walked down the aisle, Jason strolled a few paces behind, playing Wagner's *Bridal Chorus* even though this wedding was between grooms. Ben and Tim might have known they were getting married, but they were both clearly surprised by many of the guests. They kept stopping, wanting to greet people they didn't see every day. Jason kept them moving with the music, playing them all the way to the front, where Adrien was waiting. Then Jason quickly took his seat. Michelle patted his hand, while behind him, William massaged Jason's shoulders.

He felt like crying already.

"I assume you know why you're here," Adrien said, causing the audience to laugh.

"Something about parking tickets?" Tim replied.

"Oh, it's much more serious than that," Adrien said. "We have all gathered here today to make your love legally binding. And to see two handsome men kiss. Before you do, I have some vows prepared for you—"

"Actually," Ben said, "we came up with our own."

"Oh!" Adrien said. "That's great. Please, go ahead."

Ben and Tim turned to face the crowd, both of them momentarily overwhelmed by everyone there. Ben spoke first.

"I'm not very good at speeches, and Tim was nervous too. We thought about using the traditional vows, but we're not exactly a traditional couple. So what we decided to do was write each other letters." Ben pulled a folded piece of paper from his suit jacket. Tim did the same. "We haven't read these to each other yet, but we'd like to now."

"Do you want to go first?" Tim whispered.

Ben nodded, hand trembling. "To my knight in tarnished armor," he began, causing murmured laughter. "You saved me. I was a lonely teenager, one who never believed he would find love. Even when we met, you were a hopeless fantasy. I took care of you on that couch in your parents' house, pretending it all belonged to us. I liked imagining that you belonged to me and I belonged to you. I never would have guessed that all these years later, my dream would come true—that I wouldn't have to pretend anymore. But first you saved me. Not just when I was a teenager who needed hope and love, but as an adult, when my world had come crashing down and I tried to content myself with being alone. Once again I never thought love would be possible for me. But you kept showing up in my life, kept reminding me of how the impossible can happen. Especially when we're together. Being with you has been blissful, infuriating, beautiful, painful, everything I ever wanted and more. I wouldn't trade a second of it for the world, because most of all, being with you has been love. I adore you, Tim Wyman, and I couldn't be more proud to become your husband on this day. I love you."

The audience applauded, many of them blowing their noses. Then Tim cleared his throat, flashed them a smile, and concentrated on his own letter. "To the one who nearly got away," he said, voice shaking a little. "When you came into my life, I was bored with myself, bored with the world around me. I would look up at a sky filled with stars and wonder why something beautiful like that couldn't be down here on earth. Then you came, this strange, proud little guy who was so defiant. What most people would consider a weakness, you made a strength, and I admired you for that. I was almost afraid to touch you, not just because of the obvious reasons, but because you were like one of those stars in the sky. I thought I would get burned, and I guess I did… but first I asked you to teach me how to fly. And you tried. You tugged on me and you pulled, trying to get me off the ground, and maybe for a moment we flew together, but it was only your strength carrying me. When I ruined everything, when you grew tired and flew away, I knew I had missed my chance. But I never forgot you. Over the years I tried to make your memory proud, and even though you weren't there…" Tim shook his head, folded the letter and put it in his pocket. Then he took Ben's hands. "When you say that I saved you, all I did was keep showing you what you taught me. Everything wonderful that's happened, everything good about this life, it's all because of you. You're the most amazing man I've ever met, Benjamin Bentley, and I'm going to keep you safe, keep you company, and most of all, love you for the rest of our time together. I just hope it lasts even longer than those stars in the sky."

Now there was some outright crying. Jason was having a hard time keeping it together, but he didn't want tears in his eyes to prevent him from seeing what was happening. Adrien presented them with the rings, which they placed on each other's fingers at the same time. Then Tim stepped forward, whispering something in Ben's ear that caused him to smile, and for a moment they appeared so ageless and perfect. That was when they kissed. Jason decided it was the single most beautiful moment he'd ever witnessed.

Afterwards, Adrien had them sit one at a time and sign papers, Jason glad for the time to recover emotionally. And he liked the idea that each one of those signatures prepared them for the worst, would make any bad situation a little better by ensuring Ben and Tim could be together, no matter what. For the rest of their lives, they would be there for each other.

"Are you happy you met them?" Michelle asked from next to him.

"Yes!" Jason said, holding back another wave of tears. "I'm so glad I moved here."

Michelle smiled. "Sometimes I wish they had been together when you were younger. If only I could have introduced them to you sooner. I feel like you belong with them. Is that crazy?"

Jason shook his head. "They're the closest thing I've had to family since my mom died."

"I'm glad to hear that," Michelle said. "I hope you'll forgive me for telling Ben and Tim about today."

Jason's jaw dropped. "*You* told them? Why?"

Michelle's eyes sparkled. "Because it was the perfect opportunity."

"For what?" Jason asked.

Before he could get his answer, the voices around them died down as someone up front addressed them.

"I guess we were in a letter-writing mood," Tim said, another piece of paper in hand. "Do you want to read this one?"

Ben nodded and took it from him. "To our future son," he said. "There was a time when we felt like we had it all, when we thought we couldn't be happier. Then you came into our lives. We saw ourselves in you, and we realized that while we didn't need anything, we still had a lot to give. But we were wrong, because the more we got to know you, the more we realized that we did need you. Even being in love can be lonely, and you've brought so much light into our home." Ben raised his eyes to seek out Jason. "And even though you've started your own life, we feel stronger just knowing you're out there. We look forward to your every visit, and hearing about the adventures that you'll go through."

Ben glanced over at Tim, who continued for him. "When two people know they want to spend the rest of their lives together, marriage is only a formality. The wedding simply makes it official. Likewise, you already feel like family to us, Jason, but ceremonies are important, and we want the world to know—"

Ben stepped forward. "In my heart, you're already my son. Why don't you get up here and make it official!"

"Well?" Michelle said, addressing Jason. "Are you going to accept, or are you going to do something crazy like set the wedding cake on fire?"

Jason glanced over at her and laughed. Then he turned his attention back toward the front, where Ben and Tim were looking more than a little nervous. As if he would ever reject them! Jason stood, and as he walked to the front, everyone clapped. Adrien held out an arm, directing Jason to the chair. He took a seat and practically went cross-eyed at the legal document in front of him.

Adrien bent over to explain. "This simply states that you are not in a diminished capacity, and that you want to legally recognize Benjamin Bentley and Timothy Wyman as your guardians, in which case, you'll be issued a new birth certificate with their names on it. You will also be entitled to all the benefits of a biological child, as well as answerable for any responsibilities as required by law. Unless you have any concerns—and I assure you that you have nothing to worry about with these two—then please sign here."

Adrien backed away. At the bottom of the document were three names below empty spaces. Tim's name was on the left, and he appeared next to Jason on that side and grabbed the pen. "This doesn't mean you can borrow my car," he said before signing. Then he ruffled Jason's hair.

From Jason's other side, Ben took the pen from Tim. "We know we're putting you on the spot," he said. "You don't have to do this now. You can think about it, if you need to."

Jason shook his head. Michelle was right. This was the perfect time. When people got married, they became family. That's what this occasion was all about. Making family. Cementing bonds of love, be they romantic or otherwise. Jason snatched the pen from Ben and signed.

"Now it's up to you," he said, offering the pen back.

Ben smiled down at him, took the pen, and signed his name with a flourish.

"Wait!" Jason said. "This doesn't mean we're all going to be Wymans, does it?"

"It's a perfectly good name!" Tim said defensively.

"Yeah, but not nearly as cool as Bentley."

"There's been enough paperwork for one day," Ben said. "For now, we'll all keep our names. Come, let's tell everyone the good news."

Jason stood, Ben taking hold of one hand, Tim taking the other. They led him to the front where everyone could see him, then raised his arms up like a boxer who'd just won the championship fight.

"Ladies and gentlemen," Tim said. "May I present to you, our son, Jason Grant!"

Tim's grandmother leapt from her seat. "My beautiful great-grandbaby!" she cried out before rushing the stage to hug him.

That was the cue for everyone else to stand and step forward. Jason was surrounded by happy faces, shook a multitude of hands, and kept hearing the word 'congratulations.' It meant the most coming from Michelle, and he said it right back to her.

"What do you mean?" she asked.

"You said you'd find me a family one day. I didn't make it easy for you, but you did it. Best caseworker ever!"

Michelle laughed and opened her arms to take him in.

By the time the moon had risen high into the sky, most of the guests had gone home, or at least back to their hotels. A few still remained. Marcello was slow dancing with Tim's grandmother, each keeping a hand free so they could hold and occasionally guzzle a glass of champagne. They seemed to be engaged in the friendliest of drinking contests, a shirtless waiter dutifully standing a few paces away, a tray full of drinks held ready. Allison was posing for Kelly as he took photos of a mother holding her sleeping baby. If Kelly was trying to capture innocence, he was out of luck. Allison was no Virgin Mary with child. Instead she smiled like a diva, as if having a baby was the most fashionable thing possible. No innocence, no nauseating tenderness, just the unabashed pride of a mother.

Seated at a table near the buffet, Ben was feeding Tim bites of wedding cake, but he wasn't allowing him time to chew and swallow. The more Tim's cheeks bulged outward with cake, the louder Ben laughed. Farther away, Emma strolled along the edge of the fence, holding hands with her date and looking dashing in a black tuxedo.

In the middle of it all was the stage, surrounded by flowers and lit by chains of tiny white lights. Jason sat on the step and observed his surroundings. After a few minutes of this, he sighed.

"I hate when a party is over," he said.

"Really?" William asked from next to him. "Why?"

"Because endings are sad. They always make me cry."

"Even when they're happy?"

"Especially when they're happy because then I don't want it to be over."

William put an arm around Jason and pulled him closer. "I don't think of it that way. To me it's more like when a war is over. The chaos has finally ceased. Everything is calm and peaceful again."

"And kind of sad," Jason said.

"Hm," William replied. "Hey, remember when I asked you for four years?"

Jason glanced over at him. "Now I'm getting sadder."

"I know, I know. What if I asked you for four more?"

"That's not funny."

"I'm dead serious," William replied. "Except this time, I want you to come with me. On a journey. Of sorts."

Jason looked back to where Ben and Tim—no, to where his *parents*—were seated. Now they were exchanging frosting-covered kisses. From beneath the table Chinchilla grumbled in her sleep, stomach huge and round, no doubt from all the treats she had begged from guests. Jason loved this world. He didn't want to leave it, not ever, but he knew he would. If that's what William wanted him to do, Jason would leave it all behind… but he would never stop missing it. Especially the people. Ben had pulled away from Tim, eyes twinkling as he nodded once. Except Ben wasn't nodding in greeting. He was nodding toward William.

"Uh, I sort of need you to look at me."

Jason turned his head. William was holding a little black box. One that was covered with lint. He supposed all such boxes looked the same, but he could have sworn it was the same box that had once held the engagement ring Tim had given Ben. Jason struggled to remember if it had been part of the ceremony, snapping out of it when William laughed.

"Not the reaction I was hoping for," he said.

"Sorry," Jason said, "but is that from my old room?"

William shrugged. "I needed a box."

"Yeah, but it was in my underwear drawer."

William gave him an exasperated look. "Just take it, okay?"

Jason hesitated. Of course, in the back of his mind, he wondered if this was what it seemed. William wasn't down on one knee though, so it probably wasn't.

Fed up with waiting for him to react, William opened the box for him. The interior was no longer empty. Instead it was filled almost to capacity. Inside was a red and yellow ribbon, attached to it a gold medallion. William took it out and held it up, revealing it as some sort of military decoration. Jason admired it a moment before looking to William in confusion.

"It's a Lifesaving Medal," William explained. "This is the life you helped me save. I figured it's a nice symbol for what I'm asking for. A life. Together. Just give me four years. We can stay right here in Austin, if you want. And at the end of that time, when I've done my best to prove myself, I'd like to be standing right here with you."

"And what?" Jason asked.

William smiled. "And then we'll give Ben and Tim some serious competition."

Jason grinned, reached not for the medal but the back of William's neck so he could draw him in for a kiss. Then there was a flash of a camera and a cheer. Someone shouted, "I think he said yes!" before hands started clapping. Jason looked up at the smiling faces around him and felt a sense of wonder. For a moment, he saw it all through the eyes of a lonely boy who had lost his family. A boy who had never dared dream of a day like this, that a group of strangers could become so many precious things to him—family, friends, and even a lover.

"What do you say?" William asked, still uncertain despite the kiss. "Is that a yes? It didn't feel like a no."

Jason chose a different answer. "Four years," he said.

"I'm supposed to wait four years to get your answer?" William cocked his head and gave him a puzzled smile. "Is this some sort of punishment?"

"Take it or leave it," Jason said easily.

"Okay," William conceded. "I suppose that's only fair. It's my turn to wait, and when the four years are up, I'll stand on this stage with you and ask my question again. I'll say 'Jason Grant, will you spend the rest of your life with me?' And you'll say... Come on! Give me a hint! What will you say?"

Jason grinned, and rather than let words betray just how in love he was, he leaned in for another kiss. As their lips met, he realized this wasn't a sad ending, nor was it a happy one. Instead, this moment was the very beginning of it all. A lifetime of never being lonely, of never lacking love. He'd finally done the impossible. Jason had come home again, and this time it would last forever.

Jay Bell's most beloved story is now on the big screen!

Now you can listen to Ben sing, watch Tim jog, and see just how adorable Jace looks in his flight attendant uniform, in the official *Something Like Summer* movie adaptation. Find out where you can watch it at:

www.jaybellbooks.com

The Something Like... series continues in:
Something Like Lightning

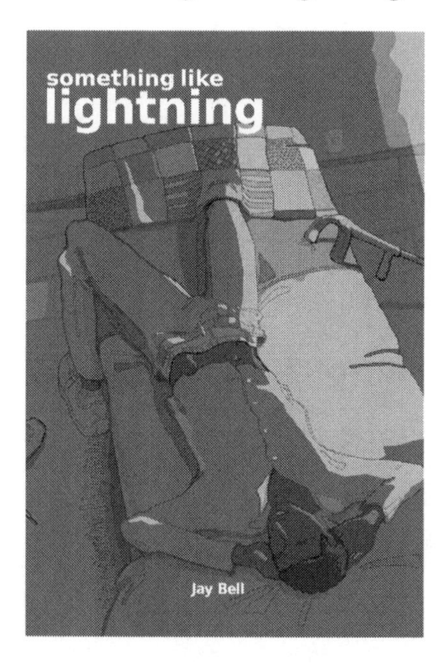

Kelly Phillips has been out of the closet since he was a young teenager, and thanks to the gay youth group he frequents, he has never been short on friends or lovers. But when you have almost everything, it's hard not to focus on what's just out of reach: A best friend, who would be Mr. Right if he wasn't already Mr. Straight. Or that handsome guy at school, who would be easier to wrangle if not for his angel wings. And then there's the one who might be a perfect fit, maybe even a soulmate… if only he wasn't convinced he didn't need anyone at all. Kelly has always been good at running. Now he must learn to chase, which will not only test his endurance, but the durability of his heart as well.

Something Like Lightning is a new beginning in the *Something Like…* saga, shifting the focus to a fresh set of characters while also revisiting a familiar face or two.

For more information, please see:
www.jaybellbooks.com

Also by Jay Bell
Kamikaze Boys

True love is worth fighting for.

My name is Connor Williams and people say I'm crazy. But that's not who I am. They also think I'm straight, and mean, and dangerous. But that's not who I am. The stories people tell, all those legends which made me an outsider—they don't mean a thing. Only my mother and my younger brother matter to me. Funny then that I find myself wanting to stand up for someone else. David Henry, that kind-of-cute guy who keeps to himself, he's about to get his ass beat by a bunch of dudes bigger than him. I could look away, let him be one more causality of this cruel world... But that's not who I am.

Kamikaze Boys, a Lambda Literary award winning novel, is a story of love triumphant as two young men walk a perilous path in the hopes of saving each other.

For more information, please see:
www.jaybellbooks.com

Also by Jay Bell:
Hell's Pawn

John Grey is dead… and that's just the beginning of his troubles.

Purgatory should have been a safe haven for souls that belong neither in Heaven nor Hell, but instead John finds himself in a corrupt prison, one bereft of freedom or pleasure. Along with his decedent friend Dante, John makes a brave escape, only to fall straight down to Hell and into the arms of Rimmon, a handsome demon. John is soon recruited as Hell's ambassador, visiting the afterlife realms of other cultures to enlist an army strong enough to stand against Heaven. As interesting as his new job is, John's mind keeps returning to Purgatory and the souls still trapped there. Somehow he must free them and stop a war he doesn't believe in, all while desperately trying to attract the attention of an incubus whose heart belongs to another.

Hell's Pawn is a wild romp through an afterlife stuffed full of adventure, romance, and fun.

Made in the USA
Middletown, DE
17 September 2023